TIPPING POIN

By

Si Rosser

Schmall World Publishing

First published in Great Britain as a paperback by Schmall World
publishing

Copyright © Simon Rosser 2011

KINDLE VERSION

TIPPING POINT

SI ROSSER

SCHMALL WORLD PUBLISHING

TIPPING POINT

"The point at which the number of small changes over a period of time reaches a level where a further small change has a sudden and very great effect on a system…"

Oxford Advanced Learners Dictionary

For Zuzana
Also by the same author;

Impact Point – Robert Spire 2

Melt Zone – Robert Spire 3

Cataclysm of the Ancients – Robert Spire 4

The A-Z of Global Warming

And AMBER LEE Adventure - VAPORIZED

TIPPING POINT is now out on AUDIOBOOK

Author's website – www.sirosser-thriller-writer.com
CLAIM YOUR FREE E-BOOK AT THE END OF BOOK!

PROLOGUE
April 5

"ONLY ANOTHER FOUR of these trips and we're done," Davenport shouted to his friend, as he looked back at the jagged cliffs rising out of the ocean on the bleak leeward side of the Ile de l'Est.

"Thank God! Don't ever ask me to sign up for anything like this again. After the year we've spent down here, I'm sure we'll both be exempt from having to do any further voluntary research for a while," Hawthorn replied.

Dawn was just breaking over the windswept isles, as the old wooden fishing boat chugged out of the make-shift port on Ile de l'Est, one of six islets that make up the French Crozet Islands in the Southern Indian Ocean. The sub-Antarctic archipelago - part of the French Southern Territories since 1955 - was uninhabited, except for a small research base on the main island, Ile de la Possession.

"You know Adam, I could think of better things to be doing during my gap year. Monitoring penguins and sea creatures doesn't feature high on the list," Hawthorn said, turning the boat towards the sampling zone.

"Don't forget it's your turn to update the catalogue with whatever marine samples we find," Davenport shouted, throwing the well-used notebook across the deck to his friend.

Adam Davenport and James Hawthorn had been based on the main island, Ile de la Possession, along with five other research scientists for the last eight months, and were now embarking on the final four months of their placement as part of an international monitoring team, studying the many different species of penguins, seals, birds, flora and fauna unique to the archipelago. The islands were in fact one large nature reserve, since being declared a national park back in 1938. The two researchers felt long forgotten by the outside world. The monthly food drop, by small plane, from the French Kerguelen Islands - some 1300 kilometres to the east - was their only real comfort.

The boat's bow rose up on the crest of a wave as they motored out of the protected inlet toward Ile de la Possession, and the buoy that marked the research area, some two kilometres out from the eastern shore.

"It sure is calm out today," Davenport said, looking out over the horizon. A group of five petrels circled above the boat as they arrived at the marker buoy.

Hawthorn cut the engine, letting the boat drift toward the orange buoy. "Pass the rope, so I can tie her up," he yelled.

Davenport threw him the frayed end of the rope, which he secured to the chain on the buoy. The boat bobbed up and down on the light swell as Davenport went to retrieve his packet of Marlboro's from the wheelhouse. "How many pots are we supposed to be pulling up today James?" he shouted over to his friend.

"Looks like we dropped eight overboard last week," Hawthorn replied, flicking through the scruffy, worn notepad which dated back to the 1960s. "It's going to look like seafood pick and mix by the time we haul them all up."

Davenport leaned over the side of the boat, taking in a deep breath of sea air. He pulled a Marlboro from the packet, licked the end of it, and placed it between his lips. "There's a very strange smell on the port side," he shouted to Hawthorn, who was getting the sampling kits ready to drop overboard.

He flipped the top of his Zippo lighter open and struck the flint. Before Hawthorn could answer him, a flash of light and heat exploded around them, completely engulfing the wooden fishing boat.

Hawthorn felt the force of the explosion as he was thrown into the shattered wheelhouse, followed by an instant of agonizing pain, then darkness.

Davenport opened his eyes. He was in the water, surrounded by flotsam and covered in burning oil. He tried to swim through it, but the task was futile. He screamed, and dived under the water. The last thing he felt was a searing pain in his lungs as he sank into the freezing depths.

CHAPTER 1

London, April 15

DR. DALE STANTON sat at his desk in the darkening room of his Russell Square apartment staring blankly at the glowing computer screen, his eyes tired and sore. His face was impassive, except for the visible, nervous, twitch in the corner of his mouth, which revealed his gathering thoughts.

He was putting the finishing touches to the presentation that he would be giving to the Intergovernmental Panel on Climate Change conference in Oslo, Norway, in a little under a week's time. Stanton had been working on his current project for almost eight months, and the conclusions he'd reached, he had little doubt, would concern the scientific world. Reaching over, he turned on the desktop lamp and rubbed his eyes, before leaning back in his chair to stretch his aching neck.

Looking back at the monitor, he started reading over the salient parts of his presentation to check it one final time before finishing for the evening. He resumed typing; making what he hoped was the final amendment to his paper.

We know the Ocean Thermohaline Circulation is an important Atlantic current powered by both heat (thermo) and salt content (haline) which brings warm water up from the tropics to northern latitudes. Without it, the Eastern Seaboard of the USA and climate of Northern Europe would be much colder. I have been re-analysing all the data amassed by the

RAPID-WATCH program and my calculations reveal that the measuring devices have been incorrectly calibrated. Twenty-five of the thirty devices used to measure ocean flow were set by the manufacturers to measure fresh water. When calibrating the data to factor in measurements for denser salt water, the figures revealed...

Stanton jumped, as the telephone on his desk rang. He took a deep breath and sighed, as he reached over his laptop to pick up the phone. "Hello!" There was no answer. "Hello!" Again, silence. He replaced the receiver. His train of thought interrupted, he sat quietly for a moment before completing the final sentence, then saved the amendments and closed the program down. He clicked on his private finance folder to check an insurance policy he knew was about to expire, and, as he did, accidentally opened the file containing a copy of his will. Perusing it, he reminded himself to amend the charitable legacies clause in order to make a gift to the team down at *RAPID. God knows, they would need all the help they could get.*

He'd had the will prepared after receiving a large sum of money from his father two years earlier. A colleague had recommended a local firm specialising in environmental law, with a promise that one of the firm's senior environmental lawyers, a Mr. Robert Spire, would be appointed as a co-executor. He closed the file, reminding himself to have the will amended when he returned from Oslo next week.

Stanton reached across his desk and pulled the research book he'd been using, from the shelf, to double check a couple of facts. He flicked through the pages to a section entitled *The Younger Dryas* period. Around 12,900 years ago - just as the world was slowly warming up after the last ice age - a rapid descent back to colder conditions occurred in as little as ten years or so, a mere blink of an eye, in climactic terms. A shut down of the Atlantic Ocean Thermohaline Circulation was thought to have been a possible cause of the rapid chill. Stanton's hair stood up on the back of his neck as he considered the possible ramifications of his latest research.

He closed the book, turned off his laptop, and ran his hands through his lank brown hair. He got up from his desk and looked out of his window at a deserted Russell Square and closed the blinds. He realised he'd been working for almost six hours, and it was now coming up to six P.M on Saturday evening.

He enjoyed living alone in his two-bed terraced townhouse apartment in London's Russell Square, one of only a few private residences left overlooking the park, but had noticed various businesses, as well as the University College of London, taking over most of the area during the last twenty years. The district was dotted with restaurants and bars, and in an hour he would be meeting up with an old friend for a well-earned drink in the Hotel Russo, not far from his apartment.

He briefly took hold of the memory stick containing his presentation, before putting it back down gently. The facts, figures and details of his paper were spinning around in his head. He knew he wouldn't be able to relax until he had given his talk in Oslo. He'd been over the calculations at least ten times to ensure they were correct. He walked into the bathroom. *Unbelievable; how could they have failed to check the calibration on the measuring equipment?*

Just as he was about to get in the shower, the phone rang again. He picked up the receiver, "Hello!" There was silence on the other end. As he replaced the phone he heard a click on the line. *Not again.* He shrugged, and stepped under the shower.

Stanton was in the middle of drying himself when a text message came through from Mathew confirming the arrangements. They would be meeting in the Kings Bar at the Hotel Russo; a warm intimate wood-panelled bar, and one of Stanton's favourite local watering holes. He finished his ablutions, went to his bedroom and put on a white linen shirt, navy blue Chino trousers, socks and leather boater shoes and glanced in the mirror. He looked and felt tired. He splashed some aftershave on his face, locked the door to the apartment and headed down the hall stairs and wandered out into the warmth of a mild spring evening.

CHAPTER 2

THE HOTEL RUSSO was situated just five minutes from Stanton's apartment on the opposite side of Russell Square. The park, one of the square's main features, looked empty, but on the surrounding streets the early evening traffic was picking up. There was a mixture of late night shoppers and taxis, collecting and dropping off their fares.

He arrived at the hotel with its imposing Victorian red brick facade just after seven-twenty, walked into the bar and scanned the room, but didn't see his friend. He should be here soon, he thought, as he sat down on a stool near to the bar.

"Can I help you sir?" an impeccably dressed barman inquired.

"I'll have a pint of bitter please."

Stanton, at forty-nine, looked a good five years younger than his age. He likened himself to *Basil Rathbone,* from the classic Sherlock Holmes films, but not quite as tall. It had been a while since he'd been out socialising; his heavy work load over the last eight months had made it impossible.

As he was halfway through his drink, he noticed an attractive dark-haired woman sit down on one of the bar stools to his left. Dressed in a smart grey pencil skirt, white blouse and grey suit jacket, he surmised that she might be a stockbroker or banker. He realised he had been staring at her a little too long, as she glanced at him and smiled, whilst shifting on her stool. She ordered a drink, some kind of cocktail, and he noticed that she had a subtle accent which he couldn't quite place. Possibly Eastern European, or maybe Russian, he considered.

He glanced at the time: it was now seven-fifty. *Odd, Mathew wasn't usually late.*

He finished his drink and looked around the bar. The oak-panelled room was intimate with soft lighting. A group of men were drinking in one corner, and two women were chatting over cocktails, near to where he was seated, but that was it. A few large brown leather chairs faced away from the bar in the corner, surrounded by lush green yucca plants, but the chairs looked empty from where he was sitting.

He went to order another drink, and, just as he was about to attract the barman's attention, he heard a lightly accented voice come from his left. "Hello, would you mind if I join you for drink?"

Stanton looked toward the attractive woman, somewhat taken aback by her forwardness. "Of course,...um, I am waiting for a friend, but, you are welcome to join me. Can I get you a drink?"

"Please, mai tai would be great."

"My name is Dale," Stanton said, offering his hand.

"Hello Dale, I am Victoria," she said, taking his outstretched hand.

Stanton ordered a mai tai and another pint of bitter for himself, his throat feeling even dryer than it had earlier. He hadn't met such an attractive woman in a long time, but her sudden interest led him to believe that she was probably a high-class escort. It had been difficult for him to meet *anyone* with the time he'd been putting into the *RAPID* project, and he knew that his socialising skills had become a bit rusty. He tried to think of something to say that would clarify her intentions. "So, Victoria, are you here on business or pleasure?" he asked.

"Well, I was supposed to be meeting friend, but she

cancelled on me last minute...I wanted drink, so I stay," she said, in broken, but perfectly understandable English.

"Well, I am glad you did," Stanton replied.

Victoria smiled, and sipped her cocktail.

Stanton sat there for a moment admiring her silky shoulder-length dark hair, and her slim, athletic figure. Her high cheek bones and angular face betrayed her Eastern European heritage. "Excuse me a moment, I should really try and call my friend again."

He called Mathew's number, but there was no response. He rejoined Victoria at the bar. "So, Victoria, what is it you do?" he asked, anticipating the worst.

"Well, I am photographer...freelance for ladies fashion magazine."

"Ah, really," he said, relieved at her response. "I'd have put you down for a banker or stockbroker myself."

Victoria gave a little laugh. "I will take that as compliment, Mr. Dale, but I know nothing about that sort of thing. Anyway that sounds boring, no?"

"I guess so," Stanton replied, somewhat embarrassed at what she might think of his line of work.

"So, where is your friend?" she asked.

"I really don't know, tied up at work I guess. He should be here shortly."

Victoria placed the cocktail straw between her lips and took a long drink. She then took hold of the end of the straw, and used it to mix the ice at the bottom of her glass. She looked at Stanton, her green eyes glinting as she moved her head to one side. "I don't wish to sound forward, Mr. Dale, but I haven't eaten yet, and wondered if you like to join me for dinner? The restaurant here is very good."

Stanton liked the fact that she called him Mr. Dale. He wasn't sure if she had misunderstood his name or if it was her broken English, but it sounded kind of charming. The thought of joining her for dinner was too much to resist. He summoned the barman over and gave a description of his friend, telling him he'd be next door in the restaurant if he showed.

"No problem, sir," the barman said, as he mopped up some spilled beer with a cloth.

Stanton paid the bill and followed Victoria next door into the hotel's restaurant, where they were shown a table near to the door. He began to feel slightly aroused as he looked across the table into Victoria's green eyes.

She gave him a long smile and asked, "So, Mr. Dale, what is it you do for job?"

Stanton cleared his throat from the bread roll he'd just eaten. He didn't want to bore her with his research, but couldn't think of anything entertaining to say. "Well, I'm actually a climate scientist for the Met Office in London, but I'm currently working on a project down at Southampton University."

"Ah really, I have read about this global warming. It is bit worrying, no? But, where I come from, we could do with things little warmer, the winters are very cold."

"Oh and where is that?" Stanton asked.

"Novosibirsk, in Siberia."

"Really? You're a long way from home," Stanton said, leaning back in his chair.

Victoria smiled. "I haven't lived there for six years or so Mr. Dale, but I still visit family whenever I can. I have only been based in London for last eight months. I enjoy my job, but I find city so big and tiring. Back home is much easier way of life, but not much to do there for girl like me."

I bet, Stanton thought.

The waitress appeared at the table and filled their glasses with water. Stanton perused the wine menu that had just been handed to him. He looked up at Victoria. "Chardonnay OK for you?"

"Perfect, I like French white...but you choose."

Stanton ordered a bottle of *Pouilly-Fuissé*, and after a short while the waitress returned with the chilled wine and filled their glasses.

"Well I guess we should drink to something," Stanton said, holding up his glass.

"Yes, here's to...an unexpected evening," Victoria replied, raising her glass.

Stanton took a decent drink. As he let the fresh, delicate flavours soak his palate, the waitress returned with their orders.

"So, you said you have read about global warming issues. Do you know much about the subject?" Stanton asked, picking up on Victoria's earlier comments.

"Oh, a little, but the subject is little depressing, no?"

There was an awkward silence. "This pasta is very good. How is your fish?" she asked.

"Great," Stanton replied, realising she clearly didn't wish to talk about the topic. "Well, it doesn't look like my friend is turning up," he said, checking his watch.

"I don't think so either, but you don't look like you are missing him too much?"

Stanton smiled. Half of the Chardonnay remained in the bottle in the ice bucket. He went to refill Victoria's glass, but she quickly raised her hand and placed it over the top.

"Not for me, Mr. Dale. I already feel little bit drunk."

Stanton smiled and filled his glass. "Well, it's been a real pleasure meeting you Victoria."

"The pleasure is all mine, but we don't have to say goodnight yet. Maybe we could go for coffee somewhere?"

Stanton was quiet for a few seconds. He felt a little nervous, and no doubt it showed. "We could go back to my apartment, perhaps? If you would like some coffee, I mean," he said, awkwardly.

"Wonderful. Do you live far from here?"

"Just across the square," he replied, relieved at her response.

The waitress appeared with the bill, and Stanton instinctively took out his wallet to pay.

"No, Mr. Dale, I pay for dinner."

"Don't be silly, I really don't..."

Victoria cut him off mid-sentence. "Please, I insist," she said, taking a roll of notes from her purse.

In the corner of the Kings Bar the smartly dressed barman and a customer were trying to lift a man who was slumped in one of the large leather chairs. The man, who was in his early forties, was out cold, and had been since around seven that evening.

The barman felt for the man's pulse. "Well, thankfully he's not dead," he said to the man helping him. "Perhaps I'd better get an ambulance."

"I think so; he's either drunk himself into a stupor, or something's seriously wrong. He's unconscious."

The barman walked briskly over to the phone on the wall behind the bar and dialled for an ambulance. At the same time, the customer felt for the man's wallet. He found it, and searched through the contents to reveal a driving licence. Printed under the photo I.D was the name Mathew J. White.

Stanton and Victoria arrived, arm in arm, at his apartment. As they ascended the steps, to the front door, an ambulance came into view with its sirens blaring, the busy London traffic appearing to ignore it.

Stanton fumbled for his key, and opened the door. He led Victoria up the hall stairs in silence. As they reached the top, Victoria put her arm around his neck, pulling his head toward hers, and kissed him. It was a long, passionate kiss and the taste of her lips and scent of her perfume was subtly intoxicating. She pulled her head back. "Time for that coffee you promised, Mr. Dale?"

"Ah yes, coffee. I'll put the kettle on just as soon as we get in," Stanton replied. He was thinking of other things, however. It was the first time in months that he'd allowed himself to be distracted from his work. He opened the front door to his apartment, flicked on the lights and walked into the lounge off the main hallway, his guest following behind.

Habit forced him to glance over towards his study as he went into the kitchen to put the kettle on. He grabbed two coffee cups from the cupboard above the kettle and pulled the plunger from the French press, which was thankfully clean. It wasn't long before an aroma of Colombian coffee wafted through the kitchen.

Victoria appeared and walked toward him, speaking in Russian, her accent soft and exotic. Stanton hesitated for a moment, a puzzled look on his face.

"Ah, sorry, sometimes I do that." She smiled. "May I use bathroom?" she asked, her Russian accent more obvious this time.

"Sure, it's down the corridor, off to the left."

Stanton admired Victoria's shapely figure as she walked down the corridor to the bathroom. He felt a combination of unease and excitement as he thought about the beautiful stranger he had invited into his apartment. He pushed the coffee press down, aroused at the prospect of the sex that he hoped would follow. He heard a click from the bathroom door as Victoria unlocked it, and his stomach turned over as nerves started to get the better of him.

He quickly searched for the remote control and hit the play button for the CD player. The melody of Simon and Garfunkel's *'The Boxer'* started drifting out of the speakers.

Victoria walked back into the room and Stanton handed her a coffee. "Here's to a fantastic evening out," he said, studying her svelte figure.

"Fantastic," she repeated, putting her cup down on the table by the side of the leather sofa, and moving closer to him.

He went to drink his coffee, but the Russian pulled the cup out of his hands and placed it down next to hers. She placed her left arm around him, and pulled him towards her, kissing him passionately. He felt her warm, soft lips, on his, and experienced an excitement he hadn't felt in a long time. The nerves he'd had, only a short while ago, evaporated, as lust took over.

The long kiss was interrupted by a sudden stabbing pain in his upper left arm, and almost instantly, he felt unwell.

Victoria pulled away from him. At the same moment he began to feel nauseous, and then a burning sensation developed in his throat, followed by rapid breathing. Twenty seconds later, darkness enveloped him. He tried to reach for the phone, but his limbs seemed no longer able to support his weight, and he fell to the floor, sucking in his last breath.

Victoria stepped back and stood there for a moment, staring at Stanton lying on the floor in a pathetic heap, his mouth still open. Simon and Garfunkel's *'The Fifty-Ninth Bridge Street'* song had just started to play. *You don't look like you're feeling too groovy now, doctor,* she thought, looking down at him.

She quickly gathered her things, left the apartment and quietly closed the door behind her. She descended the hall stairs and walked out onto Russell Square, which was deserted, apart from a group of drunken students staggering noisily along one side of the park. She ·checked the time; it was one-twenty A.M. Unnoticed, she hurried towards Endsleigh Place, where her dark Saab was parked.

CHAPTER 3

Oakdale, West Wales
April 15

ROBERT SPIRE AWOKE to the sound of birdsong coming from the back garden of his modernised stone cottage, located in the sleepy village of Oakdale, in west Wales. He rolled his six-foot one inch frame out of bed, ran his hands through his dark blond hair, and forced himself to do fifty press-ups, something he tried to do most mornings. He completed his exercise and walked sleepily into the bathroom for a shower.

As he stood under the hot water, he thought back to the hectic, daily grind of London where he had lived and worked for five years, as an environmental lawyer in the city. His work had involved defending large corporations from litigation brought against them, for problems ranging from oil spills to land contamination. It had dawned on him that he was going to be trapped in the ever more competitive game of firm management and partnership politics. He'd had a choice, either slog it out in the city, or grab an opportunity that had arisen to take over a small legal practice in west Wales, after the father of a friend had decided to retire. At thirty-eight, he felt that if he didn't make the move, he was unlikely to ever run his own law firm, on his own terms, something he had wanted to do for some time. That had been two years ago, and now he was slowly getting used to waking up to the sounds of the country; birdsong and bleating sheep, as opposed to the screeching of car tyres. The only thing he missed was the money however, but the change in work pace and being able to go scuba diving whenever he wanted, - a hobby he loved, - made up for it.

He thought about his wife Angela, who hadn't settled into their new home quite so easily. She still hankered after her life in London, which she compensated for by travelling back there regularly to catch up with friends. She also used the time to purchase gifts to sell in her small, but exclusive boutique she'd been lucky enough buy in the village, shortly after the move to Wales.

As Spire dried himself, he realised he had grown to enjoy the sleepy village that was now his home, for the time being anyway.

The time was coming up to nine-thirty on Saturday morning. He grabbed his bathrobe and wandered into the kitchen, the heat from the under-floor heating warming his bare feet as he walked in. He flicked the kettle on and yawned out loud. He heard a *click* coming from the hallway and guessed it was the postman. Sure enough, a pile of letters and a newspaper lay in an untidy heap on the front door mat. He poured two cups of coffee, and walked back into the bedroom.

"Here you go, honey," he said, placing a cup on Angela's bedside table.

Angela turned in the bed and gave Spire a sleepy smile. "What time is it?"

"Nine forty-five. What time you leaving for London?"

"Oh, in an hour or so...after you make me breakfast," she said with a grin.

Spire playfully grabbed the quilt either side of her shoulders and pushed it hard into the bed, pinning his wife down. "Oh, really?" he said, kissing her lips.

"Don't you try and hypnotise me with those blue eyes of yours, you bully. Scrambled egg on toast will do please...pretty please?"

Spire released her from his makeshift bed-trap. "OK, you've got twenty minutes," he said, as he made his way back into the kitchen.

He started preparing breakfast whilst perusing the *Independent* newspaper, which had just been delivered. Nothing much in the news it seemed, apart from an article about climate change activists attempting to block the construction of a new generation coal-fired power plant. Just like the business with Heathrow's third runway, environmental activists were increasingly venting their anger on the government for its seemingly carefree attitude to increasing carbon emissions; despite their pledge to reduce the UK's emissions by eighty per cent by the year 2050. He folded the newspaper as Angela wandered in, her hair still wet from the shower.

"Here you go," he said, placing breakfast on the kitchen table.

"Thanks, darling. So what you got planned whilst I'm up in London?" she asked.

"Well, I've got plenty of work to do on the Taunton case. I'll take some long walks along the coast; get the lads over for a party..."

"I don't think so!" Angela said, throwing a crunched up napkin at him, as she got up from the table.

"You're right; working on the Taunton case, followed by a walk on the beach, will wipe me out," Spire said, as he cleared the breakfast dishes.

Forty minutes later, Angela was ready to leave. Spire walked her out to the car and kissed her goodbye, watching as she drove her yellow Volkswagen Beetle out of the gravel driveway, up the lane, and out of sight.

As he strolled back up the drive to the cottage, he noticed that the side gate, which led to the back garden, was ajar. The wisteria which he'd cut back shortly after buying the cottage had grown back with a vengeance, and its vines had crawled over the gate, making it difficult to close. He hadn't noticed it being quite so entangled around the lock of the gate before. He pulled some of the offending vines away, and closed the gate, before wandering back inside to get on with his work.

Spire awoke with a jolt; his watch told him it was one-forty A.M. Cursing, he slowly got up from the sofa. The afternoon's work had finished him off. An old *Hammer Horror* movie was showing on the television. Apart from the flickering light of the screen, the cottage was immersed in darkness, and, to make things worse, the central heating had been off for some time.

As he reached for the television remote, a sudden rustling, from outside the lounge window made him jump. He heard the sound again, closer this time. *What the hell was that?*

He grabbed the remote control and turned down the volume. Then, slowly edging to the end of the curtains, he peeked out, his heart pounding. A fox was shaking a bin bag of its contents onto the rear patio. *For God's sake, relax*, he told himself. He knocked on the French glass door, and the startled fox bolted off, into the darkness.

He turned off the television, washed, and slumped on to his bed, drifting off to sleep within minutes of the blankets covering him.

The following morning Spire woke up to the sound of the alarm buzzing. The red digits on the clock radio displayed 7.45

A.M., and he realised he must have forgotten to switch the alarm off. He reached over to the bedside table and hit the mute button.

He stretched, got out of bed and looked out of the bedroom window. The sky was overcast and a strong wind was bending the branches on the trees outside. He went into the kitchen, switched the lights on and made himself some fresh coffee, which he took into the study. Files and papers lay on the table, from the work he had been doing the day before.

Spire's latest case was a personal injury claim, against one of the large local oil refineries. His client, Eric Taunton, an employee, together with a few of his colleagues, had been repairing one of the pipes that took liquid petroleum gas away from the refining process. The plant had been on shut-down, so the job should have been pretty straightforward and free of danger. Unfortunately for Mr Taunton, one of his colleagues had decided to light a cigarette. As Eric removed one of the valves from the pipe he had been working on - *Kaboom* - an explosion had ripped through the entire section, as liquid petroleum gas escaped, igniting as it was exposed to the lit cigarette. The explosion had thrown poor Eric a full twenty feet from where he had been working, ripping his leg off in the process. Two of his work colleagues, including the one who had intended to smoke, weren't quite so lucky, and had been killed.

Spire had commenced a claim against the refinery, on behalf of his client, for negligence, and he needed to get all the papers ready in order to issue court proceedings, which he would do next week.

He tidied the papers, and decided not to do any more work on the case today, not on a Sunday. He fancied a walk along the cliff tops, which he did regularly to keep himself fit, something he relished after practising martial arts for a number of years when living in London. In addition to the exercise, the views from the cliffs were spectacular, as good as anywhere else in the world.

Whilst dressing, he looked out of the bedroom window. The weather seemed to be getting worse; rain clouds were gathering in the distance. He grabbed the keys for his Audi from the kitchen hook, put his waterproof jacket on and left the house.

Spire reversed out of the short gravel driveway and accelerated down the lane towards Manorbier, a small village between the towns of Tenby and Pembroke, and drove down a windy, narrow country lane that led towards the beach. The grey, weathered-stone walls of Manorbier Castle loomed up from its impressive setting overlooking the bay.

He slowed to a crawl as he negotiated a right-hand bend that dropped steeply towards the beach. Passing the castle to his right, he drove up a short hill that ran along the cliffs and parked on an elevated position overlooking the bay, turned the engine off and got out of the car.

He stood looking out over the ocean, taking in some deep breaths of damp, fresh salty air. The grey clouds merged with the equally grey Celtic Sea, effectively part of the North Atlantic Ocean. The view was somewhat spoilt, however, by a large oil tanker on the horizon, slowly making its way out to the open sea. *Probably just dropped off imported oil for refining,* he guessed. Whatever it was doing, the large tanker was an eye-sore on the horizon.

Spire diverted his gaze down on the beach where a lone person was walking their dog, occasionally picking up a piece of driftwood and throwing it for their pet to retrieve. There were also three or four surfers patiently perched on their surfboards waiting for a decent wave to come in, but the sea looked calm. *They would be waiting a while,* he thought. Just as he was about to make his way down the short cliff, he heard a shout behind him.

"Robert, take it easy going down that path!"

Spire turned around to see the coastguard, David Miles, walking down toward him. "Someone fell yesterday when some of the bank collapsed. I haven't had time to cordon off the area yet."

"I know that path like the back of my hand, Dai, don't worry about me."

"I know that, but just take care. Anyway, how's life with you? Settled in to that cottage of yours yet?" Miles asked.

"Yeah, it's slowly beginning to feel like home," Spire replied, as he pointed toward the horizon. "That's a big old tanker out there eh?"

Miles followed his gaze. "Yep, sure is. Just dropped off some crude I guess. They seem to be showing up here in ever increasing numbers lately. Anyway, I gotta go. Say hello to that lovely wife of yours, will you?" Miles said, turning around to walk back up to the road.

"Will do," Spire shouted, turning to make his way carefully down the bank and onto the beach. The strong wind pummelled his face with cold, fresh air as he walked across the damp sand toward the cliffs on the other side of the bay. Halfway across the beach, he stopped and gazed out to sea. The oil tanker he'd seen from the cliff top was now barely visible, the sea haze slowly engulfing it. He moved on, the seagulls screeching and wheeling above him, as he planned out the rest of his day.

CHAPTER 4

April 17

ANGELITA DIAZ LET herself in through the front door of number 72 Russell Square. Originally from Spain, she'd lived in London for the last ten years, earning a living cleaning the houses of some very affluent clients. Although strenuous, she managed to juggle a weekend and evening cleaning job with a part-time clerking job at the nearby University College London, or UCL as it was more commonly known.

It was now ten forty-five Sunday morning, and she was running a little late. It didn't matter so much today, as her client, Dr. Dale Stanton, was away in Oslo for five days, and had asked her to come over on Sunday to ensure the flat was clean for when he returned. She walked up to the landing outside Stanton's apartment and let herself in.

As she entered the lounge, she was greeted with an odour of stale cigarettes. *That's odd*, she thought, never having noticed the smell in the apartment before. She continued into the kitchen and opened a window. As she walked back into the lounge, a pile, of what she assumed was rugs, caught her eye. She looked closer, and screamed, as she realised the pile on the floor was in fact Dr. Stanton. She dropped her bucket of cleaning products and ran over to his lifeless body.

"Dr. Stanton, Dr. Stanton; are you OK?" she cried, as she

bent down and turned Stanton onto his side, feeling his wrist for a pulse. "Oh Jesus, sweet Jesus" she cried, realising he was dead. Diaz stood up, ran to the phone and dialled 999.

"Police, fire or ambulance ma'am?" the operator asked.

"Police...and ambulance, please...hurry!"

Diaz gave the operator her name and address and put the phone down. She then slumped onto the sofa and started to cry. What seemed like half an hour passed before she heard the front door bell ring; it was the ambulance crew. She buzzed them in, and soon heard their pounding feet coming up the hall stairs. She jumped up to open the apartment door.

"Are you the apartment owner?" a stocky, muscular dark-haired man, who was holding oxygen equipment, asked.

"No, I am the cleaner. I just arrived and saw Dr. Stanton lying on the living room floor. I checked his pulse, but..." Tears started to pour down her cheeks again.

"OK...OK ma'am. We will take care of things from here. Have you any idea what happened?"

"No," Diaz said, sobbing. "I just came in and he was lying there."

Two paramedics were now stooped over the body of Dr. Dale Stanton, their radios crackling every few seconds. One of the men tried to administer oxygen, whilst the other felt for a pulse, initially on Stanton's wrist, then on his neck. "We are too late, there's nothing we can do. Rigor mortis has already set in."

"Looks like he's been dead for some time," the man holding the oxygen equipment added.

Diaz heard the sound of sirens, and assumed it must be the police. A short while later, the doorbell buzzed again, and she pressed the intercom button to let the police in.

Detective Inspector Lance Johnson and Sergeant Peter Smith appeared in the apartment and introduced themselves.

"Can you tell me what happened here please?" Johnson, the taller of the two asked, as he walked towards the body, which the paramedics had now covered with a white sheet.

"Yes, like I told the ambulance crew, I just come here to clean Dr. Stanton's apartment. He was due to be away for a while. I entered the apartment, and just saw him lying there, on the floor," Diaz said.

"I see. Did you notice anything out of the ordinary, about the apartment, when you arrived?"

"Um...No, no, everything seemed fine, as usual," Diaz replied.

"You said Dr. Stanton was supposed to be going away. Do you know where?"

"I think he mentioned Norway. He is a scientist you see, and he was always going somewhere. He is...was a very busy man."

"I see," Johnson said, as he walked into the kitchen.

"Excuse me, sir, but may I go? I really don't feel very well, and I don't think I can clean the apartment now. I can't bear to look at poor Dr. Stanton lying on the floor like that."

"Of course, but please give your details to my colleague first, just in case we need to speak to you again?"

"Yes, no problem," Diaz replied.

"Oh, one more thing, did Dr. Stanton have any family, – wife, children or girlfriend that you're aware of?"

"He wasn't married, and had no children. I wouldn't know about girlfriend. I think his parents are still alive, but I don't know where they are."

"Thank you, Ms. Diaz, make sure you leave the keys to the apartment when you go, please."

Diaz nodded and went to collect her belongings.

"What do you think?" Johnson asked the stocky paramedic.

"It's hard to say, but my guess would be a heart attack.

There doesn't appear to be any marks on the body; well, not from what I have seen. The poor chap is definitely dead though, has been for some time, maybe twenty-four hours plus. I won't be able to issue you with a cause of death certificate. I'm afraid, you'll have to arrange that with his GP, and we'll have to take the body to the mortuary for an autopsy."

"Very well," Inspector Johnson said, "I'd appreciate it if you just waited while I search for some identification."

"No problem."

Johnson rolled Stanton's body over and checked his pockets, but found nothing. Looking around for a jacket, he found one on the back of a chair, near the window. On the left inside pocket he found Stanton's wallet and mobile phone. He took both out, placing them into a clear bag in front of the ambulance crew.

In the kitchen, Officer Smith finished taking down Angelita Diaz's details. "Thank you for your help," Smith said to Diaz, as she left the apartment with her bucket full of cleaning equipment.

"Ok, we're just about done here chaps," Johnson said to the two paramedics.

The two men grabbed their equipment. "We'll be back up soon with a stretcher, for the body," the muscular paramedic said, as they both left the apartment.

"What you think, Lance?" Smith asked, adjusting his tie.

"Don't know really. Everything looks fine to me. The poor bugger may have just had a heart attack, I guess, but he looks a bit young for that. I can't see any evidence of foul play or anything to suggest anyone else being here."

"Looks like he smoked quite heavily though, judging by those fag-ends in the ashtray," Smith said, gesturing towards a half-full ashtray by the side of the sofa.

"Mm, bad habit, but all we can be sure about is that he's

been dead for a while, judging by the rigor mortis. Come on, we're no use here. Let's get back to the station and run a CRB check, then try and locate Stanton's relatives, see if we can find out who his doctor is."

"Alright, boss," Smith said, taking one last look around the apartment.

Johnson followed Smith out, pulling the door closed behind him.

Detectives' Johnson and Smith arrived back at St John's Wood police station a little while later. They were about to walk into their shared open-plan office when Superintendent Flint came down the corridor towards them, grooming his unkempt hair.

"You boys been up to anything exciting this morning?" he asked, in a deep Scottish accent.

"Is a dead scientist exciting enough, sir?"

"Really? Foul play you think? Something go wrong with one of his experiments?"

"Not really, looks like a heart attack. We'll just carry out a few routine checks, before putting the case to bed."

"Very well, I'll catch up with you both later," Flint said, as he walked briskly down the corridor to his office.

Johnson sat at his desk, powered up his computer and placed Stanton's wallet and mobile phone in front of him. "Peter, do us a favour and go and get a couple of coffees would you?"

"No problem," Smith said, disappearing to the coffee machine, situated in the back room.

Johnson brought up the CRB interface and typed in his password, then entered Stanton's details and clicked the search tab. A blue search bar moved slowly back and forth along the bottom of the screen as the computer went to work. Thirty seconds later the words 'No entries found' popped up. As he'd suspected, Stanton was clean.

Johnson then clicked on Google, re-entered Stanton's name, and hit the return key. Within seconds a list of results appeared down the page. "This is more like it," he muttered.

Harry Dean Stanton - prolific character actor...

Stanton, Harry Dean - Play.com...

Stanton Dale Dr. - Climatologist, specialising in sea level rise, associated with global warming, climate change. See also IPCC...

"Bingo!"

"Found something?" Smith asked, returning with the coffee.

"Yep, confirmation our chap was a climate scientist. Also looks like he's written some academic papers in relation to global warming. Seems to be connected with a project called *RAPID*, whatever that is."

"Here, take a look at Stanton's phone will you? I'll check his wallet."

Johnson emptied Stanton's wallet of its contents. There was a twenty pound note, some old receipts, a photo-card driving license, gym membership card, some credit cards, but that was it. Smith turned on Stanton's Nokia mobile phone. "Shit," he said, as the password prompt appeared on screen.

"Pass me the phone a minute, I want to try something."

Smith handed the phone to Johnson, who then took his own Nokia phone out of his pocket, opened it up and took the SIM card out. He then opened Stanton's phone, removed the SIM card, and inserted it into his own phone and turned it back on. "Bingo!" he said, after a few seconds. A list of names and numbers revealed themselves. Johnson scrolled down.

Adam

Atlantic Bar

Adrian

He scrolled down to *M.* "Here we are, *Mother.*"

"Well done," Smith said.

Johnson called the number and got a dialing tone. Three rings, four, five, six...Just as he was about to end the call, a soft voice answered, "Hello! Doris Stanton speaking."

Johnson cleared his throat. "Mrs. Stanton, this is Detective Inspector Lance Johnson, London Metropolitan Police. I am very sorry to disturb you, but we have some very bad news about your son. Is it possible to come and see you?"

"My son? You mean Dale? What are you talking about?" Her voice tightened.

"Mrs. Johnson, we received a call this morning from your son's cleaning lady. I'm afraid...well; she found your son dead in his apartment...a suspected heart attack."

"Heart attack? That's...that's...not possible. That can't be. You are telling me my son is dead? That can't be...it can't be true."

"I am very sorry, Mrs. Stanton. Do you live locally? Your son's body has been taken to the forensic mortuary in Westminster. The coroner will need to identify the cause of death."

There was silence on the phone.

"Mrs. Stanton?"

"Yes, I heard you. I live in Windsor. I...I just can't believe my poor Dale is no longer here."

"I am very sorry for your loss Mrs. Stanton, I know this is not a good time for you, but can you come to your son's apartment?"

"Yes...yes, I can be there in around ninety minutes." Doris Stanton started to sob and the line went dead.

Johnson grimaced at Smith as he put the mobile down.

"Ouch" Smith said, sympathetically.

Johnson and Smith arrived back at Stanton's apartment, let themselves in and waited nervously for Mrs. Stanton to arrive. One hour and forty-five minutes had passed since they had spoken to her on the phone.

Buzz...buzz. Both detectives jumped at the sound of the doorbell. Johnson stood up and went to the intercom. "Mrs. Stanton? Please come up," he said, pressing the door-entry button to let her in.

Johnson waited on the landing, and saw a plump lady with a friendly-looking face, dressed in green trousers and a black jumper with a green scarf wrapped tightly around her neck, slowly ascending the hall stairs. He greeted her as she reached the top. "Hello Mrs. Stanton, I am Detective Inspector Lance Johnson. I am very sorry about this situation."

"Please, detective, I would like five minutes here alone. Can you leave the apartment?"

"Of course...of course," Johnson said, looking over at Smith and gesturing toward the landing.

Doris Stanton entered the lounge and slumped onto the sofa. "Why, Dale? I don't understand, why you my love?" She spoke softly through her tears, and sat, staring around the room where her son's body had been found. Ten minutes passed before she got up and walked over to the entrance to the apartment, and called the detectives back in.

"I'm so sorry, Mrs. Stanton; we just needed you to check your son's apartment, make sure it was secure and everything."

"Of course, but I want Dale to have a post mortem. I know he has been under quite a lot of pressure at work recently. I need to know what caused his heart attack; he was so young."

"We will be liaising with the coroner about that, Mrs.

Stanton."

She then gave Inspector Johnson her card, containing her details, and Johnson did likewise. "Here's the set of keys that your son's cleaner had. Perhaps you might want to change the locks?"

"Thank you, I'll think about that. I will come back to the apartment in a few days, just...well, just to see to Dale's things."

"No problem. We will be in touch in a day or two, Mrs. Stanton, thank you for coming over. We'll secure the apartment for you, but you'll need to attend the mortuary."

Doris Stanton nodded solemnly.

Inspector Johnson walked her out and watched as she descended the hall stairs, and disappeared out onto Russell Square, no doubt for the saddest journey home she'd ever have to make.

CHAPTER 5

DORIS STANTON AWOKE at six-thirty Monday morning, after a poor night's sleep. Tormented by the untimely death of her son, she felt more alone than ever before. Roger, her late husband, had passed away from a heart attack only two years earlier. She looked over to his photograph on the bedside table, recalling how he had spent twenty-five years building up his pharmaceutical company, working almost every day, until the day of his death. She would never forget the last day she saw her husband alive. He had gone out for an important business lunch; unfortunately it was his last. The heart attack hit him as he was eating his dessert, and he'd ended up keeled over in his half-eaten lemon meringue pie, an extremely undignified way to go. Following her husband's untimely death, she'd inherited more money than she could ever spend. His shares alone had been worth one hundred and twenty-five million pounds. Money wasn't her problem, just the fact that her family had been taken away from her prematurely, and no amount of money could compensate for that.

She tore her eyes away from her husband's photograph and got out of bed. She needed to go back to Dale's apartment to collect some cherished keepsakes.

Doris arrived in Russell Square early, managing to find a resident permit space on Tavistock Street, not far from the apartment building. She unlocked the front door, climbed the stairs to the apartment and let herself in.

The late morning sun poured into the lounge, illuminating two large fossilised crystal ornaments that stood on the mantle over the hearth. Two fitted shelving units, tightly packed with scientific books, sat either side of the marble fireplace. She walked down the corridor and into Dale's study. Piles of papers lay scattered over the floor. Most related to climate change and sea level studies. A large stack of papers with the title; '*Grace Satellite Data on Sea Level Rise 2002-2005,*' lay untidily on the desk, a dark coffee stain covered the index on the second page.

She wandered into the bedroom; everything appeared tidy. The bedside radio alarm clock displayed 11.20 A.M, and there was a half-read *Clive Cussler* novel resting on the bed-side table, along with an empty mug. A mirrored wardrobe ran along the length of the room, which she opened. The left-hand side of the wardrobe was full of shirts and suits, the right side a mishmash of different coloured shirts and casual wear.

She closed the wardrobe, turned and looked around the room, recalling the mahogany box she was looking for, which contained some of Dale's childhood belongings. It was about the size of a small suitcase. *Where could it be?,* she wondered.

She looked at the bed and noticed the corner of an object protruding from under it. Moving closer, she could see that it was a black suitcase. She slowly bent down onto the floor, her knees clicking, pulled the suitcase out and looked inside, but it was empty. Behind the case she spotted another box, this time a dark wooden box. It was the item she had been searching for; Dale's mahogany box.

She dragged it out from under the bed, feeling a slight sense of relief knowing her son's sentimental and precious childhood items were inside. Tears came to her eyes as she remembered happier times. She opened the lid slightly and could see it was full of his belongings, but rather than open it now, she decided to look at the box's contents at home.

She pulled herself up off the floor with the help of the metal bed post, and hoisted the box onto the bed in order to get a better grip on it. She walked back down the corridor, gripping the box with both hands, took one last look around the lounge and left the apartment, carefully making her way down the hall stairs and out onto Russell Square. She looked across at the park as she walked to her car, pausing briefly to watch a few teenagers sitting eating their lunch and an elderly couple stroll through with their dog.

She arrived back at her large Elizabethan-style mansion, set in twelve acres of Windsor countryside, at just after two-thirty in the afternoon. She opened the electric wrought-iron gates with her remote control key, drove up the gravel driveway to the front of the mansion, and parked.

Once inside, she went into the kitchen to put the kettle on, placing Dale's mahogany box on the kitchen table. Unable to wait any longer, she opened it and carefully took out the items. First, an electric Flying Scotsman train, then a blue Frisbee, a pair of old slippers and two Rupert the Bear Annuals. At the bottom she saw a worn sealed brown envelope. She pulled it out and ripped it open using her silver letter opener.

There was some kind of document inside...*Dale's will!* She set it down on the table and poured herself a cup of tea, then took the document from the envelope and started reading;

This is the last Will and Testament of me, Dr. Dale Stanton, of 72 Russell Square, London, WC1.

I appoint Mr. Robert Spire, Lawyer in the firm of Denton Croft and Partners, of 455 Bond Street,

London, and my mother Mrs. Doris Stanton, of Falcon Walk, Windsor, to be the Executors and Trustees of this my Will.

I revoke all former Wills and Testamentary dispositions heretofore, made by me.

Robert Spire? I don't recognise that name. She continued reading;

I leave all my real estate whatsoever and wherever to my trustees absolutely to be divided as follows;

Seventy - five per cent, to be divided between the following charities and/or organisations;

The Allegiance for Climate Protection

The World Wide Fund for Animals

PureAir, The CleanWorld Trust

As to the remaining twenty- five percent, I bequeath to an organisation or company, solely concerned with researching the causes of, and/or to mitigate against the consequences of climate change.

Dale had left all his money to organisations connected with climate change and global warming. At least his death wouldn't be totally in vain. She sat back in her chair, thinking through what all this would mean. *Had Robert Spire known Dale? Was he still around to help administer Dale's estate?*

She poured herself another cup of tea, before checking the telephone book for the law firm's listing picked up the telephone and dialled the number for Denton Croft Solicitors.

"Hello, Denton Croft and Partners, may I help you?" a chirpy female voice inquired.

Doris introduced herself, mentioned the will and asked to

speak to Mr. Robert Spire.

The girl on the phone asked her to hold, while she transferred the call.

Doris sat patiently, listening to bland music coming out of the receiver.

"Hello, Mrs. Stanton? My name is David Croft, senior partner here. I understand that you have a will, naming Robert Spire as executor, is this correct?"

"Yes, that's right. May I speak with him?"

"I'm afraid Mr. Spire left this firm around two years ago. I've done a client record search and it looks like he was the last person to have your son's file. My understanding is that he may well have taken the papers with him. We don't have a copy of the will anymore, I'm afraid."

Doris sighed as she heard the bad news.

Mr. Croft continued, "I can tell you Robert Spire took over a law firm in Wales, west Wales, I believe. Hold on, I'll do a Law Society search against his name, see if I can find the firm."

Doris could hear the faint tapping of a computer keyboard as she waited.

"Ah yes, here we are. His firm is called *Spirelaw*. If you have a pen, I can give you the number."

She quickly scribbled the telephone number down, thanked Mr. Croft for his help, and ended the call, feeling slightly more optimistic than she had two minutes earlier.

It was now coming up to three in the afternoon; she needed to call her friends to cancel the bridge arrangements. She felt in no mood to socialise. Instead, she would focus all her energy on getting hold of Robert Spire to discuss her son's will.

CHAPTER 6

THE ASSASSIN GLANCED at her watch: it was two-thirty A.M, time to make contact with her current employer. She hoped they would have another assignment for her.

She powered up her computer notebook, typed in her password, and entered a second encrypted site, and typed a secure e-mail;

H2O has been evaporated. Please confirm transfer and further instructions.

Anyone sophisticated enough to eavesdrop would struggle to make sense of the cryptic sentence. She waited for a response. Thirty seconds later she heard a *'pflop,'* signalling the arrival of an e-mail into her mail box.

Excellent news, transfer is complete. Attend climate change conference-San Francisco in five days. Dr. Jack Bannister (CH4) will be in attendance. The methane must be burnt, same terms. Please confirm.

The e-mail was signed; *Arc Bin Quid Lo.*

She considered the request for a few seconds before agreeing to the instructions. She then logged out of her encrypted site, and signed into her Zurich bank account. Sixty thousand euros had been deposited, as promised.

Easy money, she thought, as she logged back out. She turned the computer off, poured a double measure of Vodka, and lay back on her bed.

Ksenyia Petrovsky had conditioned herself not to feel any emotion after killing. Her training with the KGB, and later the FSB, had turned her into a professional and resilient assassin.

The assignments, given to her by *Arc Bin Quid Lo,* had interested her. The fact that western scientists were now telling the rest of the developing world that they should cut back their greenhouse gas emissions, stop polluting, stop building power stations, stop virtually every industrial process that added to Earth's greenhouse gas levels, angered her. The governments of western countries were hypocrites. They had been polluting the world for the last hundred years. She didn't know a lot about global warming, but as far as she was concerned, her world had never been warm. Not her childhood, and certainly not where she had lived most of her life - Siberia.

She reached over to the side table and picked up a picture, containing a worn photograph, of a handsome moustached man, with broad shoulders, that filled his military uniform, two little girls standing by his side. She stared at the photograph of herself, her sister and her father, holding back a tear as she recalled her mother taking the picture some twenty-eight years earlier.

Caressing the photo, she thought back to when she was recruited into the KGB. She had an easy route in, after her father had served in the Russian-Afghan war. She had been nine years old when he was killed by a single gunshot wound to the chest, as his unit pulled out from eastern Afghanistan during the 1986 withdrawal. His unit belonged to one of the first in the Red Army to pull back, after orders were finally given by, the then President, Gorbachev. Another week and things would have been very different.

She thought back to those hard times, her mother struggling to raise her, and her younger Sister Irina. She recalled her burning desire upon her eighteenth birthday to find out exactly what had happened to her father, and as a result, met the man who would later recruit her into the KGB. It was the only way for her to escape poverty. Scraping a living and trying to make ends meet for herself, her mother and sister was not a life she was prepared to endure.

She had served in the KGB, and later the FSB for eight years, before deciding to go it alone. She wanted more, more adventure, more money, and wanted to get out of Moscow where she had been based. The combat training, classes in espionage and seduction, had been gruelling, but had provided her with a host of useful skills. Listening and intercepting satellite phone conversations however had become boring. It was not what she signed up for. She had wanted to see the world, and would do whatever was required to further her ambitions, and to help her mother and sister.

She frequently had to reassure herself of the reasons for becoming a trained killer. For the right price, she would now allow herself to be hired by anyone willing to pay. Her targets were usually scum, gangland bosses, drug dealers, corrupt officials, and deserved what they got.

These latest assignments were a little more unusual, but the pay was excellent, and her research had suggested that the West was now trying to prevent the developing world's desire to modernise itself, by suppressing its ability to industrialise, the explanation - global warming. *No, the scientists were justifiable targets.*

She got up from the leather chair and reached for a small suede suit case, hidden out of sight, on top of the freezer. She opened it and shuffled through the various passports inside and found her UK passport, the identification she would use for her trip to the United States. She needed to register herself with the new ESTA system; or Electronic System for Travel Authorisation. Another expensive layer of security the Americans had put in place, in an attempt to improve airline safety. She found the appropriate website, and registered herself, then booked a Virgin-Atlantic flight, leaving London

Heathrow on Friday for San Francisco, returning the following Thursday. The hotel booking could wait until later.

She refreshed her drink and walked over to the window and looked out onto the deserted street below, her thoughts wandering to the assignment that lay ahead.

CHAPTER 7

April 18

ROBERT SPIRE ARRIVED at his office at eight-thirty Monday morning, still feeling slightly jaded, following a late night catching up with Angela after her weekend away in London. The one and a half bottles of 1996 Muriel Rioja they'd consumed had no doubt contributed to his fuzzy head.

Spire's office was a small one, consisting of four rooms over a newsagent in the main street in the village of Oakdale. The rooms were bright and airy, and the walls painted off-white, complemented by colourful modern art prints. He worked alone, apart from Kim; his receptionist - come secretary - come office manager. She was twenty-eight, and her attractive looks were complemented by her tomboy personality. She was also very reliable, which was the main thing, and without her, he knew he'd be in a mess.

Above his office were a few rooms owned by the newsagents below, used mainly for storage space. A large window looked out to a reasonable sized yard, come parking area, and beyond that was a narrow lane, which arced back around to the main road.

Spire sat down and turned on his computer and desktop lamp. Whilst waiting for the computer to boot up, he picked up his *Hoyo de Monterrey* Cuban cigar, which was still in its tube, unscrewed the top, and inhaled the rich aroma. The cigar had been a gift from Kim, and he had so far resisted smoking it, but planned to as soon he successfully completed the Taunton case. The wall to the right was decorated with a large map of the world, and, on the wall to his left, a small flat screen television which was usually tuned to CNN.

He'd just started dictating some witness statements on the Taunton case when his telephone rang.

"Robert, there's a Mrs. Stanton on the phone. She says you are named as an executor in her son's will. Do you want to speak to her, or shall I tell her you're busy?" Kim said helpfully.

"Don't recognise the name. See if you can find a file, and put her through."

Doris Stanton introduced herself, the reason for her call, and how she had obtained his number from the senior partner of his old firm, Denton Croft Solicitors.

Spire hesitated before responding, trying to recall anyone appointing him as an executor at his old firm. He could not. "Dr. Dale Stanton, you say?" Spire asked, trying to buy some time, whilst searching for Stanton's name on his recently installed case management computer system.

"That's correct. I was wondering if I could meet up with you, Mr. Spire, to discuss the contents of my son's will?"

"Mm...Well of course, Mrs. Stanton. Where are you based?"

"I live in Windsor, Falcon Walk; it's just off Winkfield Road as you leave Windsor. I understand you are down in Wales. If it's OK, I could..."

Spire cut her off mid-sentence. "Actually, Mrs. Stanton, I am due to travel to London during the week," he lied, fancying a trip away from the office and west Wales.

"That would be very kind of you if you could visit Mr.

Spire. How does Wednesday sound, at say two in the afternoon?"

"Two is perfect, Mrs. Stanton. I shall see you then."

Spire ended the call, and then dialled Kim's extension. "Kim, did you find any information on Dr. Dale Stanton?"

"I've looked on the computer, carried out a file search, but there's nothing on him. Can you recall transferring the file when you left Denton Hall?"

"Nope!"

"Hold on, I'll have a look in the cabinets."

A few minutes later Kim walked into his room, holding a slim blue file. "Got it," she said, smiling.

"Well, well. Where the hell did you find that?"

"It's amazing what you can find in those cabinets when you have a proper look. It was hiding at the back of the miscellaneous section."

"Really?" Spire said, opening the empty-looking blue file. Inside, he found a few scrawled-on pieces of A4 paper, together with a copy of the will of Dr. Dale Stanton. He recognised the notes as belonging to his previous assistant, Mary-Anne, who had worked for him a year or two before he'd left the firm. He guessed she must have appointed him as executor without him knowing it, in conjunction with the client's mother, Doris Stanton, a common enough appointment.

He opened the two-page document and quickly perused it. He read the clauses providing gifts to three named global warming related organisations, all of which he'd heard of.

Hello, this is interesting. The clause giving away twenty-five percent of his estate to an organisation of the executors' choice was particularly unusual. *Dr. Stanton clearly wasn't short of cash.*

He checked his watch. It was approaching four forty-five in the afternoon, and he felt like getting away early, perhaps for a run. He powered down his computer, and then went to turn off the television. As he did, a news headline appeared on CNN;

'President appoints new member of 'Green Team' to fight global warming.'

About time, he thought, as he turned the television off and left his room. Kim was busy typing some dictation on the computer. "Oh, Kim, do me a favour and see what you can find out about Dr. Dale Stanton, would you please?"

"Sure," Kim replied. "I'll dig something up, ready for the morning."

"One more thing, blank out my diary for the next two days please. I'll be taking a trip over to Windsor."

"Off to see the Queen?" Kim asked, raising her eyebrows.

"Very funny," Spire smiled at her, as he left the office.

It was six in the evening and Doris Stanton was just about to run herself a bath when the phone rang. It was Inspector Johnson, calling to let her know that they'd received the results of her son's post-mortem.

"I'm listening, Inspector."

"Well, according to the coroner, your son's blood contained extremely high levels of nicotine, and a very strong nicotine patch was found on his arm. It seems that a combination of the patch, combined with the large number of cigarettes he'd smoked, perhaps in a short period of time, was enough to cause the seizure."

"Nicotine patch? Cigarettes? I'm a bit confused Inspector. As far as I was aware, my son did not smoke. Are you sure about this?"

"That's the coroner's finding, Mrs. Stanton. We found a

dozen or so smoked cigarettes in the apartment. Whilst the autopsy revealed no evidence of any smoking damage in your son's lungs, the evidence suggests he was a heavy smoker."

"I have never seen Dale smoke, Inspector. I just don't know what to say."

"I understand how you feel, Mrs. Stanton, really I do. The official cause of death is a nicotine induced seizure, I'm sorry. I'd be grateful if you could come to the station sometime to collect your son's wallet, mobile phone and apartment key. We will be closing the investigation at our end."

"I'll come by tomorrow morning, around eleven."

Doris put the phone down, feeling angrier and more confused than ever. *Dale had never smoked, why had he started now? What the hell had he done to himself?*

The following day Doris drove back to London, picked up Dale's personal items from the police station, then made her way back home to Windsor. She sat down at her kitchen table, opened her son's wallet, and removed his credit cards with the intention of cancelling them all. As she pulled the cards out, a glossy, black business card fell onto the table. The expensive looking card was emblazoned in gold letters with the name *Arc-Bin-Quid-Lo.*

Probably one of Dale's work contacts, she thought. The card didn't have a telephone number on it, which she considered a little odd. She put it back into the wallet and picked up the telephone to cancel her son's three Visa cards.

Robert Spire woke early Tuesday morning, ate his breakfast of toast and freshly brewed coffee, picked up his overnight bag and left for Windsor. Angela had left thirty minutes earlier, for her boutique in the village. The two-hundred mile drive up the M4 was effortless, Spire stopping once for fuel. He now found himself driving out along one of the main roads from Windsor.

"At the next junction, turn right," the reassuring female voice from the Audi's satellite navigation system, directed.

He turned into Winkfield Road, and accelerated down the empty country lane.

"You have reached your destination," the navigation system suddenly confirmed.

He slowed down and looked around. *This can't be right.*

He was in the middle of nowhere, dense woodland stretched out on both sides of the road. As he started to reverse slowly back up the road, he noticed a large pair of wrought-iron gates set back from the main road. There was a silver plaque on the gatepost with the name *Falcon Walk* printed on it. Below the plaque was an intercom. He drove up to the gates, reached out and pressed the intercom button. Thirty seconds passed and the chrome box crackled with the sound of a voice. "Welcome, Mr. Spire, please drive up to the front of the house."

Spire waited for the large gates to swing back, and then proceeded up the long gravel driveway. He spotted smoke rising from two white chimney stacks, shrouded behind a grove of large old oak trees which populated the vast expanse of lawn.

He arrived at the house, freshly painted an off-white colour, and pulled up behind a dark Mercedes. Two ten-foot conifers stood either side of an ornate columned porch, providing shelter to the large wooden double-entrance doors. As he put his hand out to ring the doorbell, one of the doors swung open. "Hello, Mr. Spire, do come in. Thank you so much for travelling all the way up here to see me." An elderly, but feisty looking, lady stood there smiling at him.

"No problem, Mrs. Stanton," Spire said, shaking her hand.

"Please call me Doris. Come in, come in."

Spire walked into a large hallway. A beige marble floor stretched out in front of him. Beyond, an opulent staircase ascended and divided in two, with each stairway appearing to serve a separate wing of the house.

Mrs. Stanton ushered him in through a door on the left, which opened up into a large living room, decorated with a cream carpet and brown leather sofas. A large black-granite fireplace containing a crackling fire was burning away, the odd ember from the freshly cut wood popped and sparked out from grate onto the hearth.

"Beautiful house you have here, Mrs. Stanton. How do you manage to keep it looking so immaculate – I mean the grounds and everything? You and your husband must have your hands full."

"Thank you. Well I certainly don't manage it all by myself. My husband passed away some time ago, but I have plenty of help from two cleaners and three gardeners, and the luxury of time." Doris motioned for Spire to sit down. "Please, take a seat, Robert. May I call you Robert?"

"Of course," Spire said, relaxing into the comfortable armchair.

"I have made a pot of tea, would you like some?"

"That would be great."

Doris Stanton disappeared, returning five minutes later with a tray of tea and an assortment of shortbread biscuits. She handed him a cup, and offered him a biscuit. "Robert, I trust you have now seen my son's will?"

"Yes, I have. I must say I don't recall meeting your son. I think my assistant at my last firm must have taken instructions from him, and appointed myself as co-executor."

"I see. Well, I'll be frank with you; I am totally devastated by what has happened. Dale was all I had left. My husband died two years ago, leaving me everything. He was extremely wealthy, as you can see."

No kidding, Spire thought, dipping a biscuit into his tea.

"Did you appreciate that Dale was a scientist with the Met Office, focusing on climate change?"

"Well, to be honest, I haven't had time to consider anything in much detail, but I guessed from the legacies he'd left that his speciality may have been in that area."

"Yes, well, he was committed to his work, and for the last eight months or so, he was working on a project down in Southampton, with the university I believe."

"I see, but what does all this have to do with your son's will?" Spire asked, somewhat puzzled.

"Well, yesterday, I received a call from the police, confirming that my son died from a heart attack, caused, apparently, by an overdose of nicotine. According to the coroner he was wearing a nicotine patch, and had smoked half a packet of cigarettes before he died. His lungs, however, showed no evidence of smoke related damage. This seems very odd to me. Dale, as far as I am aware, didn't smoke."

Spire listened as he sipped his tea, wondering where the conversation was leading.

"My son had a cleaning lady, named Angelita Diaz. I managed to get in touch with her yesterday and I asked her about Dale's smoking habit. She told me she had never known Dale to smoke either, not in all the time she had been cleaning his apartment. But, she did recall seeing an ashtray full of cigarette-ends in the lounge when she found his body, and the place reeked of stale smoke, something she hadn't ever noticed before. She forgot to mention this to the police at the time as she was in shock. This has made me a little suspicious."

"Suspicious? What of?" Spire asked.

"Well, surely if my son smoked, she would have noticed.

So, why would he be wearing a nicotine patch?"

"Well, if he was a smoker, I suppose he could have been weary about smoking at home. A nicotine patch would suggest he was trying to kick the habit," Spire said.

"Well, yes, I suppose. Anyway, Robert, as you can see from Dale's will, he left twenty-five percent of his assets, probably around three hundred thousand pounds, to an organisation of the executors' choice, on condition it is relevant to global warming. I would like to engage your services to find an appropriate home for the money. I know you specialise in environmental matters, and you have a great deal of experience in this area. My son would appreciate the fact that you were looking after his interests, I'm sure."

"Well, I appreciate the compliment," Spire replied. "Of course I can try and help. If you like, I could try and find out what your son was working on down in Southampton, if that would assist?"

"Anything would be helpful right now, Robert. Don't worry about expenses. I will pay you your hourly rate and any expenses on top. Just send me your engagement letter, or whatever you need to do, and I will sign it. I would suggest that you take a trip to Southampton University first. Maybe the organisation down there will turn out to be an appropriate home for the legacy Dale left."

"Very well, I'll make that my priority. I have a few loose ends to tie up in work, but will be able to get started next week."

"That would be fantastic. Oh, while I remember, I have Dale's wallet here. I was cancelling his credit cards when this business card fell out. You can have it, may have something to do with the project he was working on in Southampton."

Spire glanced at the expensive-looking black glossy business card, before putting it in his pocket.

"OK, Robert, I have a few things I need to do, so if you are happy with everything we have discussed, I'll have to say goodbye for now."

Spire stood up and shook Doris's hand. "Thank you for the tea. I hope I can help with your son's estate. I'll report back as soon as I return from Southampton."

Doris walked him to the front door. "Thank you again for coming so soon. Have a safe trip home."

Spire drove slowly back down the long driveway, nodding as he passed to a gardener, who was busy raking up some fallen leaves from one of the rockeries. The large black gates swung open as he approached them. He drove through and onto the main road, and accelerated towards Windsor. He had arranged to meet one of his good friends there for dinner, and was now looking forward to the company, a decent steak and a good bottle of wine.

As he drove, his thoughts wandered to the odd comments made by Doris Stanton, about not knowing her son had smoked, and about the coroner's findings. *Perhaps Dr Stanton had been under a lot of stress?*

It was certainly a very unlucky way to die, he considered, as he drove along the tree-lined avenue toward Windsor town centre.

CHAPTER 8

California, April 21

DR. JACK BANNISTER was seated at his desk in the study of his vine-covered four bedroom home, in Fairoaks, a leafy suburb of Sacramento, California. He took his glasses off and rubbed his tired eyes. He was putting the finishing touches to his presentation paper entitled;

'Arctic Ice Loss, Warming Seas, and the New Methane Time-Bomb.'

If this didn't give the politicians something to think about, nothing would, he thought, as he finalised the report's conclusions.

Bannister had worked for the National Snow and Ice Data Centre based in Boulder, Colorado, since graduating with a degree in chemistry from Berkeley, California, in the mid-sixties. He had spent most of his life studying the changing composition of the atmosphere since the early days of NSIDC. His studies closely followed the work of Dr. David Keeling who had, since 1958, until his death, been monitoring the amount of carbon dioxide in the atmosphere from a sampling base on the largest volcano on the planet - Mauna Loa in Hawaii.

Keeling's research had caught Bannister's interest as a

young freshman at Berkeley after the first ten years' worth of data had been made available, which showed an increase in carbon dioxide levels from 315 parts per million by volume in air (ppmv), to around 325 ppmv. He had wondered whether the increase would continue, and his suspicions, it turned out, had been correct. Atmospheric carbon dioxide levels now stood at 395 ppmv; an increase of around twenty-seven percent. He continued checking his almost completed paper.

My team has been looking for potential methane gas 'hotspots' around the world, in order to try and identify areas of frozen methane hydrates. These locations have been chosen using a combination of geological data, historical and current seawater temperatures, and data from NASA's Jason One and Jason Two sea-surface height satellites.

We know that higher than normal sea-surface height, indicates warmer seas, due to the expansion of seawater as it warms. So, we started looking in areas of the world's oceans which were normally much colder. An area off the French Crozet Islands, a sub-Antarctic archipelago which lies in the Southern Indian Ocean, caught our interest. In early 2009 we approached the French government to request permission to explore the continental shelf around the islands using the two-man submersible, Poseidon, on loan from our Oceanic Exploration Department. I was lucky enough to obtain one of only two licenses issued by the French Government, the other permit, I established, had been granted to a government department belonging to The Kingdom of Saudi Arabia, it seems, for fishing rights.

The Poseidon's crew discovered several plumes of streaming bubbles coming from the ocean floor, some of which reached the surface. Samples confirmed the gas to be methane, which is some twenty-three times more powerful - molecule for molecule - than carbon dioxide, when talking about its greenhouse gas warming potential. This, as many of you will appreciate is a very worrying development. Not only does it suggest that Southern Antarctic waters are warming, but that methane gas is now escaping from the ocean depths into the atmosphere, where it will exacerbate the global warming problem. We now call upon the scientific community to immediately put in place a plan to monitor, and capture, the escaping methane. An area of ten thousand square kilometres around the islands will need to be restricted and cordoned off, and discussions with the French Government will need to take place immediately...

"Darling, lunch is ready."

Bannister was immersed in his paper, and didn't hear his wife calling him.

"Darling, are you still awake?" she called again.

"Ah, yes, sorry, Margaret, I'll be right there." He put his pen down, stretched and turned off his laptop.

"How much more do you have to do today? You've been working on this paper for months. I know you're dedicated to your work, but the kids and I rarely see you anymore!"

"I'm sorry, darling, it's just about finished. A little more polishing tonight and it'll be ready."

"Thank God! Maybe you could take the kids and me on that trip to Hawaii you promised months ago?"

"It's a deal," Bannister said, smiling at his wife, as he ground black pepper on to his mozzarella and tomato salad.

"So, what time are you planning on leaving tomorrow?"

"Well, it's a good two hour drive down to the bay area; if I leave by lunchtime, I should get there for around four in the afternoon. I'll be meeting up with John and some of the other guys for dinner. I may try and finally get over to Alcatraz on

Saturday. The usual pre-conference cocktail party is on Sunday evening, and then the presentation is on Monday. After that, well...I'm all yours."

"Wow! I'm honoured," Margaret replied, forcing a smile.

"It's a shame you can't at least come to the cocktail party, but you know how boring those things can be, and besides, someone's got to look after the kids."

"Yeah, well, I'll just get busy planning our vacation to Hawaii," Margaret said, smiling wryly.

Bannister finished his lunch, and checked the time: it was coming up to one in the afternoon. "I need to go over the paper a few more times. I'll be in the study if you need me."

"Where else would I find you?" Margaret said, clearing the lunch plates away. "I'll bring you some tea in a little while. Oh, do you know where you'll be staying when you get there?"

"Yep, the office has already arranged that. It's the small friendly boutique hotel, alongside Washington Square Park, in North Beach. The number's on the fridge."

"You never know, if I manage to get rid of the kids, I might see you there," Margaret shouted from the kitchen.

Three hours later, Bannister closed the reference book he'd been using for his research, satisfied that his paper was now complete. He gulped down the last dregs of cold tea. The samples of gas taken by the *Poseidon* submersible team had arrived only six days earlier, just in time. Prior to completing his report, he'd carried out a number of tests on the gas to determine its composition. The entire sample of gas had been used up in the process, but this wasn't a problem, as the *Poseidon* would be collecting more. The tests had confirmed his worst fears; methane gas was indeed venting from the seabed around the Sub-Antarctic Crozet Islands.

He turned off his computer, stretched his arms, and got up from his leather armchair. It was six-thirty when he finally wandered into the lounge. He poured himself a small brandy and sank onto the sofa next to Margaret, who was engrossed in an episode of the detective series *Monk.*

Thirty minutes later, he drifted off to sleep, on his wife's shoulder.

Ksenyia Petrovsky left her apartment, at six on Friday morning, and stepped into the waiting taxi. Her black Samsonite suitcase was packed with just enough clothes for the seven day trip, her hair was now chestnut brown, to match her United Kingdom passport photograph. A leather case, containing her Leica camera was slung over her shoulder.

"Heathrow airport please, terminal three."

"No problem, love," the Hackney-cab driver replied, in a cockney accent. "Going anywhere decent? Getting away from this bloody awful weather, are we?"

"Just a short business trip, nowhere special," she replied.

Despite the wet morning, the traffic was surprisingly light, and the cab dropped her at Heathrow two and a half hours before the flight's scheduled departure time. She checked in at the Virgin desk and one hour forty-five minutes later had boarded the aircraft, and was now searching for her seat on the upper deck.

A flight attendant approached, and offered her a glass of Champagne. She accepted the drink and relaxed into her leather seat; thankful no-one had been seated next to her. Thirty minutes later, and with a roar of the aircraft's four Rolls-Royce engines, the plane lifted into the air.

Ksenyia finished her champagne and swallowed a prescription sleeping pill. She closed her eyes, mentally preparing herself for the eleven hour flight.

The *ping* from the fasten seat-belt sign coming on woke her from a deep sleep. A flight attendant walked by, making sure passengers had obeyed the order. She looked out of the window as the aircraft banked right, and saw the unmistakable orange-red span of the Golden Gate Bridge come in to view as the 747 flew over. She looked down on the densely built up area of downtown San Francisco, its famous undulating hills hardly noticeable from the air.

"Cabin crew, ten minutes to landing," the pilot announced, over the P.A system.

Ksenyia heard the whine from the 747's hydraulics as the wing flaps extended, followed by the dull thud of the landing gear coming down. The aircraft seemed to glide, almost silently as it descended toward the airport. The only thing visible out of the window was the blue Pacific Ocean, until the runway finally came into view at the very last moment.

She waited patiently in the international arrivals queue, before finally being called toward the immigration desk.

"Passport please, Ma'am," the officer demanded.

Ksenyia handed over her passport.

"What is the purpose of your visit?" he asked.

"I am here on business, for a photo assignment."

The officer scanned her passport, looking up at Ksenyia as she replied.

"How long do you intend staying in the United States?"

"Just under a week, I'll be leaving next Thursday."

"Thank you, madam, have a nice stay."

Ksenyia passed two armed guards, and walked out toward the baggage reclaim area, collected her luggage and made her way to the exit, where another armed guard was busy checking passports, and collecting visa documentation. "Afternoon, Ma'am; are you carrying any food products in your bag?" he asked.

"No," Ksenyia replied, smiling at the officer.

"Do you mind if I had a look in your case please?"

"Not at all," Ksenyia said, feeling her pulse quicken.

The officer ushered her over to a table screened off from the main baggage reclaim area. She noted she was the only passenger being searched.

"Is there a problem, Officer...Jaggard?" she asked, in an exaggerated English accent, spotting the guard's name printed on his identity badge.

"No problem, Ma'am, just routine. Please open the case."

She entered her pass-code into the Samsonite's built in padlocks and the case clicked open.

The officer started rifling through the case, pulling out clothes and shoes, and placing them on the table. He then took out her wash bag, which contained the nicotine solution.

Ksenyia kept her gaze locked on Jaggard as he picked out the vial of clear liquid.

"What's this?" he asked.

"Contact lens solution," she replied, pointing to her eyes.

Jaggard shook the bottle and started to unscrew the top, just as another officer appeared from a door toward the back of the cordoned off area they were in.

Ksenyia felt her heart pounding as she watched the second officer walk over to speak with Jaggard, a concerned look on his face.

Officer Jaggard turned back to her. "OK, Ma'am, you can pack your things back up and go," he said, handing the vial back to her. "Have an enjoyable stay here, in San Francisco."

The two officers hurried away, their radio's crackling.

Ksenyia took a deep breath, slowly exhaling as she repacked her case, her heart rate gradually returning to normal. She walked out into the main terminal building, pushed past some travel agents holding up name signs, and exited into the warm spring Californian sun. She got into one of the waiting yellow cabs and gave the name of her hotel to the driver.

She relaxed into the back of the cab as it sped away from the airport terminal building and onto the Bayshore Freeway, which was already choked up with commuter traffic. *Let's hope Dr. Bannister is enjoying the last few days of his life,* she thought, as the taxi edged through the traffic toward the North Beach area of the city.

CHAPTER 9

French Crozet Islands

ON THE OTHER side of the world, it was six-thirty in the morning. The two-man crew onboard the submersible *Poseidon,* were navigating slowly along a section of ocean floor, two nautical miles off the southern tip of the Il de l'Est. They had received a request to explore the southern ridge, to search for evidence of further venting gas, after having taken a sample from the northern ridge, six days earlier.

The craft's powerful underwater halogen lights penetrated the inky blackness ahead. Every so often, a squid could be seen crossing the shafts of light, before disappearing into the darkness.

Lieutenants' Rogers and Skipton, operating the submersible, could now see the island's continental shelf, rising gently on the port side, as they proceeded in an easterly direction, hugging the southern tip of the island close to where it gently rose from the ocean floor.

Suddenly the intercom sprang to life, followed by a burst of static. *"Ocean Explorer* to *Poseidon, Ocean Explorer* to *Poseidon*, please provide your status report."

"This is *Poseidon*," Rogers responded, "Depth; seven hundred-forty metres and proceeding in an easterly direction along the ocean floor, tracking side of island ridge, over."

"Continue on present course. It's promising to be a sunny morning up here."

"Thanks for letting us know. It's black as coal down here."

The intercom fell silent again. The *Ocean Explorer* was maintaining position, three quarters of a kilometre above, the vessel's multiple thrusters being controlled by the latest global positioning equipment as it tracked the submersible below.

The NSIDC registered *Ocean Explorer* had left her home port of San Diego one month earlier, for the voyage to the southern oceans. The crew of eight, including the crew operating the submersible, was now ready to return home. All that was required of them was twenty-four hours further surveillance along the Island's southern ridge, before the operation ended.

Lieutenants' Rogers and Skipton had no idea what was in the water sample they had collected six days earlier, neither did the crew on board the *Explorer*, although they surmised that the gas bubbles venting at two locations on the northern side of the island were a consequence of volcanic activity. They had seen similar vents before, near the Hawaiian Islands.

"I'll be glad to get out of this damn sardine can," Rogers said, his voice producing a faint echo within the confined space of the submersible.

"You and me both; I've had cramp for the last hour."

The submersible was configured so that the two operators sat back-to-back, with their upper bodies surrounded by acrylic glass viewing bubbles, giving them both excellent three hundred-and-sixty degree visibility. Skipton, sitting in the rear swivel-chair, was able to rotate easily, in order to operate *Poseidon's* two rear manipulator arms. Rogers was seated at the front of the craft, and had access to the controls of the two larger arms, operated by two levers on the control panels in front of him.

They continued along the ridge, the craft's underwater lights illuminating the barren ocean seabed ahead. After a while the halogen lights picked up an object, a metallic shaft, half buried in the ocean floor sediment in front of the submersible. Rogers reduced propulsion, and turned thirty degrees starboard, in order to take a closer look. "Can you see that, Dan?"

"Yep," Skipton replied, "Looks like some kind of metallic rod or something, can't quite make it out."

"Let's go take a closer look."

Rogers manoeuvred *Poseidon* towards the object, hovering the craft a few metres above the seafloor. As the area became illuminated, they could see that the shiny rod hadn't been submerged for long, as its surface was still smooth steel, and clear of barnacles or crustaceans of any kind.

Rogers delicately moved the control knob which operated the mechanical arm, extending it toward the end of the buried object. Manipulating a smaller knob, he closed the clamps around the buried object. Then, delicately operating the main controls, he pulled the long metallic shaft clear from its resting place. Clouds of sediment billowed out from the seabed, temporarily blocking all visibility. After a short while, the particles slowly dispersed, revealing the object clearly for the first time.

"Looks to me like a large drill collar," Rogers said, studying the object clamped in the manipulator arm. "It appears the drill head has sheared off. I think we are just holding the end of it. The rest may still be buried further down."

"What the hell is it doing down here? It clearly hasn't been submerged for very long," Skipton said, somewhat puzzled by the find.

Static suddenly burst out from *Poseidon's* intercom. "*Ocean*

Explorer to *Poseidon*, forty-five minutes to ascent. Please confirm."

"*Poseidon* here, forty-five minutes confirmed. We're going to check something out down here," Rogers replied.

On the surface, radar operator, Joe Martin, onboard the *Explorer,* got up from his desk to relieve himself. He'd been sitting at the sonar, monitoring *Poseidon,* for four hours without a break. As he got up he failed to notice a second image, appearing on the sonar screen, moving towards the submersible.

The *Poseidon's* underwater sonar suddenly started to ping in quick succession, prompting Rogers to tap the screen in front of him.

Skipton then heard a dull throbbing sound coming from somewhere behind him. He swivelled his chair around to look, and was immediately blinded by a powerful light. *What the hell...?*

The sound of bending metal screeched through the small craft, followed by a loud...*Crack!* Rogers and Skipton briefly felt the shock-waves from the implosion that followed, as more than seventy atmospheres of water pressure pulverised them.

Joe Martin, aboard *Explorer,* returned to his post and glanced down at the sonar screen. Previously where he had seen a green image, representing *Poseidon's* position, he saw nothing. *Shit,* he thought, as he expanded the sonar range - again nothing. *That's odd!*

"*Explorer* to *Poseidon*. Everything OK with you guys?"

There was silence.

"*Explorer* to *Poseidon,* please give your current status!"

There was no response.

"This is *Explorer*, I repeat; please provide me with your current status."

Joe Martin tried again, but failed to reach the *Poseidon*. "Christ, where are they?" he cursed. He reached up for the switch, and sounded the *Ocean Explorer's* general alarm.

CHAPTER 10

April 22

ROBERT SPIRE ARRIVED at his office just after midday on Friday. Kim either wasn't in, or she'd gone out for lunch. He turned off the alarm and entered the reception, went straight into the small kitchen and flicked the kettle on.

Damn, no fresh coffee, he realised, on opening the fridge door. He made himself a cup of instant, wandered into his office and powered up the computer, turning the television on to CNN to catch up on the latest news. A NASA news report confirmed that one of their satellites - designed to map world CO_2 levels - had failed to reach orbit, and had crashed in Antarctica. *Another zillion dollars up in smoke,* he mused, as he swivelled his chair back toward the computer screen.

On his desk was a thin A4 folder; Dr. Dale Stanton's name was printed on a white label in the top left hand corner. Inside the file were several A4 sized sheets of paper containing information on Dr. Stanton, which Kim had obtained from the internet. There was a summary of an article entitled '*Sea level rise 2002 to 2005 IPCC presentation. doc.*' There were other items of information relating to Dr. Stanton's work at the Meteorological Office, including the post he'd held at Southampton as a science liaison officer for *RAPID-WATCH 2005 to 2012.*

RAPID appeared to be a project looking into the causes of

rapid changes in climate, particularly in relation to the Atlantic Ocean conveyor, or current. There was also some information on Dr. Stanton's qualifications, obtained from Kings College London, but that was about it.

Spire heard the main office door open, and glanced up to see Kim walking in. She placed her bags down, and walked over to his open door.

"Afternoon, Robert, fancy a cup of fresh coffee? How was the trip to Windsor?"

"Yes to coffee, as for Windsor, the trip turned out to be pretty interesting. Mrs. Stanton has retained us to find a suitable home for the three hundred thousand pounds left by her son in his will."

"Three-hundred thousand pounds...wow! That's some legacy."

"Certainly is, but nothing compared to the amount of money Mrs. Stanton seems to have. She wants me to go down to Southampton, dig around a bit. Perhaps shed some light on why her son had a heart attack so early in his career. I think she just wants to satisfy herself that he wasn't being put under any unreasonable work pressure."

"Do you need an assistant to accompany you?" Kim asked, curling her wavy brown hair around her fingers.

"I need my wonderful assistant to look after the office and field my calls while I'm not here."

"Damn!" Kim frowned, as she walked back into the kitchen.

Spire checked his watch, it was eight-fifty. He figured that if he left for Southampton soon, he could be there by about one in the afternoon. "I'm going to go down and pay a visit to *RAPID* today," he shouted to Kim. "See if the organisation might be an appropriate home for the doctor's legacy. Do me a favour, open up a file for Doris Stanton and send her one of our standard letters of engagement can you?"

"No problem," Kim said, appearing from the kitchen, sipping her tea.

"Oh, and see if you can get hold of someone down there who worked with Dr. Stanton, tell them I'm coming down. I'll need a thirty minute appointment at say, one-thirty P.M if possible."

"Consider it done. Anything else? Would you like me to book you on a weekend sailing course while you're down there?"

"Very funny Kim, I'm down there working, *not* on vacation."

"Yeah, yeah, I believe you. What about your coffee?"

"Keep it hot for me!" Spire shouted, as he left the office and headed down to the rear courtyard where his Audi was parked.

Four hours, and a few hundred miles later, Spire pulled off the main road to Southampton's docklands area. A sign pointed the way to East Dock, home to the National Oceanography Centre where the *RAPID* climate change project office was based. He pulled up alongside a small hut, and into a space marked '*Visitors.*' As he was about to get out of the car, his mobile phone rang.

"Hi Rob, it's me," Kim said. "I managed to get hold of someone…after about ten attempts. A Professor Sammedi, *RAPID* scientist, agreed to see you at two o'clock."

"Sammedi?"

"Yep, that's what he said, why?"

"Nothing, isn't that the name of a henchman from one of the *James Bond* movies?"

"God knows! Anyway, good luck."

Spire ended the call and walked into an empty reception area. Cream painted walls were adorned with pictures of satellite photo's, depicting hurricanes in various stages of formation. There was also a series of pictures showing ships with cranes, placing what looked like monitoring equipment and buoys into the ocean. A sign on the wall read;

Welcome to the National Oceanography Centre,
RAPID Climate Change Project, Southampton.

A comfortable-looking sofa ran along the back wall. Placed either side of the sofa were two large yucca plants, potted in cheap-looking Chinese imitation vases. He walked over to the reception and pressed a button on the counter, setting off a buzzer somewhere inside the main building. A few moments later he heard the sound of heels walking across a polished floor, then an auburn-haired middle-aged lady, wearing spectacles, appeared from a rear door and walked into the office behind the counter. "Afternoon sir, may I help you?" she asked politely.

"Hi, yep, my name's Spire, Robert Spire. I'm here to see a Professor Sammedi. My assistant made the appointment earlier today."

"Ah yes, Mr. Spire. Would you please take a seat? Can I get you a cup of tea, coffee maybe? Professor Sammedi will be with you shortly," she said, glancing at her watch.

"Black coffee would be great, thanks. No sugar."

Spire sat down and started thumbing through a copy of *National Geographic* magazine. After twenty minutes or so, just as he was coming to the end of an interesting article on the next generation of bionic limbs, a booming voice from above made him jump. "Mr. Spire?"

He looked up. Standing over him was a tall, broad-shouldered man, with a large mouth and bulging eyes. He reminded Spire of a chameleon. "My name is Jacob Sammedi.

I am science co-coordinator here at *RAPID*. I understand that you are here on behalf of the late Dr. Stanton. His death, as you might appreciate, has been a terrible shock, just terrible," he said, thrusting his plate-sized hand out for Spire to shake.

Spire stood up, taking Sammedi's extended hand. "Thank you for seeing me Professor. Yes, Doris Stanton, Dr. Stanton's mother, has asked me to come down, just for a quick chat about a few matters, if that's OK. I know you must be busy."

"No problem, Mr. Spire. Follow me; we'll go to my office."

Spire was led down a long corridor, both sides of which were decorated with photographs showing scenes of undersea life. They arrived in Professor Sammedi's office, which was illuminated by natural light from a large window in the wall opposite the door. A floor to ceiling bookshelf stood against the side wall and a wooden desk, surrounded by various types of potted plants, took up most of the rest of the room. A large, wooden-framed map of the world hung on the wall opposite the desk.

"As you can see, Mr. Spire, from where I sit, I have a view of the entire world," he said, chuckling. "Please, sit down."

Spire took a seat opposite him.

"So, how can I help you, Mr. Spire?"

"Well, Professor, Mrs. Stanton has retained my legal services as co-executor of Dr. Stanton's will. The doctor gifted a considerable sum of money to global warming related organisations, and I have been tasked to find out whether *RAPID* might prove to be a suitable home for the legacy."

"I see." There was a pause whilst Professor Sammedi appeared to process the information. "I understand Dale died of a heart attack, in his apartment, is that correct?"

"Yes, that appears to be the case."

"Terrible, he was only a few years younger than me, Mr. Spire, and a very close colleague."

"I'm sorry, Professor. Are you able to tell me what Dr. Stanton was doing down here. Perhaps something about your organisation?"

"Yes, of course. We're working on a project called *RAPID*, looking into what can cause rapid changes in climate. The project's funded by the Natural Environmental Research Council, *NERC* as it's known. We're specifically looking into the Ocean Thermohaline Circulation. You might be aware Mr. Spire, of the Atlantic heat conveyor?"

"I know a little. Isn't the Gulf Stream part of it? Warm water is brought up from the tropics and heat is off-loaded in the process."

"Yes, very good, Mr. Spire. The Gulf Stream is a surface current, which is mainly wind driven, but you're right, it does bring warm water northwards from the tropics. The Ocean Thermohaline Circulation however is a deep water current, powered by temperature and salt. It is like a giant underwater conveyor belt. Warm water is brought up from the Equator and cools as it moves to higher latitudes, leaving behind denser, salty water. The denser water sinks, eventually returning back to the Equator, a process which takes about one thousand years to complete."

"Wow! You wouldn't want to hitch a ride on it then," Spire said, attempting to be humorous.

"No you wouldn't," Sammedi said, forcing a slight smile.

"So, what is *RAPID's* involvement in all this?"

"Well, we have been monitoring the rate of flow of the conveyor, at a latitude of twenty six point five degrees north in the Atlantic Ocean, for some time. Monitoring devices placed at regular intervals across the Atlantic measure the rate of flow of the current. It has been suggested in some scientific circles, that that if global warming melts enough of the Greenland ice sheet, the fresh water flowing into the ocean, as a result, might interfere with the drive system of the conveyor. You see, fresh water is less dense than salt water...it means the water won't sink. Bingo, all of a sudden the system breaks down."

"And what if it does?" Spire asked, intrigued.

"Well, we'd all end up pretty cold, Mr. Spire. What people don't appreciate is that if global warming causes the ocean current to break down, the result maybe a cooling over the UK and Europe. Paleoclimatologists think it's happened before, around thirteen to fourteen thousand years ago, during a period called the *Younger Dryas*. There was a sudden and rapid change from a relatively warmer climate, back to ice age conditions, possibly triggered by a breakdown of the conveyor. It is believed that glacial melt-water from Lake Agassiz near Hudson Bay in Canada drained into the Atlantic."

"So, what does your research show?" Spire asked.

"Well, there's no need to panic just yet," Sammedi chuckled. "Although the preliminary results show a possible thirty percent slowdown in the system, we believe this to be within a natural variation. Further studies and analysis may reveal more in the future. Thankfully, we've just had our funding extended for another four years."

"That's good to know, Professor, but if you don't mind me asking, what was Dr. Stanton's involvement in all this?"

"Dale was involved in analysing the data we'd obtained from each of the monitoring devices, to make sure it was being interpreted correctly. New computer software meant we had to integrate the data with the new system. We aren't expecting to discover anything unusual. Unfortunately, this will now have to be looked at again, as Dale had been working on the calculations for some months. A little longer than we'd expected, but he was always very thorough. He was going to present the findings at the *IPCC* meeting in Oslo, Norway last week, but obviously, well..." Professor Sammedi fell silent.

"I'm sorry, Professor," Spire said, glancing at his watch. I think I've already taken up enough of your time, you've been most helpful."

"It's been no trouble Mr. Spire."

I'm wasting my time down here, Spire thought, assessing the *RAPID* program to be a worthy home for Dr Stanton's legacy.

"I'll see you out, Mr. Spire," Professor Sammedi said, standing up.

Spire followed the professor back through to the reception area.

"Well, thank you for the visit, and please give my regards to Mrs. Stanton, won't you?"

"Certainly. Oh, just one last thing Professor. I almost forgot to ask, do you know if Dr. Stanton smoked?"

"You mean cigarettes? Um, no, not that I'm aware of...why do you ask?"

"Probably nothing, his mother just wanted to know. What about this?" Spire asked, showing Professor Sammedi the black business card embossed with the name *Arc Bin Quid Lo*.

"Unusual looking card, I've not seen anything like that before," Sammedi said, looking puzzled.

"Never mind, thanks for your help, Professor," Spire said, placing the card back in his wallet.

Spire walked out into the car park and took in a deep breath of fresh, sea air. Masts on yachts, moored in the nearby harbour, chimed in the breeze. A large seagull squawked, and flew off the bonnet of his car as he approached it.

His head was now spinning with facts and information about the Ocean Thermohaline Circulation. *Had Dr. Stanton discovered something about the data that had previously been overlooked? Surely, if there was a problem, RAPID scientists would know about it?*

Interesting as it was, he wondered what he was doing down

in Southampton when he should really be back in the office, progressing some of his more important cases. He'd bill Doris for his time, advise her that the *RAPID* program was a worthy venture for her son's legacy, and then close the file.

He checked his watch; it was coming up for three thirty. He calculated he'd be home by eight P.M, if he left now. He called Kim to update her, and then Angela to tell her she could expect him home for dinner.

Spire arrived back in Oakdale a little earlier than expected, and, as he drove past his office, he noticed a light had been left on. He parked his car around the back and let himself in. The first thing he noticed was the message light on his phone flashing red. It was from Kim, saying she'd had to leave the office early as her grandmother had been taken ill during the afternoon. He deleted the message and called Doris. Five rings later she answered. After exchanging a few pleasantries, Spire gave her a word for word account of his visit to *RAPID*, relaying a condensed version of what Professor Sammedi had told him.

Doris listened intently, only interrupting to clarify the odd technical phrase she didn't understand.

"So, Robert, you found nothing unusual?" she finally said.

"I'm afraid not, Doris. I even asked the professor if he knew whether Dale smoked. He didn't think he did, but he didn't sound certain. I also showed him the card...he didn't recognise it."

"Well, I am sure Dale didn't smoke, Robert. So, what do you suggest now?"

There was a pause on the phone while Spire thought of a way to let Doris down gently. "I really don't know what else I can do to help. I feel the *RAPID* program is a worthy cause for Dale's legacy. It's clearly undertaking some very important research, and I would have no hesitation in recommending the National Oceanic Foundation as a worthy recipient of Dale's money...of course, subject to your agreement."

There was silence whilst Doris digested what he was saying.

"Very well, Robert, I guess there's nothing else I can do. I appreciate all your help, and I'll certainly take on board your recommendations. Can you take care of the arrangements and send me your bill?"

Spire detected the disappointment in Doris's voice. "Of course, I'll see to it all. I hope everything works out for you, and it goes without saying that I appreciate your instructions. If there's anything else I can help you with, please get in touch."

"You can count on that, Robert," she said, sounding somewhat despondent.

The phone line went dead.

Poor old Doris, Spire thought, as he jotted down the time he'd spent on his visit to Southampton. He then powered up his computer and searched for a local flower shop, and ordered a bunch of flowers from their website to be delivered to Kim's grandmother at the hospital. He smiled to himself as he shut down the computer, knowing Ethel would appreciate the gesture.

He turned all the lights off and left the office, driving home via the off-license to grab a bottle of Chilean Merlot for supper.

The Royal Brunswick Hospital in Southeast London was having one of its typical busy evenings. A nurse walked into the patient's room carrying a cup of tea, a glass of water and some triangle-cut, ham sandwiches. "How are you feeling today, love?" she asked.

"Still groggy, but my head is clearing a bit now. Have the doctors figured out why I collapsed?" the man asked, sleepily.

"Well, it looks like you somehow received a dose of a very powerful sedative. It knocked you out for a few days, and gave you some short term amnesia. Today's the first day you've looked anywhere near back to normal."

"What the hell was it?"

"Substance called *Lorazepam*, quite unusual, but you'll make a full recovery. You should be out of here in a few days. But for now, you need more rest."

The nurse walked out, leaving him to his afternoon snack.

The patient sipped his tea and rubbed his head, trying to recall where he'd been, and what he had been doing. His last memory was from the previous Saturday afternoon, which he'd spent looking for a new car. As he tried to recall his movements, his head started to feel fuzzy again, and his body ached.

Mathew White closed his eyes, and slowly drifted back to sleep.

CHAPTER 11

IT WAS A warm spring afternoon in San Francisco as the yellow cab pulled up outside the Conquistador Hotel, on the corner of Powell and Filbert, alongside Washington Square Park, in the North Beach area of city. "Ok here for you Ma'am?" the driver asked.

"Perfect," Ksenyia replied, getting out of the cab.

"That'll be sixty-five dollars exactly," the driver said, as he walked to the trunk to get her luggage.

Ksenyia handed over eighty dollars. "Keep the change."

"Thank you, Ma'am. Enjoy your stay."

Washington Square Park was bustling with people, either walking their dogs, sitting on the grass chatting, or just strolling diagonally through the park to avoid the surrounding busy streets. The park was small, and as its name suggests, square in shape, but it provided an oasis of green amongst the hectic streets that criss-crossed San Francisco's Italian neighbourhood.

Ksenyia walked into the cool lobby of the boutique hotel, her heels clicking on the light grey marble floor as she entered. A dark wooden counter was positioned off to the right; large ferns added some colour to the otherwise empty and quiet lobby.

A slim man, with a goatee beard, looked up from his computer as she walked over. "Good afternoon. Welcome to the Conquistador, North Beach. How can I help?"

"Hi there, I booked a room from the UK a few days ago.

My name is Victoria Boothroyd," she said, faking an English accent.

"Ah, yes, Boothroyd...Boothroyd, here we are. How is London these days? I was there five years ago - love the place."

"Hectic as ever!" Ksenyia said.

"Hectic yes, but always very exciting. Are the British bobbies still walking around with their truncheons?" The concierge asked, suddenly becoming animated.

"They probably carry stun-guns now," Ksenyia replied, smiling politely.

"About time if you ask me. Ok, Ms Boothroyd, I have put you in room twenty-three on the second floor, lovely view of the park from there. Here's your key."

Ksenyia took the large wooden key fob with her room key on it.

"There's a bar through that arch over there, open until midnight, and the elevator is just ahead of you. Any problems, call concierge, someone will be here to help. Have a nice stay."

Ksenyia wheeled her Samsonite case towards the elevator, taking it up to the second floor, where she found her room halfway along the dark, wood-panelled, corridor. The room was light, and the walls decorated with floral wallpaper, which gave it a tired look, but the view over the park made up for it. She placed her case on the bed, opened it up, and took out her wash bag. The contact lens bottle containing the nicotine solution was still intact.

She had been briefed that Dr. Bannister would be arriving at around four in the afternoon, an hour from now. She went into the bathroom, turned the shower on and removed her suit jacket, unzipped her skirt, and stripped down to her ivory silk underwear. She walked back into the room and sat on the end of the bed. In need of a drink, she grabbed a miniature bottle of

Smirnoff from the mini-bar, poured the contents into one of the glasses provided, and drank half of it. The vodka warmed her stomach as it went down, and reminded her of home. She unhooked her bra, threw it on the bed, stripped off her underpants, and walked into the bathroom and under the hot shower.

Feeling clean and refreshed, she quickly dressed, this time casually, in jeans and a grey T-shirt. She towel-dried her hair, pulled on a pair of black boots, and headed down to the lobby. The concierge was nowhere to be seen and the lobby was empty.

She walked out into the sunshine and strolled over to a bench, positioned against the black iron railings of the park, which gave her a perfect view of the hotel's entrance.

Impatient American drivers, she thought, as the noise from honking car horns pierced the tranquillity of the quiet park behind. Fifteen minutes passed, and then a black Sedan pulled up alongside the hotel. Anticipating it was her target, she stood to walk back to the hotel, but stopped as she saw an old lady, her back bent over from scoliosis and old age; slowly emerge from the car, helped by her chauffeur. Another middle-aged lady got out the car and they both slowly made their way up the street.

Ksenyia sat back down on the bench and watched a group of Chinese children walk towards her, having emerged from the park some way up. They passed, chatting and laughing with each other, looking very orderly in their identical school uniforms as they marched by.

Distracted by the children, she failed to notice a yellow cab pulling up outside the Conquistador Hotel, but just caught a glimpse of a man walking into the hotel as the taxi drove off. Grabbing a discarded *San Francisco Chronicle* from the bench, she ran across the street and into the hotel, entering the lobby as the man at the desk was welcoming Dr. Bannister to San Francisco. She discreetly took a seat on one of the chairs, next to a fern, and held the paper up in front of her. It wasn't long before she had the information she needed.

"Here's your key sir, room thirty-two, nice park view. The bar is through there and you can take the elevator to the third floor, which is just over there."

"Thank you very much," Bannister said, with a soft, authoritative, voice as he headed toward the elevator.

Ksenyia watched over her paper as Bannister waited for the elevator to arrive. He was distinguished, attractive and around six foot tall, she estimated, with fairly long salt and pepper hair, swept back off his head. He stepped into the elevator and she watched as it rose to the third floor.

Bannister placed his case on the chair, took off his jacket and called Margaret from his cell phone, to tell her he'd arrived safely. He then called John, arranging to meet in the hotel bar at seven-thirty P.M. He closed the curtains, lay on his bed and drifted off to sleep.

After a brief rest, Bannister woke and checked the time: it was a little after six-thirty. He took a shower, pulled on some fresh clothes and made his way down to the bar for a drink. The bar area was small, but well equipped with a semi-circular black marble counter area and dark mahogany bar stools. Black and white pictures depicting long-ago scenes of San Francisco hung on the walls. He sat down on one of the stools, and an attractive barmaid, wearing black trousers and a white blouse, appeared from behind a ceiling-high wooden wine rack.

"Evening sir, can I get you a drink?" she asked.

"I'll get a beer please...Sierra."

The barmaid brought over his beer, together with an

assortment of nuts, and then disappeared back behind the large wine rack.

The malty, amber beer tasted good. He was halfway through his drink when a striking brunette entered the bar and smiled at him, as she sat down on the stool next to his. "Hi, I'm Victoria Boothroyd. I believe you must be Dr. Jack Bannister?" she said, in a distinctive English accent.

"Good evening, Victoria, do I know you? Are you here for the climate conference?" Bannister said, somewhat taken aback.

"You could say that. I'm a freelance photographer for the GreenTimes magazine. I'm over from London to cover the conference."

"Ah, I've not heard of that publication. Guess it hasn't made it over the pond yet?" Bannister said, smiling.

"I'm afraid not. It's a new publication, and without much funding I might add."

"That doesn't surprise me, environmental publications rarely do, but at least they had enough money to send you over."

"Yes, lucky me," she replied.

"Can I get you a drink, Victoria? I'm just waiting for a friend, but he's not due for thirty minutes or so."

"Are you sure?"

"Yes, of course. I'm having another beer."

"In that case, I'll take Vodka, over ice."

The drinks arrived, along with another small bowl of nuts.

"Have you been to one of these conferences before?" Bannister asked, as he placed his beer back down on the bar.

"No, this is the first time for me. I'm usually assigned to photograph someone standing beneath a wind turbine, or in a field of crops being grown for bio-fuel use. I know how to have fun!" she said, sarcastically.

"Do you know much about global warming?" Bannister

asked her, now somewhat intrigued by the woman.

"Well, only what I see on the news and read in the papers. It seems there's never a day goes by without something being said about it. It's difficult to know what to believe."

"That's true. But, unfortunately, you'll be hearing a lot more about the subject in the news in the future, as the problem sure ain't going away." Bannister became distracted, and turned toward a man with dark curly hair who had just entered the bar.

"There you are, Jack!" the man said, as he thrust his hand towards Bannister.

At that moment, Ksenyia saw the opportunity she'd been waiting for. Bannister didn't notice her empty the vial of nicotine solution into his glass. The contents momentarily effervesced as the colourless liquid mixed in with the golden beer.

Bannister turned back toward Ksenyia. "John, meet Victoria. She's a free-lance photographer from the UK, assigned to the climate change conference."

"Nice to meet you. I'm John Gregory, a good friend of Jack's."

"What do you fancy drinking, John? I'm on the Sierra Nevada, it's very good," Bannister said.

"Sounds good, I'll have the same."

The barmaid had already anticipated the order and was pouring another beer. She went to push a beer mat over to where her new customer had sat down, when she accidentally knocked Bannister's glass over. The thick beer glass didn't break, but the contents spilled over the counter. "Oh God, I'm sorry!" she said, blushing, as she quickly mopped up the liquid.

"I'll get you another...on the house."

"He's always had a drink problem!" Gregory blurted out, trying to make light of the incident.

"Fancy another, Victoria?" Bannister asked, ignoring the spillage.

"No thanks!" she said abruptly, getting up from her stool. "I need to get going. I have a few things to do."

"Something I said?" Gregory inquired, attempting to be funny again.

"I'll see you again, Dr. Bannister. It was nice meeting you Mr. Gregory," she said, leaving the bar.

Bannister was slightly taken aback at Victoria's change of mood, and looked on as she walked out.

Gregory shrugged his shoulders, "Ah well. Let's go out for some pasta, Jack, there's lots of great eateries around here, I'm famished."

They finished their drinks, left the bar, and walked out onto the street and headed into the heart of North Beach. Neon lights from the neighbourhood's many Italian restaurants illuminated the dusk with a variety of colours, and the aroma of Italian cuisine filled the air.

As they walked, Bannister listened to his friend chatting about the latest generation of photovoltaic cells being developed in Silicon Valley, but he struggled to concentrate as he thought about a dinner of some tasty pasta and a decent bottle of red wine.

CHAPTER 12

April 23

THE FOLLOWING MORNING Bannister awoke early and wandered down to the restaurant, where he ordered a breakfast of eggs benedict, which he washed down with a cup of black coffee and orange juice. After skimming through the *Chronicle*, he left the hotel to walk down to Fisherman's Wharf, with the intention of taking a boat ride over to Alcatraz Island.

It was a pleasant spring morning, and, as he approached the vicinity of the pier, the smell of salty air filled his lungs. Seagulls squawked noisily overhead, occasionally dive-bombing the pavement to pick up scraps of food thrown by the tourists. He passed the market stalls, and arrived at Pier thirty-three and wandered over to the kiosk, to purchase a ticket for the Alcatraz trip. The notice board confirmed the next ferry left in twenty minutes.

He followed a group of tourists onto the boat. As he stood on the crowded deck, he looked back toward the pier, raising his hand to shield his eyes from the bright spring sun glinting off the water. The sound from clicking cameras and chatting holiday-makers filled the tour boat. Excited visitors spent most of the thirty-minute crossing taking photographs of the Golden Gate Bridge, which majestically spanned the calm waters of San Francisco Bay.

Bannister looked on as Alcatraz approached. It appeared far

more forbidding up close than from a distance. White foam sprayed onto the deck from an errant wave as they approached the jagged rocks, which loomed up on both sides of the docking area.

Gulls screeched and wheeled overhead as he disembarked the ferry, and made his way over to a group of tourists who had gathered by a graffiti-covered wall. They were listening to a tour guide discuss the American-Indian's occupation of the Island in 1969, some six years after the prison closed.

Bannister left the group and entered the outer prison building, where he collected some headphones. The digital recorder started playing commentary narrated by genuine prison guards and inmates, which added considerably to the atmosphere of the place, as he walked around the sinister and crumbling interior.

After a while he began to feel queasy from the musty smell of the damp prison, and also a little claustrophobic, so decided to make his way out to the prison yard.

Forty minutes in there is enough for anyone, he thought, as he walked out into the sunshine and inhaled a lungful of fresh air.

Ksenyia, who had been following Bannister the entire time, kept her head down as she watched her target from the concrete steps that descended from the prison yard door. She hoped he'd make his way to the café for a drink, so she could administer the lethal liquid. *Alcatraz will take another life today,* she thought.

Bannister completed a circuit of the yard and walked back into the building. She followed him as he made his way back through the prison. Instead of going to the café, he walked down the stone ramp back to the pick-up point to join a small group of tourists waiting for the return ferry. Annoyed, she followed him onto the ferry with the returning passengers.

It was almost midday as the ferry approached the Pier. The ferry's deck vibrated as the engines were put into reverse, lurching as it bumped the mooring.

Bannister grabbed the rail, to prevent himself toppling forward. More tourists gathered on the quay side, ready to embark. He made his way off the boat, and walked over to one of the numerous stalls. He bought a coffee, drinking it as he slowly strolled up Powell Street and back towards North Beach. One of San Francisco's trade-mark trams, packed full of sightseers, dinged its bell as it travelled past on the way back down to the wharf.

The concierge looked up from his computer as Bannister walked into the hotel lobby. "Had a good morning sir, ya been sightseeing?"

"Yep. I've been coming here for years, but have only now managed to get over to see Alcatraz. Glad I went, but it's not the place you want to spend too much time in on a day like this."

"You bet. Coupla hours over there is enough, eh?"

Bannister stepped into the elevator, deciding to return to his room for a rest, before getting ready for the evening's frivolities. He entered his room, lay down on his bed and closed his eyes.

Bannister was woken by a loud ringing from his bedside telephone. He sleepily reached over and picked up the receiver.

"Dr. Bannister?" a man with a French accent inquired.

"Yep, this is him," Bannister said, yawning as he spoke.

"Jack, bonsoir, it's me, Francois, how are you my old friend?"

"Francois! Are you in San Francisco?"

"Oui, oui, I'm in the hotel. I arrived a few hours ago. Wondered if you fancied an aperitif before dinner tonight?"

Bannister checked his watch; it was four-thirty. "Yes of course. I must have dozed off up here. Give me an hour and I'll meet you in the bar. You can then fill me in on your latest theories on how you're going to save the planet."

"Oui, I look forward, Jack. I'll see you one an hour."

Bannister forced himself off the bed, and into the shower. He was looking forward to seeing his old friend, Professor Francois Trimaud, climate scientist par excellence, as he liked to call him. Trimaud was always working on a new project to combat climate change, in an effort to save mankind from the perils of a warming planet. No doubt, one day, he would be given the Nobel Prize for his efforts. He'd met the French scientist - now resident professor at Paris's Pierre and Marie Curie University - in Geneva, back in 1974. Trimaud had been the guest speaker back then, at what was one of the first low key climate change conferences. They had been friends and colleagues ever since.

Bannister found Trimaud sitting on one of the bar stools, chatting away to the barmaid who'd served him the evening before. "Francois! It's damn good to see you."

"Bonsoir, Jack," Trimaud said, rising off his stool. He flung his arms around Jack and kissed him on both cheeks in the customary French way.

"Can I get you a drink, sir? Sierra Nevada Pale Ale?" the barmaid asked, smiling at Bannister.

"Ah, yes please. I'll start with one of those, thanks."

"And for you sir, can I get you another glass of Californian Pinot Noir?"

"Oui, merci bien," Trimaud said.

"So, Francois, what time did you get in?" Bannister asked.

"I landed just after ten this morning. Managed to rest for five hours or so, and now...well, I feel completement de la vie - full of life again."

"Just you wait until about ten tonight, that's when it hits you!"

"Ah, oui. As long as I'm feeling fresh for your talk on Monday, that's all that matters, mon ami."

"So, tell me Francois, what have *you* been working on lately, you must be up to something?"

"Ah, well, of course Jack. I cannot tell you everything as I need to carry out one more practical experiment before I can write up the paperwork."

"Tell me, I'm intrigued?"

"Well, it's a theory I have been working on for a good while now. Let's just say it involves three ingredients - a trip to the Arctic, iron sulphate and plankton."

"Don't tell me, Francois; you're going to seed the Arctic Ocean with iron sulphate in an attempt to induce plankton growth, which will then photosynthesise and extract carbon dioxide from the atmosphere? If so, I'm disappointed my friend, I thought something more radical from you. The theory has already been tested, by a German team I believe, with only moderate success."

"Tres bien, Jack, but my work has an extra ingredient, or dimension, shall we say, which may make all the difference. We all know the Arctic is melting at an accelerating rate. Its tipping point may have already been reached, God forbid, but I *may* have discovered something to prevent this from happening."

Bannister laughed. "I *knew* there was more to, it my friend. Of course you've got something up your sleeve. I look forward to reading your paper, when it's completed."

"And I yours, Jack. Anyway, enough talk about work. How is Margaret?"

"She's well. Getting a bit impatient with the latest project I've been working on, but that's not unusual. I've promised to take her and the boys off to Hawaii to make up for it." Bannister sipped his beer. "And you, what happened with Helena after?"

"Kaput! We separated eighteen months ago. We tried to make a go of things, but just couldn't see eye to eye in the end. Usual thing, working long hours, not paying her enough attention, c'est la vie."

"I'm sorry to hear that, Francois."

Trimaud shrugged his shoulders. "Here's to ongoing scientific research, Jack; salut!"

They both clinked glasses and polished off their drinks.

"It's coming up for six now Francois. If you're hungry, I know a great Italian restaurant around the corner. Tomorrow, I have ordered a taxi, for seven o'clock, to take us to the hotel for the dinner. John is also coming. I believe you may have met him last time you were in San Francisco. He's in the solar technology business, works out of Silicon Valley."

"Ah yes, I remember him, of course. Ok, Jack, let's aim to meet back down here in forty-five minutes."

"Have a nice evening, gentleman," the barmaid said, as Bannister and Trimaud left the bar.

Ksenyia had managed to get two good nights sleep since arriving in San Francisco. It was now Sunday evening and with the jet lag now shaken off, she was preparing for the task ahead. On the bed, she'd laid out all the items she would need for her assignment. Camera, GreenTimes press pass, vial of nicotine solution, syringe and black suit.

She ran herself a shower and sat on the end of the bed, thoughts wandering to the previous week. Her London assignment had been straightforward; the English scientist had proven to be surprisingly gullible. She almost felt guilty at how easy it had been to carry out her task. A quick nicotine injection into the arm, and the rest had gone like clockwork. She had used the same method many times before. The combination of the nicotine patch and conveniently placed cigarettes always confused the authorities. A verdict of accidental death usually followed, with no further questions asked.

Bannister's death, she realised, would be slightly cruder. Any autopsy would no doubt reveal the high levels of nicotine in his blood. Questions would inevitably be asked. Questions, which she wouldn't be around to answer.

She got up from the bed to take a shower. The taxi would be collecting her in forty minutes.

Ksenyia arrived at the impressive Nob Hill Hotel before any of the other guests, and showed her GreenTimes magazine press pass, to the security guard on the main door as she entered, explaining that she'd been commissioned to take photographs of guests as they arrived, and during the dinner.

"Sure thing, Miss Boothroyd," the burly guard replied, as he checked her credentials on the pass. "You can stand just inside the hallway here. You should get a great view of the guests as they enter, but first, please put your camera and bag through the X-ray machine over there - standard procedure."

"Of course," Ksenyia said, smiling.

Her camera and bag passed through the machine without a problem. The guard then scanned her with a hand-held wand. Once through security, she positioned herself next to a large pot plant, inside the main lobby of the luxurious hotel, and prepared her Leica camera.

She didn't have to wait long. Guests started to enter and mill around in the lobby by the large revolving doors. Men wearing black dinner suits, and women in evening dresses poured into the hotel. Adrenalin started to flow through her veins as she took shot after shot of the guests as they entered, the camera's flash lighting up their faces as they smiled smugly for photographs.

Dr. Jack Bannister and his colleagues didn't notice her as they arrived. She took a photograph, managing to get all three of them in the frame as they entered the lobby. Satisfied most of the guests had arrived; she made her way into the main ballroom.

Inside, the attendees were standing around in groups, talking together and drinking Champagne, which was being served to them by the hotel's waiters and waitresses. She walked up to a group of six people chatting together, and asked them if they would stand together for a photograph.

"Yeah, sure. Where will the picture appear?" asked a plump, spectacled man, as he mopped sweat from his brow with a white handkerchief.

Ksenyia looked at the short man, who reminded her of an overweight penguin in a dinner suit. "The pictures will be appearing in the UK's GreenTimes magazine, and possibly in the local press," she lied.

"Great, I love England," the man said, beaming, "Snap away." The group huddled together, holding up their Champagne flutes toward Ksenyia as she photographed them.

She moved on, spotting Dr. Bannister and his friend John

Gregory chatting to a small group of people near the bar. She lowered her camera, and accepted a glass of Champagne offered by one of the waiters, and took it over to a small table situated in the corner of the large room. Then, acting as if she was examining her camera, she took the vial containing the nicotine solution from the camera case, and emptied it into her glass of Champagne. She took a deep breath to compose herself and then made her way over to where Dr. Bannister and his colleagues were standing, waiting for him to place his glass down on the table next to him.

She didn't have to wait long. *Enjoy your last drink, doctor.* She swiftly swapped her glass for his without anyone noticing, and then interrupted the group of chatting scientists. "Hello gentlemen, how are you all tonight?"

"Hello, Victoria. Taking plenty of snaps I see," Gregory said.

Bannister turned around "Hello, have you come over to take a group photo for that magazine of yours?"

"I certainly have. But let's drink a toast first. How about to…to preventing global warming?" she said, as she held Bannister's original glass of Champagne in her hand. As expected, Bannister reached behind him for what he thought was his drink and held it up.

"We'll all certainly drink to that," Bannister said, raising his glass higher.

"Cheers everyone," Ksenyia toasted, lifting her glass in response.

"Cheers," they all replied.

Bannister drank his Champagne and put the glass back down on the table.

"And now for a group photograph," Ksenyia said, holding up the camera. "All huddle together, please."

Bannister soon began feeling light-headed. *Good grief, that Champagne must have been strong*, he thought, his vision blurring. The flashes from the camera hurt his eyes and a splitting headache formed in his temple. He felt his heart starting to pound inside his chest, and then his throat started to constrict. He tried to loosen his bow tie as he collapsed to his knees.

I'm having a heart attack, he thought, as he fell forward onto his chest as the powerful poison overwhelmed his vital organs.

"Jack...Jack, you Ok?" Gregory shouted, as he rushed to his friend's aid. He turned Bannister over and placed him in the recovery position. "Jesus, somebody call paramedics...quick!"

Guests started gathering around, to find out what the commotion was all about. Gregory grabbed hold of one of the waiters and shouted for him to call the emergency services. He then turned back to Bannister, crouched down and started to pump his chest, but after a short while it was evident that his friend was unresponsive.

Ksenyia fired off one more shot before putting the camera down. No one had noticed her inserting a shiny black card into a Champagne flute on the table near to where Dr. Jack Bannister lay dead on the floor. *Assignment completed.*

She slipped unnoticed out of the hotel, taking a cab back to Washington Square Park. Once inside the hotel she headed straight for Bannister's room, having made a mental note of the room number the previous day. Using her hair clip to unlock the door, she quietly crept inside.

Dr. Bannister's laptop was on the desk by the television. She opened it up, turned it on, and effortlessly overrode his password prompt. She then inserted a disk which went to work corrupting the files stored on his computer. She noticed his attaché case, opened it up and pulled out a thin manila file containing some papers with the title;

'The Crozet Islands: Discovery of Underwater Methane Gas Vents.'

She removed the disk from the computer, took the folder and left the room.

Back in her own room, she powered up her notebook and entering the encrypted area, typed a secure message to her employers;

The methane has been burnt.

She then shut down her computer, undressed, and ran herself a bath. Lying on the bed, she closed her eyes, listening to the running water as she daydreamed of lying on a far off beach, the waves crashing against the shoreline. On the golden sand in the distance, she could see her family, waving their hands as they walked towards her.

CHAPTER 13

April 25

IT WAS SIX A.M, on a dull Monday morning in west Wales when Spire awoke. He planned on getting an early start in the office to work on the Taunton case, as legal proceedings needed to be issued by the end of the week. He slipped out of bed and onto the floor, where he forced himself to do eighty pushups. He stood up, tightened his cotton pyjama bottoms, walked into the kitchen and put the kettle on. Dawn was just breaking outside, and the cloudless sky promised a pleasant spring day. He made a pot of fresh coffee, and headed for the bathroom.

Spire grabbed his wallet from the bedside table and slipped quietly out of the bedroom. As he did, Angela stirred and mumbled goodbye.

Twenty minutes later, he arrived at the office, parked in his usual spot in the small gravel courtyard behind the shared building, and walked up to the back door - negotiating a pile of beer cans and cider bottles from what looked like a down-and-outs gathering the night before - and let himself in.

After an hour or so of working on the Taunton case, Kim arrived and walked over to Spire's open office door. "Morning, Rob, you and Angela have a nice weekend?"

"Not bad. Angela was in London, so I managed to catch up on some work, relaxed a little too. How about you? Oh, how's your grandmother?"

"She's a little bit better, thanks to you. You needn't have sent those flowers Rob, that was very kind of you," Kim said, handing him a small parcel.

"Well, I'm glad she's feeling better. What's this?"

"Open it."

Spire opened the neatly wrapped gift. Inside was a black plastic box, which he opened to reveal a sleek, silver lighter, the type that had an after-burner type flame, designed, it seemed, to light in hurricane-force winds.

"It's for your cigar, when you finally get around to smoking it. And for being so kind to my grandmother," Kim said, smiling.

"Perfect. That's very kind of you, Kim. I plan on treating myself to that cigar when we settle the Taunton file," Spire said, admiring the lighter, before dropping it into his inside jacket pocket.

He continued opening the morning post, which hadn't long arrived. The second letter was from Doris Stanton, thanking him for all the work he'd done. There was also a cheque in the envelope, for payment of his fees. He opened the Stanton file, and as he did, the black business card that Doris had given him fell onto the floor. He picked it up and read the odd name over to himself. *Arc Bin Quid Lo. Who the hell would have a name like that? The world's most wanted - and now dead - terrorist sprang to mind.* He stapled the card to the inside jacket and closed the file.

He dictated a letter for Kim to type, thanking Mrs. Stanton for the payment, and also a letter to Professor Sammedi at *RAPID,* confirming that a cheque for three-hundred thousand pounds would be on its way; a gift from the professor's colleague, Dr. Dale Stanton.

By the time Spire had worked on the eighth file of the day,

the afternoon was drawing to a close. It was now almost four in the afternoon, and he turned the television on to CNN to catch up on the day's events. After watching the fairly mundane news loop for twenty minutes, he got up to make himself a drink. Kim had left early to go and check on her grandmother, who needed to spend a few more nights in hospital. Whilst in the kitchen waiting for the kettle to boil, some news relating to global warming caught his attention. Always interested in the latest developments on the subject, he briskly walked back into his office.

On the television was a picture of a distinguished looking, smartly dressed, man in his early fifties. The name Dr. Jack Bannister appeared under the photograph. The image changed to a reporter, who was standing outside a hotel holding a microphone.

Spire grabbed the remote and turned up the volume. The reporter continued speaking;

"... Dr. Jack Bannister, eminent climatologist, collapsed and died yesterday whilst attending a pre-climate conference dinner. Dr. Bannister, who was due to give a talk at the National Global Warming Conference, appears to have suffered a massive heart attack last night, at the hotel behind me. Dr. Bannister was one of the world's leading climatologists, specialising in ocean chemistry, particularly on the impacts rising levels of carbon dioxide have on the ocean's acidity levels. His most noteworthy contribution to the field of climatology was perhaps discovering large methane gas deposits under the Arctic's permafrost ..."

Spire listened, transfixed to the television. *This can't be a coincidence.* He reached for the phone and called Doris Stanton. After a short while, she picked up. "Hello Doris, Robert Spire here. How are you?"

"Hello, Robert, I'm fine. I didn't expect to hear from you so soon. If you're chasing me for payment, I posted your cheque…"

He cut her short. "No, Doris, it's nothing to do with that. Have you seen the news today?"

"No. Why?"

"Well, it might be nothing, but I'm watching CNN as we speak, and it looks like another climatologist, a Dr. Jack Bannister, dropped dead at a climate conference in San Francisco yesterday."

"You are *joking* Robert. I...I don't know what to say. It does seem like a very odd coincidence, don't you think?"

"You could say that." Spire hesitated as a crazy idea came to him. "Listen, I don't know what you'll think about this, but what if I flew over there to try and find what happened? Maybe speak to some of Dr. Bannister's colleagues, even attend the conference. I could put a hold on the legacy to *RAPID* and fly over to San Francisco on the basis I'm still looking for a home for Dale's money."

"Well, Robert," Doris said, sounding a little taken aback by the suggestion. "If you think it's worth it, that's fine by me. I'm happy to provide a carte blanche for any costs involved, naturally."

"Ok, good. I'll need to speak to Angela tonight, but I'm sure she'll be fine about it. I might even take her along with me. Hold on a minute Doris, I'm just *googling* the conference now."

He typed 'San Francisco Climate Change Conference' into the search engine as Doris waited on the phone. A number of references flashed up. The conference appeared to consist of a three day event, running from Monday to Wednesday.

"Looks like the event started today, and runs until Wednesday. At a push, I could get out there by tomorrow afternoon, if I catch a flight in the morning. I might be able to get to the conference tomorrow afternoon, or on Wednesday, for the last day."

"Listen, Robert, you don't have to pursue this you know. You've already done enough to help me, but do whatever you feel is necessary. Just take care of yourself and keep me informed will you?"

"Of course; it might be nothing, just an odd coincidence, but it's worth looking into, I think. I'll give you a call as soon as I get out there."

As Spire ended the call a feeling of foreboding came over him; a mixture of nerves and excitement - in that order. He tried to call Kim, but there was no answer. He left a message on her mobile, telling her he'd be out of the office until at least Friday, and to make sure all the papers on the Taunton case were filed in court. He quickly dictated a further note on Stanton's file, telling Kim not to send the letter containing the cheque to *RAPID*. Unfortunately, Professor Sammedi would now have to wait for the money.

Spire wondered if there could be a connection between the deaths of Dr. Bannister and Dr. Stanton. *What would the autopsy results reveal?* He considered the ramifications if it turned out that the scientists' deaths were linked in any way.

Spire locked up the office, and drove home as fast as the road conditions allowed, only slowing down as he approached one of the many narrow country lanes.

As soon as he got home he went straight to his bedroom and started packing. Angela wasn't back from work yet, and he hadn't yet had time to call her either.

The time was approaching five-forty when he heard the sound of gravel crunching under car tyres, as Angela pulled up the drive. He wasn't sure how she was going to react to the last minute trip he was planning.

"Hi darling," he greeted her, as she walked through the front door carrying two bags of food shopping.

"Hi! You're home early," she said to him.

"Here, let me take those from you," he said, grabbing the bags of food and placing them on the kitchen worktop. "I managed to get quite a bit done at the office today. How was your day?"

"Not too bad. The silver bookends I bought in London, on the weekend, have already sold out. I knew I should have bought more."

"Fantastic. Listen, you're not going to believe what's happened today."

"Don't tell me, the Taunton case settled?" Angela replied, as she put the kettle on.

Spire told Angela the events of the last hour, from the CNN news story, to the conversation with Doris, then came out with what he really wanted to say, "Fancy a trip to San Francisco?"

Angela stopped what she was doing and looked at him. "Oh God, Robert, you can't be serious? You're not really thinking of flying over there tomorrow, are you? It's hardly much notice is it. I mean, I've got no cover for the shop, and I have a coffee morning already arranged, for Thursday. Apart from that, we'd only be out there for a few days - there wouldn't be time to do anything!"

"Well, that's true, darling. Listen, it's off the cuff I know, but I really think something odd is going on, and I feel a certain level of obligation toward Doris to look into this. Maybe it's coincidence, maybe not, but I think I should go and..."

"Go and do what?" Angela interrupted. "You're not some kind of international sleuth, you know. What do you expect to find over there?"

"I don't know, but I don't feel I can put this case to bed yet. I mean, these guys were both eminent climatologists, about to give presentations on matters relating to global warming. Then they both end up dead. Odd, don't you think?"

"Coincidence, more like. People *do* just die you know! I mean, they probably both had heart attacks, especially if they were in stressful jobs. Look Rob, I'm not saying you shouldn't go, just pointing out that the whole thing just sounds quite innocent to me. I feel for Doris, I really do, but just because two scientists on the opposite sides of the world drop dead, it doesn't suggest to me that anything odd is going on, that's all."

Spire sighed. "Fair point, I appreciate the trip won't exactly be much fun. I doubt there will be any time to go sightseeing or shopping," he said, now trying to put his wife off the trip.

"Count me out then," she said.

Spire could hear from the tone of Angela's voice that her initial anxiety about him going was ebbing.

"Rob, I'm not stupid, you've clearly already decided you're going. What time is the flight?"

Spire recited his hectic travel plans.

"Darling, you're crazy!"

"We'll see," Spire said. "You're not getting rid of me yet. I'll cook us a nice dinner tonight, and leave first thing tomorrow morning."

With the hard part over, he disappeared into the study, brought the flight information up, and booked the most convenient flights he could find. *Virgin Atlantic* had a flight leaving at eleven-thirty in the morning, arriving in San Francisco at two-twenty in the afternoon local time, returning Thursday. The ticket was flexible however, meaning he could return Friday, or Saturday if need be.

He then walked back to the kitchen, and over to the wine rack and pulled out a bottle of Spanish Siglo to drink with dinner. As he uncorked the bottle in the sink he glanced out of the window; a full moon hung low in the cloudless sky, bathing the back garden in moonlight. He turned the kitchen light off to get a clearer view, and gazed through the window up at the star-filled night sky. *What a magnificent sight.*

The absence of any light pollution allowed the millions of visible stars to shine brighter than ever. He looked up at the familiar constellations, turning the cork over between his fingers as he considered the trip over to San Francisco, a slight pang of apprehension forming in the pit of his stomach, as he considered whether he was doing the right thing.

CHAPTER 14

San Francisco, April 26

THE FOLLOWING MORNING Spire left home at five-thirty and arrived at Heathrow's long-term car park three and a half hours later. He grabbed his bag from the back seat of the car and headed for the lift, which took him to the main walkway leading into the terminal building. He checked in and found a quiet table where he could relax and call Doris. She wasn't in, so he left a brief message, telling her that he was on his way to the U.S, and that he'd contact her with any news as soon as he could.

He hadn't been sitting down long when an announcement on the overhead monitor confirmed his gate was open. He finished his coffee, and headed over to the queue of people waiting to pass through the airport's new 'millimetre wave' body scanning machines. After a short while, he was ushered into the machine. He waited for the flashing light to turn green, then exiting the hi-tech scanner, he made his way to the boarding gate.

On the aircraft he found his window seat, and within thirty minutes the Boeing 747-400 was slowly lifting into the skies above London. An hour into the flight and his early morning start caught up with him, and he drifted off to sleep.

A sudden metallic clatter woke Spire and he opened his eyes to see a flight attendant serving a customer some duty-free goods in the seat next to him. "Excuse me, sir, I didn't mean to wake you," the flight attendant apologised.

"No problem," Spire replied, still half asleep.

The plane banked gently left, prompting Spire to look out of the window. He could see the huge Utah salt lakes below, spreading out like vast milky puddles. Some hours later, following a surprisingly good lunch, the plane commenced its descent into San Francisco International Airport, where it was a beautiful clear and sunny day.

After clearing customs, Spire walked out of the baggage reclaim area and found the exit. On the way out, he popped into the airport shop and purchased a copy of the *San Francisco Chronicle,* together with a small book entitled, *San Francisco's Obscure Tourist Attractions*, thinking it might be useful if he had the chance to do some sightseeing later. He left the arrivals terminal and walked out onto the cab rank.

A yellow cab pulled up in front of him. "Where ya going sir?" the rotund, friendly looking taxi driver asked.

"Into the city, please. Can you recommend any hotels?"

"Yeah, sure buddy, hop in. I assume you'd like to stay downtown. If so, the Hilton has a good spot, its right next to the Transamerica Pyramid."

"That will do," Spire said, recalling the pyramidal Transamerica building; the tallest skyscraper on the San Francisco skyline.

The journey into town didn't take long. Spire took in the sights of the city as they drove through the various neighbourhoods. Looking out the window, he guessed they were passing through the financial district, identifiable by the tall grey, block-stone buildings. The route ahead suddenly darkened, despite the blue sky above, as the sunlight struggled to compete with the tall buildings ascending vertically from either side of the street. They continued through the financial district until the streets opened up again, and then the iconic Transamerica Pyramid came into view, its crushed-quartz facade glinting white in the sunlight.

The cab veered left, drove one block along, then made a right turn into the Hilton Hotel forecourt, the Transamerica building loomed up behind.

"Here ya go; you won't have a problem getting a room in there. That'll be sixty-five bucks, buddy."

Spire got out, paid the fare plus a ten dollar tip, and stood for a moment, letting the sun warm his face. After a few moments he walked through the revolving doors and up to the concierge where he made a booking for two nights. He asked the young man behind the check-in desk about the climate change conference taking place in the city. The concierge told him that he thought the event was being held at one of the city's old hotels, overlooking the park, in the Nob Hill district.

Spire thanked the young man, took the elevator to the seventh floor and found his room. He fell onto the bed and laid there for five minutes. He realised he was drifting off to sleep and forced himself off the bed. The time was coming up to three-thirty, which meant it was still the best side of midnight back home, early enough to give Angela a quick call, to tell her he'd arrived safely.

After calling, Spire showered, pulled on a pair of jeans and a white cotton shirt, and headed for the elevator. On his way down he checked the map in the corridor for the nearest exit. The sign provided a stark reminder which route to take in case of an earthquake.

The sunlight warmed his face as he walked out of the hotel's entrance, immediately rejuvenating him. He felt a pulse of adrenalin course through his veins as he thought about the next few days, and what he might discover. Unsure as to which way to go, he asked a passing couple for directions to Nob Hill.

"Sorry pal, we're Canadian, on holiday," the man said, shrugging his shoulders.

Another couple walked by, but they too were tourists. Spire gave up and walked back towards the hotel.

"Can I help you sir?" the doorman asked, as he walked in.

"Yep, I'm just trying to get directions to Nob Hill."

"No problem," the doorman said, taking out a small map from his pocket. Using a black felt tipped pen, he marked out directions to the area on the map and handed it to him.

Spire thanked the doorman, studied the route marked out on the map, and headed off down the hill.

Thirty minutes later, he was climbing a series of steep steps as he negotiated one of the city's famed 'hills', before finally arriving in the opulent Nob Hill area. He found Huntington Park, and then spotted the grandiose hotel at the far end, its prime position giving it perfect views of the park and city. It was evident that something was going on at the hotel from the assortment of large vans and trucks parked outside the hotel's forecourt, each with their own satellite dishes.

Spire made his way to the hotel entrance, passing a female reporter from *Brazilian Bahia Cable News,* who was standing in front of a man holding a shoulder-mounted camera. The attractive reporter appeared to be adjusting her hair, using the camera lens as a make-shift mirror. She glanced at him and smiled as he walked past.

He entered into the marble-floored lobby of the hotel, and spotted a gold sign on a notice board, which confirmed the climate conference was taking place in the Park Ballroom, situated on the second floor of the hotel. He noticed a long table, opposite the concierge desk, which looked like it had conference material on it, and made his way toward it. Before he could get there, a guard approached him. "Excuse me sir, could you please follow me and walk through security."

Spire was ushered through an airport style security frame, which remained silent as he walked through. The guard frisked him anyway, and moved a hand-held 'wand' scanner over his body. "You're clear, buddy," he finally said, placing the scanning equipment back down on the table. "You looking for the conference, or just staying at the hotel?"

"Actually, I'm trying to get into the conference," Spire said.

"Do you have a ticket?" the guard asked.

"No, but I was hoping I could buy one."

"Sure, if you go wait over by that desk, someone will be out to assist."

Spire thanked the guard and walked over to the tables which were covered with an assortment of leaflets and brochures of the ongoing event. A tall, skinny man dressed in a smart black suit then appeared from a door in the wall behind the table. "Can I help you, sir?" he asked, in a high-pitched voice.

"I'm looking to buy a ticket for the conference," Spire said.

"I'm sorry sir, but all public tickets would have sold out some time ago, especially after what happened on Sunday. The death of our star speaker only increased interest in the event," he replied, his squeaky voice grating on Spire.

"I appreciate that, but I've travelled all the way over from the UK to attend. I'd really appreciate it if you would check."

The man went back through the door, only to appear twenty seconds later. "I'm sorry sir, like I said, all the tickets have gone."

"Very well," Spire replied, walking away.

There's no way that idiot even checked, he thought, as he made his way over to the concierge desk to ask where the bar was.

"We have one on the first floor sir, just through there, or there's the *Panorama* restaurant bar on the top floor. Great views of the city and park from there, naturally. You can get the elevator over there," the Concierge chap said.

Spire pressed the button for the *Park Ballroom*, and the elevator rose quickly and silently to the second floor, where the conference was taking place. The doors pinged open and Spire walked out onto a carpeted foyer area. A long corridor disappeared off to the right. A sign on a wooden stand pointed left toward the climate conference. He walked around the corner which opened up into a larger corridor, and noticed a number of desks along the back wall. Behind each desk was a door, which, he presumed, entered into the ballroom where the conference was taking place. Sitting behind every desk was a hotel employee or conference organiser. It was clear that a ticket would be required to get inside.

He scanned the corridor, trying not to draw attention to himself, and walked in the opposite direction, towards the gents toilets, where he noticed an ice machine with a water fountain next to it. He took one of the small conical paper cups and filled it with ice-cold water. While thinking of his next move, one of the double doors that led into the conference room opened, and a slim, spectacled man in his fifties walked out and headed towards him. As the man approached, Spire noticed he was carrying some papers under his left arm. The man walked past and headed into the gents toilets.

Spire finished his drink and followed the man in.

"Afternoon, Doug," Spire said, as he walked over to where the man was standing, noticing the name badge on his lapel. "Interesting discussion just now, eh?"

"Do I know you?" Doug asked, looking confused.

"Ah, no, sorry, I just saw your name tag."

"Oh, yes!" Doug said, fingering his plastic name badge. "Very worrying, isn't it? If Greenland continues to melt, we might as well all buy houseboats."

"Ha! Quite," Spire said, wondering how he could bluff his

way into the conference.

Doug zipped himself up and walked over to the hand basin to wash his hands. Spire noticed that he'd placed the papers he'd been carrying on the marble sink top, and walked over to join him. "So, Doug, are you here for the full three days?" he asked.

"Damn ticket was so expensive, I'll be here tomorrow!" he replied, leaving the washroom.

Doug had left his papers on the sink. *There's my ticket in,* Spire realised, grabbing them. He walked quickly after Doug, who was now just an arm's length from the first door that led back into the conference room. "Excuse me, Doug!" Spire shouted after him.

Doug turned around, just as he was about to open the door. "What is it?"

"You forgot your papers," Spire said, holding the documents against his chest.

The lady on the desk looked up at him as he reached the door. "You left your papers in the gents," Spire repeated, smiling at the conference official.

"Ah, yes, thank you very much Mr…"

"Spire, Robert Spire," he said, ushering Doug through.

The lady sitting at the desk smiled at Spire, looking a bit bemused, as he followed Doug through the heavy oak door into the conference room.

CHAPTER 15

TEN CRYSTAL CHANDELIERS hung down from the white elaborate ceiling of the oval conference room, which was decorated with ornate plaster coving around the edges. Rows of dark-wooden chairs had been laid out on the parquet flooring in a large semi-circular fashion, following the contours of the room.

Doug made a beeline for his seat, which was about ten rows in from the last row, a third of the way into the room. Spire walked slowly along the back of the room, trying to find a chair that wasn't occupied. He estimated there must have been around three hundred guests in the ballroom. On the stage, one of the speakers was standing at a podium talking about proposals for a windfarm off the coast of California.

As Spire reached the end of the row of chairs, he noticed a conference official, sitting behind a table at the back of the room, eyeing him suspiciously. Spire then spotted a free chair three rows from the back, gave the official a slight nod, and walked toward the empty seat and sat down, smiling at the delegates either side of him.

The speaker was coming to the end of his talk on windfarms, which appeared to have sent most of the audience to sleep. As he stepped down, from the small stage, some of the attendees gave a polite clap. Then a well-dressed lady, who had been sitting at a desk behind the speaker, stood up and walked to the podium. "Thank you for that interesting talk, Dr. Seagrove. We can only hope congress approves the funding package quickly so the proposals can proceed," she said, smiling at the speaker. "Ok Ladies and gentlemen, that brings us to the end of day two, of this, the fourteenth Climate Change Conference. Please come back in the morning for a nine o'clock start. The agenda for tomorrow can be found in your conference brochures. Before we wrap up for the day, I'd like to introduce you all to our distinguished guest, Professor Francois Trimaud, who would like to say a few words about yesterday's terrible news."

Spire looked on as a short, friendly-looking dark-haired chap, wearing corduroy trousers and a blue cotton shirt approached the stage.

"Bonsoir, ladies and gentlemen, merci bien," he said in a strong French accent. "My name is Francois Trimaud, and a few of you, I'm sure, will know that I am resident professor at the University Pierre et Marie Curie in Paris, and long serving member of The Arctic Marine Council. I specialise in climate science, particularly geoengineering," he said, lowering the microphone. "Sadly, I am not here to give you a lecture this evening on the climate, but to say a few words about my dear American friend, and wonderful colleague, Dr. Jack Bannister, who passed away suddenly on Sunday evening. I'm sure many of you who knew Jack are as shocked and saddened by his sudden passing as I am. I would just like to send my deepest sympathies to his family, his wife Margaret, and to say what a terrible loss his untimely death is to the world of climatology, and me personally. I will be arranging a scholarship in his name at some point, and will let everyone here know about it in due course. That's all I want to say for now," he continued, his voice breaking. "Thank you all for listening. Merci bien."

There was a long silence as the audience digested the announcement. The seated guests slowly got up off their chairs, some of them clapping as Professor Trimaud stepped down from the platform. As the delegates started to slowly leave the room, Spire quickly made his way to the stage where he had seen Professor Trimaud standing, talking to a man in a wheelchair. He pushed his way through the crowd toward him. "Excuse me, Professor Trimaud?" he asked anxiously, when he reached him.

"Oui, hello, can I help you?"

"My name is Spire, Robert Spire. I'm a lawyer from the UK. I'm sorry to interrupt like this, but I really need to talk to you for five minutes about your friend, Dr. Bannister."

"Jack? Oui, of course."

"Maybe it would be better if we go somewhere a little more private, Professor."

"Au revoir, Dr. Bernard, I'll catch up with you soon," Trimaud said, giving the man in the wheelchair a brief hug.

Dr. Bernard nodded, and wheeled himself away.

"We can go to the bar for a coffee if you'd like?" Spire suggested, as they both walked toward the exit.

Spire and Trimaud found a table in the bar with fabulous views, overlooking the city and the park below. A waitress came over and they ordered two coffees.

Spire waited for the waitress to leave before speaking. "Professor Trimaud, I'm sure you want to know why I've brought you up here, so I'll get straight to the point," he said, before telling Trimaud how he had initially been contacted by his client in London following the death of her son, the climatologist Dr. Dale Stanton. He told him about his trip down to Southampton, and then, after hearing about the death of Dr. Bannister, to San Francisco.

Trimaud listened intently as Spire relayed the events of the last ten days. "I must say, Mr. Spire, that is an awful lot to take in. Are you suggesting that Jack's death, over here, could be related to the death of Dr. Stanton, in the UK?"

"It's possible, Professor. I mean, it could all amount to nothing, but we have two dead climatologists, both of whom...well, collapsed before they were about to give presentations relating to global warming. The coroner put Dr. Stanton's death down to nicotine poisoning, but the odd thing is, according to my client, he didn't smoke."

Trimaud interrupted. "Pardon, but I thought you said Dr. Stanton had been wearing a nicotine patch?"

"He had been, and an ashtray full of cigarette-ends was found in his apartment. I suppose he could have been trying to kick the habit, but I have been assured by Stanton's mother, and Professor Sammedi down at the Oceanography Centre, that Stanton *didn't* smoke."

"I see," Trimaud said, looking puzzled.

"As far as I am aware, nobody at the Oceanography Centre knew exactly what Dr. Stanton's talk was going to be about, or what he may have discovered," Spire continued.

"You say he was looking at the Ocean Thermohaline Circulation?"

"That's correct."

"Well, it's common knowledge that the ocean conveyor has been monitored by the *RAPID-WATCH* program for some time now," Trimaud said, finishing his coffee. "To my knowledge there isn't a problem with the Atlantic Ocean conveyor. There is some evidence that the strength of it may have deteriorated by around thirty percent, but this is thought to be within natural parameters for the system. Perhaps Dr. Stanton was just checking the figures - nothing too sinister, I shouldn't imagine."

Spire noticed a flash out of the corner of his eye, and glanced over at a woman with shoulder-length dark hair, taking photos of the view outside. He looked out to the park below, noting the fantastic vista, before turning back to Trimaud.

"Have you any idea what Dr. Bannister was working on? Or what he'd planned to talk about at the conference?" he asked.

"Well, Jack kept his research under wraps, at least until he made a presentation, or released a paper into the scientific community. His papers will be found, but it may take a while for his research to come to light. I work in the same way...I just can't believe Jack is no longer here, Mr. Spire. I was only out drinking with him last night...c'est terrible." Professor Trimaud fell silent and stared out of the window, clearly upset over his friend's recent death.

"Professor?" Spire said, interrupting Trimaud's gaze.

"Sorry, Robert, please, call me Francois," he said, turning to him.

"Francois, do you mind telling me what *your* area of research is? You mentioned that you were a climate scientist. Geoengineering, I believe you said."

"Ah, yes. Well, I lecture at the UPMC University in Paris, and I specialise in climate geoengineering. Basically, I try to come up with practical ways to tackle the negative effects of global warming - on a planetary scale."

"Nothing too difficult then," Spire said, with a wry smile.

Trimaud raised his eyebrows. "It is my passion, Robert. I will soon be taking a team to the Arctic to test a theory that I am working on. It involves seeding the Arctic Ocean with an experimental iron sulphate to prevent further melting."

The waitress came over to the table and smiled. "Can I get you gentlemen another drink, two more coffees perhaps?"

"Same again," Spire said, looking up at the smiling waitress.

Trimaud nodded in agreement.

"Ocean seeding?" Spire asked inquisitively. "I've read about that in the papers."

"Oui, my team hope the theory works...naturally. I'll be

travelling to the Arctic in around two months, on a joint French/US expedition, to carry out tests. The Arctic sea ice starts its annual melt in early summer, giving us a two month window in which to navigate up the Northwest Passage, the location for the tests. The Arctic ice usually reaches its minimum in around mid to late September each year, before starting to freeze over again."

"Well I sure hope the experiment works, Professor, for all our sakes," Spire said, holding up his coffee cup.

Trimaud did likewise. "Well, Robert, I will be talking with Jack's widow sometime soon, and when I do, I will try and find out the cause of his untimely death. I will have to let her mourn for a while, you understand."

"Of course, Francois," Spire said.

They finished their coffees and left the bar, and waited for the elevator to take them back down to the first floor.

Ksenyia, who'd been sitting three tables away, started packing her camera up. She waited until both men entered the elevator, and then walked out into the corridor to get the next elevator down.

"It's been very interesting chatting to you, Robert," Trimaud said, as they stepped out of the elevator into the foyer, "but I must say goodbye to my colleague back up on the second floor. Have a good trip back home, and I'll be in touch. Au revoir," he said, extending his hand to Spire.

Spire shook his outstretched hand. "Au revoir Francois; thanks for your time."

Spire made his way to the hotel entrance, which took him back past the conference desk. The man with the squeaky voice, who he'd spoken to earlier, was standing behind his chair, a smug look on his face.

"Very interesting conference," Spire said sarcastically, as he walked out. By the time the man recognised him, Spire was already walking through the hotel's revolving doors.

Thursday morning soon arrived and Spire paid his bill and checked out of the Hilton. Over breakfast, he'd managed to flick briefly through the small book he'd bought at the airport on the city's 'off-the-beaten-track' tourist attractions. One apt monument caught his attention. He flagged a cab, down just outside the hotel's forecourt, and asked the driver to take him to the parking lot of the *Beach Chalet Restaurant*, which overlooked the Pacific Ocean, on the western edge of the Golden Gate Park.

As Spire got into the cab, the driver glanced at Spire with a puzzled look on his face. "If you want the park, chief, there's more to see on the eastern side."

"It's not the park I want, just something near to the Restaurant," Spire replied.

"Fair enough, buddy, you're paying."

After twenty minutes or so they were driving along Fulton Street, which afforded a splendid view of the ocean up ahead. Continuing along the northern edge of the park, they reached the end of the street. Ahead, the blue Pacific stretched out, as far as the eye could see. The cab made a left turn onto the Great Highway, then, almost immediately, the driver made a sharp left into the car park of the ocean-fronted *Beach Chalet Restaurant.*

"Here we are," the driver said, looking at Spire in his rear view mirror.

"Keep the fare running please, I'll be back shortly."

"No problem, bud," the driver replied, getting out of his cab. He lit a cigarette, and leaned up against the car door, taking in the view of the Pacific.

Spire walked toward the restaurant's entrance and looked around. *Where is it?* He wondered. He walked to the opposite end of the car park, and then the obelisk he'd been searching for, standing in an innocuous position in the car park, came into view. He walked over to it and stood under the stone monument, looking up at the stone shaft and the plaque under the lead relief. The faded inscription read - *Roald Amundsen 1872-1928.*

The monument had been erected to the Norwegian explorer, whose ship the *Gjoa,* had sailed into San Francisco in 1906 after completing its exploration of the Arctic, and the first successful transit of the Northwest Passage.

Spire shielded his eyes from the morning sun as he studied the twelve foot-high pillar. As he stood there, he was startled by a brusque voice, coming from the edge of the car park. "You interested in the stone, Mr.?"

He turned to see an old man sitting on a bench, some ten feet away. "Oh, just doing a spot of sightseeing before I leave," Spire replied, making his way back to the cab.

"A brave man was Amundsen. A very brave man," the old man continued. "You know, he named that little old boat after his wife and took her all the way to the Arctic, the Northwest Passage, spending three whole years there before sailing back here to 'Frisco. Arrived in port just after the big quake of nineteen – o – six," the old man said, ejecting a line of brown spittle as he finished speaking. He wiped his yellow-stained beard, and continued slowly masticating a mouthful of tobacco.

Spire stopped, and walked back toward the bench. "You the tour guide around here or something?" he asked, half-jokingly.

"Na, just an old sailor without a boat," the man replied,

chuckling. "Not many people take the time to stop and look at this monument. In fact, not a lot of people even realise it is here."

"Well, I wouldn't have if I hadn't bought this," Spire said, holding up the small guide book.

"The actual vessel was here until seventy-two, and then the Norwegians wanted her back. Can't say I blame them, she was just rotting here, exposed to the Pacific an all."

Spire took a seat next to the old man on the bench. "Did you ever sail up that way yourself?"

The old man looked at him, his face wizened from years of exposure to the elements. "Along the Northwest Passage you mean? Yep, sure did. I made it up as far as the northern tip of Resolute Island in sixty-four. Damn cold winter it was. I got myself caught in the pack ice for ten weeks before finally breaking free. The other ship wasn't quite…ah; anyway, it was tough back then." The old man turned his head, ejecting another line of brown spit, before turning back to look at Spire, a youthful twinkle now evident in his pale blue eyes.

"Did you ever try sailing that route again?" Spire asked.

"No, never got the chance. The ice was never as navigable as it was back in sixty-four, until now that is. God damn global warming has started to melt the entire channel. Before long, every damn fishing boat, oil tanker and frigate will make the route. That's if the Canadians will let them." The old sailor let out a raspy laugh, as he coughed up more phlegm.

"What do you mean?"

"The route goes through Canadian waters. They ain't just going to let any Tom, Dick or Harry sail up there for nothing now are they? Any ship sailing that route will shave thousands of nautical miles off the usual and necessary journey around the Capes, or through the Panama Canal. If the Northwest Passage becomes ice free, then you have easy access between the Atlantic and Pacific Oceans. What we have then, my friend, is the next gold rush. At the rate the passage is melting, I might even be around to see it." The old sailor chuckled again, as he cleared his chest of phlegm.

Spire glanced back up at the stone obelisk with renewed respect. "You mentioned another ship?" he said, after a few moments.

"Other ship?" the old man said, looking serious. "How long you got, son?"

Spire checked his watch; "Shit, not long enough I'm afraid. It's been interesting talking to you Mr...?"

"Harrington. Parker Harrington," the old man replied.

"I'm afraid I really must go. I got a cab waiting, and a plane to catch. Take care, old sailor," Spire said, getting up.

"See you around, kid," the man replied, removing his cap.

Spire rushed back to the waiting cab. The driver was lying back in his seat, listening to the commentary from a baseball game. "Cheers for waiting. Straight to the airport please," Spire said.

The driver straightened up and started the car. "Right away, buddy. Find what you were looking for?"

"Sure did, and an old sailor to boot," Spire replied, with a smile.

As they drove back to the airport, Spire looked out over the Pacific Ocean which glistened in the afternoon sun. He thought about the last few days, wondering whether the trip had been worthwhile from his client's point of view. *What had he discovered?* He hadn't established the cause of Dr. Bannister's death, although a heart attack was the obvious contender. Professor Trimaud hadn't seemed overly alarmed about the death of Dr. Stanton in London, and he wasn't concerned about the Atlantic's Ocean Thermohaline current, the last project Dr. Stanton had been working on. *Could the deaths of both scientists really just be coincidence?* He wasn't so sure.

Whilst he mulled over the events of the last two days, he hadn't appreciated the cab had already pulled into the drop-off area for the terminal building.

"Here ya go, my friend. Sixty bucks I'm afraid - I let you off twenty."

Spire pulled out seventy dollars and paid the fare.

"Thanks, buddy. Have a safe trip back to England," the driver said, pulling off.

After a painless check-in, and a short wait, Spire relaxed into the comfortable seat on the top deck of the 747 aircraft, just as a flight attendant came over and offered him a glass of Champagne.

"That's just what I needed, thanks."

"I wish I could join you," she replied, a playful look on her face. She continued down the aisle, offering Champagne to another passenger a few rows behind.

"Spasibo, thank you," the passenger said.

Spire turned around to see who the Russian accent belonged to. An attractive woman, with shoulder length dark hair, and wearing designer sunglasses was sitting four rows back, in the opposite aisle. She glanced away as he looked at her.

Spire finished his drink, just as the captain introduced himself over the P.A system, before giving brief details of their flight back to London.

Before long the jet was flying toward the east, leaving San Francisco and the setting sun behind. Spire settled into his seat, soon forgetting about the attractive passenger sitting a few rows behind him.

Four rows behind, Ksenyia Petrovsky removed her sun glasses and sipped her Champagne, thinking about her new assignment. *Whatever your interest is my English friend, I will ensure that it remains extremely short lived.*

CHAPTER 16

SPIRE SLEPT FOR most of the overnight flight home, awaking shortly before the aircraft commenced its descent into London Heathrow. Fifty minutes later, he was driving his Audi out of the airport's internal road system and onto the M4 motorway, heading west back towards home. By the time he had crossed the Severn Bridge into Wales, the motorway traffic had eased off considerably. With his eyes now stinging and wanting to close, he put his foot down for the final stretch of motorway, arriving in the village of Oakdale ninety minutes later. He was struggling to stay awake as he pulled into his driveway.

Angela had left the lights on in the lounge and hall, and a warm orange glow emanated out into the dimming afternoon light. He turned the ignition off, sitting for a few moments rubbing his tired eyes. As he got out of the car he was startled by the sound of a car engine behind him. He turned to see a car accelerate along the lane, its brake lights glowing red in the dark lane as it disappeared around the corner. "Idiot," Spire muttered, as he locked the car and walked to the front door.

The following morning, Spire rolled out of bed and onto the floor, where he lay briefly before forcing himself to do his customary eighty press-ups. He stood, yawned and wandered into the kitchen, found the French press and placed a large helping of Italian coffee into it. Before long, the fragrant aroma of fresh coffee filled the kitchen. He shouted to Angela, who was already in the lounge reading the Saturday morning papers. "Fancy a coffee, darling?"

"Had one already thanks. How's the weary traveller feeling?"

"Not bad. Perhaps one of your cottage pie's later might help me get over my jet lag? Say, do you fancy a walk on the beach later? It looks like it's going to be a great day."

"Sounds good, but I need to pop into the shop first to check on a few things."

"Okey-doke," Spire said, yawning again. "I'll jump in the shower, and then we can go."

Outside the cottage, one hundred metres or so along the lane, a dark Saab was parked up against the verge. Ksenyia Petrovsky typed a message into her notebook whilst she waited;

Arrived in UK, and have followed target. I will take appropriate action and report back in a day or two.

A few minutes later she heard the sound of an e-mail arriving into her in-box.

Understood; Target's name is Robert Spire, Environmental Lawyer. You know what you must do. After, travel to Paris, further instructions will follow. The usual additional 10k applies if business card is left in a visible place - Arc Bin Quid Lo.

She liked the somewhat encrypted e-mail. For each assignment she had been able to earn an additional ten thousand euros, simply by placing a black business card on, or near her victims' bodies, a power trip for her paymasters no doubt. Paris sounded good. She had spent time there before, both for pleasure and business, and she looked forward to her next assignment, which she anticipated would be her last.

She looked on as Spire's car reversed out of the driveway, and waited as the Audi drove out of sight, before getting out of her car and strolling towards the cottage. She walked directly up the gravel drive and rang the doorbell, not expecting a reply. She'd say she was looking for a Mr. Smith if anyone answered, and simply ask for directions to Pembroke, a town she'd seen on a sign the day before.

As anticipated, there was nobody home. She peered through the window into what looked like the lounge. Having taken the car, Spire would be gone for at least ten minutes, she assumed. She moved to the side of the property and found a vine-covered side gate, which opened easily. She walked through and made her way around to a secluded back garden and spotted a rear door. She took an elongated hair clip from her pocket, formed it into a miniature torsion wrench and inserted it into the lock. After twenty seconds of manipulation, the door's bolt slid open, and she quietly opened it and slipped through into a rear utility room.

The washing machine was on and going through a spin cycle, shaking furiously as if it were about to eject its contents all over the floor at any moment. Ksenyia looked around the small room; a pair of flippers, oxygen tank and a spear gun was leaning against the wall. She walked through the utility room and kitchen and into the lounge beyond. A photograph of a tanned Robert Spire standing on a beach, mask and snorkel in hand, sat on the mantelpiece. She looked around but saw nothing of interest, and continued into the study. Papers were neatly stacked on a desk next to a computer; some blue folders were piled up on the chair. She picked one of them up and quickly perused the documents inside. It was obvious they were legal documents and letters relating to a claim of some kind, nothing to do with global warming or the dead scientists. She turned the computer on, overriding Spire's set password, *permafrost,* and opened and perused his files. Again, nothing stood out that connected him with Stanton or Bannister. Satisfied that Spire didn't appear to be involved in her business, she shut down the computer and pulled a piece of A4 paper from the printer and wrote out a message, attaching it to the computer. She left the cottage the way as she'd entered, wiping the few surfaces she had touched with a cotton handkerchief.

Tchaikovsky's *Eugene Onegin* drifted out of the car speakers, as Ksenyia relaxed in her seat. *The calm before the storm,* she thought. Earlier, she had replaced the registration plates on the Saab with false ones. The only item of equipment she needed for this assignment, a black woollen balaclava, lay on the seat beside her.

She almost missed Spire's car pulling back into the driveway. She felt the muscles in her lithe body tighten, with a mixture of anxiety and excitement, as adrenalin began to surge through her veins.

She lifted the high-powered *Sunagor* binoculars to her eyes as Spire and his female companion got out of the car and entered the house. She followed Spire's silhouette through the net curtains, as he moved in and out of the lounge.

Spire shouted to Angela, who was getting clothes out of the washing machine, "I don't know about you, but I fancy grabbing some lunch at that new restaurant we went to, for Brian's birthday, followed by that walk on the beach...what do you think?"

"Great, give me five minutes and I'll be with you."

Spire went to check his e-mail, when Angela shouted at him. "I'm ready, come on, you can do that later - It's almost two o'clock."

"You're right," he said, turning around. He walked into the utility room to check the back door was locked, and then left through the front door to find Angela waiting by the car.

CHAPTER 17

KSENYIA LOOKED ON as both targets left the cottage. *Had he seen the note? Surely not, he appeared too relaxed.* She slapped the dashboard with the palm of her hand as the Audi reversed out of the drive and down the narrow lane.

She tossed the binoculars aside and accelerated out from the grass verge after them, wheels spinning.

Spire turned right onto the main road, and as he did, noticed a dark Saab appear from nowhere, stopping abruptly at the T-junction behind him. He pulled off, and fifty metres or so further along the main road he checked the rear view mirror again, and this time could see two women in a red Mini Cooper. There was no sign of the Saab. He made a right turn off the main road into a narrow country lane, which was around two miles long.

He turned to speak to Angela, when suddenly a rear impact pushed the Audi forward with a severe jolt. "What the hell was that?" Spire shouted, looking behind. The dark Saab had returned, this time it was right on their tail.

Spire slowed down in order to find a clearing to pull over, but the Saab suddenly rammed into the back of the car again. "Jesus, what the hell's going on?" Spire shouted, fighting with the steering wheel, as he accelerated along the narrow country lane to try and escape the lunatic in the car behind.

"Bloody hell!" Angela screamed, turning around to look

through the back window.

Spire glanced into the rear view mirror to try and get a glimpse of the Saab driver. Behind the wheel was a balaclava-clad figure, barely visible inside the dark vehicle. Heart pounding in his chest, he tried to focus his concentration back on to the road in front. *Was it a teenager, high on drink or drugs perhaps?* All he knew was that the collision hadn't been an accident. Too concerned to pull over and attempt to reason with the Saab driver - not with Angela in the car - he slammed the automatic sports-box into second and accelerated along the road.

"Be careful, Robert, we're in a *country lane* for chrissake!"

The Audi surged forwards, the Saab on its tail. They arrived at a blind bend giving Spire no choice but to keep going. He could see the end of the lane approaching, but the Saab was only a metre or two behind as he braked for the upcoming junction. There was another collision, and a sound of grinding steel as the Saab shunted into the back of the car again, pushing the Audi over the junction and into the main road. A silver Mercedes swerved, just managing to avoid a collision as it drove past.

"Hold on, honey," Spire shouted, as he accelerated up the road. "If you weren't in the car I'd get out and throttle this bastard," he said, searching for his mobile phone. He found it and passed it to Angela. "Quick, get the registration plates and call the police."

Angela twisted around and made a mental note of the registration plate - NRP 880Y. "Got it," she said, keying in 9-9-9.

The speedometer was showing eighty as Spire slammed his foot on the brake in order to take a sharp left hand bend into another country lane, hoping the Saab would overshoot the turning. The route led towards the small village of Manorbier.

"Shit!" Spire shouted, glancing in the rear view mirror and seeing the Saab slow down just in time to make the turn. Accelerating hard, he planned on losing the Saab in the lane.

"Watch out Robert!" Angela screamed, as two riders on horseback emerged from a bend in the road.

Spire slammed his foot on the brakes and threw the automatic gearbox into second. The Audi's engine screamed as the car skidded into the hedgerow, causing one of the horses to rear up, throwing its rider to the road.

Behind him, the Saab screeched around the corner, just missing the fallen rider.

Spire arrived at another main road, turned right and accelerated down the hill. "We'll try and get to the coastguard's house overlooking the bay."

Angela wasn't listening; she was relaying the Saab's registration plate to the police. As the Audi skidded around a right hand bend, leading to Manorbier beach, the force of the turn caused Angela to drop the phone. "Shit, the mobile!" she screamed.

"Did the police get the number?"

"I...I think so," Angela said, shaking.

The Audi skidded around a sharp right-hand bend which led down toward Manorbier beach, forcing a couple walking their dog to jump out of the way as they sped past them.

The pedestrian cursed, raising his fist at them as they screeched by. Spire checked the rear view mirror and saw the pursuing Saab's wing mirror shatter against the pedestrian's left arm a second or two later as it tore passed them. The man bent over double in the road, but luckily appeared still very much alive.

Spire passed Manorbier Castle and accelerated up the hill toward the elevated parking area overlooking the bay; where he normally parked when out for a walk. The coastguard's house was only two-hundred metres or so further up the bluff, situated in a secluded spot overlooking the sea.

Without warning, there was another smash, this time from the rear offside. Spire wrestled the steering wheel as one of the Audi's tyres blew out, causing it to veer suddenly to the left. The car then swung violently in the opposite direction, left the road, and headed into the bracken and gorse which fringed the edge of the cliff top. "Hold on!" he shouted.

He wrenched the steering wheel in a desperate attempt to pull the Audi back onto the road, but it was too late. The car hurtled through the bracken at forty miles an hour. He reached over to Angela in a futile attempt to shield her from the collision about to follow, as he realised they were going to plummet over the cliff.

All of a sudden there was a deafening crunch, followed by a hiss, as the car came to an abrupt stop, two metres or so from the edge. He could only assume that the Audi had been brought to a halt by a large boulder, or mound, hidden beneath the bracken.

The forward momentum threw them both into the inflated airbags with brutal force. Spire opened his eyes, the fleeting tranquillity interrupted by a loud hissing from pressurised air escaping from a damaged part of the engine. He feared the worst, realising thay had to get the hell out of the car.

Ksenyia had only intended to force Spire's car off the road, to scare him, not to kill him. She felt a sense of relief when she saw that the vehicle had collided with something, preventing it from going over the cliff. She pulled her balaclava off and accelerated along the coast road, continuing for a few miles before pulling over to exchange the number plates, this time returning the correct plates onto the car.

She assessed the damaged nearside front wing and front bumper and didn't think it looked too serious. She got back in the car, returning in the direction she had come from, but taking a different route back towards the motorway. She calculated she'd be back in London for around eight.

Spire's interest in the dead climatologists would surely be extinguished, she hoped, as she accelerated along the dual carriageway towards the motorway.

Spire forced his door open, and fell out onto the bracken with a soft thud, before making his way around the back of the car to open the passenger door. Steam hissed from the Audi's crumpled bonnet. He helped Angela out of the car, noticing she had a nasty gash on her forehead, which was oozing blood.

"You ok honey? Your head is cut. Jeez, I'm sorry; I lost control after the last knock."

"I think I'm alright, but I feel a little light-headed. Who the hell was that, Rob? What's going on?"

"I don't know. Let's just hope the police catch the bastard. Come on, we need to get that head wound checked out."

A red pickup truck appeared, and quickly drove off the road down to where they were standing.

"Dai, thank God!" Spire said, recognising David Miles, the coastguard, as he walked down towards them.

"Good gracious, are you two alright? What the hell happened?" he asked.

"Some idiot in a black Saab forced us off the road, just up there," Spire said, pointing to the skid marks on the road where he'd lost control.

"Good grief, if it wasn't for that boulder there, you'd have gone off the cliff, for sure. You're both bloody lucky to be alive. Give me a minute and I'll tow the car back onto the road." Miles returned to his pick-up truck and prepared to tow the Audi from the bracken. As he did so, the front spoiler creaked and ripped off, as the car was pulled from a concealed lump of rock.

A police car sped up the hill towards them and pulled over, its light bar flashing.

Spire gave the police officer a detailed account of what had happened, starting with the first rear-end shunt in the country lane, to the final jolt, which caused him to lose control on the cliff road.

The officer looked stunned as he took down all the details, and then radioed for an ambulance. "I've never known anything like this to happen around here," he said, in a heavy Welsh accent, shaking his head. He reassured them that there was an ambulance on its way, and then returned to his car and sped off in the direction the Saab had taken.

Spire turned back to Angela, "At least we'll get that head of yours checked out at the hospital," he said, checking her wound.

"Are *you* hurt, Rob?" she asked, running her hand over her cut.

"Just a bit of a sore neck, but apart from that, I think I'm fine."

The ambulance arrived after about fifteen minutes and Spire and Angela were escorted into the back by a tired looking paramedic. "You two are lucky, we've just done a home visit up the road. Could have been waiting forty-five minutes if we had to come from Withybush," the ruddy-faced paramedic said, in a broad Welsh accent.

Angela was assisted onto one of the stretchers, whilst Spire took a seat beside her. "Well, it looks like we're going to have to re-schedule dinner," he said, smiling.

"I've lost my appetite anyway," Angela replied, sighing.

The ambulance drove swiftly in the direction of the hospital, its lights flashing.

As Spire sat there stroking his wife's head, an uneasy feeling welled up from the pit of his stomach, as he thought about the car chase which had almost killed them. *Who the hell was driving that Saab?*

The police car arrived in Pembroke, a small town seven miles from the location of the crash, and the next town the Saab would have arrived in, had it continued in its last known direction of travel. Sergeant Jenkins drove around the walled town twice before radioing back to the station. "Patrol to station. No signs of the Saab, I think I lost it. Have alerted Haverfordwest Station, will return, over."

Jenkins was looking forward to the end of his shift in fifteen minutes, and the snooker tournament taking place at The Swan Inn, his local pub. He turned off his siren and headed back towards Manorbier.

CHAPTER 18

SPIRE ARRIVED HOME from the hospital at nine-thirty. Angela had been given an X-ray, and a full check-up, and everything appeared fine, but, as a precaution, the hospital had kept her in overnight. He walked up to the front door and inserted his key into the lock. The driveway and porch were in darkness, which didn't usually bother him, but this time, he had an uneasy feeling, as if he was being watched.

He opened the door, flicked the hall lights on, and went straight into the kitchen, grabbing a cold beer from the fridge. He stood, gulping down half the bottle's contents before closing the fridge door and wandering into the lounge. He put the television on to break the silence. With his beer in hand, he walked into the study with the intention of checking his e-mail backlog.

He noticed the A4 sheet of paper stuck to his monitor as soon as he walked in. "What the hell?" he muttered, as he read the note;

Halt your unhealthy interest in global warming. Do not contact the police or you will regret it. The paper was signed; *A. Visitor.*

A Visitor, that son-of-a-bitch had broken in here! He stared at the note before shoving it in his draw, slamming it shut. *Had anything been stolen?* His earlier feeling of unease had been justified. Feeling even more unsettled, he stood and closed the study curtains. His thoughts flashed back to the chase with the Saab. Now it made sense - someone was trying to warn him off the Stanton case.

Spire could take care of himself, physically anyway, years of martial arts training had ensured that, but his concern for Angela was now amplified. He couldn't risk going to the police, not yet anyway. An equally serious concern then dawned on him. *Had the scientists been killed because of their work in the field of global warming?*

He finished his beer, then walked around the cottage to double check the doors and windows were all locked. The first thing he would do in the morning would be to call Doris; he had a plan, but it meant a trip to Paris in order to meet with Professor Trimaud again.

The following morning he woke early and called the hospital; thankfully Angela was fine, and would be ready to come home around lunchtime. Relieved, he made himself a French press full of strong coffee and sat down to plan the rest of the day. First he'd call Doris to update her on the events of the last twenty-four hours, and then he'd contact Professor Trimaud in Paris, to warn him that his life might be in danger.

He needed to purchase equipment to beef up the security around the cottage. Before he could do anything however, he had to wait for a replacement hire vehicle to be delivered to him. The insurance company had promised it by midday. He made a note of a few items he needed on a blank sheet of paper;

4 security lights, 2 motion sensor video cameras, padlocks, dead bolts, and 2 pay-as-you-go mobile phones.

That should do for a start, he thought.

He took a quick shower, and then called Doris Stanton.

"Good morning, Robert, what do I owe for the pleasure of this call, so early in the morning?" she said.

Doris listened in silence, as Spire told her about the previous day's events.

"Good God, Robert, this is terrible. Who, or what, is behind all this, do you think?"

"I've no idea, Doris, but we were almost killed yesterday. I doubt the driver meant to run us over the cliff, otherwise they wouldn't have gone to the trouble of breaking in and leaving a note for me, but that's not the point."

"Robert, do you want me to organise some private security for you? I can do it you know, it's no trouble."

"That's a kind offer, Doris, but it would just worry Angela unnecessarily. I'm going to improve the security around the cottage today, but these people, whoever they are, clearly mean business. I'd rather gather more evidence before going to the police. Who's going to believe that Dale's death in London from an apparent nicotine overdose, the death of Dr. Bannister in San Francisco, a car chase, and this break-in are all connected?"

"I suppose it does sound a little absurd, Robert. I'm very sorry about Angela, it's just terrible. I'll enhance security around my place, too."

"Doris, if Dale's and Dr. Bannister's deaths *are* linked, it's a huge concern. This could have implications far greater than we can ever begin to imagine. We just don't know what could be at stake here. I'll contact Professor Trimaud in Paris to see where we go from there, if that's Ok with you?"

"Of course, Robert, but for God's sake be careful. I mean this isn't just about Dale's legacy any more. I never imagined things would develop in this way. Anything you need, Robert, I mean financially, just let me know and it's yours."

"That's very kind, Doris; I'll bear that in mind. From now

on, I'll call you from a new mobile number, just in case the phones have been tapped. I suggest you buy a pay-as-you-go mobile too, and we'll communicate that way from now on."

Doris agreed and terminated the call.

Spire then called Trimaud's Paris number, but there was no answer. He hoped it wasn't too late, as he replaced the receiver.

He called Kim at the office, briefly telling her what had happened, and promising to try and get into the office for a few hours during the afternoon, to check the post and give her a proper update. From the tone in her voice, he could tell, she was worried. He decided not to add to her concerns by telling her about the note left on his computer.

As he put the phone down, the sound of crunching gravel prompted him to look out of the window. A pickup truck was lowering a Ford Focus onto the driveway. He opened the front door and hurried over to the driver. "Great, that was quick!"

The man looked at him. "Yes sir, we got the call early this morning. I had the Ford on the back already, so came straight over."

Spire signed a few papers, and the man handed him the keys and drove away. He walked back inside, grabbed his wallet and jacket from the kitchen table, and went into the lounge to turn off the television; CNN was on as usual, and as he picked up the remote to turn it off, a breaking news story flashed across the screen.

Mystery deepens as submersible is lost in Southern Indian Ocean...

Spire, turned up the volume and fell back onto the sofa. The scene flashed to a reporter standing outside NSIDC headquarters in Boulder, Colorado.

"A further twist has emerged in the death of climatologist

Dr. Jack Bannister, in San Francisco, seven days ago. The National Snow and Ice Data Center, who employed Dr. Bannister, appear to have suffered another terrible setback. During what appears to be a routine mission exploring the region around the Crozet Islands nine days ago, the Poseidon, one of their deep-sea exploration submarines, failed to surface on schedule. All attempts to contact the sub have failed and concerns are now obviously rising. Further updates will follow as soon as information becomes available."

Spire shook his head in disbelief. *What the hell is going on?*

Concerned at the news, he left the cottage, double checked that the back and front doors were secure, and headed into town, to the hardware store, to purchase the items he needed. He then drove the thirty miles or so to the hospital to check on Angela.

When he arrived, Angela was sitting in the waiting room drinking a cup of coffee. She looked fine, a small plaster on her forehead the only physical sign of the previous day's events. They drove home, Angela just happy to be out of hospital.

"It was pretty lonely in that bed last night, I can tell you," she said, as they drove back along the country lanes toward home.

"I bet, honey. If it's any consolation, I didn't sleep too well either," Spire replied, hiding the concern from his face.

"Have you heard from the police? Did they catch the Saab driver?" she asked him.

"Nope, not heard, I'll call them later. I went into town earlier and bought some security equipment for the cottage; lighting, cameras, that sort of thing."

"Oh, Robert, you don't think the Saab driver knows where we live, do you?"

"No, don't be silly, darling...it's just to be on the safe side."

Spire felt guilty about not telling Angela the entire truth, but the last thing he wanted to do was worry her even more.

They arrived back at the cottage and Spire discreetly walked from room to room, to check everything was as it should be. As far as he could tell, all looked fine. "Let's get you a cup of tea," he said, walking into the kitchen. "Then I'll see if I can install some of that equipment."

He handed Angela her tea. "I need to make a call to NSIDC, darling. I'll be in the study if you need me."

"NSIDC?"

"The Snow and Ice Data Center; Bannister's employers."

"Ok, you do what you have to do. I'm going upstairs to have a lie down."

Spire went into the study and quietly closed the door, powered up the computer and carried out a search for NSIDC on the Internet. He clicked onto the organisation's website, and then dialled the number listed under 'contact details.' There was a few seconds delay, followed by an international dialing tone.

"Hello, Office of the National Snow and Ice Data Center, University of Colorado, which department do you require?" a young polite woman, with a soft American accent, asked.

"Hi, I was wondering if I could be put through to the Office of Oceanic Research," Spire asked, guessing this was the most appropriate department, after looking at the website.

"Sure, hold on a moment," the girl replied.

There was another dialing tone, followed by a man's voice. "Hello, Mike Tweed, O.R office, may I help?" he asked, curtly.

"Ah yes, I hope so. My name is Spire, Robert Spire, and I'm calling from the UK. I'm inquiring about some research your organisation has been indirectly involved in, and wondered if you could assist?"

"Could you tell me what your interest might be, Mr. Spire?"

"Certainly, I'm an environmental lawyer based in the UK,

and I was recently in San Francisco with a colleague of mine, Professor Francois Trimaud, a good friend of US scientist Dr. Jack Bannister. I just heard on the news that one of your research subs has been lost, off the coast of the Crozet Islands. I hoped you could tell me something about it?"

Spire decided to take a shot in the dark with the query, hoping that by mentioning the climatologists names he could illicit some information. There was a long pause on the line.

"You say you *knew* Dr. Bannister, sir?"

"Well, not very well, but I was with Professor Trimaud only a few days ago."

"You do know Dr. Bannister is *dead*?"

"Yes, I do…shocking," Spire said, sympathetically.

"Yes, quite, he was one of our best climatologists, and a great man. We've had enough bad news for a good while." There was a long pause on the phone, before Mr. Tweed continued, his voice sounding a little more relaxed. "Dr. Bannister was leading an exploration team off the Crozet Islands, and his department had leased the *Poseidon* from us. She went down two nautical miles off the southern tip of one of the islands. We haven't managed to bring her up yet, that operation is still ongoing. We lost two good men when she sunk, tragic situation, really is." Mr. Tweed suddenly fell silent, as if he'd already said too much.

"Can you tell me what Dr. Bannister was looking for?" Spire asked, anticipating a negative response.

"I'm afraid that information is classified, sir. I couldn't tell you, even if I knew."

Spire thought he'd probably asked enough. "Thank you for your help, Mr. Tweed, I appreciate it. Good luck with the recovery operation."

"Thank you. Have a good day sir."

"Oh, one last thing Mr. Tweed; did Dr. Bannister know that

the sub had been lost before he died?"

Tweed was silent for a few seconds. "Our department tried to get hold of him whilst he was in San Francisco. A message was left on his hotel phone, but I don't believe he ever received it, Mr. Spire."

"Maybe for the best," Spire replied, thanking Mr. Tweed before hanging up.

Spire realised his instincts had been correct. *The submersible had been on hire to Dr. Bannister, but what the hell could he be so interested in around the Crozet Islands and was it connected with the work of Dr. Stanton?* He needed to speak to Francois, as soon as possible.

He shouted upstairs to Angela. "I'm going out to try and fix some of these motion sensor cameras." There was no response and he assumed she was still sleeping.

He rigged up one of the camera's overlooking the front drive, and one in the back garden. The internal monitors could wait until later. It was now coming up to three in the afternoon, and he needed to get into the office to check his post, and update Kim on the recent events. He grabbed his jacket, checked on Angela, who was still sleeping soundly upstairs, and left for the office.

Kim was typing away when he arrived; she looked up as he entered. "Where the hell have you been, Rob?" she asked, looking concerned.

"You might well ask," Spire said, sitting down. He gave Kim a detailed account of the car chase, and the break-in.

"What the hell are you going to do, Robert? This sounds serious."

"You could say that. There appears to be a connection between the two scientists' deaths, but the real question is why?" He told her of his concerns for Professor Francois Trimaud, in view of his involvement in the Arctic experiment.

"It's crazy, Robert; it sounds like something out of a movie! Do you know if Dr. Bannister's death has been explained yet?"

"Nope, no news on that, but Professor Trimaud was supposed to be getting back to me once he'd spoken to his widow, Margaret. In the meantime, Kim, just be extra vigilant, will you. I have bought a new pay-as-you-go mobile. From now on, you'd better only call me on this," Spire said, writing down the new number for her. "Apart from that, we just act as if nothing has happened, ok?"

"I…I guess so," Kim said, clearly worried.

Spire's mobile phone rang. Still holding the new one, he stared at it for a few seconds before realising that it was his old phone ringing in his pocket. He quickly retrieved it.

"Hello, Robert Spire," he said.

"Bonjour, Robert, it's François, comment allez-vous?"

"Ah, Francois, hello, I'm fine thanks," Spire said, sighing in relief upon hearing his friend's voice. He looked over at Kim, pointed to the phone as he mouthed Trimaud's name.

"Listen, Francois, sorry to interrupt, but let me call you back from another phone. What's your number there?"

Trimaud gave him his number and Spire called straight back. "Sorry about that, I might be paranoid, but after what's happened to me over the last twenty-four hours I'm not taking any chances."

"Oh? You can tell me in a moment, Robert. I'm not sure if this is relevant, but Jack's good friend, John Gregory, who was there the night Jack died, called me yesterday to say he'd found a business card in one of the glasses near to where Jack collapsed. He noticed it when he cleared some broken glass off the floor. He wouldn't have thought anything of it, but it had a very strange name on it, so he kept it. It's probably nothing but…"

Spire cut him off. "*Business card?*" he said, his heart rate accelerating. "Is it black with the name *Arc Bin Quid Lo* printed on it?"

There was silence on the phone, "Oui Robert, comment vous savez...how do you know this?"

"The same card was in Dr. Stanton's wallet. His mother, Doris, gave it to me. She assumed it belonged to one of his colleagues. Have you any idea what the name on the card means?"

"No, sorry, Robert, it's nothing I am familiar with."

"That *is* odd," Spire said, thinking about the strange coincidence for a moment.

"So, what is your news?" Trimaud asked, after a moment.

Spire relayed the news he'd just seen on CNN and Trimaud listened in stunned silence. "I've just come off the phone from NSIDC and they confirmed that the submersible that sunk was, indeed, hired out to Bannister's team, and was being used to explore an underwater region off the French Crozet Islands."

"Are you *sure,* Robert?" Trimaud asked.

"Yep, I just spoke to a chap called Tweed. He confirmed the loss of the sub, and that two crew members had died in the incident. What do you think Dr. Bannister was doing there, Francois?"

"This is intriguing. It would be something he was researching, but he did not tell me what he was doing. From what I recall, Iles Crozet are situated about one thousand kilometres from the Antarctic coast, but there is not much there, just a national park, I think. I'll see if I can find out a little more, perhaps ask Margaret if she knows anything." Trimaud paused. "So, Robert, what happened to you?"

Spire brought Trimaud up to speed with recent events. About the car chase, and the fact that he was now convinced there was a connection between the scientists' deaths and their work. He didn't mention the break in, so as not to worry Kim. "Someone wanted your friend, Jack and Dr. Stanton, dead, Francois, but we need to find out why. I'm concerned you might also be in danger, you need to be careful. I'm thinking of coming over to see you in a few days, if that's Ok? Discuss your research in more detail; see if we can figure out what Bannister and Stanton could have been working on."

"Fine with me, Robert, you're welcome to come over anytime. In the meantime I'll look into the Crozet Island link, try and find out what Jack was looking at."

"One more thing Francois," Spire said. "Only call me on this number from now on, and perhaps buy yourself a new pay-as-you-go mobile, just in case."

"Oui, ok, Robert, I'll do that," Trimaud said, ending the call.

Kim had been sitting in silence as the conversation unfolded. Spire sat for a few seconds, digesting what had just been said. He told Kim about the card that was found by Bannister's body, and in Stanton's wallet. "It more or less confirms both scientists were murdered, Kim."

"My God, Robert, won't the police do something?"

"They need to know about the link, that's for sure, but I don't want to risk anything at the moment...I mean, if these people are watching, they could come back."

Kim frowned. "I bloody hope they don't," she said.

"Kim, have a good look at this, see if you can make any sense of it," he said, handing her the glossy black business card.

She studied the card. "Very odd names," she said, screwing up her face in thought. "I'll see what I can come up with."

"Thanks. Listen, I can't concentrate on work today, but I'll be in tomorrow to try and clear my backlog, and next week I'll be taking a trip to Paris for a few days, to see Professor

Trimaud.

"Paris...do you need an assistant?" Kim pleaded.

"Nope, I need you to hold the fort while I'm away; it's the most important job!" Spire said, smiling at her as he left the office.

"Yeah, yeah," Kim said, as she resumed typing.

Spire hadn't been home long, when Angela walked down the stairs holding her empty mug.

"Hi, how are you feeling?" he asked, from his desk in the study.

Angela wandered into the room, still looking very tired, and sat on his lap. "Much better, thanks. How long have I been sleeping?"

"About four hours."

"Really? The painkillers must have knocked me out. What have you been up to?"

"Well, I went into the office to check on things and to let Kim know what's been going on. Then I called NSIDC, and spoke to Francois Trimaud in Paris about the situation..."

Angela interrupted. "Oh, Rob, you're not still involved in all this crazy business, are you?"

"What do you mean? It's not crazy. Listen, a black business card with the name *Arc-Bin-Quid-Lo* embossed on it was found in Stanton's wallet. I've just learnt that an identical card was found near Bannister's body, in a Champagne flute."

"*You're kidding!*" Angela said, appearing to be a bit more interested. "That *is* odd. Do the police know about this?"

"Not as far as I'm aware; The San Francisco police are sure to investigate, once they find out."

"So, what are you going to do?"

"I'm not sure, darling. If both climatologists *were* killed, it points to there being a connection between their work and global warming, or the environment generally. The ramifications could be serious. I'm planning on meeting up with Francois, in Paris, to see if he can shed any light on what they may have been working on. He's got the expertise to be able to help. Not only that, but his life could also be in danger. He's about to conduct an important geoengineering experiment in the Arctic." Spire paused to take a breath. "Whoever killed Bannister and Stanton may also want to try and stop Professor Trimaud from carrying out his research. The question is: why?"

"Oh, Robert, this seems all too farfetched. You're in way over your head. I mean, we moved down here for a quiet life, and now you're getting yourself involved in *this*...it's ridiculous, and dangerous." Angela hesitated for a moment, before saying, "Oh God, you don't think the car chase is connected, do you?"

It was the last question Spire wanted to hear. He felt guilty about not telling her the truth. "No, darling, I don't...I mean, how could it have been? Nobody knows I'm involved in this, apart from you and Doris."

"Are you sure? Oh, Robert, I'm worried."

"Why don't you come with me to Paris, or at least have some friends come and stay while I'm gone? You could even go to your parents."

"My parents, this is getting worse!"

"Angela, Francois has also asked me to go on the Arctic expedition with him, in a few months time," Spire said, thinking he might as well bring the trip up now.

"The Arctic! Robert, you must be bloody joking. San Francisco, Paris...I'm drawing a line with the Arctic, that's just ridiculous. You're a lawyer, for chrissake! You can take me somewhere warm instead, that's final."

Spire forced a frown and changed the subject. "I'll go make

us some lunch, then get on and finish the rest of this security stuff. I just need to work out how to connect the external security cameras with the monitors and then we're all set...it will then be like Fort Knox in here."

"Well, let's see if it all works first before making claims like that. I haven't forgotten the security lights you put up in our first place. They never worked properly," Angela said, sarcastically.

Spire wandered into the back garden with his tool box, his thoughts far from the job in hand. All he could think about was how he was going to get away with going to the Arctic, with Francois, to witness the ocean-seeding experiment.

It was something he wasn't prepared to miss.

CHAPTER 19

Saudi Arabia, May 1

THE TWO SAUDI brothers sat opposite each other on large red cushions, which gave some comfort against the hard surface of the beige marble floor of the two-story apartment they were in, situated in a tree-lined, quiet, dusty suburb just outside Riyadh. A ceiling fan moved the warm air around the room, providing a slight breeze within the muggy apartment.

Fahim was the taller brother, and undeniably more handsome than Faric, who was shorter at five foot seven, but his stocky frame made him look even more so. They both carried the physical scars from their twenty-five year long careers as geologists within Saudi Arabia's oil industry. Fahim was missing his lower right ear lobe, and Faric carried an ugly scar which ran from midway on his left cheek to the left nostril of his oversized nose. The skin under the scar was still coloured with pigments of oil, which had burnt into his flesh, following an explosion at a refining plant he'd been working in. He had been lucky to escape with his life, but the ugly injury gave the appearance of a scar full of blackheads.

They sat in silence as Fahim took a long draw on the mouthpiece of the Sheesha, filling his lungs with apple-flavoured tobacco. He passed the flexible pipe to his brother, exhaling the fragrant smoke from his lungs, before finally speaking to him in Arabic. "So, Faric, I take it the final coordinates of the Crozet field have been determined?"

"Yes, brother, I received the geologist's final report this morning, and our computer systems have been updated accordingly. We have also received the coordinates for the second exploration site, following the electromagnetic and seismic surveys. The data indicates that the new prospect contains vast pockets of hydrocarbons, trapped in a four thousand square kilometre area."

"Depth?" Fahim asked.

"Estimates place the reservoir at around four hundred metres below the seabed. The submersible is now back in position, carrying out further seismic reflection surveys of the ocean floor. It was just unfortunate that the exploration drilling was delayed by the collision, that occurred last week. The drill head used at the initial exploration site has not yet been found, the search being made more difficult now the Americans are in the area looking for their...what is left of their submersible. We have a team continuing to look for the drill. The surveillance vessel, *Bounty,* is keeping watch, and the drill ship, *Plentiful,* is on standby. A replacement collar and drill is already on site and ready to be fitted, once the area quietens down."

Fahim looked across at his brother through the cloud of smoke he'd just exhaled. "Both incidents were very careless and have caused delay with the Crozet project. You know that time is not on our side. Whilst the operations with our Russian friend have gone considerably well, the preparation for the drilling is taking longer than anticipated. Make sure there are no further delays."

"Yes, brother."

"What is the position on the Atlantic site?" Fahim asked, passing the Sheesha back to Faric.

There was a few moments silence as Faric inhaled a lung

full of the apple-scented smoke.

"Passive seismic surveys have revealed three leads, two of which show promising prospects. We have prepared the area for final scanning and I expect to be given a location for two exploration wells in a matter of weeks. From the initial two-dimensional seismic surveys, our geologists estimate that there could be up to thirty-five billion barrels of recoverable oil in the region. That's larger that our Al Khurais field."

"Excellent! And what about news on the extension of existing licenses on both sites to full hydrocarbon extraction license rights. Has this been dealt with?"

"Yes," Faric nodded. "Tarique is in Paris, as we speak; dealing with the French site, and Moussad is currently in Praia arranging the licenses for the Cape Verde location. The ministers, from the Department of Trade and Industry in both nations, are being very cooperative. Neither our French, nor our Cape Verdean friends, yet know of the existence of the oil, naturally. We will however have to relinquish ten percent in royalties of anything we recover, as dictated by the license...a small price to pay."

"Yes, of course, excellent. The Portuguese will soon realise what a mistake they made by giving up the Cape Verde Islands. Their bankrupt government could certainly do with the money now. It will only be a matter of time before the sacrifices we have made, will bring us praise, and the recognition we deserve. NewSaudOil Corp will be hailed as our country's saviour," Fahim said, smirking.

There was a knock on the door. "Yes!" Faric shouted, impatiently.

A woman dressed in black robes and slippers appeared holding an ornate tray, on top of which were two china cups and a long spouted dallah pot, together with a small plate of dates.

"Your coffee, sirs," she said, tipping her head slightly.

"Leave it, we will serve ourselves."

The woman nodded and silently left the room.

"So, brother," Fahim continued, "we have just one obstacle in our way, the French climatologist, Professor Francois Trimaud. Our latest intelligence reports tell us he is nearing completion of his preliminary work, and will be leaving to carry out the Arctic tests in a few months, subject to Western bureaucracy, and Canadian approval of his plans. We will have to assume that the authority he seeks will be granted. We will need to brief our Russian friend one last time, as the Arctic tests cannot be allowed to proceed. After that is done, we don't anticipate any further problems. All being well, every aspect of our operation will be ready to implement. Have you spoken to our Russian investors about this?"

"Yes, they are fully aware of the developments and have given us their blessing on this phase of the operation," Faric replied.

"Very well; make sure that nothing else goes wrong."

Fahim poured himself some coffee, passed the dallah to his brother, then took a long drag on the Sheesha pipe, craned his neck back, and blew the smoke up toward the ceiling fan.

Faric stared at him cautiously for a few seconds. "There's one more thing Fahim. Do you not think it wise if we have a second option in place? I mean, what if Trimaud isn't neutralised before he embarks on the Arctic trip. Should we not plan for our Russian friend to infiltrate the French/US science expedition team?"

Fahim narrowed his eyes and looked at his brother. "That's not a bad idea, see that it is done. We will meet here again in four days time, to reassess the situation. Gomez will be here shortly to take me to the desert headquarters; I want to check that our computer systems have been updated."

Faric nodded "I look forward to seeing the look on their greedy faces, once they realise the extent of our discoveries brother."

"As do I, Faric. We will teach them respect - even our father would have been proud of us."

Faric shrugged his heavy shoulders. "Our father had no time for us. He should have supported us when we needed him, but he chose not to. We could have kept our jobs, he didn't give a damn about us - never did."

"Perhaps not, brother," Fahim replied. "But do not disrespect our father's name," he said, standing to leave. "Have some respect for the man who taught us all we know."

The automatic window shutters opened as he left the room, allowing shafts of sunlight to stream in and reflect off the clouds of smoke, which hung in the air like thick white blankets. "I'll see you tomorrow," Fahim said, as he kissed his brother goodbye on both cheeks.

Faric accompanied him to the door and watched as his brother walked across the sand-covered drive into a waiting black Mercedes. The car pulled away from the white-washed apartment and headed out of the city along a long dusty expanse of road, flanked on both sides by desert.

Faric casually lit a cigarette and looked up and down the deserted street. As he turned to walk back into the apartment, a scrawny dog appeared at his feet, sniffing the ground in search of a morsel of food to eat. He looked down, inhaled on his cigarette, and then kicked the dog out towards the road, before stepping back into the darkened hallway of his apartment.

Thirty minutes later the Mercedes pulled up outside a large stone building, which rose out of the desert sand like a huge geological monolith. Virtually the same colour as the surrounding sand, the massive structure melted into its environment. The sun's rays glinted off a large gloss-black granite sign fixed on the stone façade high above the entrance, emblazoned on it in gold lettering was the name;

NEWSAUDOIL CORP.

Fahim got out of the car. "I'll be back in an hour, Gomez," he said to the driver. He walked into the air conditioned building and was met with immediate relief from the outside forty degree Celsius heat. As he stepped through the security scanners, a guard to his left acknowledged him, tilting his head as he walked past and into an open lift, where a computer synthesised voice asked which floor he required.

"Fifth floor," Fahim responded, directing his speech to the voice recognition sensors housed in each corner of the lift's shiny black veneered-marble interior.

He exited the lift, passing two workers wearing blue overalls, each sporting rectangular badges on their shoulders, embroidered with the insignia *NewSaudOil Corp- Geology Dept.* The men nodded at him as they continued along the corridor. Fahim entered his spacious, luxurious office, his shoes sinking into the thick cream carpets as he walked in.

The office was fully equipped with enough food, assorted drinks, and luxuries to allow Fahim to spend a week there, if he needed to. An ivory marble bathroom, steam room, plunge pool and wet room lay through a door on the right. A relaxation room complemented the suite, situated through another short corridor beyond the small kitchen.

He walked over to his elegant mahogany desk, feeling the cool air from the recessed air conditioning units brush over his face, sat down and powered up his computer, which was connected to three, forty-four inch monitors arranged next to each other. Dark wooden shelving units - filled with classical books - spanned two walls of the room. Directly behind his desk, a floor-to-ceiling toughened glass rectangular window overlooked a large internal garden area, which today, as usual, was bathed in sunlight. Sprinkler systems sprayed water onto lush green lawns and palm trees, in what was a huge internal oasis in the centre of the vast complex.

NewSaudOil Corp had been built from scratch, rising from the desert sand, in just eighteen months. The buildings housed the geologists, research equipment and computers necessary for the huge task that the company had been set up for - global oil exploration and recovery. The final building in the complex, the section Fahim was now sitting in, had been completed just over six months earlier.

Fahim took a deep breath of lemon and jasmine scented air and waited for the streaming data on the monitors to upload. He turned his chair to look out over the internal garden. The green tranquil area looked inviting, and he envisaged himself and his brother - in the not too distant future - walking amongst the palm trees, as they celebrated their success. He was lost in his thoughts briefly, before spinning his chair back around to study the monitors in front of him.

Displayed on the far left monitor were seismic charts and electromagnetic scans of the ocean floor and rock strata around the Crozet Islands. The data and the images provided by *NewSaudOil's* submersible revealed that there was in the region of one hundred and fifty-five billion barrels of probable oil reserves there, located four hundred metres beneath the seabed. The monitor in the middle also showed images of rock strata data for a location five hundred nautical miles off the west coast of the Cape Verde Islands, in the Atlantic Ocean. Again the information told him that the oil bearing region contained as much as thirty-five billion barrels of probable oil reserves. The two new oilfields, Fahim calculated, would have combined reserves of almost one hundred and ninety billion barrels of oil, enough to keep Saudi Arabia at the forefront of oil production for decades to come.

Fahim's mind wandered as he looked at the monitors in front of him. He thought about his team of thirty-five geologists and scientists, and the discoveries that had been made only ten months earlier, following a three year search for new oil provinces. He compared this to the feeling of disgrace and contempt he'd had after being expelled from the state oil firm by the Royal Family. His only crime was to tell them that their methods of extracting oil from the country's fields was about to cause a sudden and massive decline in production. He had advised them that their projected twelve million barrel a day contribution to world oil output, would, at some point, between 2012 and 2015, dramatically decline. His advice had of course been rejected by the majority of geologists, and not only that, he and his brother had been expelled from the company for their pessimistic and irrational beliefs.

Faric was right; their father, high up in one of the Kingdom's most important energy companies - before his untimely death - was unable, or had refused to support them. As consolation, the King's cousin had allowed them to set up their own oil company, if they could find the funding. The private Russian investor had come along just at the right time, providing five billion dollars to get the new company off the ground. There were no strings attached to the loan, apart from the fact that it had to be paid back, with interest, *if NewSaudOil Corp* was ever successful in finding oil. The investor had requested a very reasonable twenty-five percent of the value of any new discoveries.

After the first oil province was found, Fahim knew that there would be no problems repaying the loan. He smiled to himself as he thought about how events would unfold. The Kingdom would be forced to purchase *NewSaudOil Corp* and its huge reserves of oil as soon as it dawned on them that his warnings had in fact been correct.

He had compared the data from their two largest oil wells, the Ghawar and Safaniya fields, with the analysis and research carried out by the American geoscientist, M. King Hubbert who had accurately predicted that the United States would reach its peak oil production between 1965 and 1970, after which there would be a rapid decline. He had tried to convince the Kingdom's oil ministers that the bell-curve hypothesis was correct, and the water injection methods used to extract the oil - which compensated for the fall in natural oil pressure - would result in a water oil ratio which would make it impossible to extract any more oil, once a certain point was reached.

Fahim had calculated that the Saudi fields were about to hit the downward side of the bell curve, a point at which production would rapidly start to decline, by 2015 at the latest. The Minister for oil, and his deputy, simply wouldn't accept that the country's oil, estimated to be in the region of 260 billion barrels of proven reserves, would simply start to run out. In seventy years maybe, they had told him, but not in five.

Three years had passed since then, and Fahim estimated that production could start to decline rapidly in around eighteen months, and then the shit would really hit the fan. *Who would save the world and his country from an energy disaster? Who would plug the current twelve million barrel-a-day global shortfall?* Iraq and Iran simply didn't have the capacity. Any future discoveries, if large enough, would take years to come on-line. Not even the British with their latest discovery in the Falkland's, or Brazil's Tupi field would be able to pump the extra oil, but *NewSaudOil Corp* would, and he relished the thought. He and Faric would be rewarded and would become heroes. They would pay off their secret Russian investor and take all the credit; that had been the agreement.

His loyal team of thirty-five men knew nothing about the necessary 'collateral' damage the oil discoveries would cause. Their Russian investor had provided all the necessary intelligence on the scientists' discoveries and movements. How this was done, he didn't know; he didn't need to know. All he was concerned with was finding the oil, and exploiting the new fields as quickly as possible.

Fahim opened his eyes and focused his gaze to the third monitor. This showed a detailed map of the Northern Hemisphere, with magnified images of the Arctic region. A graph on the bottom right of the image displayed two sets of fluctuating digits. One set of numbers showed 3.8 million square miles, or 9.8 million square kilometres, the other 430, expressed in centimetres. Above the digits was written *NSIDC-Arctic ice coverage/thickness live data feed.* The figures represented total Arctic ice coverage, and ice thickness respectively. The data revealed that the ice covering the Arctic was less than it had been three months earlier, and that it was thinner. Fahim couldn't yet tell from the data whether this year's Arctic summer melt would beat the record lows set in September 2007.

The data was as expected, for the ice would continue to reduce until mid to late September. Historical data showed that the Arctic sea ice was in steady and persistent state of decline. A predictable, unstoppable, consequence of natural global warming, Fahim believed.

He shut down the computer and the monitors blinked off. Rising from his chair, he looked back out to the internal garden for a few moments, before leaving the room. The door self-locked behind him.

As he stepped out into the baking afternoon heat, strong

winds were starting to whip up the desert sand. He shielded his eyes and ran to the waiting Mercedes. "Take me home, Gomez," Fahim said to the driver, as he got in.

The black Mercedes drove off in the direction it had come from, the desert sand enveloping the car, rendering it almost invisible to a guard who was watching them leave from behind the glass entrance door.

Ksenyia sat at her dining table in her London apartment, her attaché case open in front of her. Traditional Russian folk music was playing at a low volume in the background. The blinds covering the lounge windows were half-closed, to deflect the strong sunlight which would otherwise penetrate the room.

An assortment of objects from the case was laid out on the table in front of her. A standard FSB issue throwing knife, a compact Makarov pistol, two miniature tracking devices, a miniature camera hidden inside a cigarette lighter, and five hundred milligrams of nicotine solution in a toughened, heat-resistant plastic container. Various passports also lay scattered in the open case.

She was in the process of cleaning and checking her gun when she was interrupted by the sound of an e-mail arriving into her inbox. She turned the computer screen toward her, entered the secure area and opened up the message from *Arc Bin Quid Lo.*

Proceed to Paris immediately. Professor Francois Trimaud. He is based at the UPMC University. French ice must be melted. Usual terms, final instruction.

Ksenyia memorised the name of the university and deleted the e-mail, then gathered the items from the table and returned them to the case. She booked herself on a suitable train to

Paris, leaving on Sunday afternoon, and found the passport issued to her in the name of Samantha Goodyear. The photo I.D showed her with shoulder-length blonde hair. She then closed and locked the case, and placed it back on top of the freezer.

She thought about the message for a while. Just like the cryptic message that had been sent for the Bannister assignment, this message also contained a clue. *French ice must be melted - a clear instruction to eliminate the professor. Could Trimaud also be working on a project connected with ice?* Whatever it was, her task was to make sure that Trimaud did not complete his work. She considered the next large payment and thought about taking a break as soon as this task was completed. She then turned the volume up on the CD player and ran herself a bath.

CHAPTER 20

Paris May 2

FRANCOIS TRIMAUD HAD just finished delivering two, one hour lectures on the relationship between hurricane intensity and ocean temperature, a developing subject area of his, and one the students seemed to enjoy. The potential destructive force of nature's most powerful wind system always proved to be a popular topic. He left the building and walked down the concrete steps to the street; it was a dull and overcast late spring afternoon. He crossed the road and walked two blocks to one of his favourite local café's, stepping inside just as it started to drizzle.

The *Café Metro* was sparsely decorated with stripped wooden floorboards and wood-panelled walls, which were adorned with pictures of Parisian street-scenes from the turn of the century.

Trimaud took off his raincoat and hung it on one of the coat stands closest to the small round table he usually took, primarily for its view of the pavement outside. A waiter came over as soon as he sat down. "Bonjour, Professor, un café? Carte?"

"Merci Alan, café c'est bon."

Trimaud took out a copy of *Le Monde* from his canvas bag and opened it to the page he'd started reading earlier that morning. The waiter returned, placing a cup of black coffee on the table in front of him, together with a small silver plate containing the bill.

He studied the paper for a while, pausing to take a drink. He glanced out of the window at the pedestrians scurrying along, trying to avoid the heavy rain which was now bouncing off the pavements. He checked the time; one-forty. He planned to get to the laboratory for about two-thirty P.M, which was when the results of the Arctic tests should be known. The test results would determine whether the Arctic expedition could proceed or not. He blanked any thoughts of failure out of his mind.

As he sipped his coffee he noticed an elegant, striking blonde walk into the café, and watched as she folded away her umbrella and sat down at a table not far from him. She smiled at him briefly, before looking toward the bar. He returned the smile, lifted his paper, and continued reading.

He read for a further ten minutes or so, but couldn't concentrate on the newspaper; his mind was firmly fixed on the Arctic test results. The possibility of the experiment - if successful - being able to prevent the Arctic from losing any more of its sea ice, or even reverse the current melting trend, thrilled him. He folded his paper up and put it back in his bag, glancing over to the table where the attractive woman had been sitting; but she was nowhere to be seen. He left five euro's for the bill, retrieved his raincoat from the stand, and walked out onto the pavement.

Since leaving the café, Ksenyia Petrovsky had been standing on the corner of the street, sheltering under the awning of a patisserie. She glanced up from the shop window as Trimaud walked past her, stopped on the corner and got into a waiting taxi. She walked briskly to the end of the street where another taxi was dropping off a fare. An elderly lady had just got out, and was in the process of searching for her purse to pay the driver. Ksenyia jumped into the waiting taxi and asked the driver to quickly follow the silver Mercedes, now three car lengths ahead in slow moving traffic.

"Un moment!" the driver replied.

"Please, I'm in a hurry," Ksenyia said, pushing a fifty euro note into the driver's hand. "I'll get the lady's fare too."

"C'est bon," the driver said, indicating and quickly pulling off.

Sitting comfortably in the Mercedes, Trimaud gave the driver directions to a large farmhouse, situated just outside the *Peripherique de L'IIe-de-France,* on the outskirts of Paris. The farmhouse incorporated a large covert laboratory and test facility, used by the French government for the production and testing of vaccines, amongst other things. A section of the complex had been allocated to him and his small team for climate change research.

The taxi dropped Trimaud off at the perimeter wall surrounding the premises. He paid the driver and walked the short distance to the main gate, turning into a small non-descript wooden hut, overlooked by security cameras. The hut was empty, apart from an old pine table in the corner, which had a few dirty coffee-stained mugs on it, and an old rusty kettle. The items were merely props, the basic hut doing a good job of concealing its hi-tech reason for being there; providing access to the lab complex beyond via a sophisticated hand-palm entry reader system.

Trimaud placed his hand onto the graphite palm reader, located in the corner of the hut. The unit lit up, glowing blue briefly, as a clunking sound emanated from three large deadlocks retracting from their locked position within the steel gate outside. Trimaud left the hut and walked through the person-sized opening in the gate, and into a large courtyard and over to a wooden farmhouse building, which housed the laboratory. The gate clunked shut behind him.

The laboratory had been constructed to blend in with the other old farmhouses dotted around the area, so as not to attract unwanted attention. Just *how* it had been built, Trimaud didn't know, as the site must have occupied an area the size of an aircraft hangar.

He walked up to a smaller wooden out-building, on the right of what looked like the main farmhouse, and entered through a barn-style door. He was standing in a small area which was empty, apart from a few bales of hay. A larger steel door was visible to the right of the stacked bales. He pushed a panel in the wall to reveal a retinal scanner, which slid silently out from a hidden compartment. He placed his right eye over the scanner, and started to count down from five down to one. Two thuds sounded from the depths of the steel door as each bolt retracted, allowing the door to slide open, with a growl from its hydraulic operating system.

Trimaud entered into a small ante-room, placed his raincoat into one of the open lockers, took out a white overall and pulled it on. He walked into the main laboratory, which was in the region of fifty metres long and thirty metres wide. White sterile work benches lined the right side of the room, which were almost invisible against the white-washed walls of the lab. On top of the benches were banks of computers and monitors. Text, digits and coloured graphs scrolled across their screens. On the left side, were a number of interconnected machines, each the size of a small car, and joined together with steel pipes and tubes. They were similar in appearance to a series of large boilers.

In the middle of the room, was a vast stainless-steel

rectangular water tank and elevated above it, were a series of gantry's and walkways, and a structure, looking like a large grain chute, which disappeared into the ceiling somewhere above. Beyond that, a large tent like construction, made from shiny, white translucent-type material, was visible. A sign on the door to the structure read;

ATTENTION - ARCTIC SIMULATION EXPERIMENT IN PROGRESS.

Trimaud walked alongside the large tank, and was greeted by his colleague, Dr. Pierre Girard. "Welcome, Professor, we've been expecting you. I'm sure you must be excited...and a little nervous, no?"

"Just a little," Trimaud replied, smiling. "Is everything on schedule, Pierre?"

"Yes, we will know shortly whether the *Blankoplankton* have been able to survive the Arctic simulation tests and absorbed the modified iron sulphate."

"Excellent! How are our single-celled friends getting on in the initial test tank; still performing well?"

"Take a look for yourself Francois. Use the steps over there."

Trimaud climbed up the metal steps, which rose up alongside the tank, to a small viewing platform. As he neared the top, he noticed a white, almost translucent, shimmering glow reflecting off the internal walls of the tank. He peered into the water-filled tank. Suspended in the water were bright white patches, like large lilies, some of which were floating on the surface, some under the surface. The phytoplankton, or *Blankoplankton* as the team had named the modified plankton, had bloomed in about half the volume of the tank.

"Fantastique!" Trimaud exclaimed.

"We have been monitoring the carbon dioxide levels directly above the surface of the water, and our initial findings confirm that levels of the gas are fractionally lower in the test tank, whilst levels of oxygen are fractionally higher than in a standard sample of air. This is as expected, for the level of photosynthesis this amount of *Blankoplankton* can manage," Girard shouted up, from the bottom of the ladder.

"What about its reflectivity?" Trimaud asked, looking down.

"The albedo effect created by the reflective surface of the *Blankoplankton* has lowered the air temperature by just under a tenth of a degree Celsius for every cubic metre of *Blankoplankton* enriched water, when compared to the test tank containing just plain seawater. The white surface area created by the *Blankoplankton* is indeed reflecting both light and heat," Girard replied.

"Just as we had predicted," Trimaud said excitedly. "As long as we can produce the same effects in the main simulator tank, we have a viable Arctic Ocean seeding experiment!"

"It would seem so, Francois," Girard confirmed.

An attractive dark-haired female, clad in white, approached from the back of the laboratory, and greeted Trimaud from behind the white mask she was wearing.

"Ah, Mari, how are you today?" he asked, as he descended the metal steps. Upon reaching the bottom he gave her a long hug.

"As excited as you surely are, Francois, we have been waiting for this moment for some time."

"How long before we can take a look, Mari?" he asked.

"Actually, everything is ready. If you'd like to come over to the Arctic simulator tank, we can begin."

As Trimaud walked over to the test tank, he thought about

his two colleagues, of whom he was immensely proud. He had studied climate science with both Dr. Pierre Girard and Dr. Mari Bonnet, at The UMPC where he was now based. Twelve years earlier they had both excelled at their chosen PhD subjects, Dr. Bonnet in *Phytoplankton and Photosynthesis,* and Dr. Girard in *Climatic Effects upon the Ocean and Atmosphere.* This was the reason he had chosen them for this task, when asked by the French Government to research the possibility of geoengineering the Arctic Ocean to try and prevent, or at least mitigate against the consequences of anthropogenic global warming. Both had jumped at the chance to work for their country, on the potentially Earth changing research.

Trimaud and Dr. Girard reached the covered tank, and Dr. Bonnet handed them both thick parka-type jackets, the kind worn by Arctic explorers. "Here, put these on. Whilst the water in the test tank is only minus one degree Celsius, the air temperature is considerably cooler."

Trimaud and Girard put the thick grey jackets on, their shadows casting shapes like two giant polar bears onto the glossy tent structure behind. Dr. Bonnet pressed some buttons on an external control panel, near to the entrance, operating the door, which slid open, with a *whoosh*. Trimaud followed his colleagues into the air-lock chamber room beyond. This was the first time he had been inside the structure, although he had been fully briefed on the technical specifications involved in its design.

The door slid closed after they walked through. "Here, put these goggles on, they will protect against the cold and the glare," Dr. Bonnet said, handing them both a pair. "Ready?"

Trimaud nodded in anticipation.

Dr. Bonnet pushed a button on the console in front of her and the inner door of the chamber opened to the interior of the structure. A blast of ice-cold air hit them in the face as they all walked into a large circular chamber containing a substantial round stainless-steel tank, which was set into the floor. Icicles hung from the mesh-work of steel struts above, making the whole set-up look like some ancient ice cave. A series of powerful fluorescent lights overhung the tank to simulate the Arctic sun, essential for plankton growth. A few patches of ice floated on the surface of the water in the circular inset tank.

"The entire interior is set to simulate early Arctic summer, when ocean temperatures reach around minus one degree Celsius," Dr. Bonnet explained, confidently.

Trimaud strained his eyes to look at the icy water, but couldn't see any evidence of the *Blankoplankton* that had bloomed in the external tank. The two scientists followed Triamaud's gaze, staring silently into the water for a few minutes, searching for evidence of *Blankoplankton* activity. Trimaud spoke first. "Unless I'm missing something, I don't see any evidence of plankton growth."

"There must be some here," Dr. Bonnet said, hesitantly.

Girard then spoke up. "I can't see anything either, something must be wrong."

Trimaud looked at Dr. Bonnet, shrugging his shoulders, the expression on his face revealing his worst fears.

They all left the chamber and waited for the outer door to close, before removing their thick coats. "What do you think could have gone wrong?" Trimaud asked solemnly, looking over at Dr. Bonnet.

"I...I'm not certain yet, Francois," she replied, clearly upset. "The process of plankton growth should have started at around the same time as in the outer tank. All the conditions were identical, except of course for temperature, and the slightly lower water salinity levels. Until I analyse the water samples, under a microscope, I won't be able to say what might have gone wrong, Professor, I'm sorry."

"Don't beat yourself up about it, Mari, we're all in this together. Just get to the bottom of the problem as soon as possible. I don't want to have to abort the Arctic expedition in six weeks. We might not get another chance until next year, otherwise."

"Of course, I'll start right away," Dr. Bonnet said, quickly walking toward a bank of computers running along the rear wall of the laboratory.

Trimaud walked, his head bowed deep in thought, to the small ante-room near to the entrance. "Pierre, could you have one of the technicians drive me back to the city, please?"

"I'll arrange it straight away, Francois. Listen, don't let this failure get you down, we'll crack this thing, I know we will."

"I hope so," Trimaud replied, removing his lab coat. "I'll see you in a day or two," he said, walking to the main door. He left the laboratory via the secure door, opened the wooden outer door and walked through the courtyard toward the perimeter gate, where a black Citroen was waiting for him. He felt a little depressed at the failure of the experiment, but reminded himself that he was working with two of the best scientists in their field. He got into the waiting car. "Sacre Coeur, Yves, I need a drink," he said to the driver.

The Citroen drove through the main gate and out onto the dusty dirt-track which led to the main road. Within twenty minutes they had joined the outer ring-road, and were heading back into the centre of Paris.

Trimaud looked out at the busy rush hour traffic, deep in thought. *What could have possibly gone wrong with the test?*

CHAPTER 21

THE TAXI DROPPED Trimaud off in Montmartre, just outside the Sacre Coeur, not far from his apartment situated at the Montmartre end of the Rue Des Abbesses. It was a little after six P.M.

The evening sun was just disappearing behind the Basilica, its soft rays bathing the domes in golden sunlight. Regardless of the day's earlier disappointment, Trimaud couldn't help but admire the beautiful view. He walked into the *Sincere,* an intimate bar and steak restaurant, taking a seat at the long black granite counter. The waiter acknowledged him and came over. "Bonsoir, Monsieur, aperitif?"

Trimaud ordered a Baileys and sat at the bar for five minutes staring blankly at the wall. *What did we do wrong?* He realised there were many factors that had to be precisely right in order for the experiment to have any chance of success, but these had all been checked, double checked even. The saline content and water temperature had to be right; seawater freezes at around minus one point eight degrees Celsius. The water in the test tank had been rapidly chilled to that temperature, and then warmed to simulate the ocean surface temperature of the Arctic during summer-time. The upper layers of the Arctic Ocean are slightly less saline than the rest of it, due to freshwater runoff; this had also been taken into account. The high-powered fluorescent lighting had been developed to mimic the Arctic summer sun, to stimulate plankton growth, and the iron sulphate had been pumped into the tank in the same quantity as the external tank. *So what could it be?*

Trimaud stared into his half-empty glass of Baileys, downed it and asked the waiter for another. He picked up a menu from the bar and perused it, ordering a steak - medium-rare, and a large glass of Merlot. He handed the menu back to the waiter, just as an attractive blonde appeared, taking the stool next to him.

"Bonsoir," she said, with a warm smile.

"Bonsoir, soiree agreeable," Trimaud replied, noticing the woman's striking green eyes.

"Yes, it is a lovely evening," she said, in English. "Do you speak English?" she asked.

"Oui, of course," Trimaud replied.

"Well, my name is Samantha, Samantha Goodyear from the UK. Nice to meet you…Mr.?"

"Trimaud, Francois Trimaud. Are you here on business or vacation Samantha?"

"Oh, just doing a little sightseeing. I love Paris at this time of year, it's so pretty."

"You can't beat it really," Trimaud replied, smiling.

The waiter brought over the Baileys he'd ordered and then looked at the blonde seated next to him. "Vouz aimez une boisson?"

"Oui, vodka tonic s'il vous plait."

"Here, allow me to get it," Trimaud said, handing the barman a twenty euro note. *She looked familiar*, Trimaud thought, as he sat admiring her.

"Merci, that's very kind of you," she said, raising her glass to Trimaud.

"My pleasure," Trimaud said. "Do you mind, I'll be back shortly." He left the bar and headed down to the toilets which were on the lower floor.

This is going to be far too easy, Ksenyia thought, as she reached into her handbag for the vial of nicotine. Discretely unscrewing the top from the plastic container, she glanced around to make sure no one was looking, and quickly emptied the contents of the container into Trimaud's tumbler of Baileys. *Assignment completed.*

Trimaud walked up to the bar, taking his seat next to his new acquaintance. He picked up his drink, and tilted the glass, moving the ice cubes around in the caramel coloured alcohol. As he raised the glass to take a drink, he heard the ice crack as it was exposed to the relatively warmer liquid.

Whilst in the gents, he'd been racking his brains trying to think what could have caused the experiment to fail. As he raised his glass and heard the ice crack, a thought suddenly came to him.

The 'whitening' of the iron sulphate, used to fertilize the ocean, was a process that took place at both high and low temperatures. The white silicon 'jackets,' had been sealed onto the sulphate crystals at fifty degrees Celsius, with a secondary sealing taking place at minus one degree Celsius. The Arctic experiment however had consisted of freezing the salt water down to minus one point eight degrees Celsius. It was conceivable that the white silicon 'jackets' had simply cracked and slipped off as they contracted under the extreme temperature, Trimaude realised. *Could it be that they had not been bonded and sealed at a lower enough temperature?*

Trimaud slammed his glass down on to the counter in excitement and turned to the blonde. "Please excuse me a moment, I have to make a call," he said, rushing outside.

Five minutes later he walked back in. "I'm very sorry," he

said to her, "but I really must go, something important has come up."

Trimaud summoned the barman over and he cancelled his food order. "It was very nice meeting you Samantha, I don't mean to be rude, but I have to be somewhere - enjoy your stay in Paris," he said, as he turned and left the bar.

She watched, her anger building inside, as he walked out onto the street and disappeared into the evening crowds. His drink remained on the bar, untouched.

CHAPTER 22

May 3

ROBERT SPIRE ARRIVED at London's St Pancreas station, forty minutes prior to his Eurostar departure. He boarded the train and relaxed into his seat. Thirty minutes later he was looking out of the window at the Kent countryside speeding past. His thoughts wandered to Professor Trimaud and the next few days. *Will we be able to discover anything further about the deaths of the two scientists?*

The view of sun-dried fields winked out as the train entered the tunnel, for its twenty minute crossing under the English Channel. The time passed quickly, and before long the sun's rays streamed through the carriage once again as the train emerged from the dark tunnel on the other side, accelerating as it weaved through the French countryside.

As the Eurostar reached the outskirts of Paris, Spire looked out at the graffiti-covered walls and high-rise apartment blocks, the cityscape looking like any other European centre as the train slowed on its approach to Paris's *Gare Du Nord* station.

Once in the station, he found the Metro diagram and looked up the nearest station to the university, where Professor Trimaud worked. He had arranged to meet him outside, at the *Place Jussieu,* at around four-thirty P.M - ninety minutes from now. He found the correct track and boarded the train for the Latin Quarter.

Francois Trimaud checked his watch; perfect timing, ʰ. thought. He had just finished his lecture, which gave him thirty minutes to grab a quick coffee before his guest arrived. The disappointment of yesterday's results was now a fading memory. Dr. Bonnet and Dr. Girard had considered his idea, and they were sure that the sealing of the white silicon 'jackets' had been the problem. They had run a computer simulation with the revised data, and the results had been encouraging. A new batch of iron sulphate was being prepared, and the whitening process was underway, this time, sealing the silicon 'jackets' at the revised temperatures. Robert Spire might even be the first layman to witness the experiment, Trimaud realised. He liked Spire, and trusted him to maintain the utmost discretion when it came to knowledge of the tests. He picked up his bag, put his cap on, and walked out on to the *Place Jussieu* and looked around for his English friend.

Spire alighted from the Metro, walked up a set of steep steps and found a stall selling cheap French souvenirs and magazines. He asked the owner for directions to the UPMC University.

"Tout droit," the store owner said, pointing up the long street.

Spire walked straight up the street and arrived in front of the university building, just as the students were scurrying out of the main doors, books gripped under their arms and chatting furiously together. He looked around for Professor Trimaud. Just as he was about to enter the building, he felt an arm on his shoulder and quickly turned around.

"Bonjour, Robert! Welcome to Paris. How was your

journey, my friend?" Trimaud asked, greeting him warmly with a handshake.

"Effortless. It's good to see you again, Francois."

"Allez – come on, let's grab a drink and I can bring you up to speed on what's been happening. I feel very optimistic again, since speaking with you last."

They found a small café on one of the side streets and ordered two beers. Spire sat there, listening to Trimaud bubbling with excitement, as he brought him up to date with the status of the Arctic experiment, explaining how the initial tests had failed, but that revised trials were now underway. "You must keep all this to yourself, Robert. I'm only telling you because I trust you, in view of your involvement in Jack's death. This is still highly sensitive information," Trimaud said in a hushed voice, finding time to sip his beer.

"Of course," Spire said, sincerely. "So, let me get this straight. Now that the silicon has been coated on and sealed at the revised temperature of minus five degrees, you think that the silicon jackets will be able to withstand the Arctic water temperature and remain in place?"

"Oui; we should see the first stages of photosynthesis taking place and the *Blankoplankton* forming tomorrow afternoon. You see, as the phytoplankton, or more specifically, the chloroplasts ingest the iron sulphate, it multiplies, and the chlorophyll in the cells absorbs the silicon, and becomes white. My design, however, allows the chlorophyll to retain its photosynthetic qualities. Hey presto, we have phytoplankton that can absorb carbon dioxide *and* reflect sunlight back into space. As you know, we have called this modified plankton *Blankoplankton,* and it should increase the albedo effect in the Arctic Ocean, hopefully cooling the Arctic region and thereby slowing or even reversing the current and escalating warming trend taking place there."

"That's incredible, Francois. I like the name; *Blankoplankton*...white plankton. The whole world will know that the idea was French," Spire said.

"Exactement! Anyway, enough of this. We'll go back to my apartment so you can freshen up and then we'll go out for dinner. I'm sure you must have lots to tell me."

They took a taxi back to Trimaud's apartment, on the Rue de Abbesses, which pulled up onto the pavement in the street outside a smart grey-stone building; each apartment had its own small balcony overlooking the street, secured by neat black wrought iron railings.

"I'm on troisiem etage," Trimaud said, as they walked into the entrance hall of the apartment block. A bank of steel mail boxes were fixed to the wall on the left hand side. Trimaud walked over to box seventeen and retrieved his mail. "Venez...come on, we'll use the lift."

Spire followed Trimaud into his apartment, which was deceptively large on the inside. He had imagined a small Pied-a-terre from Trimaud's description of it. The apartment was tastefully decorated with varnished wooden floorboards and brown leather sofas, adorned with large cream cushions. A small round glass table sat under a window, which had superb views over the Rue De Abbesses below. Books were stuffed into two large bookcases in the lounge. Two bedrooms, one double, and one single, led off from the small corridor, and a small, square but functional kitchen led off from the lounge.

"You've a lovely apartment here, Francois, great location too," Spire said, as he stood looking out of the large window onto the busy street below.

"Merci. I purchased it after my split from my wife Helena...it's a little compact, but was all I could afford, suits me just fine." Trimaud showed Spire the single room and pointed out the bathroom. "Freshen yourself up, Robert. I'll open a bottle of wine, and then we can go out for dinner. There are plenty of fabulous restaurants around here."

Spire took a few shirts out of his travel-bag and hung them up, then called Angela, briefly, to tell her he'd arrived safely. After a refreshing shower, he walked back into the lounge, where Trimaud was waiting for him with a large glass of red wine.

Trimaud handed him a full glass. "It's a Minervois, not bad," he said.

"Salut!" Spire said, raising his glass.

"So, tell me, Robert, have you found out anything else about my dear friend Jack, or Dr. Stanton?"

"Well, I've been thinking a hell of a lot about the whole thing, as you can imagine. My instincts tell me something sinister is going on, but proving it is another matter." Spire inhaled deeply and sighed. "This is what we know so far. Two climatologists on opposite sides of the world, mysteriously drop dead, one apparently from nicotine poisoning. Obviously we need to try and find out what they were working on, Francois."

"Well, we know Jack was engaged in something in the sea around the Crozet Islands."

"That's correct. We also know Dr. Stanton was working on a project linked to the Ocean Thermohaline Circulation, exactly what, we don't know. There are also the business cards, with the name *Arc Bin Quid Lo* embossed on them. One found in Dr Stanton's wallet, the other picked up by your friend John Gregory near to where Jack collapsed."

"Do we know anything more about them?" Trimaud asked, sipping his wine.

"No, but my secretary, Kim, is looking into it for me. She's astute, so may come up with something. Then there's the more sinister aspect of the car chase down in Wales. I live in the middle of *nowhere,* Francois; these people mean business if that incident is linked. How could they possibly have known about my involvement?"

"Could Dr. Stanton's mother have said anything?"

"Doris? I doubt it, I told her not to speak to anyone."

Trimaud thought for a moment. "Maybe you should get back in touch with that chap you spoke to at the Oceanography Centre...Professor Sammedi?"

"Yes, I could see if he's prepared to release any further information on what Dr. Stanton was working on – if he knows himself."

"I have asked Margaret if she could look to see if Jack kept backup copies of his computer files, there might be some information on them."

"Good. My main concern however is for *you,* Francois. I mean, if the people behind this can get to me, then they can certainly find you, especially if they know about your Arctic experiment," Spire said, in a serious tone.

Trimaud sat quietly for a moment, staring at his wine glass. "Do you think an environmental group could be behind all this, Robert?"

"I hadn't thought of that, but it's a reasonable theory. I'll get Kim to look into any organisations that might have been aware of Dr. Stanton's, or Dr. Bannister's, work. Perhaps you could ask Margaret if Jack had been aware of any campaigns, or protests, against his research."

"Bon, once we get some more evidence Robert, we should approach the police."

Spire hesitated before replying, recalling the message that was left on his computer. "Yes, of course."

Trimaud stood up. "Very well, Robert, we can start our inquiries tomorrow, but now we must look after our stomachs and dine! I know a great place around the corner. Let's eat and drink to tomorrow's, hopefully successful, test results."

"Good idea, Francois, I'm famished."

They drained their glasses of wine, left the apartment and headed out onto the Rue de Abbesses and walked in the direction of Montmartre. The area was bustling with tourists and early evening diners, mulling over restaurant menu boards. They walked past a few restaurants until Trimaud signalled he'd found one of his favourites. They walked in, taking a table overlooking the busy street. The waitress immediately brought over a carafe of table wine and some bread.

Spire filled up their glasses with the ruby-red wine. "Well, here's to tomorrow's positive test results," he said, holding up his glass.

"Bottom's up!" Trimaud replied with a chuckle, taking a large sip of wine.

Spire looked around the cosy restaurant at the couples sitting and chatting together. He then noticed two men in the far corner. The man with his back to him turned around and looked over toward him, locking eyes with Spire briefly, before glancing away. *Do I recognise him from somewhere?* He wondered, feeling a slight sense of paranoia creep over him.

The waitress brought over their order of steak and fries and Spire and Trimaud ate together whilst slowly demolishing two carafes of red wine, followed by coffee and a glass of brandy each.

As they both left the restaurant, Spire glanced over to the table where the two men had been sitting, but they had gone.

"We're going to sleep well tonight," Trimaud said, as they made their way back along the moonlit streets to Trimaud's apartment.

Spire pushed his feeling of unease to the back of his mind and hoped Francois was right.

CHAPTER 23

May 4

EARLY MORNING SUNLIGHT trickled into the bedroom through the slatted blinds covering the windows, slowly waking Spire. It was still only seven A.M, and his head felt foggy from the mixture of red wine and Cognac he'd drunk the evening before. He stretched and slowly got out of bed.

The apartment was quiet, except for the faint sound of music coming from a radio somewhere in Trimaud's bedroom. He showered, put on a pair of jeans and T-shirt, and then wandered into the lounge to be greeted by the aroma of freshly brewed coffee.

"Bonjour, how are you feeling this morning?" Trimaud asked.

"Morning, Francois, still a little groggy, but I'm sure that coffee will help."

"Here you are, my friend," Trimaud said, handing him a cup of black coffee and a French pastry.

Spire took his breakfast over to the glass table and sat down. The coffee tasted good and gave him an instant kick. "So, today's the day then?"

"Oui. We are being collected at eleven. It's only about thirty minutes by car to the laboratory, traffic permitting. After the tests, if you have time, I thought maybe we could pay a quick visit to the Louvre before you return home tomorrow?"

"That would be great; it must have been at least ten years since I've been there."

"Bon, the day is planned then," Trimaud replied.

Eleven A.M soon arrived and Spire and Trimaud walked out of the apartment and into the black Citroen waiting on the pavement outside the entrance. Trimaud greeted the driver as he got in.

"Bonjour, Monsieur Trimaud," The driver replied, cautiously eying Spire in the rear view mirror.

"Yves, meet Robert Spire, a friend of mine. He's travelled over from Pay De Galles. Robert, meet Yves, he's been driving for me for the last decade."

"Bonjour, Monsieur Spire," the driver said, in a deep French accent, his facial expression now a little friendlier.

Spire nodded and smiled, as Yves drove the Citroen off the curb into the morning traffic.

Twenty minutes after leaving Trimaud's apartment, the driver turned off the main ring road onto a potholed tarmac road, which led on to a dirt track, flanked either side by open fields. Beyond the fields lay a dense wooded area, a couple of old farm buildings were visible in the distance. "Odd place for a laboratory," Spire said, looking out across the farmland on either side the track.

"I was waiting for you to say something, Robert. The laboratory is actually disguised as an old farm building, to put off any unwelcome visitors. The French Government had some trouble with animal rights campaigners a while back, so decided to build it here to ensure privacy. It worked - no one seems interested in old farm buildings! A section of the complex is used in the development of vaccines and medicines. The French swine flu vaccine was developed here, after the last outbreak. The Department of Science and Research were kind enough to loan my team part of the complex, for climate research...I can't complain."

"Clever idea; mind, I don't favour animal testing, but I accept that certain sacrifices have to be made in the name of science," Spire said, glancing out at the picturesque scene.

The Citroen pulled up to the main gate and the driver got out, disappearing into a small hut on their right. Shortly after, Spire heard a hydraulic growl emanating from the large gate as it slowly slid open. Yves then drove them through into the farm courtyard, which was littered with bales of hay. A flock of clucking chickens fled from the vehicle's path, as they came to a stop by an old bathtub.

Spire and Trimaud got out, leaving Yves to drive off in a semi-circle, the Citroen kicking up dust as it left the courtyard through the main gate.

Four hundred metres away, near to a clump of trees in the field that ran alongside the dirt track, a high-powered sniper's rifle was trained onto the front nearside tyre of the Citroen, as it travelled back along the dusty track. The slow moving target posed no problem to the sniper, who was breathing slowly and shallowly, finger gently squeezing the rifle's trigger.

Thwack, the twenty-two calibre bullet hit the mark, ripping into the vehicle's front tyre.

Yves felt the steering wheel pull to the left, like he'd hit a pot hole. He drove on for a short while before realising he'd gotten a flat tyre. He stopped the car, and got out to inspect the damage. The driver's side appeared fine. He walked around to the front of the car, and, as he levelled with the nearside headlight, he felt a searing pain in his chest, followed by a second identical pain in his right thigh. He fell to his knees and cursed, realising he'd been shot, and then slumped to the ground as an inky darkness enveloped him.

Ksenyia was already dismantling the rifle as her target hit the ground. She folded the weapon and placed it neatly into a small duffel bag, then walked back to the rental car which she'd parked in a lane alongside the field.

Gomez, who had been watching from the end of the dirt track, drove toward the stationary Citroen. The old, tan-coloured BMW five series skidded on the dirt road as it lurched to a halt. He grabbed a large canvas bag from the passenger seat and got out, opened the boot of the Citroen and walked over to where the chauffeur's body lay in the dirt, bleeding heavily. He grabbed the dead man's arms and dragged him to the rear of the Citroen. He then reached into the open boot and pulled out the spare wheel and exchanged it for the wheel with the bullet-damaged tyre.

He then hauled the dead driver's body up and forced it into the boot of the car, slamming the lid shut. Glancing around to make sure he was alone, he picked up a tree branch from the field and used it to brush away any tell-tale drag marks the body had left in the dust. Grabbing handfuls of the sandy dirt, he threw it over the two large dark pools of blood, leaving the sticky red stains pretty much invisible.

He picked up the canvas bag he'd removed from the BMW, got into the Citroen, and drove it off the track and across the field towards a clump of bushes, hiding the car under some branches and foliage. He then reached over to the passenger seat, and into a canvas bag, grabbed a blue plastic ice-box and hacksaw which were inside, and got out of the car. He was no stranger to 'clean up jobs,' as he called them, having done a few for the brothers over the years.

He stood at the rear of the car, surveying the barren fields for thirty seconds, before opening the boot. He reached in, found the driver's right arm, pulled it out to the metal edge of the boot and starting sawing it off at the wrist.

Inside the laboratory, Trimaud introduced Spire to Dr. Bonnet and Dr. Girard, both of whom looked like they had been waiting patiently for Trimaud to arrive.

"Morning, Francois," Dr. Girard greeted him, as he hurried Trimaud along from the changing room into the main lab.

Spire followed.

"Morning, Pierre, Mari; this is Robert Spire who I mentioned to you a week or so ago."

"Bonjour, Robert," they both said in unison.

"Robert has an interest in our programme here, and has been retained by his client in the UK to look at potential global warming related science projects for a large legacy he's been asked to administer. Clearly our ongoing project fulfils the criteria," Trimaud said, a proud look on his face. "So, how are we doing? Has the iron sulphate injection process begun yet?"

"Yes, the process commenced last night. We anticipate initial formation of the phytoplankton any time now," Girard said, enthusiastically.

"Let's hope so. I'll explain to our guest what's going on here while you make the final preparations."

Dr. Bonnet smiled, nodded, and walked away.

Trimaud took Spire across to the bank of boiler-like machines on the left side of the laboratory, walking over to the first large piece of apparatus, surrounded in a spaghetti-like mesh of steel pipes and ducts. "Ok Robert, this is the best place to start. This large piece of equipment you see is the coating machine. Iron sulphate is pumped into the machine over there, under high pressure, from a large storage vessel in the next building. A special resin is then applied to the sulphate which assists the silicon 'Jackets' in binding onto the sulphate particles. The sulphate is then pumped through these pipes into the second and third machines where the 'Jackets' are finally added." Trimaud pointed to the fourth machine at the end. "Over there is where the binding process takes place. The entire process takes about four hours, to coat one tonne of sulphate."

Spire followed Trimaud along the bank of machines and interconnecting pipe-work until they were almost level with the Arctic test tent. "So, is this where the bonding of the silicon takes place?" he asked, pointing to a large stainless-steel machine.

"Oui. This last process is the key, we hope. We will, of course, shortly find out."

"So, how much of this stuff has to be dropped into the ocean to make it work?" Spire asked.

"Initially, just ten tonnes, but, if successful, we will need around twenty-five thousand tonnes for the final phase of the experiment."

"*Twenty-five thousand!*" Spire repeated, shocked at the amount.

"Oui, a large quantity, I know, but the Arctic's summer ice is retreating at an alarming rate. Winter ice cover extends to about six million square kilometres. Naturally, the sea ice retreats during the summer melt season, hitting its minimum toward the end of September each year. Summer ice coverage in two-thousand and ten was down to four point seven million square kilometres, the third lowest on record. The ice is retreating to a new minimum every few years; we feel that time is running out to prevent the Arctic ice from melting altogether. We plan to seed at least five-hundred square kilometres of ocean, using five tonnes for each square kilometre."

"You'll need an aircraft carrier to transport that amount of sulphate," Spire said, shocked at the staggering scale of the project.

"Or an oil tanker, my friend," Trimaud replied, winking.

"So, let's see if I have this right," Spire said, looking back along the bank of machines. "The iron sulphate is dropped into the ocean, which acts as a kind of phytoplankton fertilizer. The plankton then absorbs carbon dioxide - which is a principal greenhouse gas – theoretically reducing global warming?"

"Almost, my friend, but you are forgetting the most important part. The phytoplankton absorbs the *white-coated* iron sulphate which then permeates the phytoplankton's chlorophyll, turning *it* white. As you know, we have named this *Blankoplankton*. This absorbs carbon dioxide through photosynthesis and; here's the clever part, increases the albedo, or reflectivity of the entire area, by bouncing sunlight back into space, hopefully cooling the Arctic region and reversing the current warming trend. The *Blankoplankton* should reflect the sun's infra-red radiation back into space, preventing the Arctic from melting any further."

"What happens to the carbon dioxide the plankton absorbs through photosynthesis?" Spire asked.

"Good question, Robert. Well, when the *Blankoplankton* die, they fall to the bottom of the ocean, like particles of snow, locking away the carbon they have absorbed, effectively removing it from Earth's atmosphere for good."

"Incredible, Francois," Spire said, truly amazed by the grandiosity of the experiment.

"It will be if it works. It will be the world's largest geoengineering experiment to combat global warming," Trimaud said, turning around and pointed to the white tent structure. "And this section here, Robert, is where the test takes place, any minute now."

Spire looked at the tent-like structure, which was similar in appearance to a miniature version of one of the UK's *Eden Project* bio-domes. The glossy white material reflected light high into the dark void above.

"There's one more thing I must show you, Robert," Trimaud said, leading Spire toward the large steel tank in the middle of the laboratory. "Climb up to the viewing platform and have a look at the *Blankoplankton* for yourself."

Spire glanced up at the twenty foot high steel tank, and then pulled himself up the metal steps to the top. He immediately noticed an eerie white glow as he peered in. Expecting to find high intensity lighting, he was astonished to see that the water was alive with what appeared to be luminous white patches, which had formed column-like structures within the tank. The *Blankoplankton* glistened and shimmered like pieces of solid ice, but with an odd luminescence which emanated from the surface of the water.

Spire tore himself away from the sight. "It looks amazing, Francois, truly amazing," he said, descending back down the steel steps.

Doctor's Bonnet and Girard had now joined Trimaud at the base of the tank. "If you are ready, we can begin," Dr. Bonnet said, speaking in English for Spire's benefit.

Spire smiled in acknowledgement, noticing the look of apprehension on the scientists faces.

They all made their way over to the tented structure, where Dr. Bonnet handed out thick parka jackets to them. A bank of flashing lights on a control panel near to the entrance blinked from red to orange to green. Dr. Bonnet pressed one of the buttons, activating a hidden door which slid open with a hydraulic *whoosh*. "The air-lock is needed to maintain the internal temperature at precisely three degrees Celsius to simulate the beginning of Arctic summer," Dr. Bonnet said, as they walked through.

The outer door then closed, and thirty seconds later the inner door slid open to reveal a miniature Arctic landscape. Spire shivered at the sudden change in temperature and looked up to see a complex steel framework, covered in ice, dripping water as it thawed. A digital readout above the door displayed one degree Celsius in red numerals. A large circular tank took up most of the internal space.

"This is the moment of truth, Robert. We should be able to see patches of *Blankoplankton* forming in the water, just like in the external tank," Trimaud said, anxiously.

Spire looked at each of them, a nervous knot forming in the pit of his stomach. He peered into the tank, the air from his lungs forming white mist as it condensed in the cold air as he exhaled. Then he saw it; patches of shimmering white *Blankoplankton* floating on top of the near frozen water, just like in the external tank.

"*There it is!*" Trimaud exclaimed, unable to contain his excitement.

All four of them stared silently into the tank, mesmerised by the glowing water. Dr. Bonnet and Dr. Girard turned and hugged each other in relief.

Dr. Bonnet took a long wooden stick and stirred up the shimmering white plankton floating on the surface. The luminescent *Blankoplankton* coated the stick, which glowed eerily for a few seconds before dripping off.

"Fantastic news! Mari, Pierre, tomorrow please make initial preparations for the Arctic expedition. We can keep the arranged time frame...Robert, now you *must* come along, no exuses. Tonight we all go out for dinner to celebrate, I insist!"

After admiring the *Blankoplankton* for a few more minutes they all exited back into the relative warmth of the main laboratory. "I'll call Yves to pick us up," Trimaud said, as he motioned for Spire to follow him toward the changing room at the end of the laboratory.

"See you both at seven," Dr. Bonnet said, a big smile on her face, as she walked with Dr. Girard back toward the test tank.

Spire removed his overalls, thinking about how he could break the news to Angela about the Arctic trip. Francois was right, he had to go.

Trimaud called Yves' mobile phone, and after a few rings, was met with his answerphone. He tried again, but got the same response. "That's odd, he's not answering. He must have been taken off driving duties. I'll call a cab instead, but we will have to walk to the perimeter gate, as the cab won't be able to enter the courtyard," he said.

"Ready when you are," Spire said, looking forward to getting some fresh air.

"We can have a spot of lunch at the Louvre, if you'd like to save time," Trimaud suggested, walking through the main security door.

"Sounds perfect," Spire said, following Trimaud through the barn door.

They walked through the courtyard; it was early afternoon and the sky was now overcast and grey. Spire looked out across the empty fields. In the distance he could see Paris, dark thunderclouds gathered above the cityscape, giving the capital a sombre and gothic feel.

CHAPTER 24

KSENYIA AND GOMEZ waited in their cars in the underground car park of the Metropole Hotel in the centre of Paris.

In the rear of Gomez's BMW, covered by a blanket, was the ice box containing the Citroen driver's severed hand.

Ksenyia's mobile phone beeped. It was a text message instructing her to take the lift to the fourth floor of the hotel, room 408. She checked her pistol was loaded, and then tucked it into the small of her back, pulling her jacket down to cover any evidence of the small bulge.

Gomez received the same instruction, got out of his car, and followed the Russian up, taking a separate lift to the fourth floor.

Ksenyia reached room 408 and knocked on the door, wondering why her paymasters, *Arc Bin Quid Lo,* had decided to request this meeting now. *Were they angry that she had failed to eliminate Professor Trimaud as planned?*

The door opened, and a tall, athletic, handsome Middle-Eastern man held the door open for her. "Enter, I am Fahim," he said, with a soft middle-eastern accent.

She smiled, noticing that the last inch of the man's right ear lobe was missing, although this didn't detract from his good looks.

"Come in, please…sit down. Can I get you a drink, tea, coffee, something stronger perhaps?" he asked.

Ksenyia followed him into the room. "I'll take vodka, straight, over ice, please."

"Of course, vodka, I should have guessed," he smiled.

Ksenyia returned the smile. There was another knock on the door and Fahim walked over to open it. "Ah, Gomez, come...come. Meet Ksenyia, our Russian friend."

Ksenyia stood up and shook hands with Gomez, a short, thick-set Middle Eastern man, who clearly already knew Fahim.

"Our Russian friend here is drinking vodka, what will you have?"

"Coffee, with cream is fine," Gomez replied in a gruff voice.

"Very well. Please, both sit down," Fahim said, gesturing towards the comfortable looking sofas. He then disappeared into an adjoining room, before returning with another man, who was a little shorter but similar in appearance. Ksenyia immediately noticed a deep scar which ran down his left cheek, mottled with black spots. His scarred face spoilt his otherwise good looks.

"I am Faric, you must be Ksenyia?" he said, holding out his hand. "Gomez," he said, nodding toward the short stocky man.

Another man then appeared, holding a tray, which he placed on the table in silence, before disappearing back into the adjoining room.

"Your vodka, as requested," Fahim said, handing the glass to Ksenyia. "It's *Stolichnaya*, acceptable, I hope?"

"One of the best; the unmistakable flavour of Siberian Birch charcoal...the vodka is filtered through it," Ksenyia responded, with a smile.

"Ok, we don't have much time," the man with the scar suddenly spoke. "Rather than try and deal with matters from Riyadh, we decided to arrange this meeting to ensure that nothing further goes wrong, at this crucial stage. Sources tell us that the French scientist will be collected from his laboratory at one-thirty today, so I will get straight to the point. You have both carried out your tasks impeccably so far, but time is running out. The Frenchman must be prevented from continuing with his Arctic experiment." Faric's voice suddenly changed tone. "Unfortunately, he was not persuaded to drink the nicotine solution, and as you know, it is not our style to blatantly kill our targets, for obvious reasons...except for today, that is. We had no choice but to kill Trimaud's chauffeur, for reasons that will shortly become clear." Faric paused before continuing. "Until now, neither of you will have appreciated why we might be doing this. Perhaps you have guessed, but I very much doubt it."

"It is not our concern," Ksenyia interrupted, worried that if too much information was disclosed, problems could arise later on. She didn't want any reason to be involved with this group after her current assignment had been completed.

"That is true, but time is now of the essence, and we both feel, as does our Russian investor, that you should appreciate what the stakes are, because failure is not an option."

Faric stood up and tapped his spoon against his teacup as he paced back and forth along the room, seemingly deep in thought. "You see, we are at a turning point in our nation's fortunes. Our country's oil, we believe, is running out. If our operation fails, our beloved country will crumble, our magnificent buildings, culture, wealth, way of life, will end...return to the sands of the desert. We will, of course, not allow this to happen."

The tapping of the teaspoon against the china cup increased in intensity, until, suddenly, the teacup cracked in Faric's hands. There was silence for a few seconds, as he placed the broken pieces on a table next to the sofa.

He then continued, as if nothing had happened. "So, this is the situation. In a matter of weeks, Professor Francois Trimaud will embark on an expedition, to the Arctic, to test something he has been working on. We believe it is a form of geoengineering experiment, the purpose of which will be to attempt to slow down the current melting trend taking place in the Arctic. We don't know the exact details yet, but that is unimportant. What *is* important is, the expedition must be stopped. They think that man-made global warming is responsible for the Arctic's melting ice. As usual, their arrogance blinds them to believing that they can prevent what nature has already decided upon. Well, we won't let them alter the course that nature has chosen. The joint French/US venture will not be allowed to succeed. It suits our needs, and that of our future clients, if the Arctic becomes, and remains, ice free during the summer months…and preferably all year round."

Fahim then spoke. "You see, with the area ice free during the summer we can navigate the Arctic's waterways. An ice-free Northwest Passage will allow for the transport of our newly discovered oil between the Atlantic and Pacific Oceans. This is an essential element of our operation. The transit time for transporting our oil from our Atlantic oil fields will be cut by at least two thirds."

Ksenyia finished her vodka as she processed what was being said.

Faric spoke again, the tone of his voice softening. "So, with your help, and God willing, we will put an end to this final obstacle, but it might prove a little harder than the previous assignments. This is why we decided to meet here in Paris. Sending electronic commands over a computer is so impersonal, don't you think?"

Ksenyia nodded nonchalantly. Whilst she had received cursory briefings about climate change and global warming as part of her ongoing FSB training, she knew little about geoengineering the Earth's oceans. It all sounded a bit sinister to her. She was a trained assassin, not a scientist. She considered what was being said. If the Americans and French were indeed meddling with the Earth's oceans, perhaps they did need to be stopped.

"So here is what we are going to do," Faric continued, his voice sounding less anxious than a short while ago. "Gomez, you have the driver's severed hand I take it?"

Gomez nodded. "Of course, Faric, it's in the boot, as instructed."

"Good. Access to the Lab compound is by a palm reader situated in a small hut near to the main gate. Thanks to Trimaud's chauffeur, we can now gain entry into the laboratory courtyard."

Gomez chuckled to himself as he drank his coffee. He looked up. "He came in very handy, eh?" he said, shrugging his shoulders.

Faric ignored the joke, and continued. "Ksenyia, you will join Gomez and follow Professor Trimaud, as soon as he leaves the laboratory later today. All *you* have to do is make sure he is dead before midnight tonight. For security, and in order to ensure his Arctic test never gets off the ground, we will penetrate the laboratory and...well, that's not your concern. The destruction of the laboratory will create a news story for a few weeks, but I'm sure the French media will not dwell on it for too long. The government won't want to publicise the true nature of the laboratory's purpose in any event. Once these tasks are completed, that will be the end of the matter. Ksenyia, you will receive one further payment of one hundred thousand euros. Gomez, Fahim and I will return to Saudi Arabia, and life will go on as before. Is everything clear?"

"It sounds straightforward enough, gentleman," Ksenyia

said, eager to leave.

"Are there any questions, before you go?" Faric asked.

There was silence in the room.

"Good," he said, in a softer tone. He looked at Ksenyia. "You and Gomez will travel separately to the lab and wait for Trimaud to leave. Follow him and carry out your orders. Gomez will be there to ensure there are no hiccups, and in case the Englishman Spire complicates your task."

"Very well," Ksenyia said, looking over at Gomez.

Gomez walked over to both brothers, and in turn, took hold of their arms and kissed them both on the cheeks. Faric then handed Gomez a key. "Take the freezer box and place it in the boot of the black Mercedes parked in bay sixteen, leave the key inside."

"Of course, Faric," Gomez said, nodding to acknowledge the instruction.

Faric turned to Ksenyia. "God willing, we will not meet again, my Russian friend. May Allah be with you."

"And you," she replied, trying to sound sincere, as she headed for the door. As she reached to open the door, Faric put his arm out, preventing her from opening it fully. He stared at her with penetrating dark eyes. "One last thing, make sure Trimaud's death looks like an accident."

Ksenyia paused for a second, the threat angering her. Restraining herself, she smiled at Faric, "Of course," she said, ducking under his outstretched arm into the corridor.

She walked with Gomez back to their cars in silence. When they arrived in the basement Gomez went to retrieve the blue ice box from the BMW and placed it into the boot of the black Mercedes as instructed. Ksenyia waited by her car for him to return.

"You can follow me to the end of the track, which leads to the laboratory. We wait there for the scientist, and then follow him as he leaves. We'll take both cars, in case one of us loses him," Gomez said.

"Very well," Ksenyia replied, getting into her car. She checked the time; it was 12.45 P.M.

As she drove towards the outer ringroad, she thought about what the brothers had said. She certainly felt no guilt eliminating Professor Trimaud, now that she knew what he was attempting to do. *Nature should be left to take its own course.*

Her dislike for the man she now knew as Faric was even greater and she would happily dispose of him too, given the chance. *Get the job done, get paid and disappear as quickly as possible*, she concluded, as she accelerated along the ringroad toward the laboratory.

CHAPTER 25

The Louvre

THE TAXI CARRYING Spire and Trimaud slowly made its way along the dirt track, passing the clump of trees off to the left where the black Citroen had been driven, bushes and foliage now concealing it from sight. The busy Paris outer ringroad came into view in the distance.

Unnoticed by either of them, two vehicles pulled out from the layby, just off the dirt track, as they drove out onto the main tarmac road, and all three vehicles merged onto the ringroad and headed toward the centre of Paris.

"So, my friend, you said you haven't been to the Louvre for some time?" Trimaud asked.

"That's correct, maybe seven years or so. I don't suppose much has changed though. I take it the Mona Lisa is still there?" Spire replied, smiling.

"Ah yes, as well as plenty of other marvellous paintings by old masters," Trimaud said enthusiastically. "Robert, did you know that the Louvre was built, not as a museum originally, but as a fortress? It was constructed back in the late Twelfth Century to protect what was then Europe's largest city from the Anglo-Norman threat. A rampart was built around the whole of the capital; the Louvre became a reinforced fortress within."

"Really; it goes back that far?"

"Of course, the reigns of Louis Thirteenth and Fourteenth

had the most impact, that's when extensive and ambitious building works transformed the original building into the Louvre we see today."

Fascinating, Spire thought as they continued down Boulevard Saint Michael, which gave a fantastic vista of the Seine as they crossed over onto the Ile De Le Cite. The taxi then made a left turn onto Quai Francois Mitterrand, where the grand buildings of the Louvre came into view on the right.

Dark clouds were now massing overhead, and it looked like there was going to be a downpour at any moment. The taxi then turned right into the Place du Carrousel and the modernistic glass Pyramide du Louvre came into view, flanked either side by the huge wings of the Louvre galleries.

"Almost our stop, Robert," Trimaud said. "I asked the driver to drop us at the Esplanade and Galerie du Carrousel end; it's a little more dramatic."

"Sounds great," Spire replied, trying to hide his ignorance.

The driver pulled over and stopped along the Carrousel, allowing Spire and Trimaud to get out, just as a couple of Gendarmes approached and waved the taxi along.

Ksenyia and Gomez had followed the Renault along Quai Francois Mitterand, soon realising that the Louvre was the most likely destination for their targets. Gomez called Ksenyia and suggested that she park her car in the main car park, located on the Avenue du General Lemonier. He would follow the Renault for as long as he could to ensure they were in fact going to the Louvre, and then confirm with her, double back, and park there himself.

Gomez looked on as the scientist and the Englishman got out of the taxi on the Place du Carrousel, and then head towards the main entrance of the Louvre. He called Ksenyia -

who was just parking her car, to confirm the position.

Trimaud and Spire walked through the Pyramide du Louvre and purchased two entrance tickets. "The glass pyramid is fantastic, non?" Trimaud said, looking up as they passed through American architect Leoh Ming Pei's contribution to the museum.

Groups of tourists were gathered at various spots within the main foyer studying their hand-held maps, trying to work out which wing to investigate first.

"Allez - this way, Robert," Trimaud said, walking past the hordes of confused looking tourists. "We'll go straight to the *Cour Carree* wing; some of my favourite European pieces are housed there."

Spire followed Trimaud to one of the main staircases off the large foyer, and ascended three flights to a large landing area. A group of American tourists on a guided tour moved slowly into one of the Louvre's long corridors, temporarily holding them back.

Some distance behind, Ksenyia pushed her way past some agitated tourists into the main foyer, desperately searching for the two men. Groups of tourists were gathered around chatting and pointing to various stairwells leading off from the concourse.

Where the hell are they? She wondered, looking up at the staircases. She then caught a glimpse of two men on the landing area at the top of one of the far staircases, pushing their way through a crowd of visitors. One looked to be around six foot tall with dirty blond hair, the other shorter, with dark hair poking out from under a cap. *That had to be them.*

She moved toward the staircase, running up the steps two at a time. As she ascended, she bumped into a Japanese tourist, accidently knocking his oversized Nikon camera out of his hands.

"Excuse me," she apologised, continuing past. She reached the landing and looked down the corridor. A group of tourists were gathered, being given a guided tour, and beyond them, about half way along the corridor, she saw Trimaud and Spire studying one of the Louvre's many paintings.

She composed herself and walked slowly down the corridor towards them, passing the noisy group of sightseers blocking the corridor. She called Gomez, telling him her current location, whilst feeling in her handbag for the syringe of nicotine solution. She had discussed the plan with Gomez earlier; he would immobilise Spire, while she injected Trimaud with the nicotine. It would be quick and discreet; no fuss, no trace. They would be out of the Louvre before the paramedics arrived on the scene. *End of Trimaud, end of assignment, and the end of her relationship with Arc Bin Quid Lo.*

She quickened her pace as she moved down the corridor, trying not to let her thoughts stray as she eyed Trimaud and Spire, a short distance ahead, studying another painting.

"Robert, this is one of my favourites. It's the *Allegory of Victory* by Mathieu Le Nain," Trimaud said, pointing to a winged helmeted female standing in triumphant pose atop a naked female body. "The winged figure stands over her quarry, supposedly meant to represent deceit or intrigue. The interesting thing about this painting is that X-rays revealed another painting underneath. Perhaps the artist started something he didn't like, deciding to paint over it. Or, maybe the owner commissioned the artist to paint this painting on an old canvas? It remains a mystery."

"Interesting, Francois, but why is it one of your favourite paintings, out of the thousands in here?" Spire asked.

"Actually, there's around thirty-five thousand paintings housed here. The reason I like this one? As a boy, my mother used to bring me here on a Saturday, once a month. She would stop and admire a painting that used to hang next to this one. It didn't interest me, but this one...well, I found it intriguing, and it just stuck with me. Anyway, come on, Robert, there's lots more to see." Trimaud pointed enthusiastically, walking briskly along the corridor.

Spire followed him, just managing to keep up.

Gomez entered the main foyer, found the staircase leading to the Cour Carree wing and briskly walked up to the third floor corridor, and found the Russian, who was standing looking at a painting of an angel standing on top of a naked body, its wings spread. "Where are they?" he asked, taking no interest in the painting.

"Over there, at the end of the corridor," Ksenyia replied, looking discreetly toward them.

Gomez looked, and saw the targets studying another painting, some ten metres away.

They both watched as Spire and Trimaud continued around the corner and out of sight, and then hurried after them, almost bumping into their targets, who were now mulling over another painting only two metres along the corridor from the corner. They continued past them, before stopping, as if to admire a painting on the opposite wall. They listened as, behind them, Trimaud discussed the painting with Spire.

"This is another one of my favourites, *The Consecration* or *The Coronation of Napoleon,* as it is more commonly known, by Jacques Louis David. The artist was actually present at the ceremony and painted the picture, once he returned to his studio," Trimaud said, pointing to a figure in the painting. "The curious thing is that the Pope, originally painted with his hands *on* his knees, was re-painted upon Napoleon's instructions, to show him making a gesture of blessing."

Spire admired the painting whilst Trimaud discussed the painting's history. "Very interesting, Francois, but I'm afraid Napoleon's coronation is going to have to wait - I need to find the gents."

"Au revoir, Napoleon...allez - this way, Robert," Trimaud said, chuckling.

Spire followed Trimaud along the corridor, turning right at the end where he saw a sign for the gents about halfway down. They passed an open balcony; quiet chatter from the Louvre's visitors drifted up from the busy level below. Apart from that, the corridor was surprisingly empty.

Spire walked into the gents, leaving Trimaud in the corridor admiring a *Baron Regnault,* oil on canvas.

Outside, Ksenyia pulled the syringe from her handbag, and edged closer to Trimaud, who was still studying the painting in front of him. Just as she was about to jab the syringe into Trimaud's upper left arm, she felt a tap on her shoulder. *Had security been watching?* She froze, lowered her arm, and turned to face whoever had interrupted her.

"Excuse me, this fell out of your handbag," a little girl said, holding out a silk handkerchief, which Ksenyia recognised as her own.

The girl's father looked on from the open balcony area and

smiled.

Ksenyia knelt down and took the pearl coloured handkerchief from the girl's hand and forced an appreciative smile in response. The girl then ran back over to her father, gave Ksenyia a shy glance, and grabbed his hand.

Spire had just pulled his zip up when a sudden and powerful blow to his back sent him crashing into the porcelain urinals. The impact caused him to slip onto the floor, where he landed on his left shoulder.

What the hell? As he fell to the floor, he caught a fleeting glimpse of his attacker - a stocky, powerful, Greek-looking man - who was now stooped down with his right hand clasped around a beige dagger-like object, his arm pulled back ready to lunge.

Spire instinctively swept his right arm in a powerful arc across his attacker's ankles, managing to force the heavily-built man off balance. The man lunged at him with the dagger, but missed, hitting the back of the urinals instead with a sickening crunch. The dagger fell out of his hand and clattered onto the floor.

Despite what must have been at least one broken knuckle, the stocky man didn't flinch, and before Spire could react, the man head-butted him in the face. Spire heard the sickening crunch of his own nose breaking. He'd felt the same pain many times before during martial arts training sessions; and was used to it, but it still hurt like hell. Adrenalin pumped into his veins and he lunged at the man's groin in response, buying himself enough time to rabbit-punch his attacker in the neck. The heavy man fell back, clearly in pain. Spire jumped up from the floor and kicked the lethal looking plastic dagger away.

The man got up a split second later and threw another

punch, but Spire was able to side-step out of the way. The swipe threw his attacker off balance. Spire grabbed the man's right arm and spun him around into the sinks behind. The assailant's shoulders crashed into the mirror, shattering it in the process. At least ten sections of glass shattered onto the tiled bathroom floor.

The man seemed injured, and then suddenly, he grabbed a shard of glass from the floor and threw it. Spire ducked, slipping back onto the floor in the process, just avoiding a nasty sliver of glass. Before he had time to get to his feet, the man turned and ran out of the restroom.

In the corridor, Ksenyia turned around, ready for a second attempt at stabbing Trimaud with the syringe, but he had moved along to look at another painting. Before she could follow, Gomez, bloodied and startled, came charging out of the gents toward her, glaring at her as he passed. The look on his face could mean only one thing - *Leave.*

She dropped the syringe into her handbag, and walked briskly past the toilets and down the first stairs she could find, which took her back down to the main concourse area.

Had Gomez killed Spire? She cursed to herself, realising that another chance to complete her task had just been screwed up.

CHAPTER 26

TRIMAUD HEARD THE commotion and turned to see a man half running, half walking out of the restroom, down the corridor and out of sight, just as two of the Louvre's security guards came sprinting towards him, and then disappeared into the restroom.

Trimaud followed the guards in, and found Spire stooped over one of the sinks, washing blood from his nose, ignoring the two guards who were shouting at him in French.

"Robert, what the hell happened?" Trimaud asked.

"Francois, do me a favour and tell these idiots I've just been assaulted. Instead of shouting at me, they should be out there looking for the bald stocky man who just ran out," Spire replied calmly, holding his nose.

"Tell me exactly what happened here, Robert and I'll relay it to the guards."

Spire did as he was asked.

"Robert, they are asking if you knew your attacker. Was robbery the motive?"

"I didn't recognise him, and I don't think he was trying to rob me either," Spire said, pointing to the knife on the floor. "He looked Greek, perhaps Middle Eastern, I couldn't quite tell."

One of the guards walked over, and using a handkerchief, picked up what appeared to be a strong plastic dagger, perhaps made from some type of polymer composite. He studied it carefully, speaking into his radio before leaving the restroom. Two cleaners then entered and started clearing up the shards of broken glass from the floor. Another cleaner placed a no-entry sign near to the door.

"Robert, the guard would like you to look at some security tapes. He also suggested that you go to hospital."

"I think I'll be fine, Francois. Maybe another broken nose, but there's not much anyone can do for that. Come on, let's go look at the tapes," Spire said.

They followed the guards along the now sealed-off corridor. Spire turned to Francois. "Did anyone approach you after I had gone into the toilets?"

"No, I was studying *The Three Graces*, when I heard the commotion. That's when I saw the two guards running down the corridor. There was a woman behind me, and a young girl with her father, but apart from that the corridor was empty."

They both followed the security guard down one set of stairs and along another corridor to a door marked *Prive*. The guard unlocked the door and ushered them in to what was, obviously, one of the Louvre's main security rooms. Banks of monitors displaying internal images of the museum switched between different locations within the building.

Spire glanced at the largest screen, recognising the main concourse area. The guard who had led them in spoke to a large man who was sitting behind one of the monitors. The man rolled his chair along to the end screen and pressed a few buttons. He then turned a dial which enabled him to freeze and reverse the images on the central screen. The guard motioned for Spire and Trimaud to move closer to the monitor.

Spire recognised himself and Trimaud looking at the Napoleon painting, just before they moved off down the corridor towards the toilets. The CCTV controller then fast-forwarded the video until a man could be seen running out. He paused the video, reversed it, and then replayed it in slow motion. The man's face was in shadow, but his dark forehead and balding scalp were visible, as was his large bulbous nose. He looked Greek or Middle Eastern, as Spire had described.

The security guard spoke to the controller, who then pressed another button. A laser printer on the desk, next to Spire, zipped into action, printing off the image displayed on the screen. The guard pulled the A4 glossy image off the printer and handed it to Spire. "Is this the man who attacked you?" he asked, in a heavy French accent.

Spire confirmed that it was.

The controller then continued playing the surveillance tape. A woman could be seen approaching Trimaud, and then suddenly turning around. A young girl appeared to be handing her something. The brunette, her face hidden, walked off frame in the opposite direction to Spire's attacker.

The security officer then spoke to Trimaud, who translated for Spire. "Robert, they are going to run some checks on him, and the knife, see if they have any information in their database, or with Interpol. I have given them my contact details for now, just in case they need any further information."

Spire nodded. "Fine, come on, Francois, let's get out of here, I need a drink."

Spire and Trimaud exited the Louvre through the glass pyramid and walked out into the courtyard, leaving via the Rue de Rivoli entrance. They crossed the road and found a small open-air bar which had cast-iron tables laid out, each with its own parasol. They sat down at a table near to a large, old tree and ordered two beers. They both sat in silence until their drinks arrived. Spire poured the chilled bottled beer into his glass, and took a large gulp before speaking. "Christ, Francois, that was close; do you think that whoever is involved could be on to us already?"

"Certainly looks like it, but why go for you? We must go to the police. We need some protection, Robert."

"No, Francois, we can't. Not yet anyway."

"Pourquoi?" Trimaud asked, looking puzzled.

"There's something I didn't tell you. I had a break-in at my home. A note was left on my computer, threatening me if I went to the police. I'm worried about Angela; I haven't told her, or anyone else apart from you and Doris. I have to try and get to the bottom of this thing myself…that's why I can't risk going to the police just yet."

Trimaud shook his head. "Good God, Robert, what are we going to do?"

"I'm not sure yet, but if we can find out what Dr. Bannister and Dr. Stanton were working on, we might be able to figure out what the hell is going on."

Spire finished his drink and looked around for the waitress to order another. As he did, he scanned the bar to see if anyone was watching them. The paranoia he'd had the previous night was coming back in full flow. Tourists were milling around, chatting and taking pictures, but everything appeared normal. "I'll call Kim, see if she's discovered anything," Spire said, suddenly realising he hadn't checked in at the office for two days. He dialled the number from his pay-as-you-go mobile. The phone rang three times before Kim picked up.

Kim sounded in her usual happy, carefree mood, and he was glad to hear her voice. "Listen Kim, this is just a quick call. I'll be coming back tomorrow, but I need to know if you had any luck with deciphering that business card I gave you?"

"Not really, Rob. I entered the name on the card into a search engine hoping to get something, and played around with the words, without any luck. I've also tried entering all variations into a Greek, Latin, French and Egyptian language translator tool, but got nothing...I'll keep trying."

"Well done, Kim. What about the environmental groups, any luck there?"

"Nothing; the only groups active over here are the well regarded ones; The World Wildlife Fund, Friends of the Earth, and Greenpeace. None of them have had any connection with the dead scientists, from what I can see. There's a group in the States called *Finish Fossil Fuels*, and they mention Dr. Bannister's work on their website, but Bannister's name is used in *support* of their cause, not against it. I'll continue looking later on this afternoon, Rob."

Spire ended the call, and relayed the discussion back to Trimaud, who sat silently sipping his beer.

"Jack's wife promised to call me if she discovered what her husband was working on. I guess she's not found anything yet, but I'll chase her tomorrow," Trimaud said, trying to sound optimistic.

Spire buried his head in his hands; his nose had started to throb again. "Should I cancel dinner tonight?" Trimaud asked.

"No, no, I'm fine," Spire sighed. "We can't do anymore today. Let's go out for dinner as planned and celebrate your scientific breakthrough, nothing's going to get in the way of that."

"I must say, Robert, whoever attacked you today probably had a bit of a shock. Where did you learn to handle yourself like that?"

"I can take care of myself, Francois. I trained at the *Yuck Kung Foo* martial arts club, in London, for fourteen years. It's a good job he ran off when he did, or I'd probably be sitting in a French jail, waiting to defend myself on a murder charge."

"Well, I know a good lawyer!" Trimaud replied, chuckling.

Spire managed a brief smile in response to his friend's

always present sense of humour.

Trimaud paid the bill and they found a cab. They both sat in silence as the cab slowly made its way back through the city traffic to Montmartre, and finally Trimaud's apartment.

After leaving the Louvre, Ksenyia had driven back to the *Hotel Metro,* a non-descript two star hotel, a stone's throw away from the Champs Elysees. She had been unable to contact Gomez since the aborted attack.

She sat on the end of her bed in the small room. The sounds of the capital, car horns and never ending traffic noise intruded through the open bedroom window, from the busy city streets below. She was furious with herself for failing to dispatch her target for the second time. A twenty-two caliber bullet would have been a much quicker and simpler solution. She cursed as she powered up her laptop, entered her secure area and typed an e-mail to the Saudi brothers.

French ice remains frozen. Please advise.

She got up from the bed and started to pace up and down the small room. Five minutes later she heard the sound of an e-mail arriving into her mail box. She sat down, pulled her laptop toward her and opened the message.

Gomez has updated us on the assignment. The situation is unfortunate; Spire appears to be a formidable obstruction. We will melt the ice ourselves. Please remain where you are and await further instruction and payment.

She slammed her laptop closed, walked into the bathroom and ran herself a shower, deciding to give the brothers twenty-four hours to get back to her, or she would leave the country and treat the assignment as terminated.

CHAPTER 27

French Crozet Islands
May 5

THE RECOVERY SHIP *Deep Quest* maintained its position one hundred nautical miles off the southern tip of the Crozet Islands in the Southern Indian Ocean, aided by the latest computer controlled dynamic positioning system, which constantly adjusted her bow and stern thrusters against the moving ocean currents. The shadow cast by her twenty metre-high crane bobbed up and down on the waves, which in turn, gently rocked the high-tech recovery vessel.

The *Deep Quest* had recently arrived at the location to relieve the *Ocean Explorer;* its mission, to attempt recovery of the lost submersible, which had been located, thanks to its lithium-ion powered radio beacon, which continued to emit signals from almost one kilometre down on the seabed.

The crew had worked around the clock to secure the huge recovery slings and lifting devices needed to pull the sub up from its inky-black resting place. The affectionately named *Gert* and *Daisy,* two of the *Quest's* remotely operated vehicles or ROVs, had been down to the sub to tether lifting slings around her bow and stern sections. The agile ROVs with their powerful underwater lights had completed the job in a little less than nine hours. The ROV's operators, Lieutenant's Frank Williams and Jimmy Marshall were now exhausted and catching up on some well-earned sleep in their bunks, after having worked non-stop throughout the night securing the lifting equipment to *Poseidon's* hull. Everything was now in position and the crew was on standby for the final and most critical part of the recovery operation.

On the bridge, Captain Skip Majors sounded the *Quest's* alarm, before speaking to the crew over the ship's P.A system. "Crew, please take up your positions, let's get the job done as quickly and safely as possible, so we can all go home."

There was a flurry of activity aboard the ship, as the crew responded to the order.

Captain Majors, a silver-haired man in his late sixties, and a veteran of salvage operations, scanned the surrounding waters with his binoculars. In the distance, he observed two wooden fishing trawlers flying the Saudi Arabian flag. *Odd, he thought. What were they doing out here?* He watched as they hauled in their catch from the night before.

Deep Quest's siren sounded again, and the huge winch, with its three-inch-diameter steel cables, creaked to life, pulling taut on the fifteen tonne weight tethered far below. The crane's gears groaned and screeched, as the *Poseidon* was winched up through the water. Seagulls began to gather on the crane-head, and on the surface of the ocean around the steel cables where they disappeared into the depths below. Six of the ship's crew stood lined up along the port side, ready to report visual contact of the wreckage.

Drake, a ten-a-day cigar smoking ex- marine, was busy at the crane's winch controls, ensuring the gears were operating within their designed operating tolerance. The lift was also being monitored by the *Deep Quest's* sonar operator, who was passing depth readings to Captain Majors as the sub was pulled up.

The cable-length monitor told Drake the sub had just risen up through one hundred and fifty metres. He prepared to slow the ascent to a crawl as the sub neared the surface.

"Crew, standby, please, for visual contact," Captain Majors ordered, as he looked down from the bridge at the cables slowly rising from the ocean.

Private Scot Ramsey, standing alongside his fellow crew members, strained his eyes as he searched over the port side for the telltale dark shadow of the sub, which would soon be visible just below the surface of the ocean. He didn't have to wait long. He was the first to see the eight metre long dark shadow appear, just before the sub breached the surface. Ramsey - along with the other crewmen - could see that the *Poseidon* had been crushed like an old tin can, her hull a tangled mass of metal. Only the sub's powerful exploration arms were recognisable and intact as she was pulled clear of the surface. Seawater cascaded from the craft's imploded interior like miniature waterfalls.

Drake manoeuvred the crane, slowly swinging the *Poseidon* around onto the *Quest's* thirty-metre long by fifteen-metre wide internal recovery area. The mangled steel and titanium remnants of the sub creaked as it was lowered onto the deck. Seawater streamed out from the crushed hull, containing an assortment of ocean life; a lobster, crabs and numerous small fish washed out onto the recovery deck. Seagulls that had been watching keenly from the crane above dived down, scooping up the stranded fish in their beaks. The lobster and crabs, along with a few lucky fish, escaped back into the ocean via the large drainage grates situated on the edge of the recovery deck area.

Captain Majors addressed his men over the P.A system. "Well done, crew. Recovery team please release recovery equipment and secure the hull." Majors left his position on the bridge, temporarily handing control to his second in command, Officer Bill Trent, whilst he went to join his crew on the deck in order to take a closer look at what was left of the recovered submersible.

He descended the three sets of freshly painted white steel steps to the deck below, returning a salute to the crew lined up along the port side.

Drake, the crane operator, was just releasing the steel lifting cables that had been tethered to the lifting slings as Captain Majors walked to the edge of the recovery deck. "Captain," he said, nodding in acknowledgment as he placed a fresh cigar into his mouth. "She sure was heavy for a crushed piece of titanium; the poor bastards didn't stand a chance. It looks to me like she imploded following a hull breach."

"Jesus; what a mess," Majors said, looking at the sub. "Good work on pulling her up, Drake. The forensic engineers back home will have their work cut out for them," he said, shaking his head as he eyed the mangled wreckage.

"What do you suppose that is, Captain?" Drake said, pointing his smouldering cigar at the four metre long shaft clamped in the *Poseidon's* exploration arm.

"Let's go and take a closer look." Majors replied, clearly intrigued.

Drake followed Majors onto the recovery deck, treading carefully so as not to slip, and walked over to the bow of the submersible where the two large exploration arms protruded from the mangled forward section of the sub. One arm was clamped around a shiny steel shaft, clearly not part of the craft. Judging by its shiny surface, the object hadn't been under the sea for very long. Drake studied the metal cylinder and noticed what looked like a groove just before the end of the shaft. He ran his fingers along the narrow channel and across the shattered end of the thick steel rod. "Captain, look here," he said, pointing at the groove, whilst exhaling a plume of cigar smoke. "I think we are looking at the shattered shaft of a drill collar."

"Are you certain?" Majors said, raising his eyebrows.

"I know a drill collar when I see one, Captain, and that's what this is."

Four hundred metres away, on the bridge of the Saudi Arabian fishing boat *Plentiful,* a heavily-built bearded man watched the recovery operation through high powered binoculars. *Well well, it looks like the Americans have found their sub.*

He barked an order to a crew member below, who was busy hauling in empty lobster traps in an attempt to maintain the facade that the vessel was on an innocent fishing trip. "Prepare the ship; we're moving on to the next sector."

The man looked up. "Yes, Mustafa, right away," he said, scurrying toward the stern of the ship.

The bearded man replaced the binoculars back on their stand, picked up the Satcom phone and reported the find to his superiors.

CHAPTER 28

THE TAXI PULLED up outside Trimaud's apartment on the Rue Des Abbesses; it was just after five P.M. The weather had cleared up, and Montmartre was bustling with sightseers and diners who were strolling around, making the most of the last day of the weekend.

Trimaud paid the taxi fare, and Spire followed him up to the apartment. "I'll take a shower if you don't mind, Robert, then I'll give Mari and Pierre a call to let them know tonight's plan. Make yourself at home, there's beer in the fridge, help yourself...you need it."

"You're not kidding!" Spire replied, walking into the small kitchen and grabbing a bottle of *Gavroche* from the fridge. He opened the bottle and wandered back into the lounge, found a spot on the sofa and sank back into the soft cushion, taking a long gulp of beer. He placed the cold bottle of beer beside the bridge of his nose and closed his eyes. His thoughts flashed back to the incident at the Louvre. Everything had happened so quickly, but the features of his attacker, his balding head, large bulbous nose and round face was seared into his memory. The man reminded him of the actor *Bob Hoskins*- only an ugly Greek version. *Was it a random attack, or had he perhaps been mistaken for Francois?*

He suddenly felt very tired, thinking of all the possibilities and reached for the T.V remote, turning the television on. He flicked through the channels, until he found CNN. A news anchor was discussing a story about a missing dog being reunited with its owner after eight years. Then the breaking news banner came up, and the screen flashed to another newsreader, a male in his thirties, standing on a dock;

"The submersible Poseidon - missing for thirteen days - has been found off the French Crozet Islands in the Southern Indian Ocean..."

Spire heard the bathroom door close. "Francois, hurry, come and take a look at the news. The *Poseidon* has been *found!*" he shouted.

Trimaud rushed into the lounge, his towel still wrapped around his waist.

The CNN newsreader continued talking. *"The Poseidon, one of the latest deep-sea class submersibles, belonged to the Oceanic Research division of the National Snow and Ice Data Centre, and was, it is believed, on loan to a team led by the late climatologist, Dr. Jack Bannister, who died suddenly before a lecture he was due to give in San Francisco at the National Climate Change Conference. The US Navy salvage vessel Ocean Quest was involved in the salvage mission, and is believed to be sailing back to her home port of San Diego in order for investigations into the loss of the submersible to begin. We now go over to our science correspondent to assess what might have gone wrong..."*

The screen flicked over to CNN science correspondent Jack Livery who was standing in a studio, in front of a computer generated diagram of the *Poseidon* submarine.

"We can only speculate at this stage as to what might have happened, but from first accounts, a fatal incident seems to have led to a hull breach, resulting in the submarine being crushed under the enormous pressures that exist almost one kilometre under the ocean. The Mark IV Deep-Sea class sub was operating well within her design tolerances, and marine investigators will be looking at possible design faults or for

signs of a collision of some kind as being a possible cause or contributory factor..."

"Another coincidence, do you think?" Spire said, taking a gulp of beer, "Or sabotage?"

"It doesn't look good, Robert. We've got two hours before we meet the others for dinner. Let's spend the time checking the internet, see if we can find out what Jack might have been using the sub for. You never know, we might find something."

"Ok, I'll take a quick shower first, if you don't mind, I need to freshen up." Spire walked into the bathroom and looked in the mirror. A red-black bruise was already starting to develop beneath his right eye, and if his grandmother had still been alive, she'd have told him he looked like he'd been dragged through a hedge backwards. He smiled at the thought, and jumped under the shower.

After showering, Spire rejoined Trimaud who was on his computer searching the internet for anything relating to his old friend, Dr. Jack Bannister. He spoke without taking his eyes off the screen. "I just got off the phone with Margaret; she hasn't been able to find anything relating to Jack's work unfortunately, but will continue to search." Trimaud hit the return key and Bannister's homepage flashed up on the screen.

The website had been updated with news of his sudden death in San Francisco eleven days earlier. No mention was made of his proposed talk; just that it was in relation to '*The latest research and discoveries in the field of global warming related science.*'

"Do you mind if I take a look?" Spire asked, studying the website.

"Help yourself."

Spire minimised the page, opened another window and typed into a search engine; '*Dr. Jack Bannister and global warming.*' A list of references relating to Bannister's work came up. The most recent entry was two years old and related to a paper he'd written on methane gas release from the Arctic permafrost. Spire continued searching, and then a recent news article caught his eye. It was in relation to the greening of the Arctic tundra; the worrying fact that as the area warms, a greater amount of vegetation had started to grow there, which in turn would cause further warming. Dr. Jack Bannister was quoted;

'Vast amounts of methane gas trapped under the tundra are now at risk of being released into the atmosphere, as a result of the changes taking place there. This in turn will fuel global warming, and could prove to be the Arctic's final tipping point, after which, further warming will become unstoppable.'

The words *tipping point* and *unstoppable* played over in Spire's mind. "That sounds a bit ominous," he said, looking at Trimaud.

Trimaud shrugged. "Oui. Jack had been trying to tell the scientific community, and the US Government, for years that this was going to happen. It's incredibly serious, Robert. Arctic methane release is thought to have caused a rapid rise in temperature towards the end of the last ice age. The climate warmed up in a matter of decades."

Spire shook his head as he thought about the worrying implications. He pulled the keyboard towards him and typed in *'Crozet Islands and global warming.'* The search returned no results. He tried *'Crozet Islands and methane.'* Again, there were no results. "There must be something here, Francois. What the hell could Bannister have been working on down there?" he said, placing his head in his hands in frustration.

"Jack must have been using the submersible to study the ocean ridge around the Crozet Islands, maybe to look for previous evidence of global warming, coral bleaching, maybe taking sediment cores, that sort of thing. The only way we are going to find out my friend, is if Margaret can find his paperwork. She's looked at his computer, which was returned to her from Jack's hotel room in San Francisco, but she says the hard drive is empty."

Spire looked up. "Jeez, it must have been wiped clean. I'll get in touch with Professor Sammedi when I get back home, see if he can shed any more light on what's going on."

"Very well, Robert, In the meantime, let's at least enjoy dinner tonight to celebrate the success of the *Blankoplankton* experiment, eh? I've booked a little place called *Le Petit Arbre de Chene*. I think the English translation is, *The Little Oak*. The food is exquisite there, you will love it."

"That sounds great, Francois."

"Tres bon, mon ami. The taxi will be here in twenty minutes. Mari and Pierre will meet us at the restaurant."

They arrived at *The Petit Arbre de Chene,* in the Pigalle area of the city, at a little after seven-fifteen. Dr. Girard was alone, enjoying a drink in the lounge-bar which was decked out with dark-wooden floors and brown leather sofas.

Spire and Trimaud walked over to a bunch of comfortable leather chairs arranged around a stylish modern smoked-glass coffee table. "La ou est Mari?" Trimaud asked, as they sat down.

"I left her in the lab this afternoon; she wanted to work on a bit. She said she'd be here for around seven. She'll be here soon, I'm sure," Girard replied, speaking English, for Spire's benefit.

"She needs a break from work," Trimaud said, with his characteristic chuckle.

A waiter brought some menus over and Trimaud ordered three beers and a bottle of *Dom Perignon* Champagne with four glasses.

Spire and Trimaud updated Girard on the day's events, leaving out the attack on Spire at the Louvre. It was only when the waiter came over to ask them if they would like to go to their table that they realised Dr. Bonnet still hadn't turned up, or even called.

"It's not like Mari to be this late," Trimaud commented, as he took out his mobile phone and punched in her home number. He let it ring, but there was no answer. He tried her mobile again, but there was no answer. He then called the lab; she didn't appear to be there either. "She must be on her way. We'll give her another ten minutes and I'll try again."

A further twenty minutes passed and there was still no sign of Dr. Bonnet. With the ice in the Champagne ice bucket melting, Trimaud grimaced and called the three contact numbers he had for her again. "I think Mari may have a problem, perhaps some car trouble. Robert, do you mind if we go over to the lab to make sure her car hasn't broken down?"

"Of course not," Spire said, finishing his beer.

"Pierre, you'd better stay here in case she turns up."

"Ok, my car is parked just down the street, use it. Here, take my keys," Girard said, handing them to Trimaud.

"Merci bien. Come Robert; let's take a quick drive to the Lab."

They found Pierre's silver Golf just outside the restaurant and drove toward the ringroad. The time was seven-fifty and the traffic was light. It wasn't long before they saw the sign for the village of St-Azure, close to where the lab was located, and turned off.

Trimaud drove off the main tarmac road, up toward the farmhouse. There was no sign of life as they travelled along the quiet country track. Spire opened his window; the night was silent, apart from the occasional rasp of a cricket coming from somewhere out in the fields. Gravel crunching under the vehicle's tyres broke the silence as they pulled up outside the perimeter wall. Trimaud got out of the car. The area was in darkness, apart from a small spotlight which blinked on as Trimaud approached the entrance gate access hut.

Spire got out and looked around. *Surely Mari couldn't still be here?*

Moths and other flying bugs fluttered around the bright light above the hut. A sudden sound from the trees made him jump, and he turned around to see an owl which had been sitting quietly on a tree branch next to the hut, hoot and fly off, vanishing into the darkness. The brief silence that followed was disturbed by another sound, this time from the perimeter wall's hydraulic gates as they slowly slid open.

"Come on; we'll drive into the courtyard," Trimaud said, getting back into the car.

They drove through the gates and parked the car. The farmhouse was in darkness, apart from a dim light emanating from somewhere within the laboratory. There was no sign of Dr. Bonnet's Citroen. Spire followed Trimaud up to the barn door that led into the lab and then onto the second steel entrance door. Trimaud went to the hidden panel, and activated the retinal scanner to gain entry.

While waiting for the secure door to open, Spire looked around the dimly-lit featureless entrance area, catching a glimpse of the dark courtyard beyond. The wind suddenly picked up, blowing the barn door which creaked on its hinges as it slammed shut. The main door then slid open, and Spire followed Trimaud through into the laboratory ante-room. As he did, Spire glanced back at the rattling barn door, a feeling of unease rising from the pit of his stomach.

CHAPTER 29

THE MAIN LIGHT in the ante-room was on and a white technician's coat lay on the floor, near the laboratory entrance.

"That's odd," Trimaud said, "It's unlike Pierre or Mari not to tidy up after them."

"Hold on," Spire said, taking hold of Trimaud's arm. "Let's be careful, I have an uneasy feeling about this."

"It's ok Robert, this lab is totally secure. Unauthorised entry is impossible, in view of the security measures in place," Trimaud said, reassuringly.

Spire thought about it. Trimaud was right of course; any intruder would have to overcome the external palm scanner, and then the internal retinal scanner to gain access to the lab. "Of course, Francois, ignore me; I'm still on edge after yesterday."

Spire followed Trimaud into the main lab, which was deathly quiet, apart from a low hum emanating from the main power supply. A light was on at the back of the lab, but the building looked empty. The area they were standing in was in darkness, apart from the glow from the sequential blinking of red, green and orange lights from the banks of computers running along both sides of the hanger-sized laboratory.

They walked further in, Spire straining his eyes to see in the dim light. An eerie translucent glow still emanated from the large test tank up ahead containing the *Blankoplankton,* which appeared to be emitting light, relative to the dim light within the lab. They continued to a point where they were almost level with the main test tank. "Bonsoir, Mari! Are you here?" Trimaud shouted.

"Looks like someone just left a light on; hardly surprising after today's excitement," Spire said, breathing a sigh of relief. He followed Trimaud further in. The light they could see was coming from behind the Arctic test tank. They walked toward it, their footsteps echoing above the quiet hum of the lab's power supply as they made their way across the tiled floor.

Spire rounded the Arctic test tank and saw a figure seated half in shadow, hunched over one of the computers at the back of the lab. The lights on the computer monitor were blinking slowly, from amber to orange to green and back again. He glanced at Trimaud, who shrugged back at him. As he got closer to the hunched over figure, he realised it was Mari.

Dr. Bonnet appeared to be working; her long dark hair lay over the keyboard in front of her. Her low cut, black evening dress revealed her slender neck and upper back, but something didn't look right. *What the hell was she doing still working at this time of night?* Spire wondered.

Trimaud called out as they got closer, "Mari, what are you doing? You should be at the restaurant, celebrating with us."

Dr. Bonnet did not turn around, she didn't even respond. Spire was the first to notice the black piece of material tied tightly around her head. He hadn't seen it from further back as it was hidden against her dark hair. As he levelled with her chair, Dr. Bonnet's shocked and tear-filled eyes stared up at him, her cheeks streaked with black mascara. She had been gagged and her hands bound tightly under the desk in front of her, and her ankles were tied around the base of the chair.

Spire felt his stomach turn over as he realised she'd been restrained. "*Jesus!* What the hell happened to…?" As he spoke, he felt a sudden, searing pain on the back of his head, and then darkness.

Trimaud opened his eyes; his vision, blurred at first, slowly started to clear. Shivering, he soon realised where he was. He looked over to his right and saw Dr. Bonnet, still tied to her chair, Spire was lying on the floor a short distance away. He raised his head and looked up at the dark figures of two men standing in the entrance to the Arctic test tank.

"Ah, Professor, good of you to join us," one of the men said.

Trimaud stared at him, unable to say a word, trying to place the accent; he was sure it was Middle Eastern.

"You do not know us, Professor, but, because of your work, we know you, and that's the way our relationship will stay." The dark figure stood silently for a few seconds before continuing. "Surely, Professor, you of all people must realise that no matter what mankind comes up with to try and prevent the Arctic, or its glaciers from melting, it won't be able to. Global warming is unstoppable; it's a natural process; a cyclic process the Earth has gone through for eons. So, we will save you the trouble, of trying to prevent, what is unpreventable. Luckily, you both seem to enjoy working in cold climates, so you will enjoy your last few hours in here. Au revoir."

The men turned and left through the facility door. Twenty seconds later the door slid shut with a hiss, its seals operating as designed, locking in the freezing air. Trimaud looked up to the electronic temperature monitor above the door as the red digits flashed to minus two degrees Celsius and seconds later minus three. He knew it was only a matter of time before they would all freeze to death.

CHAPTER 30

OUTSIDE THE ARCTIC test tank, Faric pulled a canister from his small shoulder pack and sprayed the liquid contents onto the door entry control-pad. The hydrochloric acid burnt into the door opening mechanism, wrecking the entry panel.

Gomez pulled an axe from the wall, and walked over to a bank of computers, bringing the axe down on them, smashing them to pieces. The monitors sparked and blinked off. He then raised the axe and struck the interconnecting pipe-work, rupturing it in several places. He threw the axe into what appeared to be a large central water tank, laughed, and followed Faric through the laboratory and back out the main door, which self-locked behind them.

They quietly walked out into the expansive courtyard, slipping through the narrow opening between the wall and perimeter gate. The spotlight above the wooden hut blinked on as they walked under its sensor range, bathing the hut and surrounding area in light. Gomez went into the hut, took the chauffeur's severed hand out of the pull-string bag he was carrying and held it against the palm reader. The graphite reader lit up and the heavy steel door closed with a loud clunk. He walked outside and removed his balaclava. Faric did likewise, and they gave each other a satisfactory nod, before jogging down the dirt track in darkness towards the hidden Citroen, Gomez lighting their path ahead with a small penlight.

Two kilometres away, the headlights of vehicles travelling along the ring-road punched through the night sky like World

War II searchlights.

Faric jumped into the rented flat-bed truck and drove the short distance to the outcrop of bushes where the Citroen had been hidden a few days earlier. Gomez directed him with the penlight and connected the truck's winch hook to the back of the hidden vehicle.

Faric pulled the Citroen out of the foliage and up onto the flat-bed. Gomez secured it, tossed in the bag containing the chauffeur's severed hand and got back into the truck. They drove slowly along the track and headed for a small village on the outskirts of Paris, some five kilometres away.

They passed through the sleepy village of St-Azure, found the sign they had been searching for and turned off into the entrance of the breakers yard. The industrial area was quiet, the businesses closed. Gomez stepped out of the cab and walked over to the main entrance gate and cut through the heavy duty chain securing the old rusted gate with a pair of bolt cutters. The chain and heavy padlock fell to the ground with a thud.

Faric drove into the yard, spotted the yellow compactor machine and headed for it. Mangled car and van parts lay strewn all over the ground; the automobile equivalent of a graveyard. He searched for a ramp, and found it next to the huge steel compactor, and reversed the truck up the slope, bringing it to a stop close to the edge. He flicked a switch on the dashboard, and the truck's flatbed rose into the air. The Citroen on the back creaked, before gravity slowly pulled it off the truck and into the jaws of the compactor below.

Faric stepped out of the vehicle and looked over the side. Very good, he thought. The remains of the driver's body would be indistinguishable from the oil and hydraulic fluid mix sloshing around at the bottom of the mechanical crushing machine.

He drove off the ramp and back through the main gates,

where Gomez was waiting for him. He secured them once again and jumped back in the truck.

Five minutes later they were heading toward the truck-hire company, located some ten kilometres from the small private airfield they were heading for. Faric pulled into the rental company's car park, and they both got out and locked the vehicle. They then drove Gomez's BMW the remaining two kilometres to a small, officially disused, airfield where *NewSaudOil Corp's* Gulfstream 650 jet was waiting on the dimly lit runway.

Faric and Gomez boarded the aircraft and sank back into the soft leather seats of the jet's luxurious interior. Within minutes, the aircraft was taxiing down the short runway.

Faric poured himself and Gomez a glass of sixteen year-old malt whisky. "Good work, my friend," he finally said, holding up his cut-glass crystal tumbler. "Now that Professor Trimaud and Robert Spire are out of the picture, we can continue our work without further interruption."

"To our success," Gomez said.

They sipped their whisky as the jet took off, and headed in a south easterly direction, taking a route across France and on to Saudi Arabia.

CHAPTER 31

SPIRE'S EYES FELT like they were stuck together with invisible glue as he attempted to open them. The back of his head was throbbing and his vision blurred. Focusing, he realised he was tied up and lying on his side on a very cold surface, looking straight at the edge of the Arctic test tank.

He started to shiver as the blood slowly crept back into his aching limbs and rolled onto his back, looking around the test facility, his eyes slowly adjusting to the dim light. As he stared at the glistening walls of the Arctic simulator facility, a red blur distracted him. His vision now clear, he realised he was looking at the red digits of the temperature display above the door, which was showing – 8 C.

"Shit!" he cursed, his breath condensing into white mist. He craned his neck and saw Dr. Bonnet sitting motionless over to his right, tied to a lab chair. Trimaud was a short distance from her; his head slumped on his chest, his ankles tethered to an identical chair.

Spire rolled himself toward Trimaud, his skin freezing as he inched his way across the concrete floor. He knocked into Trimaud's chair in an attempt to nudge him awake, but he remained motionless. On the third attempt, the professor slowly raised his head.

"Thank God," Spire said, sighing in relief. "What the hell happened here, Francois, are you OK?" Realising his friend had been gagged; he sat up and managed to get onto his knees and turned his back towards him so that his tied hands were now level with Trimaud's head; then using his fingers, he pulled the gag from his friend's mouth.

Trimaud groaned, as he inhaled a few deep breaths of cold air. "Robert, w…we were attacked; you were hit on the head, and we were dragged in here. We will freeze to death if we don't get out soon. This facility can simulate temperatures down to minus forty degrees Celsius," Trimaud spluttered.

"How the hell do we get out, Francois? Tell me how to stop the temperature dropping."

"M…Mari has the code," Trimaud said, through chattering teeth.

Spire shuffled over to Dr. Bonnet. Her gag had fallen away from her mouth and was now hanging loosely around her neck. He knocked her chair with his shoulder, causing it to jerk back against the edge of the test tank. It was enough to wake her. "Ro…Robert?" she whispered, slowly opening her eyes.

"Yes Mari, it's me. Listen, we're locked in the test facility. I need you to tell me the exit code so we can get out."

She closed her eyes again.

"*The code Mari, I need the code,*" Spire repeated.

In a barely audible voice she relayed the four digit code to him. "Two-Zero-One-Two."

Spire crawled over to the test tank, positioned his back against it, and pushed hard with his legs, raising himself to his feet. He then jumped over to the control-pad situated near the door and lifted his tied hands level with the key pad, and slowly punched in the first three numbers of the code using the knuckle of his right forefinger, turning each time in order to check he'd entered the digits correctly. Glancing up, he noted that the temperature had dropped further. The thermostat was now displaying - 11 C.

Positioned over the pad again, he punched in the fourth digit and waited; his hands now completely numb. A few seconds passed, and then a hydraulic hissing sound emanated from the door, followed by four clicks…

"Thank God," Spire whispered.

And then…silence.

The door had failed to open.

"Shit!" Spire cursed, checking the panel again to make sure he'd entered the correct numbers. 2-0-1-2 was displayed on the control-pad; the code *was* correct. He frantically punched the digits into the pad again - the hydraulics hissed, but again the door failed to open.

Spire slumped to the floor, exhausted and frozen, finding it difficult to concentrate any longer. He wondered if he was about to pass out. His thoughts were barely forming, just a scramble of images coursing around his head. He craned his neck to check the temperature above the door, the red digits now displayed – 15 C.

Feeling his life-force draining away, all he felt like doing was sleeping. As he closed his eyes, an image of himself standing in a desolate Arctic landscape came to him; Professor Trimaud appeared through the swirling snow with a smile on his face, holding a test tube in one hand and a Bunsen burner in the other. He spoke in an excited tone, as if he had just solved a theory he had been working on, "*Fire, ice and brimstone, mon ami. Fire, ice and brimstone,*" he repeated, over and over.

Spire opened his eyes, suddenly recalling the gift Kim had given him in the office a few weeks earlier; *the lighter. Am I dreaming? Where have I put it?* He asked himself. Tensing his muscles, he rolled onto his side to see if he could feel a bulge or something to indicate the presence of the lighter in his jacket pocket; he couldn't. Kneeling in a praying position, he jerked his upper body, whilst keeping his shoulders and torso pointing toward the ground. On the fourth attempt he heard a metallic clunk. Glistening on the frosty floor underneath him was the silver lighter Kim had given him.

He sat upright and felt around on the floor behind him, trying to grab the lighter with his frozen fingers. He picked it up and tried to ignite it, but it slipped from his grip. He picked it up and tried again, this time managing to push the button down. The powerful wind-proof flame ignited, its roar resonating around the confined space. Spire expelled a chest-full of air, relieved to see the flickering red and orange glow of the flame bouncing off the walls within the dark facility. Angling the lighter away from his back, he burnt through the ropes tying his wrists together, and then yanked his arms forward. The smouldering ropes snapped and fell to the floor.

He quickly removed his jacket and set it alight, then burnt through the ropes tying his ankles together. Feeling slightly better, he moved over to Trimaud and Dr. Bonnet who were now slumped in their chairs, motionless. He removed the gags from around their necks, throwing the black cotton material on top of his smouldering jacket. He looked around the freezing lab, and noticed a temperature conversion chart on the wall, which he ripped down and threw on the fire. He also found the wooden stick that Dr. Bonnet had used to dip into the *Blankoplankton* and tossed it onto the burning material.

With the fire now burning away and warming the freezing room, he wheeled his friends towards the middle of the room and the glowing fire and untied their hands from the chairs.

He placed his own hands over the flames to warm them up, and looked around the facility again, and spotted a small wooden table in the far corner, which he hadn't noticed before. He walked over, picked it up, and smashed it against the side of the Arctic test tank. The table broke into five or six individual pieces of timber which slid across the frozen surface of the tank. He jumped up onto the frozen surface and carefully collected the pieces and threw them on the fire.

The tinder started to crack and pop as it burned, bathing the whole facility in an orange glow as the flames danced up from the burning material.

Dr. Bonnet was the first to come around. She glanced at the fire, then towards Spire, her face glowing red from the flames. "H... how did you do that?" she whispered.

"We're going to be fine, Mari, I promise. The heat and the smoke from the fire should set the alarm off and release the door-lock mechanism."

Trimaud then opened his eyes. "What's on fire?" he spluttered.

"Don't worry. I'm going to get us out of here," Spire said, relieved that his friends were still alive.

"Thank God," Trimaud stuttered, the colour slowly returning to his face.

Sure enough, the sound of a fire alarm could just about be heard ringing in the main lab outside. The temperature had also increased markedly, the readout above the door now displaying -2 C.

As they all sat warming themselves by the fire, a metallic clunk echoed around the room, followed by a hiss of air. The test-lab door then slid open, causing a veneer of ice that had formed on the inside surface to dislodge and shatter on the floor like a sheet of glass, just missing them by inches.

Spire helped Dr. Bonnet and Trimaud out of the facility into the small ante room, and then through the second door into the main laboratory. He felt the warm air on his skin as he stepped out, but the fire alarm system was deafening. Puddles of water had formed on the tiled floor, fed by the gushing sprinklers above. "Where's the alarm stop button?" he shouted, running his hands through his soaked hair.

"Over in the corner, behind the steel pillar," Dr. Bonnet replied, pointing.

Spire cautiously walked over and found a large lever and yanked it upwards. The emergency lighting blinked off, the sprinklers stopped, and the alarm fell silent. He walked back over to the computer terminal where Trimaud and Dr. Bonnet were sitting. Trimaud's forehead was bloodstained, his suit drenched. Dr. Bonnet's face was still blackened from smudged mascara, her soaked evening dress clung to her like black cling-film. He found the three parka jackets that they had worn earlier and handed one to Trimaud, then placed the other around Dr. Bonnet, who was shivering uncontrollably. "Here, these should help until the medics arrive," he said.

"At least we're still alive, thanks to you, Robert," Dr. Bonnet said, through chattering teeth.

"Now I really could do with that Champagne!" Trimaud joked.

"I'm sure Pierre placed it on ice. Come on, let's get the hell out of here," Spire said, helping them both to their feet.

A door creaked from the direction of the ante-room, startling them all. A thudding sound from the front of the lab became louder. "What the hell happened here?" Pierre Girard shouted, as he ran over to the three of them.

"You just scared the life out of us, Pierre," Trimaud said. "Come on, help us out, you're not going to believe what happened here."

The four of them left the lab and walked out into the dark, quiet courtyard. Through the open perimeter gate in the distance Spire could see red flashing lights, then, the sound of sirens became audible.

"We're going to have some explaining to do here," Trimaud said, as they walked toward the gate.

Spire looked at him. "Let's hope no serious damage was done eh?"

"We should be fine. The water will have wrecked the

computers, but the data is all backed up, and the main equipment is water-proof. We should be back in business in a fortnight," Trimaud replied, winking.

As they walked through the perimeter gate, the first of three ambulances pulled up, and a paramedic jumped out, ran over to them with a pile of thermal blankets, handing one to each of them. "Les couvertures thermiques, les ont mis dessus," he said.

"Thermal blankets to warm us up," Trimaud translated.

The paramedic then helped each of them into the back of the waiting ambulance.

As the ambulance pulled off, Spire looked out of the small square window in the back of the vehicle, just as the police started to arrive, sirens blazing. He slumped onto the small soft bed, suddenly feeling exhausted. The ambulance moved hastily back through the fields surrounding the complex. Through the small window, Spire could see the ambulance's flashing light-bar illuminate the surrounding dark woodland with streaks of red and blue light.

Thank God for Kim's lighter, he thought, as exhaustion got the better of him and dragged him off to sleep.

CHAPTER 32

MONDAY MORNING WAS overcast and unusually humid for May. Inspector Lance Johnson sat down at his desk and cleared away two empty plastic coffee cups from the evening before. As he powered up his computer, the phone rang. It was Marjorie on the main switchboard. "Morning Inspector, there's a Lieutenant-Colonel Luc Bertrand from the Fifteenth Arrondissement police station in Paris holding; he asked to speak to you."

"French police, for me?"

"That's what he said."

Johnson pressed the flashing red button on the phone. "Hello, Inspector Lance Johnson speaking," he said.

Monsieur Bertrand introduced himself in a heavy French accent, confirming that the reason for his call was because of a minor incident having taken place the previous night involving a UK citizen.

Johnson cleared his throat. "A minor incident?"

"Does the name Robert Spire mean anything to you?" Bertrand asked.

"Doesn't ring any bells," Johnson replied, somewhat puzzled.

"How about Dr. Dale Stanton?"

"*Dr. Stanton?* Yes, how do *you* know about Dr. Stanton?"

"Well, Monsieur Spire, and two of our climatologists are currently at the Saint-Pierre Hospital here in Paris, recovering from their ordeal last night."

"Ordeal?" Johnson repeated, even more confused.

"Oui. I have briefly spoken to Professor Trimaud who tells me that Monsieur Spire happens to be an environmental lawyer, who is over here visiting him. I understand they are friends. Anyway, my point of calling you is to tell you that the incident may have something to do with the death of Dr. Dale Stanton, in London, some weeks back." He hesitated. "I don't wish to discuss this any further over the phone. Perhaps you might want to take a trip over here to speak to Monsieur Spire personally. He's being kept in hospital until tomorrow morning, but after that he's free to go, naturally."

"Um, yes, of course. Sorry Monsieur Bertrand, your call has caught me somewhat off-guard. What makes you think this might have something to do with the death of Dr. Stanton?" Johnson asked.

"We have spoken briefly with Professor Trimaud, and what he has told us is very...well, intriguing. Like I said, it's best I don't discuss it over the telephone. If you can get here, before tomorrow, morning you can speak with Spire yourself."

Lieutenant Bertrand gave Johnson directions to the 15th Arrondissement Station, and arranged to meet him tomorrow afternoon, then ended the call.

Johnson put the phone down. "Peter's never going to believe this," he mumbled to himself, as stood up to get a coffee.

Spire opened his eyes and raised his head, which felt like a lead weight. He looked over at the bedside table; a digital clock displayed 9:15 A.M. The events of the night before then came flooding back, and he suddenly realised Angela was expecting him home around lunchtime. *Shit*, he thought, as he placed his head back down on the pillow, just as a nurse entered with a cup of tea for him. "Bonjour, Monsieur Spire. Comment allez-vous. How are you today?" she asked.

Spire watched the petit blonde-haired nurse as she walked around his bed, straightening the sheets as she did.

"Bonjour. I've felt better," Spire replied, rubbing his head in a futile attempt to get rid of his pounding headache.

"Oui, I am sure! You are very lucky. I am told you were exposed to temperatures of minus fifteen Celsius. Any longer in those conditions and you would be dead, for sure."

Spire rubbed his eyes, "Jeez, I guess we are lucky. How are my friends?"

"They are both fine, sleeping next door."

Spire propped himself up against his pillow, the action making him feel instantly dizzy. "What time can I get out of here?"

"You all need to be kept in for a further twenty-four hours, just to be on the safe side, so hopefully sometime tomorrow."

"You're joking! I need to get back to the UK today," Spire said, the sound of his own voice exacerbating his headache.

"Mr. Spire, I don't joke with you. I'm sure you will be well enough to travel tomorrow, until then, you need to rest. You are lucky to be alive. Now drink your tea and take your medication please. Dr. Sergey will be in to see you in a little while." The nurse flashed a brief smile at Spire and left the room.

Spire sipped his tea, and swallowed one of the tablets the nurse had given him, and closed his eyes, hoping for the throbbing in his head to subside.

He slept for a while, waking to the sound of muffled voices talking in French. He opened his eyes to see a figure standing over him. The sterile white walls of the comfortable hospital room quickly brought him back to his senses. His head was still throbbing, but it now just felt like a mild hangover.

"Ah, bonjour, Mr. Spire, welcome back to the land of the

living. My name is Dr. Anton Sergey. How are you feeling now?" the man asked.

Spire opened his eyes wider. A tall, slim man, clean cut with short dark hair and wearing standard doctors whites was stooped over him, flanked either side, by two attractive female junior doctors. "A little better now thanks," he said sleepily, propping himself up. "My head is still throbbing a little."

"Good, you're a lucky man. Just lean forward for me please would you, Mr. Spire."

Spire moved forward, allowing Dr. Sergey to place the end of the stethoscope over various parts of his back and abdomen. "Everything sound OK in there, doctor?" he asked.

"Everything's fine, but I'm not surprised your head still aches. You received a serious knock to the back of it from a blunt instrument - and you almost froze to death. Had you and your two friends been locked in that cold room any longer, you would have all lapsed into stage four hypothermia, and you'd all be lying in the morgue instead of in here. You managed to get out just in time. Lucky for you, you're a fit guy, and should be back to normal in no time," Dr. Sergey said, giving a reassuring smile.

"I'm grateful for all you have done," Spire said, pushing himself up further on his pillow.

The two female doctors smiled in response to his comments.

"Is there anything you need, some more tea or coffee perhaps?" Dr. Sergey asked.

"A strong black coffee would be great, thanks. Oh, and a telephone. I need to call my wife in the UK," Spire said, glancing at the clock. "She's expecting me back today."

"Of course. Oh, one more thing, I have been advised that a Lieutenant Bertrand of the French Police is coming in to see you and your colleagues this afternoon. I have told him he cannot stay more than one hour, if he does, he'll have me to answer to. He just wants to ask you a few questions, in view of what happened last night."

Spire sighed. "I guessed as much."

Dr. Sergey rolled up his stethoscope and placed it in his pocket. "No need to be concerned. Anyway, the important thing is you'll be fine. One more night's rest and you should be ready to leave in the morning. In the meantime, I'll make sure you get a decent cup of coffee…and a phone."

"Thank you, Doctor," Spire said.

The two assistants smiled again, and followed Dr. Sergey out of the room.

There's no way I can stay in here another night, Spire thought, concerned at what he would say to Angela if he did.

Twenty minutes later, the petite blonde nurse came back into his room with a pot of coffee and a small plate of biscuits. She took a cordless phone out from the pocket of her gown and handed it to him. "Doctor's orders," she said, with a smile, as she turned and left the room.

Detectives Johnson and Smith walked toward the metro station through the Gare Du Norde, having just disembarked the Eurostar from London. They boarded the Metro Line for the Port de Versailles Station, which would take them to the 15th Arrondissement, a short walk away from the police station where they were due to meet Colonel-Lieutenant Luc Bertrand.

The grey quarry-stone building which housed the police station was situated across the road from a small park, on the left bank of the Seine, a few minutes walk from the metro stop. Upon arrival, Johnson and Smith were greeted by a casually dressed, dark-haired man, wearing a blue open collared shirt. To Johnson, his square jaw and neatly trimmed moustache gave him the appearance of a young Robert Shaw.

"Ah, gentlemen, very good of you to come all this way, at such short notice," Lieutenant Bertrand said, as he proffered his hand to both of them.

"No problem," Johnson said, nodding. "This is Sergeant Peter Smith, my colleague; he assisted me on the Stanton case."

Bertrand ushered them into a side office and offered them seats around a drink-stained wooden desk. As they sat down, Johnson asked, "So, Lieutenant, do you mind telling us what the hell is going on here?"

"Yes, of course, let me explain. My department received an urgent call from the fire department around nine P.M Sunday evening to advise us that the Sancerre Research Facility - a high tech laboratory on the outskirts of the city - was on fire. Luckily, it wasn't, but the fire department responded to an emergency call after the alarm system had been triggered. When they arrived, your English friend Monsieur Spire and two of our climatologists were found, soaked and freezing. They had been locked in an Arctic simulator facility and were seconds away from freezing to death."

Johnson looked at Smith and frowned. "Freezing to death?" he repeated.

"Oui. I don't know much more than that, I'm afraid. The laboratory, as I said, is government owned, and used for developing and testing vaccines. It seems Spire was granted clearance to witness one of the experiments taking place there, but we're all somewhat in the dark about it. Professor Trimaud, the French climatologist involved in the project, obtained top level clearance for Monsieur Spire a few days ago. He has done absolutely nothing wrong, I might add. Professor Trimaud mentioned they were 'attacked,' at the facility; said it might be connected with the deaths of UK scientist Dr. Stanton and a Dr. Jack Bannister, over in the USA."

Johnson digested what had just been said in silence. "Dr Bannister? *Who is he?*" he finally asked.

"Well, I have made some inquiries, and it seems Dr. Jack Bannister, a US climatologist, dropped dead of a suspected heart attack in San Francisco two weeks ago."

"Really? That's news to us," Smith said.

Bertrand looked at Johnson. "Can you enlighten me on your investigations into the death of Dr. Dale Stanton?"

Johnson told Bertrand what he knew about the death of Dr. Stanton and the results of the official post-mortem. "We have closed our file; his death was put down to misadventure - an accidental nicotine overdose. I must admit though, the news of a second climatologist dying in San Francisco, whilst probably just coincidence, is a little odd."

"Oui, it might be worthwhile following the matter up with our American counterparts. Whether last night's event is connected remains to be seen. Anyway, mon ami, let's get over to the hospital to have a chat with our three friends before they are sedated again."

Johnson looked at Smith and shrugged his shoulders. They both stood and followed Bertrand out of the small room.

Spire dialled Angela's number for the fifth time, but didn't get a response. He threw the phone on the bed in frustration. *Where the hell could she be?* A mixture of panic and helplessness crept over him. He looked around the room; in one corner was a chair with small table next to it, a plasma TV was on the wall opposite, and some monitoring equipment on a rail was positioned against the back wall. Over to his right was another chair, on top of which were his neatly folded clothes.

He considered the possibility that something may have happened to Angela, and quickly pushed the thought to the back of his mind. He pulled the stiff white bed clothes back, and slowly swung his legs over the side of the bed. He felt better than he had earlier, but still not entirely back to normal. He removed his thin cotton gown and pulled out the intravenous drip from the back of his hand, grabbed his clothes from the chair, and quickly dressed. He then found a sheet of paper and a pen and scribbled a note for the hospital staff, or the police, if they found it first.

He opened the bedroom door slightly and peered out. Apart from the sound of a phone ringing in the distance, the corridor was quiet. The passage to his right was about twenty metres long, and it opened into a larger area, where he could see lights and a desk. The corridor on the left was much shorter and darker, ending with some double doors marked *Interdit*. Before the doors, the corridor branched off and continued around to the left and out of sight.

He pulled the bedroom door closed behind him and walked to the first room on the right, slowly opened the door and looked inside. On the bed lay Professor Trimaud, monitoring equipment quietly beeping behind him. He quietly slipped into the room and walked over to the bed and gently shook Trimaud who appeared to be sleeping. "Francois, wake up! It's me, Robert."

Trimaud opened his eyes slowly, then wider as he recognised his friend. "Robert, what are you doing here? Did they let you out already, I thought..."

Spire cut him off mid-sentence, explaining that he needed to get home as he was worried about Angela.

"Ok Robert, of course, you go. I haven't seen you. I'll tell the police what we know, which is very little. I won't be able to tell them any details about the experiment, and I'd appreciate it if you kept quiet about it too, for now."

"Of course, Francois, I'll see you soon. Take care, and say

au revoir to Mari for me," he said, slipping silently out of the room. He turned left and headed toward the double doors at the dark end of the corridor.

CHAPTER 33

SPIRE HURRIED ALONG to the end of the corridor and looked around the corner; it was clear. He found himself in a shorter corridor with doors on either side; at the end, another set of double doors led to an adjoining corridor. A sign on each door said *Prive*. He walked past the single doors and was about to go through the large double door, when he looked through the inset square glass pane and saw a nurse walking toward him. It wasn't just any nurse, but the petit blonde-haired nurse who had attended to him earlier.

He quickly turned around and tried the handle to the door on his left, but it was locked. "Shit," he cursed under his breath as he tried the door opposite - also marked *Prive* - just as the nurse walked through the double swing doors. Thankfully the door opened, and he quickly backed into the room beyond.

He turned around to face a group of surgeons, or possibly trainee doctors, all gathered around an operating table, on top of which lay a life-sized human prosthetic model.

The room fell silent as they all looked up at him. "Peux je vous aide?" one of the members of the group asked.

"Excusez-moi!" Spire replied, quickly turning and exiting back into the corridor, which was now empty. He hurried through the double doors in the direction the nurse had come from, out into a larger passage and turned right.

The three police officers walked through the double-glass

entrance doors of the Hospital Saint-Pierre and over to the reception area, situated just to the left of the entrance. Lieutenant Bertrand introduced himself to the receptionist, flashed his badge and asked which rooms Spire, Trimaud and Dr. Bonnet were in.

The receptionist looked over her black rimmed spectacles at the three of them, forcing a brief smile, and pulled a plan out from behind the desk, and marked a route to the rooms and handed it to Bertrand. "Merci," Bertrand said, turning to Johnson and Smith. "This way gentleman, we'll take the lift to the third floor."

The three of them walked around the corner and down the corridor to where the building's four lifts were located, two on each side of the passageway.

Spire hurried down the long corridor, looking for an exit sign. Two doctors walked past, but paid no attention to him. He wondered how long it would be until the nurse alerted staff to his absence. His heart started pounding as he began to semi-jog along the corridor. As he turned the corner he heard the ping of a lift's doors opening; three nurses walked out, together with a workman wearing an orange jump suit carrying a tool-box. They all disappeared down the corridor in the opposite direction.

He walked over to the lift, pressed the button and waited. He watched the lift's floor-level indicators turn green in sequence as the lift rose from the ground floor. The lift arrived and the doors slid open. He went to step in, but stepped out of the way as three men in suits walked out, glancing towards him as they exited. Spire dipped his head and slipped into the waiting lift, certain that the men were policemen.

He let out a sigh of relief as the lift descended to the ground floor. He stepped out and headed straight for the exit, walking out into the afternoon sun. He took a few deep breaths of fresh air, feeling his pulse slow slightly as he turned right and headed down the one-way street, back to the main road.

He found a line of waiting taxis and jumped in one. It was now just after midday, giving him ninety minutes or so to get over to the Gare du Nord station to catch the one-thirty Eurostar back to London.

Lieutenant Bertrand was greeted on the third floor reception desk by Dr. Anton Sergey. He introduced himself and officer's Johnson and Smith, telling the doctor they had come over from the UK to interview Monsieur Robert Spire.

"Welcome," Dr. Sergey said, in almost perfect English. "Your friends all had a good rest last night, and are recovering well, I am pleased to report. There will be no lasting effects from the hypothermia they suffered."

The three detectives looked at each, and then nodded at the doctor.

"Follow me, gentlemen, I'll take you to his room," Dr. Sergey said, walking off towards a set of double doors that led from the reception area. He arrived at Spire's room and knocked on the door three times, before proceeding in. "Your visitors are...Mr. Spire...? Un moment, perhaps he's in the bathroom." Dr. Sergey walked over and knocked on the closed bathroom door. There was no answer. He opened the unlocked door. "Merde, he's gone!"

"You're joking! Could he have gone to the shop or something?" Johnson asked.

"What's that?" Bertrand said, pointing to a note on the pillow.

Johnson picked up the folded piece of paper and read the

note out loud;

Sorry, gentlemen, I wouldn't normally check myself out of hospital, but I need to get home as soon as possible. Enjoy your stay in Paris.

Yours,
Robert Spire.

CHAPTER 34

THE *DEEP QUEST'S* large crane lifted the *Poseidon's* mangled wreckage off her recovery deck to a waiting transporter vehicle. Drake lowered the sub and released the coupling. The hydraulic suspension on the eighteen-wheeled truck sagged, as it took the full weight of the wreck. He then swung the crane-head back toward the *Quest's* recovery bay and released the steel chains and sling. He watched as they fell to the deck below like steel snakes spiralling down through the crane's winch-head, coiling up on the hard surface.

Drake mopped his brow, took a fresh cigar out of its tube and jammed it between his teeth. He shut down the crane, stepped out from the cab, and walked across the gangway onto the dock. He hadn't set foot on solid ground since leaving port over six weeks ago, and it felt good. He stretched and looked over toward the *Blue Anchor*, a small but popular drinking den frequented by off-duty mariners and other local San Diegan dock employees, mainly hookers.

After the time he'd put in, he needed a cold beer. His current contract meant he worked six weeks on, three off, and from this moment he was off duty for the next three weeks, and he intended spending much of that time in as many bars as possible. He took a long pull on his cigar and walked over to the *Blue Anchor*.

The driver of the transporter vehicle drove slowly along the dock road, heading for the NSIDC Underwater Research Facility which was located in Area E, some three miles from the main dock.

NSIDC'S team of marine specialists were assembled and waiting to get started on the investigation, to find the cause of the catastrophic failure of the Mark IV deep-sea class submersible, the newest in their fleet.

The driver pulled up to the main hanger door, stepped down from the cab and unclipped the stabilising struts on each corner of the vehicle, before hydraulically lowering them onto the asphalt. He got back into the truck and elevated the crane, just enough to take the slack from the chains attached to the lifting plate, upon which rested the wreckage of the *Poseidon*. He got out and walked over to the hanger door and pressed the intercom button. "Charlie, it's Mike. I got your sub on the truck, ready for transfer."

There was a faint crackle of static, then a short silence. "Very good, the team will be out in a couple of minutes," a metallic voice replied.

The driver took a *Lucky Strike* from a soft pack and lit it. A few minutes passed, and then a loud clunk came from the hangar's main door which extended almost the entire side of the building. The steel door rolled up toward the roof of the structure, revealing a vast internal space. The driver took one last drag on his cigarette and stepped it out on the floor, as three men walked out to greet him.

"Mike, how you doing, pal?" the short, chubby man asked, greeting him with a handshake. Charlie Goodman was NSIDC's Chief Marine Science Officer, and was responsible for overseeing the investigation of any ocean recovered object.

"I'm good, Charlie. You got yourself one hell of a mangled mess on the back there - best of luck trying to figure out what happened."

"Don't worry; we got a great team, as usual, to give us the answers."

Another group of men walked out alongside a slow moving yellow long-armed forklift truck, which had a large steel plate resting on top of its forks, ready to receive the *Poseidon.*

"Ready when you are Mike," Goodman called, rubbing his hands together.

The driver got back into the cab, powered up the crane and lifted the steel plate holding the Poseidon slowly into the air, hydraulically extending the crane the required distance until the plate carrying the *Poseidon* slid neatly onto the steel plate being held by the forklift truck. With the transfer complete, the forklift slowly reversed back into the hangar.

The truck slowly made its way to section R5, or Recovery Area - Grid Five. Various teams of scientists were gathered around, one set examining an old Spanish galleon, another, a recovered World War II Thames-class submarine. The forklift driver lowered the large steel plate to the floor, reversed and drove off down the sectioned-off vehicular access route running along the length of the hangar.

Charlie Goodman was joined by two of his colleagues, Bert Rogers and Joe Bernstein, both Mark IV deep-sea submersible design engineers, as he walked over to take a cursory look at what was left of the *Poseidon.* "Ok, initial observations gentleman," Goodman said. "Obviously, a catastrophic hull breach, but there are no obvious signs of projectile penetration of any kind, and there doesn't appear to be any evidence of major external hull damage. Rivets around the most vulnerable sections, upon initial glance, look intact, with no sign of failure there either," he added.

Rogers and Bernstein walked around the wreck, studying the *Poseidon's* mid section, which was completely caved in. The double circular housings for the acrylic viewing chambers where the operators sat, were now elongated, and barely recognisable, the pressure having crushed the chambers, forcing the hull inwards. All that was left of the acrylic viewing domes was the rubber seals, still visible around the elongated chamber housings. Both bow and stern sections were more or less intact, not surprisingly, as they were the strongest part of the submersible's hull.

Bernstein walked around the stern, and studied the double propulsion screws, recessed in their protective steel mesh. They looked to be in almost perfect condition. He noticed his reflection in the submersible's bright yellow hull which glowed under the hangar's lighting. Studying the rectangular stern section more closely, he noticed five horizontal grooves which started just above the rear dive planes. He directed his torch onto the area, and noticed a tiny indentation, and what looked like a small hole, which appeared to have punctured the outer hull. "Think I found something," he said to the others, as he scrutinised the damage.

Goodman and Rogers were studying the *Poseidon's* mechanical arms, and were just about to examine the steel rod clamped in the right arm, when they were distracted by Bernstein. They walked around to examine the small indentation he'd found.

"Looks like this could be the smoking gun," Goodman said, looking through a powerful hand held magnifying glass, which revealed a small hole in the outer hull. "May well be the reason for the catastrophe, but the cause still eludes us gentlemen," he said, after studying the puncture mark for a few moments. "Let's have a look at the object clamped in her arm. I think I know what it is, I just want your view," he said to his colleagues, as they walked back around to the bow.

Bernstein and Rogers inspected the four foot long steel shaft, clamped vertically in *Poseidon's* mechanical arm. A section had sheared off at a forty-five degree angle. "Some kind of dummy projectile, from a training exercise perhaps?" Rogers suggested, looking slightly puzzled.

"It's a drill-collar bit," Bernstein said, matter-of-factly.

"How can you be so sure?" Goodman asked, a slight grin spreading across his chubby cheeks.

"I spent two summers, many moons ago, on a rig out in Baja California. Saw hundreds of them. The diamond-carbide head has sheared off the top here. The collar would have been about three metres long. My guess is that it was either manufactured in China or here in the US. I suggest we ask our friends over at Vortex, they might know."

"Who is Vortex?" Rogers asked.

"Only one of the largest drill-bit producers in the world, based over in Houston," Bernstein said.

"Ah! Yep, they might just know," Rogers said, feeling outclassed by his colleague's knowledge of the oil industry.

"We can also run some tests on it, spectrum analysis, that sort of thing, may help us come up with a country of origin, perhaps even a manufacturer?" Bernstein added.

"Very good, gentlemen," Goodman said, after he was sure Bernstein had finished. "Let's get the spectrometer and X-ray equipment over, get her photographed inside and out, then we can analyse and prepare our initial reports. Meanwhile, we'll release the drill collar and take a closer look at it."

"What do you think the bit was doing in the vicinity of the Crozet islands? There's no oil or gas around there, is there?" Rogers asked.

"Not that I know of," Goodman replied. "The fact it's in such good condition indicates it hadn't been in the ocean for long. If we find out where it was manufactured, we might find out what it was doing there." Goodman slowly shook his head and patted the *Poseidon's* titanium hull as if it was a large sleeping animal. "Whatever happened down there, at least it would have been quick for those poor buggers. Come on, let's go grab a coffee and make a start on some inquiries with Vortex."

Rogers and Bernstein followed Goodman over to a metal stairway in the corner of the hangar. As they ascended the steps to the offices above, Bernstein educated Rogers on the design complexities of the latest generation diamond-carbide drill-bits currently being used in the oil industry.

CHAPTER 35

SPIRE ARRIVED HOME at just after seven P.M. The journey from Paris had taken seven hours, door to door. Ominously, a black cat darted in front of his car as he got out. *I could do without that,* he thought, as he walked wearily up to the front door to let himself in. The security lights blinked on as he approached the house. Just as he was about to insert his key into the lock, the door swung open - it was Angela. She threw her arms around him, and started to sob.

"Honey, what's wrong?" Spire asked, dropping his case and embracing her.

"I've been worried sick about you. I arrived home, after work, to get a telephone call from the police. I've been trying to get hold of you for the last four hours, what the hell happened? What's wrong with your phone?"

Spire sighed, pulling Angela closer to him. "I'm sorry, the battery on my mobile went dead somewhere near Reading, and the charger was in the boot. I didn't stop, as I wanted to get home as soon as possible. Come on, let's get inside and I'll tell you all about the trip."

Angela made a pot of tea, and then sat down at the kitchen table. "What happened over there, Rob?" she asked, wiping smudged mascara from beneath her eyes.

Spire pulled up a chair, sat down and drew a deep breath. He told Angela all about the trip, his visit to the French laboratory, Francois' hospitality, and how everything had been going well - until his visit to the Louvre yesterday.

Angela leaned forward. "My God, he actually attacked you in the loo?" she said, a look of shock on her face.

"Yep, but by the time I finished with him, he probably wished he hadn't."

"But he could have been carrying a knife, Robert, *what then*?"

Spire had made a decision not to tell Angela about the weapon the man had been carrying, for fear of worrying her even more. "I was lucky. He gave me a sore nose, but that was about all," he said. He went on to tell her about being locked in the Arctic test lab, but emphasised it had been an accident, in case she became hysterical.

"My God, Rob, I'm scared, *what next?* First our car gets rammed off the road, and now this. What the hell is going on?"

"Calm down, honey, it's going to be OK. I'm sure the police will be paying me a visit very soon. I'll tell them all I know, then, perhaps you...we, should go and stay with your parents in London for a while, let this whole thing blow over. I need to spend some time down here for work, but I'd feel much better if I knew you were with your folks."

"What about the boutique? I can't just close it."

"Could you get Carla to fill in for you for a while, even if it means only keeping the shop open for three days a week? It'll only be temporary."

"I guess so," Angela said, resigned to the suggestion.

"Whatever's going on, it's serious. I'm convinced the climatologists' deaths *are* linked; how, or why, I just don't know. I'm involved in this thing now, whether I like it or not, and I want to get to the bottom of it. Francois may well be in danger."

The phone rang, making them both jump. "This could be the police," he said, as he picked up the receiver.

"Bonsoir, Robert! How are you feeling mon ami?"

Spire covered the mouthpiece to let Angela know it was Trimaud. "Francois, I'm glad to hear from you. I've just walked in. How the hell are you, my friend?"

"Bon, a little tired, but doing OK."

"And Mari, is she OK?"

"She'll be fine. She's gone to visit her parents in La Baule after I insisted she take the week off, should keep her out of mischief for a while."

Spire detected a smile on the Frenchman's face as he spoke. "Good, so how did the interrogations go after?"

"After they finished cursing you, things went as expected. I cooperated with Monsieur Bertrand naturally. Told him about the events at the Louvre, what I could recall from Sunday night, and brief details about the experiment. He knows he'll need a warrant, and official clearance, if he wants the specifics."

"So, what do we do now Francois?"

"We continue as before. The damage to the lab will be repaired in the next ten days or so. I have prepared a briefing for the Department of the Environment who will then make recommendations to the Arctic Marine Council and the senior scientific team for consideration. If both they and the Canadian government are satisfied, we're in business."

"Do you foresee any problems?"

"I shouldn't think so. The Canadians don't want their coastal waterways used as a highway, which will happen if the Arctic melts. And, all parties have an interest in finding out if the tests work. The local Inuit population might not be too happy as they seem to be enjoying the warming climate up there. It's bringing them all sorts of opportunities they didn't previously have."

"Perhaps, but they'll think differently if the ice vanishes all together and the oil companies decide to move in. I'm sure the polar bears aren't laughing, either!"

"Very true, Robert. Anyway, the main reason for my call is to tell you that the expedition will be getting underway in a little under two months. By the start of July the Arctic ice will have melted sufficiently to allow us good access along the Northwest Passage. A Chinese merchant ship, albeit with ice-breaker assistance, has already passed through this season. We will be joined by two scientists and a technician from the US team, and there will be four of us, including you of course." Trimaud paused for a moment. "I hope you can still come along Robert, it would be a shame for you to miss the field tests, after all that's happened."

"I'll see what I can do Francois. It shouldn't be a problem," he lied.

"Bon. We'll be joining the research vessel *Mercure Blanc* at her home port of Marseilles, and we'll be sailing to Resolute Bay off Cornwallis Island, almost halfway along the Northwest Passage - ice permitting. Don't worry, I will fill you in on all the details, once on board," Trimaud said, unable to hide his enthusiasm.

"Ok Francois, call me if there's any problems; we'll talk soon."

Spire placed the phone down, and smiled at Angela, who had been sitting patiently on the sofa, listening to the conversation. "At least he's Ok. The police will want to ask me a few routine questions, I guess, but that's all. Come on, let's get an early night, we both need one."

The following morning, Spire arrived at his office and pulled into the rear car park, relieved to see it was empty. He entered the office through the back door, and tapped in the entry code on the alarm keypad. *That's odd*, he thought, realising the alarm wasn't set. He quietly ascended the rear stairs and inched the main office door open at the top. He could see the back of Kim's head and shoulders above the rear of her chair, motionless. As he looked at her, he was hit by a flashback of Mari sitting at her desk in the French laboratory. A chill rushed down his spine. "Kim?!" he shouted.

"Oh, bloody hell," Kim screamed, spinning around in her chair. "What the hell are you doing sneaking up on me like that?"

"Sorry about that," Spire said, a wave of relief flowing over him. "I was worried - the alarm wasn't on. After the weekend I've had you'll realise why I'm a bit jittery."

"Tell all," Kim said, wandering into the kitchen to make some coffee.

He waited for her to sit down, and then filled her in on the events of the weekend. She sat there, her facial features alternating between amusement; surprise and finally concern over the space of ten minutes, as Spire recounted his trip. "I'm sure the police will be here shortly," he added.

"Oh God, Rob, I wish I'd never found that damn file now."

"Don't be silly; you know me, I'm not one to back down from a complicated case, especially one involving the environment. If it hadn't been for you finding that file, old Doris would never have instructed me."

"I suppose, but what if whoever attacked you decides to come back?"

"The thought had crossed my mind. Listen, if you want to take time off in the hope that this will blow over, then that's fine. I don't want you worrying."

Kim swivelled her chair back and forth, then shook her head. "No, I'll be fine. Anyway, who would do all your typing if I wasn't here?"

Spire smiled. "What would I do without you, eh?" He stood

up and walked into his office to call Doris, and open the morning's post. Just as he was about to pick up the phone, he saw Kim walk over to the main office door, opening it to two smartly dressed men, whom he recognised from the hospital lift in Paris. He sighed as he placed the phone back down.

He didn't wait for Kim to call him. He walked out of his office and over to the men standing by the door and introduced himself.

"The elusive Mr. Spire," the taller of the two said, as he shook Spire's hand. "Detective Inspector Lance Johnson and this is my colleague Sergeant Peter Smith," he said.

Spire gave a polite smile. "We can talk in my office if you like; it's a bit more private."

"Wherever you like," Johnson replied.

Kim sat back down, raising her eyebrows at Spire before returning to her work.

The detectives followed Spire to his office. Spire sat down and motioned for his guests to take seats in front of him. "Can I get either of you a drink, tea, coffee perhaps?"

"Two coffees would be good, thanks," Johnson said.

Spire called Kim and placed the order. "I guess I owe you both an apology," he said, leaning back in his chair.

"An explanation would be helpful," replied Johnson.

"Ok, the truth is, I felt I had to get back home as soon as possible, in case my wife was in danger. I couldn't reach her on the phone, so naturally I was concerned."

"I see, but why might your wife be in danger Mr. Spire? What's there to be afraid of down here in Oakdale?"

There was a knock on the door, and Kim entered with a tray of cups and a French press full of fresh coffee and placed it on the desk.

Spire poured the coffee, telling the detectives the events of the past two weeks, the reason for his trip to San Francisco, meeting Professor Trimaud, and how he had ended up in Paris on the weekend.

"And you think this entire thing links back to the death of Dr. Stanton in London?"

Spire told them about his involvement with Stanton's will, but not about the terms of his confidential retainer with Doris. "I'd be happy to call my client for authority to discuss the nature of my instructions with you, if you'd like?"

"That can be done in due course," Johnson said, taking a sip of coffee. "Let me get this straight; you're telling us that the car chase down here last week, Dr. Stanton and Dr. Bannister's deaths, and the events in Paris are all linked?" he said, turning to Smith, who had a slight smirk on his face.

"Well, all these events have occurred since I became involved with the administration of Dr. Stanton's estate, but I can't prove anything, of course."

"Do you think we could be dealing with some kind of lunatic environmental group, or something?"

"The thought had crossed my mind, but why go to such lengths? Surely, the research Banister and Stanton were involved in would have benefited the environment, not harmed it."

Johnson was silent for a moment. "Mr. Spire, you must have made some enemies in your time. You've sued some pretty large companies over the years; maybe someone just got pissed off?"

Spire looked at the officers, suppressing his desire to tell them what he thought of the ridiculous theory. "I guess it's possible," he responded with a smile, "but unlikely, in my view. Why would my so called 'enemies' be involved with the deaths of Bannister and Stanton. I had no knowledge of either scientist until my client contacted me following the death of her son."

The detectives looked at each other, appearing to realise he was probably correct. Johnson then reached into his wallet, removed a card, and tossed it across the table toward Spire. "Have you seen this before?"

Spire picked up the black card, recognising it as soon as it landed on the desk. "Actually, my client found the same card in her son's wallet. Where did you find this one?"

"French police teams combed the area around the laboratory. This was found on the ground near to a clump of trees, some two-hundred metres from the dirt track leading to the facility. Not the sort place somebody would be handing out business cards," Smith said, looking at Spire, his eyes narrowing.

"It's very, odd I agree," Spire said, flipping the card over in his fingers, before handing it back. "I've no idea what this card means, or who it belongs to."

"So, what's your take on it all?" Sergeant Smith asked, smugly.

Spire drained his coffee cup. "Well, like I said, at first I thought that it must be some kind of environmental group behind it all, perhaps disgruntled at the scientists work. After the weekend though, I've discounted that theory. Now I have no idea, but I think something sinister is going on."

"Sinister? What exactly do you mean?"

Spire picked up a recent copy of the *Oakdale Metro* from his chair and tossed it across the desk to Johnson. The headline on the front page read:

NORTHWEST ARCTIC PASSAGE BECOMES
NAVIGABLE.

The report told of a Chinese merchant vessel that had managed to navigate the fabled route for the first time this year, with assistance from two Canadian ice-breakers.

Puzzled, Johnson and Smith read the headline, and then looked at Spire, waiting for an explanation.

"There isn't a single day that passes without a story about global warming in the news. *Two* climatologists have just dropped dead under mysterious circumstances, and Professor Trimaud's research lab was sabotaged in Paris on the weekend. Not only that, but I seem to be a target, just because of my legal involvement. These people, whoever they are, seem intent on covering something up. Environmental activists, terrorists, I've no idea, but something is clearly going on."

The look on both detectives' faces suggested they were either out of their depth, or they thought he was crazy, Spire couldn't tell which.

"So we have two suspicious deaths, a road-rage incident and a sabotage attempt, and you're asking us to accept that these events might all be linked to global warming?" Johnson said, laughing.

Spire shrugged his shoulders. "You asked for my opinion."

The detectives stood to leave; Johnson picked up the paper from the desk and looked at Spire. "Do you mind if I keep this?"

"Be my guest."

"Thank you for the interesting theory, but please don't wander too far from the end of a phone, we might need to contact you again," Johnson said.

"No problem," Spire replied, walking the officers to the door.

Kim glanced up from her computer as they walked past.

"Thanks for the coffee, young lady," Johnson said, as he reached the door.

Idiots, Spire thought, as he watched the detectives descend the hall stairs and leave through the back door.

CHAPTER 36

May 7

MONSIEUR CLAUDE DUPONT, the minister in charge of French Environmental Affairs, sat at his desk in the Environmental Ministry building on the Champs Elysees, staring at the manila folder in front of him. He removed the cord securing the recently acquired dossier, marked '*Eyes Only,*' and took out the eight typed A4 sheets of paper, entitled '*L'operation Recogelent.*'

He read the folder's contents detailing the experiment, *Operation Refreeze,* that had been funded by his government at their test facility, on the outskirts of Paris. The report dealt with the recent sabotage, and details of the expedition to be led by their chief climatologist, Professor Francois Trimaud, leaving for the Arctic in six weeks or so. The report confirmed the latest findings of the police investigation, including the search results made against the surveillance images from the Louvre's security cameras. According to the report, all cross-checks against known criminals and terrorists with Interpol, US and UK security service databases had drawn a blank. Whoever these people were, they were off the radar, Dupont surmised.

The success rate for the experiment was estimated to be around sixty-two percent, certainly sufficient to press ahead. The folder also contained a few notes on the rate of Arctic ice loss, together with NSIDC graphs comparing Arctic ice coverage between the years 1980-2011. They showed a clear downward trend. Importantly, a list of 'risk data' had also been prepared, dealing with any potential consequences to the Arctic environment, should the tests fail.

After reading through the report for a second time, Dupont anticipated that his task, when he met with the other members of the Arctic Marine Council or AMC, later that afternoon, would be an easy one. *Surely they would have no hesitation in recommending that the Arctic tests proceed,* he surmised, as he closed the folder.

The council had been set up in 1992 to determine the threat posed by climate change to the Arctic and its environs. Each country, whose borders fringed the Arctic Circle, had a permanent member on the AMC, and each country would have their environmental minister and scientific advisor present at the meeting.

Dupont glanced at his wall clock, which was showing eleven-thirty: Just enough time to finish up the report he had been asked to prepare, on the effects a warmer climate would have on the wine growing region of the Languedoc, Southern France. Vineyard owners wouldn't be happy with the report's findings, when it became known that one in three summers may be so hot that it will result in grapes being roasted on the vine, he considered.

The intercom on his desk buzzed, taking his attention away from the document he was reading. It was Monique, his secretary. "Claude, the Canadian and Russian ministers have arrived, with their scientific advisors. They are a little early, so I have taken them to the stateroom where refreshments are being served."

"Thank you, Monique, you can tell them I will join them shortly. Please send our other guests up when they arrive."

"Very well sir."

Dupont placed the dossier in his brief case, and glanced at himself in the wall mounted mirror. He adjusted his tie, groomed his hair, and checked that his teeth were clean before leaving his office for the stateroom two floors above.

He knew his counterparts well, which meant the meeting should be informal. He entered the room, which was decorated in late Sixteenth-Century French Renaissance style. Oak cabinets carved with characters from Greek mythology lined both sides of the room, with one end adorned with a floor-to-ceiling double book shelf. The centrepiece was a large oval sculptured walnut table, complete with twelve, high-backed comfortable matching chairs. Along the right side of the room, three large floor-to-ceiling windows, framed by thick oak frames and sills, let modest light into the room from the central courtyard outside.

Only two of the stateroom's lights had been turned on, so Dupont flicked the remaining six lights on as he entered. "Bonjour, gentlemen; I know we are all trying to reduce our carbon footprint, but I think we can spare a few more lights for today's meeting," he said, smiling at his guests.

The Canadian and Russian ministers returned the smile, standing to greet him. "Good morning," they both replied. The group all spoke to each other in English, their common language, which made for a variety of different accents resonating around the stateroom.

"I see you are all being looked after," Dupont said, gesturing to the silver tea and coffee pots standing in the middle of the walnut table.

"The coffee tastes exquisite," the Russian minister said, taking another sip from his cup.

The Russian and Canadian scientists, who had been talking together, greeted Dupont, taking it in turn to shake his hand. "Dr. Aidan and Professor Titov, I'm glad you could both make it," Dupont said. He then placed his case on the table and removed his dossier. Copies had been placed around the table, below the place-names of each of the AMC members.

"Sit down and enjoy your coffee gentleman, our Norwegian, Finnish and Dutch guests should be with us shortly." As he spoke, there was a knock on the door, and Monique entered with the three ministers and their respective scientific advisors.

"Ah, excellent, perfect timing, gentlemen, take a seat."

After everyone had greeted each other, the AMC members took their respective places around the table. Only three seats remained empty. Dupont opened his folder, and commenced the meeting. "Thank you all for coming today, at such short notice. I have received apologies on behalf of our American and Icelandic colleagues. Last minute problems meant they couldn't make the meeting, but they have given their approval to the report's recommendations. Professor Trimaud, of course cannot attend either, for obvious reasons. As you all appreciate, we had to bring the meeting forward due to the somewhat urgent nature of the situation, following the attempted sabotage of our laboratory facilities, by, as yet, unknown, assailants."

The ministers nodded solemnly and muttered their concern over the break-in at the French laboratory.

"Luckily, Professor Trimaud and his team were left with no serious injuries, and the experiment has only been delayed by ten days or so. This was mainly because of Professor Trimaud's lawyer friend, Monsieur Robert Spire, I might add. Full details of the attack on the facility, and Monsieur Spire's involvement are contained within the report."

There was a low murmuring in the room as the attendees flicked through the papers in front of them. The Norwegian minister, a tall thin man, wearing octagonal spectacles then spoke up. "It looks as if we owe Mr. Spire a debt of gratitude. He may well have saved Professor Trimaud's life, not to mention the experiment."

"I think we can safely say that gentleman. Mr. Spire will be commended by this council at the appropriate time, once we have a clearer picture of things."

Everyone nodded their heads in agreement at Dupont's suggestion. Dupont then took the council through the salient points of the report, including the risk analysis aspect of the experiment.

Dr. Buskirk, the Dutch science advisor cleared his throat. "You appreciate we represent our Inuit friends here, who's main concern is the potential of the experiment affecting fish and shrimp stocks, if something were to go wrong. What tests have been done to ensure the safety of the Arctic's marine life?"

Dupont turned to Dr. Buskirk. "Professor Trimaud has assured me the silicon 'jackets' used to coat the iron sulphate are inert. Any animals or marine life that ingests the modified plankton shouldn't be harmed or poisoned in any way."

"Very well, that is satisfactory from my point of view; thank you minister."

"What is of greater concern, gentlemen," Dupont continued, "is the increasing number of earthquakes we are recording in the region. It seems that the entire continent of Greenland is destabilizing as the weight of the ice covering it, decreases."

"This is a major concern. Satellites have recorded the fact that the continent is rising, by up to an inch a year around its coastal regions, but there is of course little we can do about it, apart from try and prevent the glaciers and ice from melting any further," Dr. Buskirk added.

Dimitri Madov, the Russian minister looked around the table. "Have we any idea why an attempt was made to sabotage the experiment?" he asked, changing the subject.

"Not really," Dupont answered. "The authorities, in our

country, the UK and the USA are looking into that now. So far, we have no leads. The CIA and MI6 will be working closely together on this, I can assure you."

The Russian minister continued. "If we agree to the experiment proceeding, I assume any agreement does not override the claims made by each member country to its territorial limits, and mineral rights in the Arctic generally?"

"No, minister, subject to the safety recommendations following the Deepwater Horizon disaster being implemented, the existing Arctic Treaty will not be affected by this proposal. The experiment, gentlemen, is purely to establish whether or not we can successfully geoengineer the Arctic Ocean to sequester carbon, and to prevent any further Arctic ice loss."

Dr. Aidan then spoke up. "We all know, gentlemen, the Arctic is at a tipping point, which may have been already reached, God forbid. The Arctic acts as a thermostat for the entire globe, and if it melts, we have no way of knowing how our planet's climate will change," he paused. "We may well not have any requirement for the riches that undoubtedly exist there, because we will be more concerned with the survival of our own species. Our priority *must* be to prevent the Arctic from becoming ice free, for the sake of the entire world."

An ominous silence filled the room. Even the ornate wooden-carved Minotaurs which flanked the Renaissance cabinets appeared to be looking on, taking heed of Dr. Aidan's warning.

Dupont looked around the table at the men. "Your votes please, gentlemen. May I take it that the expedition has the green light?"

The group raised their right arms and nodded in response.

"We have made the right decision. Thank you very much for attending the meeting today. Dinner will be served in the dining room at seven-thirty P.M; I take it you will all be dining?"

The solemnity of the last few minutes of the meeting quickly lifted, as all the members confirmed their presence at dinner, and chatted amongst themselves as they left the stateroom, the serious business of the day having been dealt with.

CHAPTER 37

Saudi Arabia
May 10

FARIC TOSSED A copy of *Le Monde* onto the desk in front of his brother, who was busy studying the computer screens in front of him. "What is it, brother?" Fahim asked, looking up.

"Look at page five."

Fahim opened the paper and quickly thumbed through to the article at the bottom of page five, carrying the headline;

MONTANT ARCTIQUE D'EXPEDITION.

"Arctic expedition proceeds!" Fahim translated. The article confirmed that after a serious setback at the French laboratory, caused by a 'technical problem,' the French led Arctic expedition would be proceeding, as planned, in a matter of weeks.

"I thought you and Gomez had taken care of things. How can this be?" Fahim barked.

"It seems that somehow, the French climatologists managed to escape from the Arctic simulator tank, no doubt with the Englishman's help. We left them for dead, I cannot explain this."

Fahim stared at his brother for a few seconds. "You are right, the Englishman Spire is more tenacious than we thought, and there is no end to the Frenchman's luck."

Fahim slammed the paper down on the desk. "Get hold of Petrovsky and make sure she gets invited on the expedition. Have all contingencies been considered?"

"Yes, brother. Her I.D has been prepared; her credentials confirm her as being a marine biologist technician, graduating from San Diego State University. She will be called upon last minute to cover for a colleague."

"And what about that colleague, how do we ensure she is unable to make the trip?"

"That has been taken care of, brother. The original team member will...be too ill to embark on the voyage to the Arctic."

"Very well; alert our Russian friend and tell her to make immediate arrangements to travel to Marseilles. Make sure nothing goes wrong. This will be our last chance, Faric."

Faric exhaled with a grunt, took the paper from his brother's hands, and walked out of the operations room.

Fahim turned his chair and looked through the large windows to the internal gardens beyond. A technician was repairing one of the sprinklers, near to a cluster of palm trees, which appeared to have failed. As he looked out, he became distracted by a parakeet which had landed on a tree branch just outside the window. The bird moved its head in jerky bursts, as if dancing to a rhythmical jungle beat. Fahim sat, deep in thought, staring at the bird. *How could this lawyer be jeopardising my life's work?*

The brightly coloured bird flew off toward the garden, prompting Fahim to turn his chair back around to look at the monitors in front of him. Apart from this latest news, everything was going well. His team of geologists was now just weeks away from moving the semi-submersible rigs into place at both locations, and importantly, mineral licenses had finally been obtained from both the French and Cape Verde Governments.

He looked at the monitor in front of him, displaying the Crozet field data, and picked up the phone, punching in the number that would connect him to Mustafa, captain of the *Bountiful*.

The monitor told him that the *Bountiful* was positioned two nautical miles off the southern tip of the Crozet Islands. The call connected.

"Fahim, to what do I owe the honour of this call?" Mustafa asked.

"I trust our plans are proceeding as envisaged?"

"Yes, of course, Fahim. Now the Americans have gone, we can make up for lost time. We are currently positioned over the second prospect, and will be ready to commence drilling in about six hours. The first site is spudding in now, and will be ready for the rig to move in shortly. We can move into the third sector in around ninety-six hours from now."

"Good. I trust you will inform me immediately if you have any more unwelcome visitors."

"The only visitors we have, Fahim, are a flock of petrels from the islands, nothing too troublesome. I'm sure they can just smell the oil."

"Let's hope so. I'll check on progress in forty eight hours," Fahim said, placing the phone down.

The Bountiful is certainly worth her weight in gold, he thought, as he stared blankly at the monitors. A state-of-the-art drill ship, which had, at some considerable cost, been painstakingly disguised to look like an old wooden sea-worn fishing boat by the engineering department of *NewSaudOil Corp*. Fahim smiled to himself as he imagined the catch the *Bountiful* would soon be hauling in – *black gold*.

He focused his attention back to the second monitor.

Streaming data, direct from the NSIDC satellite feed ran across the screen. The Arctic was now beginning its summer melt, but it would be the end of September before the full extent of the ice loss was known. The figures on the screen looked promising, certainly on track to equal or beat the record lows set in 2007, when Arctic ice cover reduced to around 4.13 million square kilometres, or 1.59 million square miles. "Interesting," Fahim muttered, as he studied the data-feed for ice thickness. The figures suggested a new record low would be set. The ice was indeed thinning at a rapid rate, leaving the Northwest Passage navigable - even now - with assistance from ice breakers.

Casting his eye to the third monitor, which displayed information on the Atlantic project, he studied the four leads identified at latitude fifteen degrees north and longitude thirty degrees west. This happened to correspond with the location where Dr. Dale Stanton had planned to deploy additional ocean flow monitoring equipment, to expand the *RAPID-WATCH* surveillance of the North Atlantic Current. *Unfortunately for Dr. Stanton, this location was exactly where the new oil fields were located. Anywhere else, and he would still be alive.*

A knock on the door interrupted his thoughts. "Come," Fahim shouted.

A heavily built man entered, wearing standard blue overalls embroidered with the *NewSaudOil Corp* logo on the lapels.

"Ah, Mousaf, come, come. Is this the geologist's report we have been waiting for?" Fahim asked.

"Yes, Fahim, it has just come through. Everything is as expected," Mousaf said, nodding.

Fahim took the report, glanced at it and thanked Mousaf, who turned and left the room. He read the three page report in silence, which confirmed that methane gas had been found in the seabed off the southern and eastern sides of the Crozet

Islands. The report concluded that as long as drilling didn't take place within five hundred metres of the gas vents, it would not have any affect on the natural phenomena. Fahim closed the report, smiled to himself, and input the data into the computer.

Faric walked along one of the interconnecting clear glass corridors back to his office. The sandstone blocks which secured the large glass panels in place were the same colour as the marble floor, which in turn, mirrored the colour of the desert sand below the suspended walkway. It gave anyone walking along the corridor the illusion that they were actually floating above the desert, an unnatural, but calming sensation.

Faric entered his office, closed the door behind him, and sat down at his desk. He opened his laptop, entered the secure area, and started typing;

French/US Arctic expedition is imminent. Commence operation Fonte d'Arctic.

He smiled to himself; he liked the irony of giving the operation a French title. He hesitated before hitting the return key, feeling a pang of guilt, knowing his brother had no knowledge of the plan he was about to set in motion. The Russian assassin, even himself and Gomez had failed to prevent the French scientist from proceeding with his tests. *What if the Russian failed again?* He knew his brother would thank him in time. He hit the return key, and powered down his laptop.

Former Vice Admiral Valentin Dashkov was sitting at his desk, in his make-shift office on the southern edge of the Russian Naval base at Severomorsk on the Kola Peninsula, when the e-mail came through from his Russian contact. Dashkov grinned, as he read the message and drained the last drop of vodka from his tumbler. Having retired from the Russian Navy in 1995, his services were now hired by anyone who needed goods or materials, but usually weapons or drugs, moved discreetly by sea. This time his skills were being bought by a wealthy Russian businessman, he knew only as Zablozky.

His small crew of dependable comrades had been on standby for the operation. He had sailed with them all whilst in the navy, but the money he was now able to offer them, ensured their loyalty once again, only this time not for their country, but to him.

He picked up the phone and called Captain Tabanov on his secure mobile line. "Captain, the mission will be proceeding. Prepare the *Rezky* and gather her crew. I will personally oversee the transfer of the OTMs from the secure warehouse to the ship. We'll be leaving the base in two days, for the Northwest Passage."

"Very well, Admiral, the men are ready and eager to get going. I'll meet you at the dock warehouse, east entrance," Tabanov replied.

With military efficiency, the small, but well paid crew prepared to load the *Rezky*, a Natya - I class minesweeper, with the necessary equipment for their Arctic mission.

CHAPTER 38

June 1

THREE WEEKS HAD passed since the police had visited Spire at his office, and, thankfully, they hadn't been back. He had broken the news to Angela about his intention to join Trimaud on the Arctic trip, and, as expected, her reaction had been less than enthusiastic. She had however, resigned herself to the fact that no matter what, she wouldn't be able to change his mind, so had reluctantly agreed to go and stay with her parents in London until his return. Her best friend, Carla, had also been happy to take over the running of the boutique for a while.

Spire had dealt with all outstanding legal paperwork on the Taunton file, and he was now standing over his bed, throwing the last couple of items he needed for the Arctic trip into his travel case. He'd arranged to spend the night at his in-laws house in London, but had promised Doris he'd stop off to see her on his way, in order to catch up with her before he left for Marseille. Satisfied he had packed all he needed, he headed for the kitchen to make sure everything was turned off. He went to throw half a pint of milk down the sink, when he recalled the neighbourhood fox he'd scared from the garden some three months earlier. *Was it really that long ago?*

He opened the back door, and poured the milk into an old ice-cream container, in case the fox returned, then walked around the cottage one final time to check that everything was secure. Finally, he made sure the security cameras were all working, and then he left for Windsor.

He arrived at Doris' Windsor mansion at a little after two P.M. She ushered him into the lounge, where the usual pot of tea was brewing, along with a plate of biscuits. Doris opened the French doors to let some welcome fresh air into the stuffy lounge, before sitting down in her beige Regency period armchair opposite him.

"Now that Angela is safely with her parents, the police will need to know as soon as possible if there is a link between Dale's death and Dr. Bannister's over in the States," Spire said. "Dr. Bannister's widow has confirmed that the coroner's final report will be given in a matter of days, and I have a feeling it won't be long before the San Francisco Police Department will be treating Bannister's death as murder. It will then only be a matter of time before Dale's case is re-opened."

Doris put down her tea-cup. "I hope so, Robert, that's what I want. I just know that Dale didn't die from simply smoking a packet of cigarettes. I'll be waiting for Inspector Johnson's call."

Spire finished his tea. "Good. Well in that case, I'd better be on my way. I'll try and keep in touch, but all being well; I'll be back in around three weeks. You never know, the police may have even made an arrest by then."

Doris smiled and walked Spire to the door. "Take care, Robert. We'll meet up when you return, and don't forget to send me a bill."

"I'll do that once we decide on a home for Dale's legacy," Spire said, smiling warmly at Doris as he got into the car.

He drove slowly down the long gravel driveway towards the main gates, passing a gardener who was attending a rockery. The gardener stopped and raised his arm at Spire as he drove past. Spire reached the main gate, turned right and headed in the direction of Windsor, calculating he should be able to make it to his in-laws' house within the hour.

After an enjoyable dinner the evening before, Spire got up early the next morning, showered, and left the house before Angela's parents awoke, not wanting a big fuss made over his departure. "Don't speak to anyone, except the police, honey; I'm sure they will be in touch at some point. Just stay here and relax for a while," he said to Angela, as he opened the front door.

"You're the one putting yourself in harm's way, Rob, for what, I just don't know. Please don't do anything stupid. I want you back in one piece, in three weeks time."

"You know me, I'll be fine," he said, before kissing Angela goodbye, and leaving for the waiting taxi.

The flight from London Gatwick to Marseilles-Provence Airport took less than two hours. Spire collected his luggage and walked out of the terminal building into the 25 degree Celsius June sunshine. He put his sunglasses on, found a white Citroen taxi waiting by the curb, and asked to be taken to the Old Port, or Vieux-Port as it was locally known.

The taxi travelled through the city for about ten minutes, before the driver made a right turn down a hill toward the sea. Spire looked out to his right and saw the shimmering blue Mediterranean stretching out in the distance. The car jerked as the driver carelessly clipped the curb as he took another sharp bend.

Spire sensed they were getting close to the port area as they went around a large sweeping left-hand bend, taking them past

Fort Saint-Jean, built by Louis xiv in 1660, which marked the entrance to the old port.

"Where exactly you want?" The driver asked, in broken English.

"The front of the Grand Hotel Beauvau will do," Spire said, leaning forward.

They continued along past numerous pontoons, with endless restaurants, opposite which yachts, cruisers and speed-boats of various shapes and sizes were berthed. They drove further along the port road until a tight right bend took them to the end of the large port inlet. A number of grandiose-looking hotels loomed up on the left side of the road. The driver made a left turn and pulled up abruptly in front of one of them. "L'hôtel est ici," the driver said, getting out of the taxi to help Spire with his luggage.

Spire paid the driver and looked around the bustling harbor. He noticed a large, sleek super-yacht moored right opposite the hotel. The vessel's gleaming bow rising majestically out of the water, the name *Solaris* displayed in silver letters on the side. The French Tricolore was visible on her stern, gently flapping in the light breeze.

After admiring the yacht for a few moments, Spire spotted Trimaud and the rest of his group standing near the entrance of the hotel opposite. He grabbed his suitcase and backpack, and walked over to join them.

"Bonjour, Robert, good to see you, mon ami. How was your journey?"

"Very good, I think the taxi ride here was the worst part!"

"Bon, at least you made it! Come on, let's grab a coffee."

Spire greeted Dr. Bonnet and Dr. Girard, and followed them into the hotel to a quiet area in the bar and they ordered some drinks. "How long will the voyage take, Francois?" Spire asked, once he was seated.

"Well, it's around twenty-two hundred nautical miles, something like that. Cruising at around eighteen to twenty knots, we should get there in around six days, weather permitting."

Spire let out a long whistle. "That's some trip!"

"Then, my friend, we can start our journey along the Northwest Passage."

Spire tried to recall whether he'd packed his sea-sickness tablets as he drank his coffee.

"Tres bien," Trimaud said, once they'd all finished their drinks. "It's time we made our way to the ship, mon ami."

Spire collected his bags, and followed the three of them out onto the hotel's forecourt, crossed the road, and over onto the esplanade that ran around the port. The *Solaris* super yacht rose up out of the water in front of them, gleaming in the June sunshine.

They found the adjacent pontoon, and walked down the wooden jetty toward the end. Spire spotted the bow of a large vessel tethered to the pontoon in front of them. Just above the anchor outlet, the name *Mercure Blanc* was clearly visible. The ship's hull was white for the most part, except for the lower half, which was shiny, unpainted steel. *Probably ice-strengthened*, Spire thought. The vessel's bridge and superstructure were painted sky-blue, and a large crane was positioned on the deck, amidships, which looked capable of hauling almost anything out of the ocean.

As they approached, Spire saw a tall, burly man, dressed in a white shirt and blue trousers talking to another man, who was untying a double set of ropes from the quayside. The ropes disappeared into a hole into the ship's bow. The man in the white shirt had a ruddy complexion and thick 1970s style greying sideburns.

Trimaud walked up to him. "Jacques, how are you, mon

ami? Let me introduce my colleagues, Dr.'s Mari Bonnet and Pierre Girard, and not forgetting my new friend, environmental lawyer, Mr. Robert Spire." Trimaud turned around. "Everyone, this is Captain Jacques Deville."

Spire took Captain Deville's large outstretched hand. "Good to have you on board," Deville boomed, crushing Spire's hand with his powerful grip. "Please go aboard, the rest of the team are already settling in – I'll be with you in a short while," he said in a deep, throaty French accent.

Spire followed the three scientists up the gangplank and onto the deck of the ship, from where there was a great view of the bustling port. He shielded his eyes from the sunlight glinting off the white hulls of the yachts in the marina, as he followed the French group through a side door into the superstructure.

They entered a cabin; a sign on the door confirmed it was the Storage and Laundry Room. A laminated plan of the ship was bolted to the corridor wall opposite, which revealed there were at least six decks; four above their current level and two below. A steel stairway off the corridor led upwards to the other decks. In the storage room, boxes of tinned and other foodstuffs were stacked in one corner. Arctic weather gear, including black parka jackets, boots, goggles and even skis lay on wooden shelving units running along the left-hand side of the cabin.

"Phew, it stinks of oil in here," Dr. Bonnet said, screwing up her face. "I hope our luggage won't be left in here for too long?"

"I'm sure someone will collect it once we are in our cabins. This is where the captain asked us to leave our things, and sign ourselves in using that logbook over there," Trimaud said, pointing out a tattered, old, red leather book, lying on a dark-wooden desk near to the boxes of food.

They all left their bags in one corner, and signed in. The entries in the log confirmed that there were already three other passengers on board. "So, how do you know Deville?" Spire asked, as Trimaud signed himself in.

"This will be the third time I've sailed with him. He's a good man, hard as nails and very brave. He also takes safety on board very seriously. You'll see what I mean when he gives the departure briefing."

Just as he finished talking, Captain Deville appeared in the doorway. "I can see you are all eager to find a more comfortable cabin. Come on, I'll introduce you to the rest of the expedition crew," he boomed.

They followed Deville up two flights of steel steps and into another narrow corridor, entering a much larger cabin, marked Library/Conference Room. The cabin's walls and ceiling were tastefully decorated in stained stripped wood, and the walls punctuated with large round stainless steel-rimmed portholes. Five large leather sofas filled the cabin, complete with coffee tables, and a large plasma television, which was fixed to the cabin's back wall. A set of double book cases, filled with novels and scientific journals stood at the end of the rectangular shaped cabin. The floor was overlaid with stained wooden floorboards, giving the cabin a feel of being in the lounge of an up-market boutique hotel.

"Wow!" Spire said, as he entered.

"C'est bon, eh? We had a refit only a few months ago," Deville commented, as they all walked in.

Three fellow passengers, who were sitting down chatting, stood to greet them as they entered the cabin. A short, chubby man, with a pencil wedged behind his ear was the first to greet Trimaud. "Professor, damn good to see you, and I see you've brought your team along," he said, in a soft American accent.

"Dr. Vernon Mathews, It has been a good while, mon ami.

You haven't changed a bit."

"Well, I'm not so sure about that," he replied, patting his stomach. "This continues to grow! Did you ever meet my colleague Dr. Ruth McBride?"

"I don't believe I have, but I did read your paper on the life-cycles of Zooplankton and Phytoplankton; fascinating," Trimaud said, shaking her hand gently.

"I'd like you to meet Dr. Pierre Girard and Dr. Mari Bonnet, colleagues of mine from UPMC. Without them, this project would never have got off the ground. And, not forgetting my friend, environmental lawyer, Mr. Robert Spire, who's here for the ride," Trimaud said, slapping Spire on the back. "And who is this charming young lady?" Trimaud asked, turning to the third member of the group.

"Ah, last, but not least, this is Dr. Alice Sinclair; she's along for the ride too, acting as Ruth's assistant. She kindly agreed to step in at the last minute in place of Dr. Louise Green. Poor girl suddenly fell ill, so couldn't make the trip. Dr. Sinclair recently graduated with a Marine Science degree from San Diego University. She'll be a great help, I'm sure," Dr. Mathews said, smiling at them all.

Ksenyia smiled at Trimaud. "I've heard a lot about you," she said, shaking his hand. Ksenyia had coloured her hair light brown, and had it pulled back in a pony tail. Her green eyes disguised behind brown contact lenses. She was dressed in dull, old clothes, looking a far cry from her usual self. As hoped, Trimaud clearly didn't recognise her from their last brief meeting in the Paris bar.

Spire introduced himself, keen to get the introductions and formalities over with, in the hope of being able to get a cold beer as soon as possible. "This must be a great trip for you to come along on, even if it was without much notice," he said, shaking her hand.

"Indeed, I'm very lucky. I am very much looking forward to experiencing the Arctic. I hear it's a very dangerous place, Mr. Spire, but also very beautiful."

"Beautiful I like the sound of, Miss Sinclair, dangerous-let's hope not," he said, letting go of her hand. He took a seat next to her as Captain Deville - who had been standing silently in the doorway - pushed away from the door frame and stepped into the cabin.

CHAPTER 39

CAPTAIN JACQUES DEVILLE sat down on a small wooden coffee table facing them all and sucked in a deep breath of air, before addressing them in a gruff voice. "Now that you have all been introduced to each other, I need to say a few words before we depart for the Arctic. Safety on board my vessel is paramount. I don't give a damn about your scientific experiments. If that container out there endangers my ship, I'll jettison it, without a second thought. My job is to get you safely to the drop-off zone, and back here to the port of Marseilles, without incident - understood?"

Spire found he was nodding his head, almost involuntarily, along with most of the rest of the group. A chorus of yes's then followed.

Deville continued the briefing. "Good; so, some information about the vessel which will be your home for the next three weeks. She was built in Saint-Nazaire in 2002, designed for exploration in both the Arctic and Antarctic regions. Her hull is made from double skinned, ice-strengthened steel, capable of penetrating ice up to two metres thick." He punched the palm of his open hand - as if simulating an impact - before continuing. "We wouldn't normally get very far up the Northwest Passage without the strengthened hull, but at this time of year, any ice that remains should be fairly thin. Maximum cruising speed is an impressive twenty-five knots; fast for a vessel of this nature, but we'll be weighed down, en-route, by the ten tonnes of experimental iron sulphate on board.

Once that's offloaded, our return trip should be a little quicker. The *Mercure* has a range of three thousand nautical miles, but we have enough spare fuel on board for the entire round trip. We continue up the Northwest Passage until reaching Resolute Bay off Cornwallis Island, the seeding location. We'll spend one day and night at the site, before returning home. Are there any questions?"

Dr. Winston Mathews spoke up. "What does the weather hold in store for us?"

"It shouldn't bother us on the way up. A low pressure system is expected to move toward Greenland in a week or so, bringing with it some bad weather, but we'll be well on our way back by then," Deville said, his eyes narrowing slightly as he spoke. He continued talking about the vessel's specifications. "The *Mercure* has four laboratories on board; a general scientific lab, a plankton lab, and two smaller biology labs, which you have unrestricted access to. Officer Henri Boucher, who's currently preparing for our departure, will show you all to your staterooms shortly. And don't worry, he's nowhere near as blood-thirsty as his name suggests!" Deville let out a hearty laugh before continuing. "Apart from Officer Boucher, we have two engineers on board, and two cooks, who you will meet later on. There's a plan of the ship on each corridor, near the stairwells and access points." He scratched his right side-burn. "I think that's all you need to know for now. Are there any other questions?"

There was a brief silence before Deville spoke again. "I'll give you a chance to find your cabins and settle in. Once we are out of port, I'll be calling a mandatory lifeboat drill. After that, you can relax and enjoy a drink in the bar upstairs; you'll find it's well stocked."

"Now that sounds like a good idea," Spire piped up, glancing around the cabin.

"I think you'll find something in the bar to suit your tastes, Robert, I usually do," Deville replied, getting up from the coffee table. "Very well, unless there are any more questions, I'll get myself up to the bridge. We depart in fifteen minutes."

As Deville stood up, another man entered the cabin. "Ah! Meet Officer Boucher, he'll show you to your cabins now and make sure your luggage finds its way back to you," Deville said, leaving the cabin.

A balding, somewhat shy looking man in his mid-forties, wearing jeans and a grey polo-neck jumper introduced himself. "Ok everyone, if you'd all like to follow me, I'll take you to your staterooms," he said, smiling nervously.

Spire had a quick look around his twin-berth stateroom, and tossed his newly arrived luggage onto the bed. Already feeling claustrophobic in the confined cabin, he left and made his way up to the deck for some fresh air, and to watch the *Mercure* as it made its way out of port.

Trimaud and Girard were outside chatting on the stern of the ship when he arrived. He walked over to join them. "Is the captain always so curt?" he asked.

"Ah, Captain Deville's abrasiveness often gets mistaken for arrogance, a trait left over from his navy days, no doubt. He's a superb sailor, and a safe one. He might be sixty years old, but he's as fit as a fiddle. Don't worry, Robert; I'm sure you'll get to know him a little better over the next three weeks."

Spire craned his neck and looked up towards the blue sky, letting the sun's rays warm his face. *God, that feels good*, he thought, as he inhaled a deep breath of fresh, sea air.

A metallic grating sound from the front of the ship broke the silence as the anchor was winched in, followed by a low rumble beneath their feet, as the vessel's diesel-electric engines powered up. Spire looked down onto the quay. The man who had been talking to Captain Deville earlier was still standing there, looking on as the *Mercure's* bow thrusters slowly pushed her away from the pontoon. With the ship's bow now facing toward the port's exit, a second low rumble reverberated from below, as the engines powered the large vessel forward. The man on the quay raised his arm, turned and walked back along the pontoon toward the dock.

"Come on, we better go and get ready for the lifeboat drill," Trimaud said.

Spire nodded. "I don't know about you two, but as soon as we've done that, I'll need a cold beer."

"I'm with you there, Robert," Girard said, as they headed back inside.

The *Mercure Blanc* cruised past Fort Saint-Jean and out into the bay of Marseilles, on a course that would take it out to the Balearic Sea, past the island of Mallorca, through the Straits of Gibraltar and into the Atlantic.

CHAPTER 40

San Francisco
June 2

AT SAN FRANCISCO'S Medical Examiner's Office, Dr. Harvey Weinburger M.E pulled the white evidence sheet over the body of Dr. Jack Bannister for the final time. He had just completed a full autopsy and tissue analysis. A few weeks later than he'd hoped, but the results confirmed his initial suspicions of nicotine poisoning. He removed his gloves, overall and gown, washed his hands and walked out of the autopsy suite and down the corridor to his office. He sat down, picked the phone up and keyed in the number for the SFPD, while swivelling his chair 180 degrees to look out of the window to the streets below. His view was of the grey granite Hall of Justice building which housed the Superior Court, the D.A's Offices and a jail. He watched a police car pull up to the curb. An officer got out, dragging a man in handcuffs out of the car and into the building. His gaze was interrupted by an impatient sounding man answering the phone, "Gus Mitchell, SFPD."

"Hey Gus, it's me; Harvey. I just received the toxicology tests on your Dr. Jack Bannister."

"About time, Harv, I'm all ears."

"I'm afraid it looks like nicotine poisoning, odd thing is, the deceased's lungs show no evidence of smoking related damage. Tissue examination confirms Bannister ingested the poison, either in food or drink. Gus, it looks to me like you got a homicide on your hands."

"Are you sure about that, Harv?" Mitchell asked, after a short silence.

"As sure as night follows day; Gus, the man had about sixty milligrams of the stuff in his blood when he died, the equivalent of smoking twenty cigarettes...in one go."

"Poisoned, eh? Thanks for your help, Harv, looks like I got some work to do."

"No problem, Gus, you take it easy," Weinburger said, ending the call.

Mitchell put the phone down and drained his plastic cup of cold coffee. Now for the part he dreaded; telling Dr. Bannister's widow the results of the autopsy, and the fact that they would now be treating her late husband's death as a homicide.

Mitchel called Margaret Bannister and broke the news to her. There was a moment's silence whilst she took in the revelation. "But why would anyone want to kill Jack?" she sobbed. "All he was concerned about was his research, and trying to make the Earth a better place – it doesn't make any sense."

"I'm sorry, Mrs. Bannister, but that's what I need to try and find out. Do you know of anyone who may have wanted to harm your husband, sabotage his work perhaps?"

"No, Jack had no enemies. Have you spoken with the British or French police?"

"No. Why?"

"Well, my husband's Paris-based colleague, Professor Francois Trimaud, had his research laboratory partially destroyed a few weeks ago, and was also attacked. Dr. Stanton, a British climatologist, died in London in similar circumstances to my husband…I assumed you knew about all this?"

Mitchell cleared his throat, "I wasn't aware of those events, Mrs. Bannister, but I'll certainly be checking out all leads."

He took down the French professor's contact details and hung up. After searching the internet for Trimaud's name, he eventually found a link to the French paper *Le Monde,* and a small article under the headline *Montant Arctique D'expedition,* which he translated to read 'Arctic Expedition Proceeds.' The story also mentioned the attack at the French research laboratory.

This is odd, could the deaths be connected? He checked the time, and calculated forward eight hours. It was coming up to nine-thirty A.M in London. He punched in the number for the London Metropolitan Police and was transferred to the main switchboard, before being put through to an officer from the Homicide and Serious Crime Command Unit. After explaining his involvement in the US investigation, the officer checked, but was unable to identify any investigation involving a Dr. Dale Stanton. Mitchell thanked the officer and hung up.

He relaxed back in his chair, picked up the phone and called his assistant two floors below. "Tony, it's me, Gus. Do me a favour and pull up everything we have on a Dr. Jack Bannister, climatologist. He dropped dead on April twenty-fourth at the Ravenbeck Hotel, in Nob Hill. Meet me in my room in say two hours - we got a homicide to work on."

Mitchell had been a homicide detective for just over eight years, and during that time, he'd managed to solve all but one of the eleven homicide cases that had come his way. The only one that had eluded him, involved the murder of a young mother found lying on the sidewalk, near to the entrance of Golden Gate Park. Her throat had been cut from ear to ear. He wouldn't forget that freezing February morning back in 2004 in a hurry.

He pushed the thought of that cold case to the back of his mind and re-focused on the coroner's report, e-mailed through from Harvey Weinburger's office thirty minutes earlier. Perusing the documents in the folder, he jotted down some facts that jumped out from the papers;

Global warming, National Snow and Ice Data Centre, Climatologists, Nicotine, Methane gas, Francois Trimaud, Research lab Paris, Dr. Jack Bannister, Arctic expedition, Dr. Dale Stanton, Robert Spire-UK Lawyer.

He stared at the notes for a while, trying to make sense of the facts. The most obvious place to start was to speak to someone at the National Snow and Ice Data Centre, then make inquiries at the Ravenbeck Hotel, where Bannister collapsed. According to the toxicology report, Bannister would have died within five minutes of ingesting the nicotine, meaning his killer had to have been in the hotel with him.

Inspector Johnson sat in the kitchen of his two-bed flat in Peckham, South London, finishing his breakfast. He wasn't due to go into the station until midday. The morning news came on the radio, and the main story, as usual, was taken up with more bad news coming out of Afghanistan. Two US Apache helicopters on routine patrol had collided, killing all on board. The final news item then caught his attention;

"The UK's Met Office believes that this year could be the hottest so far, eclipsing 2005 which currently holds the record equally with 1998. Scientists point out however that 1998's temperature was boosted by a strong El Nino effect. Increased greenhouse gas levels are believed to be to blame for the rising temperatures, and the trend is expected to continue in the years ahead."

Johnson looked out of the kitchen window. It was the start of a very wet and windy June. *Global warming my ass, how can the scientists say that?* He wondered, as he looked out at the rain bouncing off the rooftops.

He finished his coffee, casually glancing at the *Oakdale Metro* that Spire had given him. *Maybe there is something in what Spire had said?*

He found the number for the San Francisco Coroner's Office in his diary and called from his cordless phone. He was eventually put through to Dr. Weinburger's personal assistant.

A woman picked up. "Inspector Johnson?" she said, in a mildly irritating high pitched voice. "I can confirm that Dr. Weinburger has completed the autopsy, but I must advise you that the matter is now in the hands of the SFPD, so you will need to contact them. Have a good day." The line went dead.

Interesting, Johnson thought, as he searched for the number for the San Francisco Police Department on the internet. He found the website and called the non-emergency number given. He was placed on hold for a while, before a man with a Californian drawl greeted him. "Gus Mitchell, SFPD."

Johnson introduced himself to Mitchell, wasting no time in telling him about his involvement with Dr. Dale Stanton and Robert Spire. "Obviously, I'm keen to know the results of the autopsy, just in case we need to have another look at things our end," Johnson said, listening to the sound of papers being moved around at the other end of the line.

"I'm very pleased you called, Inspector Johnson, I just called you guys, but the officer I spoke to advised me that there was no ongoing investigation," Mitchell said.

"He's right, there isn't, not yet anyway."

"Well, I think that will change, Inspector. As of this

morning, I am investigating the homicide of Dr. Jack Bannister from nicotine poisoning, which shouldn't come as much of a shock to you."

"Are you serious?" Johnson took a deep breath and briefed Gus Mitchell on the Metropolitan Police's involvement in the investigation to date, their inquiries over in France, and the assistance given to them by Robert Spire.

"So, what is Mr. Spire's involvement in all this?" Mitchell asked.

"Spire is an environmental lawyer, seems to have got caught up in everything. He was contacted by Dr. Stanton's mother after she found her son's will, which named him as an executor. Doris Stanton, a widow, was left a considerable sum of money by her late husband, some of which went to her son, hence the will."

"Is there anything suspicious about Spire? I mean, have you considered the possibility that he might be involved in all this?"

"Involved? I don't think so, he seems clean. He's a lawyer for Chrissake. He thinks that the deaths might be linked to some environmental group, possibly trying to suppress information relating to global warming from getting out. I thought it was a bit farfetched myself," Johnson said, glancing again out of the window at the rain, still lashing down outside.

"I think we should run a check on Spire, see if he has any financial motives. What if he plans to close up shop and disappear into the sunset with his client's money? It sure as hell wouldn't be the first time such a thing has happened."

"Well, we hadn't considered Spire a suspect, but you're right, we need to look into that."

"What's the position with the French investigation?" Mitchell asked.

Johnson briefed him of the attack at the Louvre and the

subsequent break-in at the French laboratory. "An Inspector Bertrand is heading up the investigation their end. He's promised to e-mail me the complete Louvre surveillance footage as soon as it's ready. I'll send you a copy when I get it."

Mitchell thanked him and confirmed he'd make contact again in a few days to see where they were in the investigation. He then ended the call.

Johnson put phone down and stared out of the kitchen window. The rain was at last beginning to subside a little. He thought about Mitchell's comments, recalling how Spire had acted oddly by leaving France so quickly. He picked up the newspaper Spire had given him at the office and studied the headline again. *Could there really be something in this global warming hypothesis?*

CHAPTER 41

KIM HAD JUST started typing the last letter on the *Brown* file, when the phone rang. It was Inspector Johnson, asking to speak to her boss. "Morning, Inspector; I'm afraid Robert won't be in for another three weeks, he's with Professor Trimaud on the Arctic expedition. Didn't he mention it to you?"

"No, he didn't!" Johnson replied, sounding surprised. "Your boss certainly gets around. I guess I'll have to wait until he returns. Do you have a mobile number I can contact him on?"

She gave the Inspector Spire's mobile number, and hung up.

Kim finished typing, and placed the *Brown* file back in the cabinet and went to make a coffee. She returned to her desk and occupied herself with an anagram word game from *High-Life* magazine. After completing half of it, she placed the magazine back in her bag. Just as she was about get the next file to work on, she noticed the glossy-black business card from the Stanton file on her desk. She picked it up, reading the name over to herself; *Arc-Bin-Quid-Lo. Could the name on the card be an anagram for something?*

She found a blank sheet of paper and scribbled down all the letters randomly, writing down any words that jumped out at her;

Crab-Liquid-No;

Cad-Bin-Liquor;

Iran-Bloc-Quid.

She stared at the sheet of paper, unable to think of any more combinations. None of the names made any sense. She sent a text to Robert with the results, and then picked up another file and resumed typing.

Spire wandered up to the bar, on the upper deck of the *Mercure Blanc,* to get himself a cold beer. They had now been at sea for thirty-six hours, and would shortly be passing through the Straits of Gibraltar. The next land they would see would be when they reached Southern Greenland, in several days' time. Once through the Straits of Gibraltar and the protected Alboran Sea, the Atlantic would be waiting for them, and Spire suspected it wouldn't be quite so forgiving.

He walked into the bar and sat down on a stool, near to the large porthole, and grabbed a bottle of *Kronenbourg 1664* from the small fridge on the counter. He looked out of the porthole at the Spanish mainland in the distance. The ocean was calm, with just a gentle side-to-side rocking motion as the ship cruised towards the Straits. He thought about Kim at the office and reminded himself to give her, and Angela, a call before they headed out into the Atlantic. Once out in the open ocean he knew that all mobile signals would be lost, and the only means of communication would be with the ship's *Inmarsat* communications phone, an expensive piece of kit to use. As he sipped his beer, he heard voices behind him. He turned to see Dr. Ruth McBride and Dr. Mathews talking in the corridor. "Can I get you guys a drink?" he shouted across the cabin.

"I can see you have *some* use on board!" Dr. Mathews replied, smiling.

"I don't mind playing barman, whilst you lot do all the hard work," Spire retorted.

The two of them entered and sat down at the bar. Spire got them each a gin and tonic. "So, what do you think the chances are of the experiment succeeding?" Spire asked, as he sat back down.

"Chances?" Dr. Mathews said, clearing his throat. "That's a difficult one to call, Robert. The complexities involved in this kind of geoengineering experiment are immense. If the chemicals bonding the silicone jackets, covering the sulphate, detach for any reason, then it's going to fail. We might see a plankton bloom, but if we can't successfully reflect the sun's heat back into space, we won't have any chance of reversing the warming trend currently taking place in the Arctic. The sea ice will continue to melt, further decreasing the albedo effect, which in turn, will cause further warming in the area. God only knows what will happen then. There may also be acceleration in the melting of Greenland's glaciers. If they melt totally, we expect to see a sea level rise of twenty-three feet or so, which will inundate swathes of all continental shores."

Dr. McBride grimaced in agreement, as she sipped her drink.

Spire recalled a paper he'd read on the melting polar ice caps. A twenty-three feet sea level rise was unlikely, but disastrous if it occurred. "Jeez," he replied, taking another gulp of beer. "So what's your role in all this?" he asked Dr. McBride.

"My job is to monitor the effects the iron sulphate has on marine life, once the container's contents have been dropped overboard. We'll place chemical monitoring devices in the ocean to record the spread and size of the plankton bloom, make sure no chemical imbalances occur, and that no sea life is harmed in any way."

Spire shook his head. "You guys sure have a thankless task. It seems to me that if you make the slightest error of judgement, the public will always be quick to side with the sceptics, happy to believe that global warming is a complete myth."

"Well, most of the scientific community agree that anthropogenic global warming is now occurring. But you're right; the difficult task is trying to convince the public. The sceptics out there will find it increasingly difficult to maintain their stance however, as the physical evidence mounts."

"Let's just hope things don't get that bad," Spire said, grabbing another beer.

The ship's P.A system suddenly crackled to life with a burst of static. "Afternoon, good people," Captain Deville's voice boomed. "I hope you all have your sea legs on as we'll shortly be passing through the Straits of Gibraltar and out into the Atlantic. Anyone wanting to make a last call home should do so in the next hour. Dinner will be served at nineteen-hundred hours prompt."

"That told us!" Spire said, as they all got up from their stools.

"Yep, we'd better go and make those calls," Dr. McBride added, smiling.

Spire left them both and headed for the deck, to take in the view as they passed through the Straits of Gibraltar.

Charlie Goodman sat at his desk in his small room overlooking the main hall at NSIDS's Marine Research Facility, in San Diego. He was awaiting delivery of a circuit board for the Ocean-Terrain-Contour-Online-Mapping software, or OTCOM, for the latest generation underwater ROV's, when the phone rang.

"Charlie, it's Dan over at Vortex, I just got the metallurgy results back on that drill collar you sent over a few weeks back. We have an I.D on the manufacturers for you. It's a Chinese company; the name's Xenlanping."

Goodman leaned back in his chair. *No real surprises there.*

He recalled that the Chinese were one of the world's largest manufacturers of drilling equipment. "The name rings a bell; good work, Dan, now I just have to find out who they supplied the part to."

"No need, we managed to get that information too. Spoke to a very helpful clerk, who was even more cooperative when I told him we were about to place an order for fifty of the same drill collars. I said I wanted to speak to their customer directly before we placed the order, seemed to do the trick. That collar you pulled up from the seabed was purchased by a new kid on the block; a private company based in Riyadh, Saudi Arabia, called *NewSaudOil Corp.*"

CHAPTER 42

KSENYIA PERUSED THE science book she had brought with her; Marine Ecology: Processes and Systems, and after updating herself on its contents, closed the thick book and placed it on her bedside table. Earlier, she had carried out a detailed study of the ship, its cabins, communications and basic hydraulic systems, in preparation for the task that lay ahead. First, she needed to get to the bridge to release the locking clamps holding the steel container of experimental sulphate in place. She ran herself a shower and started to prepare for her final mission.

Spire called Angela, catching up briefly with events back home. All was fine. As he went to turn his phone off he found the text from Kim. *Ah, good girl, what have you found?* He scrolled down through the anagrams she'd sent, and in order to give them proper attention, decided to have a look at them after dinner. He turned his phone off, walked into the bathroom, and looked in the mirror. He felt tired; three days of stubble covered his face, and, the modest sun tan he had, gave him a weather-beaten look. He sprayed some aftershave on, and left his cabin.

He made his way to the upper deck and wandered to the stern of the ship. The sun was low in the sky and the *Mercure* had now slowed to around five knots or so. He looked back at the Straits of Gibraltar, some two miles behind them. The coast was dotted with pinpricks of light, which emanated from the numerous hotels and apartments that populated the coastal resorts. Down on the lower, main deck, the massive steel container loomed up. *Could the contents really save the Arctic's ice from melting?* He wondered.

Spire made his way back into the superstructure and toward the restaurant cabin. The *Mercure's* restaurant was painted a warm beige colour. Oil paintings adorned both walls, depicting seascapes, ranging from old galleons struggling in stormy seas, to modern research vessels sailing through calm oceans. The large rectangle windows were covered by thick dark blue velvet curtains, giving the cabin a warm, welcoming feel to it.

Dr. Mathews and Dr. McBride were already sitting at the long wooden dining table, along with two of the ship's engineers. Four bottles of wine had been placed in the middle of the table, two red and two white, together with two large jugs of water.

Spire sat down by Marcus Roux, one of the engineers, just as his three French friends came in, followed a few moments later by Dr. Sinclair, who sat next to him.

Trimaud took a bottle of white wine and filled everyone's glasses in anticipation of the first course.

"Is the precious cargo safe, Francois?" Spire asked.

"I hope so. The retaining clamps seem to be doing their job."

"Don't worry, Professor; those clamps have been designed to secure an object, weighing thirty tonnes, through a force nine storm," Roux said, grinning.

"That's good to know," Trimaud replied.

Captain Deville entered the cabin. "Evening, ladies and gentlemen, I trust you are all suitably hungry?" he boomed, as he took a seat at the head of the table. "Here's to a successful mission, and a safe return to Marseilles," he said, holding up his glass of wine, before downing it in one.

"Salut, everyone," Trimaud said, raising his glass.

There was a knock on the door; a man entered wearing chef's whites and placed a tray of sizzling, steaming king prawns down on the table. A mouth-watering smell of tangy marinade filled the cabin. "Help yourselves," Deville said, gesturing toward the sizzling platter.

The first course was followed by a choice of steak, or fresh fish, which had been caught earlier. The chef appeared with a second plate of fries, together with two more bottles of Argentinean Medoc.

Spire opened a bottle, and filled everyone's glasses.

"So, Robert," Captain Deville said, in between swallowing mouthfuls of steak, "you appear to be the odd one out here. I know your interest lies in environmental law, but how did you end up on this trip?"

Spire took a gulp of wine. "I guess, mainly for the adventure, and to witness a potentially world-changing experiment. Francois' invitation was too much to resist for me."

"That's if the experiment works, of course," Deville replied. "As for adventure, you'll certainly experience that. Not many people have navigated along the Northwest Passage, that's for sure. Isn't that correct, Dr. Mathews?"

"It certainly isn't the choice for most people's vacation plans!" Dr. Mathews replied, chuckling.

"You see, Robert; many mariners have lost their lives navigating the passage. For hundreds of years, explorers have attempted to travel along the fabled route. Some have made it, but most haven't."

"I'm well aware of that, Captain," Spire said, recalling his research on the Arctic route. "Most of those sailors had no choice but to navigate the route in wooden ships, and during the winter it would seem," Spire replied.

"I didn't realise you were such an expert on Arctic maritime history, Robert?"

"Well, I wouldn't say that. But I've done my research. I recently met a man in San Francisco, who claimed he'd attempted to traverse the route back in nineteen sixty-four. He said he was forced back because of the harsh conditions. I'm also aware that Amundsen sailed the passage in nineteen hundred and six, and made it back, in one piece, to tell the tale."

"Well, Robert, that's more than I knew," Dr. McBride said, looking impressed.

Captain Deville took another gulp of wine and sat in silence for a few seconds. A serious look descended upon his face. "The man you met in San Francisco, can you recall his name?"

Spire sat back in his chair, slightly taken aback by the question. "His name? I think he said it was Harker…or Park, something like that, why?"

"Not Parker Harrington?" Deville asked.

"I think it was! How the hell did you know that?"

The rest of the group listened intently to the unfolding conversation, eyes fixed on Captain Deville.

"Well, I remember the fateful voyage very well," Deville continued. "A good friend of mine, Maurice Loquhart was skippering the *Vanquish* with a crew of twenty-five. I had just started my service with the French Navy at the time, but Loquhart decided to go private, sailing for whoever offered him decent enough pay. There was good money to be earned undertaking specialist sailing work, if you could get it. Anyway, Loquhart and another captain, whose name escapes me, sailing the *Terminus,* journeyed up the Northwest Passage. The trip was sponsored by one of the American oil companies, who'd offered a million dollars to any vessel able to complete the east to west crossing. It was done as a gimmick, but if the expedition had been successful, it would show that oil could actually be transported between the Atlantic and Pacific Oceans, without taking the usual route around the Cape or through the Panama Canal."

"So what happened?" Spire asked.

"Well, the voyage was struck with disaster. The *Terminus* became trapped in the pack-ice a third of the way along the Lancaster Sound. The ship's ice-strengthened hull failed and she was holed beneath the water line. By the time Captain Loquhart and the crew of the *Vanquish* knew, it was too late. They set off across the ice to try and assist the stricken vessel, but the pack ice moved again, releasing the vessel from its grip. She sank in a matter of minutes."

"Were there any survivors?" Dr. Mathews asked.

Deville looked at Spire. "All souls lost, apart from your friend Parker Harrington. He was the only survivor. Loquhart dragged him from the ocean, and managed to free the *Vanquish* from the ice pack, before sailing back. I don't believe he ever captained a ship again. Of course, they didn't get their million dollars either, and the whole thing was forgotten about - by the oil companies anyway."

There was silence for a few seconds, only broken by a steady creaking as a wave caught the port-side of the ship. Spire reached out and caught his wine glass as it almost slid off the wooden table. "The poor bugger didn't tell me any of that," Spire said, feeling slightly humbled.

"And where did you say you bumped into this chap, Robert?" Trimaud asked.

Spire told them about the stop he made to see the Amundsen monument on the way to the airport, after attending the climate conference in San Francisco.

The cabin fell silent.

After a few moments Dr. McBride spoke up. "That is an odd coincidence," she said, sipping her wine.

There was another creak, as a wave caught the *Mercure's* starboard side, gently rolling the vessel in the opposite direction.

"Well, I'm done," Deville said, getting up from the table. "I'll see you all in the morning. We'll be maintaining a speed of around fourteen knots, weather permitting, so we'll be making good time overnight."

Spire finished his wine, suddenly feeling very tired. "I'm off to bed too; I think the wine has done its job on me." He got up, said goodnight to the team and left.

Once back in the cabin, Spire slumped down onto his bed, and closed his eyes. The cabin creaked quietly as the ship gently shifted from side to side on the rising swell. Recalling the texts Kim had sent him earlier; he fumbled for his mobile, turned it on, and studied the message again. He read the anagrams Kim had produced from the name on the business card. He found a scrap of paper and jotted down the name *Arc-Bin-Quid-Lo* alongside some of the variations Kim had come up. He played around with some of the letters, writing down his own variations. As he thought about the different word combinations, he glanced out of the porthole at the dark sea beyond. The wave peaks were illuminated with a silvery-white glow by the large crescent moon above. The ocean reminded him of home, and of Manorbier Bay. He thought back to the large oil tanker he'd seen making its way out to the open sea, and looked down at the scrap of paper again, filled with jumbled letters.

The words *Ocean*, *Water*, and *Oil*, were at the forefront of his mind. Suddenly a word jumped out at him from the letters on the paper - LIQUID. He concentrated on the remaining letters, writing down *Crab On* and *A Bronc*. Then it came to him - CARBON. *Could the name on the card be an anagram for Liquid Carbon?* He lay on the bed thinking for a moment. *Could this whole thing be about oil?*

He tried to process everything that had happened over the last three months, but as he lay there, he found it harder to concentrate. Within five minutes, a combination of the gentle rocking motion of the ship and the wine he'd consumed earlier sent him into a deep sleep.

CHAPTER 43

Greenland
June 3

THE INUIT SETTLEMENT of Samutaat, located on the southern coast of Greenland - some twelve hundred kilometres from the capital Nuuk - lay nestled below the towering terminus of one branch of the Helheim glacier. It had done so for over two-hundred years. A mixture of igloos, used mainly during the colder winter months, and Inuit tents made from animal hides, driftwood and bones, formed a village around the base of the glacier. Columns of smoke, the only evidence of the small thriving community living there, rose through make-shift chimneys in a number of the tents, becoming temporarily invisible against the white face of the glacier, before rising indolently into the azure blue sky above.

Uyarasuk was waiting for her husband, Talirik, to return from his hunting trip, which he had embarked upon earlier that morning, with a group of hunters from the village. Her two daughters, Akaka and Aariak, were playing outside in the snow. A fire danced inside a stone hearth within the tent, burning driftwood and animal fat, ready to start cooking a seal stew as soon as Talirik returned.

"Aariak, Akaka, come, your father will be home soon. We need to get ready to eat," she shouted, prompting the two girls to look up from an animal they had been carving from the snow.

Out on the frozen ocean, some two kilometres from the settlement, Talirik and three other hunters were making their way back, across the receding summer ice, in a traditional Qamutik dog sled. Eight Siberian Huskies, in tandem formation, were dutifully pulling them across the frozen expanse towards home. A Uniaq boat made from wooden frames and animal skin was attached to the back of the sled, carrying two seals, testimony to the day's successful hunt.

The huskies suddenly howled and veered left to avoid a large melt-pool that had formed on the surface of the frozen ocean, causing one of the dead seals to roll off the Uniaq and slide across the ice. "Tavrani, tavra!" Talirik shouted to the huskies, bringing them to a stop. He got off the sled, reached into a bucket tied to the back, and pulled out some fresh chunks of seal flesh, and tossed it to the dogs. He then walked back with his three friends to where the dead seal lay on the ice. With two at each end, they lifted the heavy mammal back on to the sled. The four men then tracked back to the area the dogs had avoided to see what the problem was. Talirik could see a large pool of water, forming a shallow surface lake, perhaps ten centimetres deep spreading out before them. "Sea never melts this much before, so close to coast," he said to his friends.

Tiquana, the eldest of the group, crouched down and placed his hand down into the melt-pool. As he pulled it out, he shook his head, a look of concern upon his face. "I tell you, this has never been so bad. Every season we come here, the ice melts more. Ten years ago, we could travel by sled for eight kilometres before having to use the Uniaq, now it's only two."

Talirik gestured up to the blue sky. "Last night, I saw

tupilak - the spirit lights - dancing; they were unusually bright; I sense something is wrong."

The three men listened intently, frowning as Talirik spoke. "Come, let's get home, our families will want to eat."

The four hunters followed Talirik back onto the sled. They all looked around the empty expanse of white, then toward their settlement, which was just about visible in the distance, nestled at the base of the vast glacier. Talirik shouted to the huskies, still lying patiently on the ice. The dogs jumped up, howling as their powerful shoulders took the strain of the sled, moving it slowly at first, before picking up speed, as they obediently pulled the hunters toward home.

Talirik's wife and daughters were standing outside the tent when the group arrived, and looked on as the men divided the morning's kill into four equal sacks of freshly cut seal meat. Talirik waved his friends farewell and greeted his wife with a kunik nose-rub, "Is fire burning bright?" he asked, affectionately ruffling his youngest daughter's hair as he walked into the tent.

"Yes, come, the fire is ready."

Talirik sat down to warm his hands. The aroma of spices and cooked seal meat wafted from the cauldron as it stewed over the fire.

One hundred and sixty kilometres inland from the settlement, a low rumble resonated up through the ancient glacier, as if it were groaning after being awoken from a thousand year sleep. A large chasm suddenly opened up, disappearing into the depths of the glacier, forming a moulin or shaft down to the bedrock below. The melt-water pooling on the surface, started to cascade down, drilling deeper into the moulin where it formed a sub-glacial river flowing along the bedrock, lubricating the mountain of ice above it. Another loud cracking noise reverberated through the glacier to the surface, opening another fracture, which instantaneously travelled twenty kilometres along the length of the glacier toward its terminus on the coast.

A loud thunderous rumble pierced the tranquillity of the Inuit settlement at the base of the ice cliff. Talirik placed his bowl down on the small wooden table, pulled back the loose flap of hide, and hurried out of the tent. A few of the other Inuit had also left their tents upon hearing the thunderous crack. The evening sky was clear, and everything appeared normal. He returned to the warmth of the tent. "I sense something is wrong, Uyarasuk. Last night, I saw the spirit lights dancing brightly in the night sky, and now there is thunder from the mountain."

"Everything is fine. You know that sometimes tupilak can be seen clearly at this time of year; it's nothing unusual, Tarilik, please, sit and finish eating."

He smiled at his wife and children, and sat back down on the Caribou skin to finish his seal stew.

Allan Mackintosh was seated at his desk, at the British Geological Survey station in Edinburgh, finishing his cup of tea. He spun around in his chair and away from the computer screen he'd been watching, and shouted over at his colleague Jim Cullen, who was sitting at his desk writing a report. "Jim, you got any more of those chocolate biscuits, mate?"

"You finished them off this morning, Mack," his colleague replied, from across the other side of the modest office. "Anyway, you'll be off home soon, it's nearly five. Some of us aren't so lucky; I'm doing the bloody grave-yard shift tonight."

"Poor bastard, what did you do to deserve that?" Mackintosh jested.

"You might well ask."

Mackintosh turned his chair back around to the computer monitor. The screen revealed that there had been three minor earthquakes in the UK during the last month; a 2.2 magnitude quake off the Isles of Scilly and smaller tremors in Bargoed, South Wales, and in Derbyshire; both under 1.6 in magnitude. The pattern was normal, Mackintosh told himself - Just three of the one-hundred and forty or so earthquakes that occur in the British Isles each year.

"Jim, keep your eye on the screen will you, I gotta go and take a leak," Mackintosh shouted, getting up from his chair. Just as he was about to leave, multiple readings started streaming in from the single vertical seismometers located in Cape Wrath and Scourie in Northwest Scotland. "Hello, what do we have here?" Mackintosh said, sitting back down. "Jim, better come and take a look at this quick. It looks like we have a 4.5 magnitude earthquake somewhere in the Greenland region."

"Are you sure?" Cullen shouted, rushing over. "That'll be the fourth this year. Make a call to the Lerwick station in the Shetlands, would you; check they have the same readings."

"I'm on it," Mackintosh replied, as he connected through to the Lerwick Seismology Station. "Yep, reading confirmed, 4.5 mag. Time was 18.47 and 16 seconds, latitude and longitude readings put the quake around one hundred miles inland from the southern coastal region. Not far from the last quake, I'd say."

"Good grief, Mack, looks like it's happening! Nothing on this scale was supposed to occur for another decade, at least. They didn't bloody mention this at Copenhagen, did they?"

Mackintosh frowned at his colleague. "You'd better make the call to our friends in Denmark, verify the quake with them, and then make a call to the Minister for the Environment."

In the North Atlantic Ocean, the Russian Minesweeper *Rezky* turned northeast, toward Southern Greenland. Admiral Dashkov was on the bridge, a pair of binoculars pressed to his face. He panned the horizon until he made visual contact with a small fishing boat that was showing up on the *Rezky's* radar. He scrutinised the vessel, which was flying the Norwegian flag, before placing the binoculars back on their stand. He pulled a Golden Fleece cigarette from his breast pocket, lit it, and took in a long hard drag. "Just a Norwegian fishing vessel, Captain," he said to Tabanov, who was standing by his side.

Down in the communications room, Lieutenant Brilev sat in front of a monitor with a set of headphones on, listening for any unusual sounds coming from the ship's sophisticated underwater hydrophones. The silence was suddenly broken by a series of sound pulses. Brilev sat upright as he pressed the headphones to his ears.

The hydrophones fitted to the Zvezda towed array system were picking up the sound waves generated by the Greenland earthquake. He listened intently for a minute, before contacting Captain Tabanov on the bridge "I've picked up an underwater contact, Captain."

"Are you sure, Lieutenant? Can you identify it?"

"I'm working on it; doesn't sound like a submarine. Hold on, I believe it could be subterranean…possibly an earthquake."

"Earthquake? Are you certain? Keep listening, and give me two-minute updates."

"Very well, Captain," Brilev said, as he concerned himself with the pulses of sound being picked up by the underwater hydrophones. He hadn't heard many under-sea earthquakes before, but he knew the signature of a submarine, and it certainly wasn't a sub he was listening to. He called Tabanov two minutes later. "It's definitely an earthquake, Captain."

"Very well, should your opinion change, let me know straight away."

Admiral Dashkov stubbed his cigarette out. He was aware that there had been a number of seismic events in and around Greenland over the last twelve months, as he'd been monitoring them himself from Russia. *That had to be what the hydrophones were picking up.*

He picked up the phone and called down to the weapons room. "Officer Charkov, make sure the cargo is secure, we're going to be hitting some rough sea soon."

"Yes, Admiral," Charkov obediently responded.

Down in the weapons room, which once contained the anti-submarine ordinance, Petty Officer's Charkov and Donskoy were keeping watch over the eight objects secured on top of steel racking, arranged in two lines of four. The objects looked similar to a child's wooden spinning top, but each the size of a small car, and black in colour. Displayed on the side of each device in Russian and English was the inscription OCEAN TEMPERATURE MODIFIER. A yellow and black radioactive symbol was displayed clearly on the side of each object, above what looked like a control-pad.

Officer Charkov got up and walked by each of the OTMs, to check the holding clamps once again. The devices weren't going anywhere. He walked back into the cabin off the main weapons room, where Donskoy was sitting, and resumed their game of Blackjack.

In the Southern Indian Ocean, the *Bountiful* moved into

position above the second drill site, one nautical mile off the Crozet Islands. Mustafa checked the radar; there were no other vessels within five hundred nautical miles of them. The ocean was relatively calm, with just a light breeze blowing from the northwest. This is perfect, he thought, as he gave the order for the drilling derrick to be raised from its concealed horizontal position.

On the deck below the men started to remove the make-shift wooden cabins that had been erected over the steel drilling tower. The motorized units on each side of the steel structure were activated; groaning under the weight of the derrick, as they slowly raised it into position. The tower contained the necessary equipment, piping and machinery needed to power the drill-bit. The huge piece of apparatus creaked as it was elevated to its vertical drilling position.

Mustafa, overseeing the operation from the bridge, turned on the vessel's Dynamic Positioning System, to ensure the *Bountiful* did not drift from the drilling location. Four successive loud thuds resonated up from the deck, indicating that the bolts securing the tower had slid into place. He then addressed the men, on the deck below, over the ship's P.A system. "Prepare to lower the drilling template onto the drill site."

There was a flurry of activity from the ship's crew, now centred on the drilling platform, which overlooked the moon-pool. The moon-pool went right through the hull of the *Bountiful* to the ocean below, allowing the drilling equipment to extend through to the seabed.

Mustafa watched as his men lowered the drilling template down through the moon-pool, which would enable a small hole to be drilled into the seabed before the template was secured in place, allowing the main well to be drilled accurately. He looked on as the men watched the cables connecting the drilling template to the drilling platform uncoil from the deck, as the template descended into the calm water of the moon-pool to the well site below.

The drill-ship rocked from side to side on the light swell, the electric motors on the underside of her hull providing the necessary propulsion to maintain position above the drill site.

Three hours later, with the necessary drill pipes connected, and in place, the ship was ready to drill the template hole in preparation for drilling the main well into the bedrock, seven hundred metres below them.

Mustafa checked the radar again, to ensure the vicinity was clear of any unwanted visitors. Satisfied they were all alone, he grabbed the satellite phone, and called Fahim. Forty seconds passed before Fahim answered the call. "Fahim, I am pleased to report that the drill template is in place and we are ready to proceed, with your blessing, of course," Mustafa reported, wiping sweat from his brow.

"Good work, you may proceed. Let me know as soon as oil is found," Fahim said.

The line went dead. Mustafa shrugged and continued his work.

Fahim ended the call and turned back to the monitors he'd been studying. They showed the position of the semi-submersible rig, now being tracked by GPS, as it was slowly being brought into place from Port Elizabeth in South Africa where it had been built by *NewSaudOil* contractors. The rig should be on site in a matter of weeks, Fahim judged. A second rig was also being brought into place over the Atlantic site, and would be ready to drill in just under a week.

Fahim smiled contentedly and got up from his desk, contemplating the future. *When the Kingdom's largest oil well dries up, NewSaudOil Corp would step in to help - for a vast sum of money and inevitable glory.*

CHAPTER 44

INSPECTOR JOHNSON STARED at the surveillance images on the computer screen in front of him. He'd finally managed to speak to Inspector Bertrand, who had e-mailed the Louvre footage over to him late the night before. Johnson took a gulp of coffee as he replayed the edited video from the multiple security cameras in the building.

After viewing the footage, he called Smith over. "Do me a favour will you and get this picture over to Interpol, see if they have anything on this guy. Also call Inspector Bertrand again in Paris to see if he has any more footage of the main foyer area, just before Spire and Trimaud ascend the stairs – I'm interested in a dark-haired female who appears to be moving quickly toward the same staircase."

"No problem, Inspector. Is there any news on Spire yet?" Smith asked.

"Nope, he appears to be out of contact at the moment, somewhere in the middle of the bloody Atlantic, according to his secretary. I'll send the footage over to Lieutenant Mitchell in San Francisco and then I'm off to see Doris Stanton again. I want to speak to her about the legacy left by her son, just to make sure she's happy with the way Spire is dealing with it."

"Good luck!" Smith said, returning to his desk.

Johnson typed a message and attached a copy of the Louvre video to Gus Mitchell, over in San Francisco;

Enclosed is Louvre footage, as promised. Take a look at the dark haired woman seen fleetingly in some of the clips – could be of interest? Perhaps you'll change your mind about Spire when you view this. I'm going to re-interview Doris Stanton today - Regards, Inspector Lance Johnson.

Johnson sent the message, turned off his computer and checked his watch. He calculated that he would be able to make it to Windsor by around five thirty P.M.

Gus Mitchell walked into the ornate marble-floored lobby of the Ravenbrook Hotel in San Francisco's Nob Hill district, flashed his badge to the security guard on the door, and asked to see the hotel's manager. He was ushered past a young couple at the check-in desk and taken to a small room behind the main concierge.

He sat and waited for ten minutes, before a rotund man in his early sixties wearing a dark, three-piece suit walked in and introduced himself as Mr. Martin Baker, the hotel's manager.

"Thanks for seeing me, Mr. Baker. My name is Lieutenant Gus Mitchell, San Francisco Police Department," he said, flashing his badge again. "I'm investigating the death of Dr. Jack Bannister here, on April twenty-fourth – I'm sure you remember it?"

"Oh, of course," the manager said nervously. "But didn't the gentleman die of a heart attack? What's your involvement, detective?"

"He did, but his heart attack was brought on by a lethal dose of nicotine, administered, it seems, in some food or drink perhaps."

"Good gracious!" Baker said, sitting down on a dark leather sofa positioned against the rear wall of the room. "How...how can I assist in the investigation?"

"I need the names of anyone who might have been involved in the preparation of food for Mr. Bannister during his stay here. Also copies of his hotel bills showing what he purchased and when; bar tabs, room service, that sort of thing. Oh, I'll also need the names and addresses of everyone who attended the climate conference, if possible."

The manager took out a handkerchief from his suit pocket and mopped his brow. "Of course, detective, I can get that information to you in twenty-four hours, it's not a problem."

"Good. By the way, do you have any security cameras at the hotel?"

"Ah, yes, we have two in the main lobby, just behind the check-in desk."

"Are there any in the ballroom where the conference was held?" Mitchell asked.

"No, I'm afraid not. The main ballroom has no surveillance cameras installed – it was never felt necessary."

"Very well, if you could get me the footage from the two check-in desk cameras, that will be helpful," Mitchell said, as he stood and handed Baker his card. "If you think of anything else that might be relevant, please give me a call."

"Of course, detective," Baker said, nodding his head. "Oh, before you go, you might want to speak to Jim Myers. He was the security officer on the door during the climate conference. He's in today, and might be able to give you some information."

Mitchell thanked Baker and walked back into the main lobby, where he spotted the security guard - a heavily built black man - sitting down near to the main entrance, reading a copy of *Baseball America* magazine.

"Jim?" Mitchell called, as he approached him.

The guard lowered the magazine and looked up at Mitchell, who was already holding up his police badge.

"How can I help, officer?" the guard asked, standing up.

"I've got a few questions to ask you about the climate

conference that took place a few weeks ago. I just wondered if you recognised either of these two men," Mitchell said, showing him the photographs.

The guard studied the two pictures for a while. "Isn't that the scientist who dropped dead here? And this man," he said pointing to the photo of Spire, "I searched him as he entered the hotel. Said he wanted to attend the climate event. I directed him over to the climate conference stand, which was over there." The guard pointed to a door leading off from the lobby.

"Notice anything suspicious about him?"

"No – nothing, he just wanted to get into the conference, is all."

"Notice anything else that night, anything at all?"

The guard thought for a moment, slowly shaking his head. "Not that I can think of detective."

"Fair enough," Mitchell replied. "Think of anything, let me know, here's my card."

Mitchell left the guard holding his card and walked through the revolving doors, and out onto the hotel's forecourt. An attractive female jogger ran past wearing nothing but an I-pod, sports bra and tight white shorts. Mitchell whistled under his breath, as he let his gaze follow the jogger as she disappeared into Huntington Park. He took a few steps, when someone shouted his name.

"Detective Mitchell!"

He turned to see the guard come bounding over to him.

"There's one thing I just remembered. Probably nothing, but on the evening of Dr. Bannister's death, I remember letting in this brunette. Said she was over from the UK, working for some kind of environmental magazine and would be taking photographs. She was here all evening, I think."

Mitchell scribbled a few notes down in his notebook. "Can you describe her in a bit more detail Jim? Do you recall the name of the magazine she worked for?"

"Something like Green-people, Green-days...*Green-Times!* That was it. I sure remember her though. Very attractive; five-nine, green eyes, long brown hair, a cross between *Cindy Crawford* and the actress *Milla Jovovich* – a great mix, eh?" The guard said, with a wink.

"You could say that," Mitchell replied, trying to visualize the striking combination. He thanked the guard, put the notebook back into his breast pocket, and headed back down the hill along California Street.

He considered the situation and the two suspects - Spire and the female photographer. He assumed that Spire had flown over after hearing about Bannister's death, no doubt to carry out his own investigations. He looked up at the cloudless sky, letting the late morning sun warm his face and thought, *Spire needs to be careful. Involved or not, he's now linked to the deaths of both climatologists.*

CHAPTER 45

Atlantic Ocean
June 4

A LARGE WAVE hit the *Mercure's* port side, rolling her thirty degrees to starboard, waking Spire with a jump. He stretched, yawned loudly and rolled out of bed and onto the carpeted floor. He attempted to do some push-ups, only managing seventy-eight before the ship pitched on another wave, throwing him off balance. He stood and looked out of the porthole onto a rolling, grey ocean. Sea spray dowsed the window every few seconds, as if someone was standing out on the deck with a bucket, tossing the foamy contents deliberately at his cabin.

He checked his watch; it was coming up to eight A.M. He grabbed his towel and clawed his way to the shower, holding on to the doorframe to steady himself against the increasing pitching and rolling motion of the ship. He quickly showered, dressed, left his cabin and walked up two sets of stairs to the bar. He glanced in and saw one of the chefs, Roberto, clearing up some broken green glass.

"Morning, Mr Spire. Disaster, we lost four bottles of Kronenbourg," he said, as he continued mopping up the mess.

"That's a catastrophe. I hope there's more on board?" Spire said, grinning. "Anyone else up yet, Roberto?"

"Not seen anyone, I think you're the first. Captain's up on

the bridge, if you want to go up. I'm sure he'll be glad of your company."

Spire nodded and found the stairwell that led up onto the bridge. As he got to the top, he lost his footing on the steel deck as the ship rolled to port, as it was slammed by another large wave. He grabbed the handrail and knocked on the thick steel door, that led onto the bridge.

"Come!" Captain Deville hollered from inside.

Spire walked in. Deville was standing at the wheel, looking out at the ocean through the large sloped windows.

"Choppy enough for you, Robert?" he said, raising a pair of binoculars to his face to examine the horizon, just as another large wave struck the ship's bow. The *Mercure* sank into a trough, water spraying onto the deck and windows.

"How long is this going to last?" Spire asked, grabbing onto the table.

"This storm was forecast. We'll be through the worst of it in another three hours, or so," Deville said, taking a slim cigar out of a fresh packet. "Can I tempt you with one of these?" he said, offering the pack to Spire.

"Sure, why not," Spire replied, placing the slightly sweet tasting cigar into his mouth. Looking down at the table, he noticed an unfolded map covering half of it. A red line had been drawn between the Straits of Gibraltar and the southern tip of Greenland. "What's our current position?" Spire asked, pointing toward the line.

"We're roughly a third of the way along. We have another sixteen hundred miles to go. We should reach the drop zone in another three days," Deville replied, both hands firmly gripping the *Mercure's* wheel.

There was a knock on the door and Trimaud walked in, wearing a thick jumper and waterproofs. "Bonjour, gentlemen," he said, rubbing his hands together in an effort to keep warm. "Coffee and breakfast is being served in the restaurant, if you can stomach it?"

"I can always manage breakfast," Spire said, stubbing out his cigar. "Do you think we should check the cargo first, Francois?"

"Good idea, Robert. If you don't mind, I was just about to suggest that."

"If you're going out on deck, put your life jackets on. I can't afford to lose either of you overboard just yet!" Deville added.

Spire and Trimaud made their way down to the storeroom, where they had first signed themselves onboard. Spire found two life jackets, and handed one to Trimaud. "Here, take this as well," he said, also giving him a thick parka jacket which had been hanging on the wooden racking. Spire grabbed another for himself and pulled it over his life vest, zipping it up as far as it would go.

They both made their way up to the main deck, and exited, through the steel door, onto the port side. Spire held the door open for Trimaud, and was immediately buffeted in the face by a biting cold wind. He gripped the handrail, and carefully made his way along the deck.

Trimaud followed behind.

They arrived on the main foredeck, where the large steel container loomed up in front of them. "You go around that way, I'll start on this side," Spire shouted, as they approached the steel cube.

Spire held onto the side of the container and studied the large clamping arms which formed a secure triangle against the corners of the steel box, extending about twelve centimetres along the length of each side. Grabbing the sides of the container, he made his way around to the next corner and knelt down. The clamp was fixed tight; the container wasn't going anywhere.

He continued shuffling around the steel cube, to the exposed port-side of the ship. As he rounded the corner, he caught a face-full of freezing seawater as a wave smashed into the side of the vessel. He could see Trimaud crouched down checking the corner clamp opposite him. As Spire stood up, another wave hit the ship's port side, sending a torrent of foaming water over both of them. The torrent caused Trimaud to lose his footing, throwing him to the deck and sliding him out of sight.

"Francois!" Spire shouted, as he hurried along the side of the container to the corner where Trimaud had been standing. The stormy grey overcast sky merged with the white-tops of the rolling ocean, severely limiting visibility. It was a few seconds before he saw Trimaud, who was now clinging onto the railings on the starboard side of the deck, slowly trying to pull himself up.

"Francois!" Spire shouted again, as he quickly made his way across the deck to him. "Jeez, I thought I'd lost you," he said, helping the professor to his feet.

"Merci, mon ami. I lost my footing back there," Trimaud said, catching his breath. "Come on, let's get back inside before we're both washed off the deck. At least the container is secure."

They both made their way to the starboard door, stepped over the small steel lip and into the superstructure. Spire pulled the door tightly shut behind him, blocking out the strengthening gale and unzipped his parka. "We'd better hook ourselves onto the railings next time we go out."

"You won't catch me out there again, until the storm passes," Trimaud replied, still out of breath. "Allez, let's go and get some breakfast."

Spire and Trimaud joined Dr. McBride and Dr. Mathews in the restaurant cabin, who were both discussing going out and taking some samples.

"What do you have in mind, Ruth?" Trimaud asked, drying his hair with a hand towel.

"I want to take some water samples at varying depths, check salinity, temperature and phytoplankton levels, that sort of thing. I can compare them with existing data at various points on route to the Arctic Circle," Dr. McBride said.

"Expecting to find anything unusual?" Spire asked.

"Well, hopefully not. We just need to compare the samples with the last decade's worth of data, see if there have been any changes. The sea temperature varies of course, plus or minus a few degrees, depending on the time of year. Salinity and phytoplankton should be more or less stable. I really needed to get readings at a position forty-five degrees north, more or less level with the Bay of Biscay, but I'll have to wait for the return journey now."

"What's so special about that position?" Spire asked, reaching over for a chocolate croissant.

"Well, it's more or less the point at which the Gulf Stream, part of the Atlantic Current, makes its way, northeast, across to the UK. We're monitoring salinity levels and temperature at that point to make sure there are no changes. The current is of vital importance to the temperature of Europe."

Spire glanced at Trimaud, and then looked back at Dr. McBride. "Isn't that part of the Ocean Thermohaline Circulation?" he asked.

"That's correct, Robert; the Gulf Stream is a surface current and a feature of it. I understand the late Dr. Stanton was involved in the monitoring project *RAPID-WATCH*, currently being conducted in the Atlantic at twenty-six point five degrees north. At present there is no monitoring in place at latitudes above forty degrees north. This project will hopefully assist in gathering the missing data."

"I'd be very interested to see the results when they are available, if possible?" Spire said.

"Of course, as soon as I can get the sampling vials overboard, I can get the water into the lab for analysis."

Spire finished his coffee. "That's better; there's nothing like your first cup of coffee to blow the cobwebs away. Oh, by the way, has anyone seen Dr. Sinclair this morning?"

"Yep," Dr. Mathews replied. "I bumped into her just before breakfast, said she wasn't feeling too good, needed to lie down until the storm passed."

"Can't say I blame her," Spire said, getting up from the table. "I'm going to do the same. I'll see you all in an hour or so."

Spire left the restaurant and made his way back to his cabin. Once inside he lay on the bed, trying to piece together all that had happened over the last three months, trying to make some sense out of it all - the scientists' deaths; the assault at the Louvre, and the terrifying ordeal at the French laboratory. Now he was in the middle of the Atlantic, on his way to the Arctic. All the events were as a result of being named as a co-executor in the will of Dr. Dale Stanton. He shook his head in disbelief at the whole thing. *Perhaps Dr. McBride's tests would shed some light on the late Dr. Stanton's research?*

A knot began to develop in the pit of his stomach as he thought about the possibility.

CHAPTER 46

SPIRE OPENED HIS eyes and found himself looking up at the white emulsion ceiling of his cabin. He checked the time and realised he'd been asleep for almost three hours. He rolled off his bed and looked out of the porthole, relieved to see a relatively flat ocean spreading out as far as the eye could see. The dark clouds had given way to patches of blue sky and the sun's rays now penetrated down to the surface, illuminating the ocean like spotlights over a theatre stage.

He pulled his parka on, zipped it up and left the cabin to look for the others. As he exited via the port door, a screech from above prompted him to look up. Three or four gulls circled overhead, no doubt searching for any scraps of food that maybe on offer. On the deck, the three French climatologists were chatting together, watching the two Americans removing pieces of apparatus from a large plastic container positioned on the deck in front of them. Spire walked out to join them all. "What's going on?" he asked, checking his watch.

"Dr. McBride is just getting ready to drop the first set of Niskin bottles, overboard to take water samples for analysis. The captain will be bringing us to a stop any time now," Dr. Girard replied.

Spire looked on as Dr. Mathews handed Dr. McBride a cylindrical object made from clear thick plastic, attached to a long thin steel cord, the end of which was connected to a small motorised winch on the *Mercure's* deck. As the ship slowed,

Dr. McBride lowered the Niskin bottle over the side, dipping the sampling bottle a metre or so below the surface of the ocean, before reversing the winch and pulling the full container back up. She then transferred the water into another bottle and handed it to Dr. Mathews, who marked on it, 'surface sample.' She then took out a black and white disk, similar in size to a Frisbee, which was attached to a rope, and lowered it over the side.

"What's that?" Spire asked.

"This is a Secchi Disk. It allows us to look at water transparency to determine plankton and detritus levels. We should get an overall snapshot of the water quality this way." Dr. McBride repeated the process another three times, on each occasion lowering the water sampling bottle deeper into the ocean, with the final sample being taken from five-hundred metres below the surface. "That should do it," she finally said. "I need to get these samples back to the lab straight away, to check the water chemistry, and importantly the chlorophyll and salinity levels."

"How long before you have any results, Ruth?" Spire asked.

"As long as the lab's centrifuge is working properly, and the test kits are up to date, I should be able to determine chlorophyll, alkalinity and salinity levels within a few hours. Water samples will need to be frozen, so we can check nitrogen content when we get back to Marseilles."

Captain Deville then appeared on the deck, lighting up a cigar as he approached. "Get your samples, Doctor?" he asked, looking down at the large plastic container.

"Certainly did, Captain, thanks for getting us to the spot," McBride said.

"Good, you can give me the coordinates for the next stop, after lunch." He turned to Spire and offered him a cigar.

"I'm alright, thanks, the one I had this morning was

enough." Spire said.

"Well, you certainly got your first taste of the Atlantic today," Deville said, exhaling a plume of fragrant smelling cigar smoke.

"I'm hoping that's as bad as it gets. I thought I'd almost lost Francois earlier, when I saw him go down."

"You have to be careful out here, at all times. The weather will be fine for a while now, but it looks like the storm I mentioned before we left Marseilles will be rolling in, after all. We should make it to the seeding spot first, but it will catch up with us on the way back at some point. I'll be briefing everyone in a day or so," Deville said, looking at Spire.

"I don't like the sound of that," Spire said, looking out over the ocean, inhaling the cold, fresh air. He turned back to Deville. "I sure hope it's all worth it."

"Trimaud knows what he's doing. If he's prepared to come all the way out here to dump a couple of tonnes of iron sulphate into one of the remotest oceans on the planet, believe me, it's got to be worth it."

At that moment, Trimaud came over to join them. "Only another forty-eight hours, Jacques, and hopefully your ship will be a few tonnes lighter."

"You just make sure you drop the stuff in the ocean Francois, and not on my deck!"

"Don't worry about that, the contents are too valuable."

"Allez, chaps, I believe lunch is about to be served in the restaurant. Eat while the ocean is sleeping," Deville said, mashing the end of the cigar on the ship's rail.

"Damn good idea. By the way, has anyone been to check on Dr. Sinclair recently?" Spire asked.

"Not seen her all day," Deville replied, as the three of them walked along the deck and back inside the ship.

Once inside, Spire decided to go and check on Dr. Sinclair.

He found her cabin and knocked the door. "Dr. Sinclair, you in there?" he shouted.

There was no answer. He tried the door, but it was locked. He then placed his ear against the door to check for any sound from within the room. He listened, but couldn't hear anything.

A female voice suddenly startled him. "Are you always so inquisitive, Mr. Spire?"

Spire spun around to see Dr. Sinclair standing behind him, awaiting an explanation. "Only when I'm bored," he joked. "I just came to check you were still alive - clearly you are."

"As you can see, I'm fine," she replied, her voice a little softer. "I understand lunch is about to be served. If you don't mind, I'll have a quick shower and join you all in thirty minutes."

Spire stepped aside, letting Dr. Sinclair walk into her room. Once inside, she promptly locked the door behind her. He waited for a moment, and then put his ear back against the door. He could hear a faint tapping, like computer keys being hit. He listened for a few moments before walking down the corridor and back to the restaurant cabin.

After lunch Spire joined the others and followed Dr. McBride down one deck level, to the *Mercure's* science laboratory. Two white melamine worktops ran along the port and starboard side of the cabin, and various pieces of apparatus and lab equipment filled half of one work surface. The rear wall consisted of part cabinet, part bookshelf, and was filled with science books and periodicals. Rectangular windows ran along both lengths of the cabin, filling the lab with natural light. A square workbench was fixed to the floor in the middle of the cabin, on top of which sat three large microscopes.

"Welcome to the *Mercure's* science lab," Dr. McBride said, as she walked over to one of the work surfaces. "OK, this piece of kit is where most of the samples get analysed," she said, pointing out a white machine, about twice the size of a household breadmaker, which was making a distinct humming sound. Dr. McBride pushed a button on the control pad and the humming stopped. "This is a centrifuge; it does most of the hard work for us," she said, lifting the top cover of the machine to expose a series of test tubes radiating out from a central core. She removed one of the tubes and held it up for them all to see.

"What are your initial observations?" she asked, handing the test tube to Dr. Sinclair, who had just joined them.

Ksenyia took the sample, hesitating for a moment before holding it up to the light. She looked intently at the water in the small glass cylinder. "Well, plankton and detritus levels look normal," she said confidently, highlighting the dark matter that had assembled at the bottom of the glass tube. "To be certain I'd need to have a look under the microscope."

"Be my guest," Dr. McBride said, gesturing to one of the microscopes on the bench.

Spire watched as Dr. Sinclair nervously reached for a small glass slide and a pipette from the central table, and placed a few drops of the seawater onto it. She then inserted the slide under the microscope, and looked through the eye-piece at the sample. After a few moments she straightened up and looked at them. "Well, the sample looks healthy enough to me, Ruth. I can see the expected concentration of diatoms and protists there. Take a look for yourself."

Dr. McBride raised her eyebrows, stooped down, and peered into the microscope, and after a few moments said; "Mm, yes, I agree with you, but oddly enough I can't see any *rotifers* in the sample, an organism I'd normally expect to see," she said, quietly impressed by Dr. Sinclair's observations. "Feel free to take a look," she said to the rest of them as she moved away from the microscope and back over to the centrifuge. "I need to carry out a few more tests on another sample to determine salinity levels," she said, pulling another test tube from the machine.

Spire lined up behind the others to peer through the microscope at the water sample. He was about to look through the eyepiece when Dr. McBride walked towards them from the back of the laboratory, a look of concern evident on her face.

"What is it, Ruth?" He heard Dr. Mathews ask.

"This is quite unusual," she said, holding up the test tube in her right hand toward the light. "This sample suggests that salinity is down to thirty-three parts per thousand."

"That's not possible!" Dr. Mathews said, taking the computer printout from her hand. "Normal Atlantic salinity levels should be around thirty-five ppt at this latitude," he said, in a worried tone.

"I'll re-run the tests," Dr. McBride said, taking another test tube from the centrifuge.

"What's the problem?" Spire asked Trimaud.

"The results are a bit of a concern, Robert. The sample has come back showing extremely low salinity levels, suggesting a large amount of surface precipitation. It's possible the sample was contaminated, but unlikely."

Dr. McBride tested a second sample, the results checked; thirty-three parts per thousand. "We are going to have to take further samples, as we get closer to the Arctic, see if there is any kind of pattern here," she said.

Trimaud placed his hand on Spire's arm. "Let's meet in the bar for a drink," he said, a slight frown on his face.

Down in the *Mercure's* engine room, situated on the lower aft-deck, the twin Bergen diesel engines were silent. Normally Luc Morel, the ship's first engineer, would be taking the opportunity during the short stop to check oil levels and carry out a quick visual inspection of the ship's propulsion system. Instead, he lay unconscious, slumped in the far corner of the room, the drug *Lorazepam* pumping through his bloodstream.

As Captain Deville re-started the engines, the vibration caused a loosened valve on the liquid-to-liquid heat exchanger, on engine number two, to work its way free. As he increased engine propulsion, the valve fell onto the steel deck, where it rolled between Morel's outstretched legs, almost like it was homing in on the only person that would be able to put it back where it belonged. Ten minutes after Deville increased power, the engine began to overheat.

CHAPTER 47

FAHIM STUDIED THE monitor on the desk in front of him. The tracking device taken aboard the *Mercure Blanc* by the Russian assassin revealed the ship had just started to move again, after having been stationary for a few hours, some six hundred nautical miles south of Greenland. A few more days and they would be closing in on the designated experiment location, he realised.

His thoughts were interrupted by his desk phone ringing. He reached over and picked up the receiver.

"Sir, a Mr. Charlie Goodman from the NSIDC Underwater Research Facility, is holding for you. Would you like to speak to him?" his assistant asked.

Fahim hesitated for a moment. "What the hell do they want?" he snapped back, wondering how they got his number.

"Shall I tell him you are unavailable?"

"No, put him through," Fahim barked.

"Afternoon, at least I think its afternoon with you. My name is Charlie Goodman, chief scientist over at the NSIDC Research Facility in San Diego, USA. I understand you are the director of *NewSaudOil Corp?*"

"You are correct in your thinking, Mr. Goodman, how may I help you?"

"Well, we appear to have something that belongs to you. A broken drill-bit was brought up clamped in the mechanical arm of one of our submersibles, the *Poseidon,* which recently sank off the coast of the French Crozet Islands. The drill-bit has been traced to your company, and I was hoping you might be able to tell me how it ended up on the seabed in that location?"

Fahim leaned back in his chair, considering an appropriate response. "Ah, yes, I read about the tragedy with the submersible. Please accept my condolences for your organisation's loss Mr. Goodman. The drill-bit…yes, we had an unfortunate mishap with that. I take full responsibility for the equipment ending up on the ocean floor. The drill had been sitting in dock at Jizan waiting to be sent for repair. Somehow, it found its way onto one of our fishing vessels operating in the area and unfortunately got caught up in one of the nets, and was lost overboard," Fahim said, pausing for a few seconds for time to think. "I can assure you the *Blue Fin Fishing Company* will be heavily fined when they arrive back in port. I would be very grateful if the drill could be returned to us Mr. Goodman. We will pay for its repatriation costs, naturally." Fahim chewed the end of his pen, awaiting a response.

"Well, that's one hell of a story, sir. I must say, we were a bit confused finding a pristine drill-bit on the seabed at that location. It's not as if there is any oil in the region, is there!" Goodman said, chuckling. "We can send it back, no problem. Our accounts department will be in touch to sort out the shipping costs."

"Of course, thank you for the call," Fahim said, replacing the receiver. He stood up and slammed his fist down on the desk, almost toppling one of the computer monitors. He pulled his mobile phone from his jacket pocket and called Faric. There was no answer, so he left a message. "Meet me at the house in two hours. Your incompetence has resulted in the Americans tracing the lost drill-bit to *NewSaudOil*. Bring all the paperwork and licences in respect of the drilling rights – both the Crozet and Atlantic site. I sincerely hope they are all in order."

He left his room, rode the lift down to the foyer and walked out into the heat of the desert sun. A strong wind was blowing in from the south, whipping up small dust devils in the sand near to the main entrance. A black Mercedes came into view, and pulled up in front of the building. Fahim got in and the car accelerated along the long desert road, toward the outskirts of Riyadh.

Charlie Goodman sat at his desk typing an e-mail to the repatriation division, to confirm that the the *Poseidon* could now be shipped back to NSIDC headquarters in Boulder, Colorado. As soon as he sent the message his phone rang again. He put down the doughnut he'd just bitten into, wiped his fingers, and picked up the phone. "Charlie Goodman, NSIDC Marine Research Office."

"Mr. Goodman? My name's Lieutenant Gus Mitchell, San Francisco Police Department. I'm investigating a homicide over here, and wondered if I could ask you a few questions?"

"SFPD you say? Sure, Lieutenant, how can I help?" Goodman asked, slightly puzzled.

"I understand that a submarine hired out to climatologist Dr. Jack Bannister and his team sunk off the Croet Islands a few months back?"

"That's correct Lieutenant, and it's Crozet with a Z by the way," Goodman said, correcting him. "Yes, funny you should call now; I just finished the accident investigation report."

"Good, then you should be able to tell me what may have caused the disaster. I'm trying to establish whether there was a link between Dr. Bannister's death and the loss of the submersible. I have to follow up every lead you understand."

"Of course, Lieutenant, but I can't discuss the report with you, I'm afraid, that will be up to NSIDC. We're just the marine research section down here," Goodman said, reaching for his half-eaten doughnut.

"Listen, Mr. Goodman, I don't want to have to go to the trouble of getting a subpoena and coming down there personally, or to Colorado, wherever the hell I need to go. All I want is your thoughts on the matter."

"Ok, Ok, Lieutenant, I'm just covering my ass here," Goodman replied, dropping the doughnut. "Basically the *Poseidon* had an underwater collision, with what, we don't know. The hull was ruptured - *Kaboom*. The poor sons-of-bitches on board probably didn't know anything about it."

"You're referring to submariner's Skipton and Rogers I assume?"

"That's correct."

"You have no idea what caused the collision?"

"Nope, the sonar operator on board the *Ocean Explorer* didn't see a thing - all very odd. This is the first major accident involving a Mark IV deep-sea class sub, as far as I'm aware," Goodman said, hesitating for a moment. "There's one more thing, Lieutenant, when we recovered her, there was a diamond-carbide drill collar - the kind used for oil drilling - clamped in her mechanical arm. They must have recovered it from the seafloor before the accident. We just traced it to a Saudi oil firm called *NewSaudOil Corp*. I spoke with the director, just now. His explanation for it being there was somewhat unusual. Said it had fallen from one of their fishing boats operating in the area. Make of that what you will, Lieutenant."

Mitchell thanked Goodman for the information, confirming he'd be back in touch if he needed to, and hung up.

Goodman shrugged, finished his doughnut and gulped down the rest of his tea.

Inspector Lance Johnson arrived at St John's Wood Police Station, and nodded at Marjorie in reception, who was busy taking a call. He wandered over to his desk, placed his raincoat over the back of his chair and went to make himself a coffee. It was eight-thirty A.M and only three other officers appeared to be on shift.

He sat down and noticed a folder on his desk, which hadn't been there the day before. A label on the front told him the file related to the Stanton case. He opened the thin blue manila folder to reveal an A4 sheet of paper, which had a typed attendance note from a telephone call made to Highbury and Islington Police Station by a Mr. Mathew White five weeks ago. The note confirmed the caller had been taken ill and admitted to the Royal Brunswick Hospital with suspected poisoning. After spending seven days there recovering, and a further week convalescing at home, he'd discovered that his best friend, a Dr. Dale Stanton, had died of a heart attack. It had taken him ten days to appreciate this fact, due to severe amnesia caused by the tranquiliser discovered in his blood stream.

As Johnson read the rest of the report, he realised the information could give them the break they'd been waiting for. He called the number in the file, and arranged to meet Mathew White at his home at five-thirty, later that evening.

Just as he was about to leave his desk to brief Sergeant Smith, his phone rang again. He picked up the receiver.

"Inspector Johnson?" a man with an American accent inquired.

"Lieutenant Mitchell? You just caught me, what can I do for you?" Johnson asked.

"Morning, Inspector, I just wanted to touch base with you on the Stanton/Bannister case. I discovered some useful information, thought I'd better share it as it could assist both of us."

"Sure, I'm all ears Lieutenant."

Mitchell told him about the conversation he'd had with Charlie Goodman over at NSIDC.

Johnson made a note, not that it made much sense, or appeared to have any bearing on the case. "Who or what is NSIDC?" he asked.

"National Snow and Ice Data Centre - Bannister's employers," Mitchell clarified.

"Oh, yes, of course. Do you think any of this can be connected?" Johnson asked.

"Doesn't figure, Inspector, but my gut tells me to look into it further. Have there been any developments your end?"

"There's been one. We've traced a witness, a Mr. Mathew White, apparently a good friend of Dr. Stanton. He was supposed to meet up with Stanton at about seven-thirty P.M on the night of his death, but never showed up. Seems he was given some kind of sedative, I assume by the killer. I'm seeing him later today to take a full statement, but from what he says, he may well be our only eye witness."

"No kidding! Ok, keep me updated on that if you would. If I dig anything else up over here, I'll let you know. Give me a call on my mobile, any time. Take it easy, Inspector."

Johnson put the phone down and called Sergeant Peter Smith and arranged to meet him at Mathew White's home at five-thirty P.M. He then grabbed his raincoat from the coat-stand and went to find Superintendent Flint to update him on the latest developments.

CHAPTER 48

THE *MERCURE BLANC* rolled violently on a rising swell, passing through longtitude sixty degrees west, in the Labrador Sea. Officer Boucher was on the bridge, having taken over from Captain Deville a few hours earlier to allow him a much needed rest. His view through the bridge's windows was of an early morning mist, which hung over the ocean like a thick blanket.

Spire had been jolted awake at five-thirty A.M; unable to get back to sleep, he'd been sitting in the bar for the last few hours. He looked out over the grey ocean, rolling in deep regular swells. He calculated they must now be only two-hundred and fifty nautical miles or so away from southern Greenland. It had been five days since they'd left Marseilles, and he hoped - all being well - that they would reach their destination within the next forty-eight hours. He poured himself a fresh coffee, his thoughts wandering to Oakdale and Angela. He was missing her and his walks on the beach. He even missed the office.

He drank the coffee, thinking back to yesterday's experiment. Dr. McBride had been concerned about the ocean's low salinity levels, although it appeared no meaningful conclusions could be reached until further samples were taken later today, when they were closer to Greenland. *What did the results mean?*

Ksenyia quietly approached the door to the bridge, holding a small tray containing a pot of tea for Officer Henri Boucher. She had gone down to the galley herself earlier and persuaded Marco to let her take Boucher his morning tea on the premise that she was interested in seeing the bridge – the vessel's command room. She knocked on the door.

"Oui, c'est overt," came Boucher's muffled shout.

Ksenyia opened the heavy door and walked in. Boucher turned his seat around from a bank of controls he'd been monitoring, appearing pleasantly surprised to see her.

"Morning; is that for me?" he asked.

"Yes, I just thought I'd bring you some tea. I'd also love to see the bridge - hope you don't mind."

"Of course not," Boucher said, taking the tray from her. "Ever been on the bridge of a ship before?" he asked, enthusiastically, taking a large gulp of tea.

"No, I was hoping for a quick tour," Ksenyia said, looking at the bank of instruments and electronic displays in front of her. A large circular radar screen was positioned to the right of the wheel, a green line making a revolution of the screen every few seconds. Nothing appeared to be within radar range of their position.

"Of course," Boucher said, appearing happy that she was showing some interest in him. "Well, this wheel, of course, controls the *Mercure's* rudder, and these two levers here," he said, pointing at a set of levers which looked like the thrusters on a commercial jet, "control left and right engine throttle. Over there is the ship's radar, and here we have the sonar. This bank of equipment contains the vessels navigational aids as well as GMDSS - Global Maritime Distress Safety System, and the all-important DPS or Dynamic Positioning System."

"What's that exactly?" Ksenyia asked, searching the bank of switches for something that looked like the controls for the hydraulic clamping system that held the container of iron sulphate in place.

"DPS is a computer controlled system which allows the ship to maintain an exact position in the ocean, by using its own thrusters and propellers - really is very clever."

"And what about those controls over there?" Ksenyia asked, spotting something which looked like it could be what she was looking for.

"That's the control console for the ship's external winches, cranes and deck clamps, and those lights blinking on and off, that's the Inmarsat communications system."

Boucher placed his mug of tea on the bulkhead shelf. "Can you do me a favour and stand here for two minutes, while I go and check the stores? Don't worry, no need to touch the wheel or do anything - the autopilot is engaged."

"OK, but don't be long," Ksenyia said, smiling at Boucher as he left the bridge. She listened for his receding footsteps, and then went straight over to the bank of controls housing the external winches. Small labels under each confirmed what the levers and buttons were for, but the explanations were in French. She identified four buttons, coloured red; the label underneath read 'Brides Hydrauliques.' She depressed two of the buttons, which flashed green. As she did, she heard two faint, but distinct thuds, coming from somewhere outside on the deck. She looked through the salt-stained, water-streaked, windows onto the stern deck, where the large container was fixed in position. Suddenly the ship rolled to starboard, as a large wave struck the port side. The bridge creaked, but outside, she could see the container had become dislodged from the clamps, perhaps a foot or so out of alignment.

She smiled to herself. All she needed now was for the storm to strengthen.

Boucher reappeared and made straight for the wheel. "That

must have been a large wave," he said, raising the binoculars to his face. "Looks like we're going to hit some rough weather; you'd better go down and warn the others, I'll make an announcement shortly."

"Will do, Ksenyia said, as she left the bridge. "Oh, and thanks for the tour."

"Thank *you* for the tea," Boucher said, winking at her.

Spire pulled on his parka jacket and ventured out of the port door, tugging the toggles tight against the stinging wind. Gripping the side-rail, he looked out over the rough sea. Waves were building in height, rising to three metres or so, rolling in increasing, regular swells. A feeling of apprehension rose from the pit of his stomach. *Another storm was clearly developing.*

He looked toward the bow and guessed the *Mercure* must have been cruising at around eighteen knots or so. Freezing, foaming water sprayed onto his face from a large wave as it crashed onto the deck. He strengthened his grip on the rails as he watched another large wave approach the port side. As it struck, the *Mercure* responded by slowly rolling starboard as the wall of water passed underneath the hull.

Above the sound of the roaring ocean, Spire heard an unnatural, metallic sound, clearly much closer. "What the hell was that?" he muttered, as he shuffled along the deck toward the stern.

He rounded the superstructure, and stood, momentarily frozen to the spot as the huge steel container, now free of its holding clamps, slid towards him. Another wave hit the ship side on, causing it to roll toward the port side.

The container responded to the laws of physics, sliding even quicker in his direction. In the split second he had to react, he darted along the rear, of what he guessed, was the *Mercure's* science labs, just missing the huge steel cube, which smashed into the superstructure. The other corner of the container hit the ship's rail, which buckled under the impact.

As Spire tried to get his bearings, the *Mercure's* alarm sounded, almost deafening him. He clawed his way along the rear of the superstructure and glanced at the retaining clamps; two of them were in an upright position, as if they had sprung open, or failed somehow. He quickly made his way along the side of the ship, and back in through the starboard cabin door, slamming it shut behind him. He loosened his parka and ran along the corridor and up one level to the bar. Inside, Trimaud and Girard were frantically zipping up their jackets. "What the hell has happened, Robert?" Trimaud shouted.

"Looks like the clamps have failed, Francois; the bloody container is sliding about on the stern deck. Another large wave and we've had it."

"Merde, merde!" they both shouted. "Those clamps were secure, how did it happen?"

"No idea, Francois, I was out on deck and heard something, then saw the container slide toward me, damn thing nearly crushed me."

Captain Deville appeared at the door. "Trouble?" he asked, matter-of-factly, as he quickly pulled his trousers on over a pair of long-johns he must have been sleeping in.

"The container has broken loose, Jacques - retaining clamp must have failed," Trimaud shouted.

"C'est impossible," he bellowed. "We have to secure it. We can use the overhead crane. If I can pay out some cable, someone's going to have to try and get on top of the container and hook the cable onto the eyelet. We can then try and slot the damn thing back into the clamps. Quick, I'll meet you out on deck. If that thing moves toward you, don't try and stop it. I don't need any dead heroes - that's an order, now GO!"

Deville made his way to the bridge, whilst Spire, Trimaud and Girard hurried along the corridor toward the port door as Dr. McBride came running along the corridor toward them. "What's happening?" she yelled.

"Container's broken free. Stay inside, don't come out, whatever you do," Trimaud ordered, as the three of them made their way out on to the port deck, just as the *Mercure* took another starboard hit from a wave, rolling the ship to the right.

Spire led the way, clinging to the railings along the deck towards the stern. The container was still resting against the port barrier and railings, looking as if it was somehow jammed between them and the rear of the main superstructure.

As the ship righted itself from the last wave, a metallic screeching, followed by a popping sound, resonated along the deck. The three of them watched helplessly as the container broke free from the railing and slid out of sight along the deck toward the starboard rail. A dire crunching sound followed.

They hurried around to the rear of the superstructure to find the steel cube had come to rest on the starboard railings, this time, wrenching them from their circular mountings. The corner of the container was now perched perilously over the side of the ship.

From inside the Captain's Lounge, Ksenyia looked down at the chaotic scene outside. *Surely they wouldn't be able to save the container now.* She stood in the warm room - Dr. McBride and Dr. Mathews by her side - looking through the salt stained windows at the events unfolding on the deck below.

Spire heard another noise, above the roar of the ocean, and looked up to see the crane amidships slowly arcing toward the stern, its thick steel cable paying out until it reached just below the height of the steel container.

Searching the main superstructure, Spire noticed a deck area on the next level, which must have been a small sun terrace belonging to the ship's bar. "Stay here, you two. I have an idea," he shouted, as he made his way back along the side of the ship and through the port door. Once inside, he ran along the corridor, up the stairs and into the bar, where he spotted a small side-door which looked like a window. He hadn't noticed it before. He opened it, and walked out onto a small rear terrace, overlooking the aft-deck area.

He was now standing about a metre or so above the level of the container. The steel cable from the crane swayed wildly above him as the ship pitched and rolled on the stormy sea. The container still appeared to be wedged in the starboard railings.

Spire shouted down to Trimaud and Girard who were still standing there, unable to do anything. They were joined by Captain Deville, who rushed over to the four clamps where the container had previously been locked in place. He then signalled up to the bridge, and, within seconds, Spire heard two loud thuds, as the two securing clamps were released, ready to accept the container once again.

Spire took a deep breath, and, without hesitating, grabbed the cable which was now dangling just in front of him. Just as he took hold of it, the crane swung toward the container, dragging his upper body, and then his legs over the low rail fixed to the terrace. His hands slipped down the oily cable as the crane-head lurched toward the steel cube, just as the *Mercure* then rolled starboard on another wave. At the same moment, three loud pops resonated out across the deck, as the weight of the steel box snapped the rivets securing the three uprights holding the rail to the main deck.

The container slid further over the edge.

Spire slid down the length of the oily cable onto the top of the container; grabbed the large hook at the end of the cable, and pulled it toward the central eyelet. Another wave struck, causing the ship to lurch sideways, but he managed to hook the cable into place. The force of the wave, and the tilt of the ship proved too much however, and the container toppled off the deck.

Spire grabbed the cable as tightly as he could, his forearms burning, and closed his eyes as the crane briefly took the full weight of the container as it dangled perilously over the side of the vessel. The crane groaned as it held the load, just long enough for the *Mercure* to right itself. The container responded like a pendulum, half landing, and half being dragged back toward the centre of the deck.

Spire released his grip; his forearm muscles spent, and then lowered himself over the edge of the container, dropping the short distance to the wet deck, landing in an exhausted crumpled heap on the cold steel.

Twenty minutes later, with the assistance of the crane, the container, along with its precious cargo, had been secured by Deville and Trimaud. The clamps were repositioned, and the cable, as added security, was left in place, held taut by the crane above.

In the Captain's Lounge, Dr. McBride shook her head in disbelief. "Thank God for Robert Spire. I think he just single-handedly saved Professor Trimaud's experiment!"

Ksenyia looked on, unable to utter a word. She wanted to kill Spire. She bit her lip, trying to maintain her composure. She knew now that she had no choice but to immobilise all the crew if she was to succeed with her final assignment.

CHAPTER 49

INSPECTOR JOHNSON PULLED up outside number 17 Arlington Road, southeast London, and waited for Sergeant Peter Smith to arrive. Mathew White had to be interviewed, and quickly.

Smith pulled up in his unmarked Ford Mondeo and walked over to Johnson, who was waiting in his car. They both walked up the short path to the front door of number 17 and rang the doorbell. A dark-haired, unshaven, man opened the door. He looked to be in his mid-forties. "Mr. Mathew White?" Inspector Johnson asked, showing his badge.

"That's me. You must be the police, I assume? Please come in," White said, clearly expecting them.

Johnson introduced himself and Sergeant Peter Smith, and they both followed White into the dining room at the rear of the house, taking a chair each at the dining table, which had a view through some patio doors to a small, but well kept garden beyond.

"Can I get either of you a tea, or coffee?" White asked.

"Two coffees would be great, one without milk," Johnson said.

White disappeared into the kitchen for a while, then brought back three coffees and handed them each a cup. "So, I assume this is all about Dale's death, or murder more like?" White said, pointing to a copy of the *Daily Mail* on the table, which had a headline on the front page;

MET OFFICE CLIMATOLOGIST DEATH - POISONING NOW SUSPECTED.

"Bloody press; no idea how they got the story, but unfortunately their report is more or less accurate. Can you tell us what you recall from that night, Mr. White?" Johnson said.

White recounted his movements during the afternoon of Saturday 15th April, up until the evening. "It's the evening which is still a little sketchy for me I'm afraid, but I do remember arranging to meet Dale at the Kings bar of the Russo Hotel, over in Russell Square at around seven, seven-thirty P.M. I hadn't been at the bar long, when a very attractive woman, shoulder length brown hair, with a slight...I'd say Eastern European accent, started...well chatting me up, I suppose. I told her I was meeting a friend, but she didn't seem too concerned. I recall walking over to some comfortable chairs at the back of the bar, and that's about it. My mind is a blank from then on. Next thing I knew, I woke up in hospital. I did call the police about six weeks ago, told them what I'm telling you now."

Johnson scratched his head. "Yes, we appreciate that, Mr. White. Details of your call have only just reached us, unfortunately. How can you be so sure she was Eastern European?"

"Well, I can't, but she didn't look British, her accent certainly wasn't from around here."

"Have you seen her anywhere before?" Smith asked.

"No, not that I know of, think I'd remember her face, she was gorgeous."

"How tall was she, Mr. White, any other features you can recall?" Johnson continued.

"I'd say around five-nine, slim but athletic looking, and, oh yes, her eyes, a beautiful green colour."

"Would you be able to assist in an artist's impression, down at the station, if we can arrange it?" Smith asked.

"I could certainly try."

"Are you aware of anyone who'd want to harm Dr. Stanton? I mean, did he seem concerned about anything?" Johnson asked.

"No, of course not - he was a very gentle and private man. He took his work very seriously. He certainly didn't ever mention anything to me. I knew he'd been involved with some project down in Southampton, looking at the Atlantic current I believe, adjusting the data for new software, I think," White said, shrugging his shoulders.

Johnson and Smith made some notes, finished their coffees, and thanked White for his time.

They both walked through the hall to the front door. "Oh, one more thing, Mr. White; do you know a Mr. Robert Spire by any chance?" Johnson asked.

"Spire...Spire," White hesitated for a moment. The name does ring a distant bell....Yes, I know; I'm sure Dale mentioned that name in connection with his will. He told me how pleased he was that a Mr. Spire, a senior environmental law specialist, was dealing with his estate. He was rather concerned a year or two ago, after his father died leaving him a lot of money."

Johnson nodded. "Thank you again for your help Mr. White. We'll be in touch about the I.D sketch."

"Sure no problem, anything to help," White said, closing the door.

Johnson and Smith walked back to their cars. "Come on Peter; let's get back to the station. I need to contact Gus Mitchell over in San Francisco. We'll need Interpol in on this, I think. Spire maybe right, we could be dealing with something big here."

As soon as Johnson and Smith arrived back at the police station, Marjorie on the switchboard handed Johnson a telephone note from Gus Mitchell SFPD. "You're popular today; Superintendent wants to speak with you too - about the Stanton case."

"Thanks, Marjorie," Johnson said taking the note, "I'll go and see him now. Catch up with you after, Peter," he said, as he walked down the corridor to Superintendent Flint's room. He took a deep breath and knocked on the frosted glass-panelled door and walked in.

"Ah, Inspector, just the man, take a seat," Flint said.

Johnson sat down on the other side of the paper-covered desk.

"I need an update on the Stanton case," Flint said, tapping his pen on the desk. "Not only have the press got hold of the story, but I've had a call from Commander Farthing, over at Scotland Yard - looks like they have been following the case with interest, and now MI6 want to get involved. They are concerned that we might be dealing with some kind of international terrorist plot. Do you think they are right?"

"Well, they might be, sir; it seems the mystery is deepening," Johnson said, bringing Flint up to date on the interview with Mathew White, and the potential Eastern European suspect. "It's quite possible she might be Stanton's killer."

"We need to get this White character in ASAP. Get him to help with a police sketch of the suspect."

"That's already in motion, sir."

"Good. Is there any news from the USA? Lieutenant Gus Mitchell is working on the Bannister case over there, isn't he?"

"Correct, sir, I need to call him now, he's already tried to contact me today."

Johnson's mobile phone rang. He fumbled in his breast pocket and pulled out the phone to silence it, but saw Gus Mitchell's name was displayed on the screen. "Sir, it's Mitchell, I'll take the call."

"Hello, Lieutenant, Johnson speaking, what's the latest?"

Mitchell filled Johnson in on the latest news as Flint sat impatiently across the desk, tapping his pen on a pad of paper. After five minutes, Johnson ended the call, and looked over at Flint. "Sir, looks like Mitchell has made a breakthrough over in San Francisco. SFPD technical team have been analysing the surveillance footage taken in the Louvre. They have been able to enhance and reconstruct the images that were of interest. Mitchell has interviewed Bannister's friend, a Mr. John Gregory, and the security guard on duty, at the Ravenbrook Hotel, when Bannister died. Looks like the woman in the Louvre video, and the photographer calling herself Victoria Boothroyd, are one and the same person. According to both witnesses there was a very attractive female photographer who said she worked for *GreenTimes* environmental magazine, based over here in London."

"And?" Flint said, leaning forward in his chair.

"Well, Mitchell has carried out some checks, the magazine doesn't exist. Turns out a Victoria Boothroyd passed away peacefully in an old age home down in Brighton, in two-thousand and ten. Looks like a simple case of stolen identity, false passport etc. Same passport was used to book a Virgin-Atlantic flight from London to San Francisco the week Bannister died."

Flint shook his head. "Looks like she could be our killer," he said. "Once Mathew White has assisted with the sketch, we can see if there's a match. Get Mitchell to send the images over so White can see them."

"Will do, sir."

"Oh, and Johnson, try and get hold of Robert Spire will you, he needs to be kept in the loop in all this. The car that nearly rammed him off the road down in west Wales, the attempt on his life at the Louvre, must all be connected."

"I'll try, sir, but you do know he's on his way to the Arctic with Professor Trimaud on the French/US geoengineering expedition."

Flint looked at Johnson, his face screwed up. "Geo what?" he boomed.

"I read up on it, sir. The idea is to seed the ocean with iron sulphate, fertilizing it essentially, in order to create a plankton bloom which then absorbs carbon dioxide – the main greenhouse gas, sir."

"It seems we have a lawyer who thinks he's James Bond. Well, I'll give it to Spire, he's got some balls. At least he should be relatively safe all the way out there, especially if this whole thing does involve some sinister plan to kill our climatologists. Make this case top priority, Johnson, and expect a call from Scotland Yard."

"Of course, sir. I'll keep you informed of all developments," Johnson said, as he got up and left the room.

CHAPTER 50

Rezky, Davis Strait
June 6

THE *REZKY* SLOWED to ten knots as Vice Admiral Valentin Dashkov guided her through the semi-frozen waters of the Davis Strait. Scattered chunks of sea ice, that had recently broken free from the still solid coastal ice further up the channel, floated idly by. The Davis Strait wouldn't be completely free of ice for another two months or so, but the *Rezky's* ice-strengthened hull had no difficulty forcing its way through the thin, scattered sheet ice, weakened from the Arctic summer thaw.

The ship's radio suddenly burst to life. "This is the Canadian coastguard calling from Nanisivik refuelling station," a stern voice said. "We are tracking your vessel. Please identify yourself, and confirm purpose of transit through the Davis Strait, over."

Captain Tabanov, who was standing with Dashkov, picked up the radio, and exhaled a plume of smoke from a freshly lit cigarette before speaking. "This is Captain Mickail Tabanov on the retired Russian minesweeper *Rezky*. We are conducting navigation training manoeuvres along the Northwest Passage. Transit course and details were registered with your department last week. We request permission to continue along present route, through to the Beaufort Sea, over."

There was a thirty second silence, before the radio crackled to life again. "*Rezky*, you're cleared to proceed. The entire channel is pretty-much navigable; transit time will be around seven days at your present speed. If you require ice-breaker assistance on approach to the Melville Trough, let us know."

"Thank you for the offer, over."

The radio went dead. Tabanov winked at Admiral Dashkov and took a last drag on his cigarette before stubbing it out on the steel edge of the bulkhead. He pulled the binoculars from their stand and pressed them to his eyes. The ocean ahead was littered with ice-bergs of moderate size, and sections of flat, floating, broken pack-ice. Nothing looked out of the ordinary for the time of year.

Dashkov picked up the radio and called down to the communications room. "How are we looking down there? Any sonar targets showing?"

The radio crackled with static. "Channel ahead is clear, Admiral," Lieutenant Brilev reported.

"What about radar?"

"Nothing in sight; we're on our own here."

Dashkov radioed down to Officers' Charkov and Donskoy in the weapons room. "Get the first OTM ready for jettisoning, we're approaching the first drop zone," he said, calmly. "Double check the coordinates," Dashkov said, nodding to his comrade.

Tabanov checked the chart. Their orders had to be followed precisely; the first OTM was to be dropped in the middle of the Davis Strait, approximately one hundred and thirty-five nautical miles along the channel from Nuuk, and just inside the Arctic Circle. Two more would be dropped in the channel as they navigated into Baffin Bay, with a fourth dropped at the entrance to the Northwest Passage proper, under the

Canadians' noses, as they rounded Bylot Island. The remaining four devices would be dropped as they navigated through the Northwest Passage in the waters of the Lancaster Sound and Melville Trough.

"So, Admiral, let me get this straight," Tabanov said, looking up. "When activated, the devices will heat the water around them to a temperature of ten degrees Celsius. Convection then ensures that the heated water radiates out from the device to a distance of one hundred nautical miles, creating columns of warm water that will rise to the surface."

"That is correct, Captain. Once activated, no more ice will form along the Northwest Passage. Not even during Arctic winter. The channel will be almost as warm as the Mediterranean." Dashkov smirked. He moved over to a bank of instruments and checked the *Rezky's* global positioning equipment, which confirmed they were approaching the first drop zone. He killed the engines, slowing the *Rezky* down from fifteen knots to a crawl, its wake no longer strong enough to push the floating chunks of ice away. Small icebergs started to surround the ship, as if being pulled toward it by a strong magnet.

Down in the weapons room, Officer Charkov attached the sling from the overhead crane to the first OTM, and pulled the hand-held control-pad from its hook on the side of the steel shelving. He yanked the black cable from its storage pouch, and pressed the green button. There was an audible click, as the crane sprang to life. Using the small control knob, he carefully lifted the car-sized object from its steel resting platform. The racking groaned as if relieved at the reduction in weight, as the OTM was lifted half a metre or so into the air.

The crane was fixed to an overhead gantry, which ran along

steel rails fixed to the ceiling of the weapons room. The rails continued out into the corridor, where they turned and travelled toward the port side of the ship, ending at the hull. A large, modified compartment had been designed there, for the purpose of jettisoning mines out into the ocean below. The OTMs were heavier than a mine, but the gantry's forty tonne operating capacity was more than adequate to lift the twenty-five tonne thermal devices.

Donskoy radioed up to the bridge, "Standing by, Admiral."

"Good. I'll start filling starboard ballast tanks one and two now," Dashkov responded.

Charkov moved the object into the centre of the weapons room and nervously manoeuvred the device using the portable control pad. The chains creaked under the weight of the OTM as it swayed in the sling. "The quicker we get this radioactive water-heater out of here, the better," Charkov moaned.

"Concentrate on the task," Donskoy ordered, "I'll steady it as it moves along the gantry."

As they reached the end of the room, they heard the hissing of pressurised water being pumped into the *Rezky's* starboard ballast tanks, to counteract the weight of the thermal device as it was transferred toward the port side of the ship.

The two men slowly followed the shiny-black ocean heater as it was moved toward the corridor. Five minutes later they reached the end of the gantry runners, and the OTM was positioned up against the port-side hull.

Charkov punched a series of digits into the head-height key pad, at the end of the dimly-lit corridor. A hydraulic hiss followed as a large panel in the ship's hull dislodged, allowing sunlight, and a cold blast of Arctic air to rush into the corridor. Moments later, the panel slid between the ship's inner and outer hulls creating a large rectangle aperture, the length of a family car, in the side of the *Rezky's* hull, seven metres or so above the water line.

Officer Donskoy took the radio from a clip on his belt, "Admiral, the device is in place; standing by."

There was a short burst of static. "You may release the OTM when you are ready, comrade."

Donskoy attached the radio back on his belt clip, nodded to Charkov, then slid back between the object and the corridor wall to where Charkov was standing. Taking the control-pad, he pressed the *Eject* button.

There was a metallic whine as two rails, previously hidden, extended out beyond the side of the hull, carrying the device out over the ocean. Two popping sounds followed, as the hook holding the sling opened, dropping the OTM into the ocean below.

Charkov and Donskoy hurried to the aperture and looked out over the side of the ship. The device had landed on a large slab of melting pack-ice, cracking it in two. In stark contrast to the white ice, the jet-black Ocean Temperature Modifier looked like a lump of coal sitting on the pristine ice, as it briefly bobbed on the surface, then slowly sank beneath the ice-strewn, grey ocean.

Admiral Dashkov started the *Rezky's* engines, powering them up to twenty knots, setting a course that would take them along the Davis Strait to Baffin Bay, the location for the second drop zone, some two hundred and fifty nautical miles from their current position.

CHAPTER 51

Mercure, Labrador Sea
June 6

SPIRE WAS SEATED in the ship's lounge draining his fourth bottle of *Kronenbourg* as the *Mercure* continued its cruise through the North Labrador Sea, around one hundred nautical miles southwest of Greenland. The storm had passed, and a calm, dark ocean extended out from the ship in all directions. He had been in the bar since around five P.M, nursing a pulled shoulder-muscle, brought on by hanging from the cable when trying to reconnect the container cable.

Captain Deville and Trimaud entered the lounge and walked up to the bar. "How's Indiana Jones doing?" Deville asked, a large smile was visible under his grey beard. "That was a very brave thing you did out there, Robert, but don't try anything like it again - not on this ship anyway."

"Understood, Captain," Spire said, raising his hand to mimic a salute.

"Jacques, don't be so harsh; without Robert here my experiment would probably be over before it started."

"Pass me one of those beers, will you, I need a drink," Deville said, gesturing to Spire.

Spire reached over and grabbed two more bottles, handing one to Deville.

"Here's to nothing else going wrong - salut!" Deville said,

raising his bottle, and downing the contents in five large gulps.

"So, where exactly are we now, Captain?" Spire asked.

Deville checked his watch; "We'll be entering the Davis Strait in about three hours, passing into the Arctic Circle shortly after that. The Strait is about four hundred nautical miles long. Plan is to hug the coast of Greenland as we navigate up, usually less ice on that side. Then we'll head for Baffin Bay and Bylot Island, where we'll turn northwest and up through the passage. Thirty-six hours from now and we should be at the seeding location," Deville said, looking at Trimaud for affirmation.

"Oui, that's about right," Trimaud replied, sipping his beer. "The site for the ocean seeding is around five hundred-fifty kilometres along the Northwest Passage, a body of water named the Lancaster Sound, not far from Resolute Bay."

"You scientists' can then start having fun!" Deville said, raising his empty bottle. "At twenty-five knots, ice permitting, it'll be around twelve hours from Bylot Island to the seeding location," Deville added, shrugging his broad shoulders.

Spire was distracted by Dr. Bonnet, who had just entered the lounge. She walked up to them, a look of concern on her face. "Bonsoir, Professor, Robert, Captain," she said, looking at them in turn. She spoke to Trimaud in French, clearly articulating something important.

Trimaud reacted with surprise.

"Pardon," Dr. Bonnet said, "but I have just explained to Francois that the test results, from the water sample we took today, were not as expected. Dr. McBride has asked the professor to come to the laboratory to take a look."

Trimaud looked at Spire. "Come on, Robert, the salinity levels are, once again, very low. Let's go and see what's going on."

Captain Deville threw his empty beer bottle into the bin.

"I'll leave you guys to the science. See you at dinner," he said, as he left the bar and headed for the bridge.

Spire followed Trimaud and Dr. Bonnet down two decks to the rear science laboratory, where Dr.'s McBride and Mathews were hunched over a computer screen.

"Ah, Ruth," Trimaud said, as he walked over to the computer, "Mari just broke the news. What have you found?"

Dr. McBride turned around. "Francois, yes, I thought you'd be interested in seeing the results. They don't look good."

Trimaud studied the computer monitor, as Dr. Mathews pointed at a set of graphs, clearly visible on the screen. Trimaud started shaking his head as he analysed the results.

Spire heard footsteps and turned toward the door to see Dr. Sinclair walking in.

"Hello, I heard there was some news," she said.

"Yep, bad by the sound of it," Spire replied, walking over to the monitor. "What have you found?" he asked.

"Well, the water samples we took today from the Labrador Sea should show salinity levels commensurate with this graph here, taken from data obtained in nineteen eighty two. You see the North Atlantic Deep Water, NADW for short, acts as the engine - in simple terms - for the Ocean Thermohaline that we talked about earlier. As the highly saline water in this area sinks, it drags the waters of the North Atlantic Drift northwards. The test samples show that the salinity levels are down by forty percent."

"So what does that mean exactly, in layman's terms?" Spire asked.

"Basically there is an unusually large amount of fresh water in the upper-most layers of the ocean. They are the lowest salinity levels that have ever been measured, as far as I'm aware. There's only one source for this amount of fresh water, and that's melting ice. As the salinity of the ocean is diluted, the normally heavier water can't sink, which affects the entire ocean conveyor."

"Wouldn't you expect that anyway, as the Arctic ice starts its summer melt?"

"Yes, Robert, but this computer program has factored those calculations in. The measurements reveal something far more significant than that. These dilution levels suggest a massive influx of fresh water is taking place, and the only source of that can be Greenland."

"We need to relay these findings back to the *RAPID-WATCH* team in the UK as soon as possible," Dr. Mathews interjected, as he printed off the graphs from the monitor.

"Well, it certainly makes your ocean seeding experiment all the more imperative, Francois. It would appear that fresh-water run-off from melting glacial ice is increasing," added Dr. McBride.

Dr. Sinclair stood there, a pensive look on her face. "What would the effects be, if the ocean conveyor slowed down?" she asked.

"Well, all sorts, and none of them good," Dr. Mathews continued. "If the conveyor slows, or God forbid stops, then warm water will no longer be brought up to the Northern Hemisphere from the Equator. The UK and the Eastern Seaboard of the United States and a large part of Northern Europe would suddenly get much colder. And, if Greenland's glaciers melt, ocean levels could rise by six metres or so, about twenty one foot, swamping many of the world's coastal cities."

"And how would Professor Trimaud's experiment prevent this from happening?"

"Well, the most unique aspect of my experiment," Trimaud added, "is the ability of the modified *Blankoplankton* to increase the albedo effect in the Arctic - essentially the ability of a surface to reflect light. If we can increase this effect, then we have every confidence that we can lower temperatures over a vast area, and slow down, possibly even reverse the current warming trend, as more sunlight gets reflected back into space."

Spire couldn't help noticing Dr. Sinclair shaking her head, looking somewhat despondent. "Are you OK?" he asked.

"Yes, sorry, I…I was thinking about something, that's all."

"Something you'd like to share?" Dr. McBride asked.

"Oh, no, I was just thinking about the experiment, I have a bit of a headache actually. I think I'll go and lie down," she said, leaving the laboratory.

Odd, Spire thought, as something niggled at the back of his mind. Something he couldn't quite put his finger on. "Francois, shall we pop up to the lounge for a chat?" he suggested, switching his thoughts back to the seemingly worrisome test results. "Do you think this could have been what Dr. Stanton was working on? Maybe he also discovered the low salinity levels?"

"I shouldn't think so," Dr. McBride interrupted. "I looked at the results taken from the Atlantic sampling survey at the *RAPID-WATCH* monitoring site only last month, they were normal."

"How can that be?" Spire asked.

"Well, we wouldn't expect the fresh water run-off from the melting glaciers to have reached down to that latitude yet, especially if it's only a relatively recent thing."

Spire shook his head, desperate to know what Dr. Stanton may have been working on. A thought then crossed his mind. "Could Dr. Stanton have had access to this recent data?"

"Unlikely," Dr McBride shrugged. "We are the first team to take samples at this latitude, as far as I know. Dr. Stanton was simply synchronising the older data with the new software, as far as I'm aware."

"Come on, Robert," Trimaud said, "let's go up and try and figure out what these results could mean, and then we'll call Southampton."

Spire followed Trimaud, who was armed with the data print-off from the computer, out of the lab and up to the bar.

Ksenyia locked the cabin door behind her and lay down on the bed, suddenly feeling drained. She thought about Professor Trimaud's comments. She now knew what was in the container - some kind of super plankton initiator, and why it was so important. She now appreciated the seriousness of it all. Before, she hadn't really thought about it, or even believed that global warming was occurring. Now, she could see that something was indeed going on, and Trimaud might actually be trying to prevent an environmental disaster, not actually cause one. She closed her eyes and thought about the engineer lying dead in the engine room, shortly to be discovered. Her head was spinning, It was too late; she had set in motion a chain of events that were now unstoppable. She needed to act, complete the task she'd been assigned. She shook her head instinctively, knowing that she couldn't allow herself to be distracted from the job that lay ahead. She would complete her mission, and then rendezvous with the *Rezky,* which would finally take her home to Russia.

Marcus Roux yawned as he left his cabin. He had overslept, but still felt tired from his initial twenty-four hour shift. He shook his head vigorously in an attempt to wake himself up, feeling guilty for not relieving Luc from his duties two hours ago, as scheduled. "Merde," he cursed under his breath as he made his way down to the engine room.

Up on the bridge, Captain Deville checked the radar screen. The route ahead on their approach to the Davis Strait was clear. He increased propulsion to twenty-five knots, planning to make up some lost time. He also wanted to try and beat his own personal best time for travelling from the tip of Greenland to Resolute Bay, which he'd managed back in 1992. He glanced at the radar screen again. All of a sudden, a red light started blinking on one panel in front of him.

"Ce qui est ceci?" Deville muttered, as he tapped the temperature gauge above the flashing light. A buzzer abruptly sounded, indicating engine number two was overheating. "Merde," he shouted, as he throttled back the engines and engaged the autopilot. He picked up the phone and called down to the engine room. "What the hell's going on down there? Morel, pick up...Roux? Is anyone there?" He slammed the phone down and headed for the engine room.

As Roux opened the engine room door, he noticed a strong smell of burning rubber. "Sorry, Luc I overslept again, I hope you..." He stopped mid-sentence, as he walked into the smoke-filled engine room. "Merde, Luc, what's going on?"

He hit the emergency lighting switch and grabbed a mask and goggles from the safety rack by the door. The emergency lighting bathed the room in a red glow. Smoke was billowing out of one of the valves near to the heat exchanger on engine number two. The drive shaft for the propeller was still revolving, but clearly slowing down. He punched the engine's emergency stop button, whilst almost slipping onto his back from the fluid that had accumulated on the deck from the leaking valve. As the emergency ventilation engaged and sucked the smoke out of the compartment, he noticed a dark figure slumped in the corner of the room.

"Luc," he shouted, as he ran over to his friend. "What the hell happened?" he said, dragging Morel's lifeless body toward the door. He placed him in the recovery position and felt for a pulse, but didn't find one. He started pumping his chest, blowing air into his friend's lungs, but it was too late. Luc Morel had succumbed to the engine fumes.

"Non! Non!" Roux screamed, as Captain Deville came charging down the corridor toward him.

CHAPTER 52

THE FENNEC EUROCOPTER flew low over the Southwestern Territories on route to the Inuit settlement, having left the Danish military base of Station Nord in Northern Greenland some hours earlier. Anders Jensen, glacial scientist from Denmark's Technical University was on board, along with three student climatologists.

Following the recent Greenland earthquake, the university had put together a team to fly out to the epicentre to collect data, and to assess the threat from the increasing level of seismic activity in the region.

"Twenty minutes to Samutaat," the pilot reported, as they tracked along the coast of Greenland.

"Stay at least ten metres away from the fault line," Jensen reminded the team, who were all now dressed in Arctic all-weather clothing.

"No problem with that request, Anders," Olsen, a rugged blond-haired man said, pulling the draw strings tight on his canvas bag. The bag contained seismic sensor pods to place in the glacier along the length of the crevasse, which would be used to monitor any further tremors or ice movement.

The chopper's rotors thumped a rhythmical beat as the pilot banked left and headed inland. The small Inuit settlement of Samutaat came into view, overshadowed by the towering face of the terminus of the Helheim Glacier.

Jensen looked out of the window as they flew over the vast expanse of ice, when three kilometres further inland from the glacier terminus, the massive fissure came into view.

The men looked down in awe as they studied the split in the ice. "Another quake here and the glacier will crack in half," Jensen said, studying the crevasse which travelled inland as far as the eye could see.

"Proof that Greenland is officially rising," Thomsen, an overweight ruddy-faced man said, as he looked down at the glacier through the small round window.

"Certainly looks like it," Jensen replied. "As the glaciers melt, the reduction in weight is causing seismic events as the continent rises back up. Something we'd been predicting for some time. We just didn't expect it to happen so quickly."

The pilot banked sharp right and started descending to a level area, some fifty metres or so from the gaping crack that had opened in the glacier. The rotors downward force blasted snow and ice away in all directions in a swirling mass of white, as the helicopter touched down on the surface of the glacier. A short distance away, melt-water cascaded down into the moulin that had formed on the surface.

The pilot flicked a number of switches on the control panels in front, and above his head, as the rotors powered down. He then turned to the men in the back. "You got thirty minutes, gentlemen, to plant the sensors. I'll be cranking up the motor at 15.45. Make sure you're all back on board."

Jenson nodded, pulling the handle to open the door. A blast of cold air and swirling snow entered the cabin. The four men jumped out, ducking under the whining rotor blades as they ran clear of the helicopter.

"Remember, no less than ten metres from the danger zone. Any sign of movement, we get the hell out of here," Jensen shouted.

The men walked gingerly towards the designated distance from the void. Thomsen took a series of photographs, whilst

Olsen pulled out a seismic sensor from his canvas bag and turned it on. He then pulled a small rubber-headed mallet from his belt and carefully hammered the pod into the ice as close to the crevasse as he could get. Olsen and his two colleagues repeated the task, leaving a gap of some twenty metres between them along the length of the glacial crack.

With the task completed, the men returned to the waiting helicopter and were flown further inland where the process was repeated again. A further fifteen pods were inserted into the ice along the crevasses length, some five kilometres from the glacier's terminus.

Exhausted and back on board the helicopter, Jensen requested the pilot take them back to the Inuit settlement situated at the base of the glacier, so he could deliver a message to the Inuit elders from the Danish government.

The pilot lifted the helicopter off the ice-mass, banked and tipped the nose down and navigated back toward the coast, and along the glacier toward the terminus and the settlement of Samutaat nestled at its base.

Talirik was inside his tent, playing a board game with his children using small pebbles, when he heard the distinctive, repetitive, thumping, which he recognised as the sound of the steel bird. He stood up and pushed the tent flap away, and stepped out into the afternoon sun. Shielding his eyes, he saw the craft descending from the blue sky into the swirling snow.

The Fennec Eurocopter landed a short distance away from the tented settlement. The pilot turned off the rotors and jumped out onto a patch of grass, recently thawed from its usual ice-covered state. He looked on as the scientists walked towards a group of Inuit who had assembled near to one of the larger tents.

Jensen greeted the elder, who he recognised from previous trips. "Amaguq, it's good to see you again, how are you?"

"Hello, Jensen, we are fine. Come, come inside and have some tea. What brings you and the steel bird back to Samutaat?"

The men followed Amaguq into the large tent, and sat down on some small wooden chairs arranged around a central fire, over which hung a steel kettle, its contents boiling.

"I'm afraid we bring bad news, Amaguq. There was a large earthquake four days ago, only five kilometres from here. The epicenter was eighteen kilometres below the surface. Massive fissures have opened in the ice on the glacier, and we are worried that any further seismic activity could destabilise the ice and endanger the entire settlement."

Amaguq poured the men some tea, eyeing Jensen and the other men cautiously as he did. A few moments passed in silence. "We live here for one hundred and fifty years. We see and hear a lot of things during that time. We hear loud scream coming from glacier at time you mention, but everything is ok. We see Tupilek the spirits dancing in sky, they warn and protect us."

"You mean the *Aurora Borealis?* This time the night spirits won't be able to help you, Amaguq; you must listen, please, the entire settlement is in danger. The Danish Government wants to help relocate you all to a safer location."

At that moment, Talirik entered the tent, greeted the scientists and sat down. "What news do you bring?"

Amaguq explained to Talirik what the men had just said.

"Do you think serious this time?" Talirik asked, his dark eyes narrowing.

"Yes, I was just explaining to Amaguq that the glacier is melting. Tremors and underground earthquakes are increasing right across the continent, caused by the landmass rising, as the weight of the melting ice covering it decreases. This process will continue for decades to come."

Talirik spoke slowly. "We know the ice is melting. We see larger and larger melt-pools on ice, earlier and earlier each year when we go hunting. I saw Tupilek in sky, at same time as large roar came from glacier four moons ago. I know something is wrong."

"I'm afraid your settlement is in danger. Our government wants to relocate you to an area two hundred miles along the coast. You will be safer there."

"This is our home," Amaguq said. "We have to meet with the elders of the settlement to discuss your proposal, they will decide if we move or not. They will ask the spirits and then deliberate on the matter, but we thank you for coming to warn us."

"You must advise the elders of the danger you are all in. The glacier could split or collapse at any time, and your homes lie right under its terminus. Please, you need to move, Tupilek can't help you this time."

Talirik looked up at the men. "Is the hunting as good over there? We must be able to hunt seal."

Jensen looked at the others for assistance. Thomsen spoke up. "Yes, I believe it will be the same. The seal population is pretty much stable around the entire coast. You will not notice any difference," he said, glancing at his note book.

"We will consult the other elders," Amaguq repeated.

Talirik nodded in agreement, a look of concern spreading across his face.

Jensen and his men finished their tea, and left the tent. A sled skidded past, pulled by eight huskies, a fresh kill of seals tethered to the back of it. The men looked around the small settlement, and at the towering glacier, glinting in the sun a short distance away.

The peaceful and modest settlement was facing peril; the scientists knew that anthropogenic global warming was melting Greenland's glaciers at an alarming rate. The settlement was in imminent danger of being destroyed, either by melting ice, rock fall, or both.

"Come on, let's get back, we can't do any more here today," Jensen said, as they turned and walked back to the waiting helicopter, its blades already turning.

As they rose into the azure sky, the men looked down on the small group of Inuit, who had gathered below to wave them off. The Eurocopter circled the settlement once, before tracking back along the coast toward Station Norde. They would return in a week, with a final offer to repatriate the Inuit from their settlement to their new home further along the coast.

Below them on the glacier, three of the sensor pods placed along the crevasse, started picking up low seismic signals, emanating from deep within the massive ancient ice flow.

CHAPTER 53

LUC MOREL'S BODY was taken to the ship's laboratory, where it was laid out on one of the work benches. The crew gathered around as Captain Deville held a brief service for the engineer, who had served alongside him in the French Navy many years earlier.

Officer Henri Boucher was on the bridge, guiding the *Mercure* up the Davis Strait at fifty percent throttle, a speed of only twelve knots, while the engine repairs were completed. Fortunately the *Mercure* had been carrying two spare heat exchangers in her provisions room.

"Jeez, if I was superstitious, I'd swear this trip was jinxed Francois," Spire said, rubbing his aching shoulder as they left the laboratory.

Trimaud shook his head in disbelief. "Why didn't Luc just get out, sound the alarm...something? He didn't have to suffocate like that."

"I agree," Girard said, "It makes no sense."

"We should get the water sample results back to Professor Sammedi's team in Southampton as soon as possible," Spire suggested.

Trimaud spread the computer print-out on the bar in front of him and collated the two data-sets collected from the Niskin bottle samples from the North Atlantic and Labrador Sea. A quick calculation confirmed that salinity levels from both locations were down forty percent and fifty-five percent respectively. "Bon, let's go," Trimaud said, after checking the data. "Pierre, you'd better go and see if Mari needs any help."

"OK, I'll come with you, Francois, just in case Professor Sammedi wants to speak to me," Spire said, as they all left the lounge cabin.

They arrived on the bridge and asked Officer Boucher if they could use the Inmarsat phone.

"No problem, it's right over there. Don't worry; I'm sure Jacques will send you the bill," Boucher replied, chuckling.

Spire looked out of the bridge's windows. The sea outside was slate-grey, chunks of ice floated in the channel over toward Baffin Island, visible on the port side. The snow-covered coastline of Greenland rose out of the ocean to their starboard side, but the water ahead looked ice-free. "Looks quite clear out there," Spire commented.

"Oui, on this side, the warmer water of the West Greenland Current keeps the route pretty much clear, at this time of year," Boucher said, as he surveyed the ocean ahead with his binoculars.

"Afternoon," Trimaud suddenly shouted down the Inmarsat phone. "Sorry for the static, but I'm calling from the research vessel, *Mercure Blanc*, currently in the Arctic. I need to speak with Professor Sammedi, or someone from his team. Yes, I can hold," Trimaud replied, after a few moments silence.

Spire turned his gaze from the view outside and waited, wondering what Professor Sammedi would think of the data samples.

Trimaud spoke again, introducing himself to Professor Sammedi, and the reason for his long-distance call. He then relayed the Niskin bottle data to him, and the exact coordinates the samples were taken from.

After a moment, Trimaud nodded, "Yes, sure, he's with me now." He lowered the receiver. "He needs to speak to you, Robert," Trimaud said, handing the phone to Spire.

Spire took the phone. "Mr. Spire," Sammedi boomed, "I hope you are all keeping warm out there?"

Spire listened through the static as Sammedi told him that he'd been looking over the data from the *RAPID-WATCH* project, and had discovered that some of the calibration on the measuring devices was wrong. He was still investigating, but he was sure it was what Stanton had probably been looking at.

"Listen," Sammedi continued, clearly concerned, "there are reports coming through from the US Geological Survey of increased seismic activity under Greenland. You need to be careful up there. Oh, and a Detective Johnson came to see me two days ago, asking about Dale. He said he had some important information for you. He mentioned that the UK and US police were now looking into the theory that a female is linked to the scientists' deaths. The Louvre footage has been examined, and Dale's friend, Mathew White has been interviewed. They think the woman at the Louvre, the reporter from the Ravenbrook Hotel in San Francisco, and the girl Mathew White bumped into at the Hotel Russo on the night of Dale's death are one and the same. Are you listening Robert? They think she's -"

The line went dead.

"Professor Sammedi…Professor?" Spire shouted down the phone; nothing. He handed the Inmarsat phone back to Boucher who placed it back on the consol and tried to reconnect the call.

"Looks like we have lost the signal, I'm afraid. Odd, as we should still have satellite coverage at this latitude," Boucher said, just as the lights on the console blinked out. "Merde," Boucher cursed, "looks like communications have gone down!"

An ominous feeling welled up from the pit of Spire's stomach. *Communications down, what next?* He hastily relayed to Trimaud what Professor Sammedi had told him.

Trimaud scratched his head. "The seismic activity is a real concern, Robert," he said, his voice faltering for the first time. "Come on; let's leave Henri to concentrate on getting us to the seeding point. We should be there in another twenty-four hours."

Spire followed Trimaud off the bridge and back to the lounge deck. "Francois, if you don't mind, I'm going to go back to my cabin. I need to lie down for a bit and get my head around a few things. I'll see you later, knock if you need me."

Dr. Ruth McBride knocked on Dr. Sinclair's door with the intention of going over the salinity and plankton data they had gathered. There was no answer. She tried the handle, the door was unlocked and it creaked open.

"Dr. Sinclair, you there? It's Ruth," she said, opening the door further. She entered the cabin and the first thing she noticed was an open science book on the bed. She picked it up and noticed it was the latest edition, only three months old. She placed it back down and went to walk out, when she saw a black case protruding from under a towel. Intrigued, she pulled the towel back and revealed an attaché case. She lifted it upright and slid the locking buttons outwards - the latches sprang open.

The contents of the case confused her. Expecting perhaps to see some scientific equipment, she was shocked to see an assortment of passports, handgun, and a container of clear liquid. She picked up one of the passports and flicked through it. It was a British passport showing Dr. Sinclair with blonde hair, the name under the photograph, Victoria Boothroyd.

The discovery unnerved her and she tossed the passport back into the case, but couldn't resist picking up the container of liquid. She gripped the cap and started to unscrew the top so she could smell it.

Ksenyia made her way back up from the ship's Electronics Room situated on the lower deck. After studying the *Mercure's* electronics systems, it had been relatively straightforward to disable the communications equipment. The *Mercure Blanc* was now alone; all external communications were down. She wiped dark brown oil from her hands as she made her way back along the corridor to her cabin. She needed to change her clothes and take a shower.

As soon as she turned the corner she noticed that her cabin door was ajar. Adrenalin surged through her veins as she stealthily approached the open door and peered into her room. She could see the back of Dr. McBride, hunched over her open attaché case. She slipped quietly into her room, closing and locking the door behind her.

CHAPTER 54

DR. RUTH MCBRIDE heard the door creak behind her and spun around, almost dropping the open container of nicotine solution she was holding. "Oh…Dr. Sinclair, there you are, I…I just came to see you," she stammered.

"You won't find anything of interest in there," Ksenyia replied, making no effort to hide her Russian accent.

"May I ask what the hell you doing with a gun, Dr. Sinclair? Not to mention all these passports?"

"Please, slowly place the container back down on the table."

Dr. McBride started backing up to the porthole behind her. She felt trapped, had nowhere to go.

"I'm afraid I can't tell you what's in the container, or my reason for being here. I just need you to put it down, and to sit on the bed," Ksenyia said, moving towards her.

Ruth McBride had never felt so scared or threatened in her life. At a loss over what to do, she threw the container of liquid at her entrapper, and then lunged for the gun lying in the attaché case.

She knew she had missed as soon as she threw it. The full container hit the cabin door, spraying the contents over the wall. "Don't move any closer, Dr. Sinclair," she shouted, pointing the gun at the imposter, her hand trembling.

"That's not a good idea," Ksenyia said, continuing towards her.

"I mean it, I'll shoot!"

"You Americans are all the same," Ksenyia responded, shaking her head. "Suddenly feeling brave with a gun in your hand? Surely you prefer the touch of a cold, glass, test tube?"

Dr. McBride pulled the trigger, but the recoil and explosion she'd been expecting didn't materialise. She pulled the trigger again, but the pistol just clicked.

"Looking for this?" Ksenyia said, pulling the ammunition clip from her pocket.

Before Dr. McBride could respond, the imposter lashed out at her with a quick, powerful punch to her neck. The choking blow sent her flying back into the porthole behind. She felt her head crack on the steel rim of the window. Her legs buckled from under her and she slid to the floor, darkness enveloping her.

"I told you it was a bad idea," Ksenyia muttered to herself, as she grabbed a silk scarf from her wardrobe and gagged Dr. McBride with it. She then dragged her limp body over to the open wardrobe, lifted her torso in, followed by her legs, and then swivelled the doctor around lengthways. She then pulled a cord from her attaché case, and tied Dr. McBride's hands behind her back, closed the wardrobe, and wrapped some of the same cord around the handles, securing it tightly shut.

She cleared up the mess, inserted the ammunition clip back into her pistol, and locked and hid her attaché case, something she should have done earlier.

After showering, she left the cabin to let the others know that Dr. McBride wasn't feeling well, and had asked not to be disturbed for the next twelve hours.

CHAPTER 55

ROBERT SPIRE LAY on his bed, thinking about the anagram *Liquid Carbon* he'd created from the name on the business card - *Arc Bin Quid Lo*. He considered Professor Sammedi's comments about there being a female link to the deaths; the reduced ocean salinity levels, and the fact that Greenland was becoming increasingly unstable. *This is turning into a nightmare.* The effects of global warming appeared to be occurring rapidly in the Arctic, and to make matters worse, it looked like somebody was intent on preventing the bad news from being made public. He wondered how Dr. Stanton had spent his last evening. *Had he been seduced by a femme fatale?*

He closed his eyes, his thoughts drifting to Angela and home. It seemed like an age since he'd felt her warm body against his, her soft kisses. She'd be worrying about him, no doubt. The last contact he'd had with her was four days ago, as they passed through the Straits of Gibraltar.

Refocusing on the anagram, Spire knew that there were probably vast reserves of oil under the Arctic, waiting to be exploited by the nations which had mineral rights there. *But could the scientists' deaths really be linked to oil? Or was this whole anagram thing just a ridiculous idea?* He jumped off the bed, eager to share his discovery with Francois, to see what he thought.

Spire knocked on Trimaud's cabin, not having been able to find him in the lounge or the science lab.

"Oui," Trimaud shouted from inside.

Spire found Trimaud lying down, going over the ocean salinity results. "Francois, I think I've discovered something."

Trimaud looked up from his papers.

"Remember the odd-looking business cards found on Dr. Stanton and close to where Dr. Bannister was found dead? I think the name on it may be an anagram for something."

Trimaud jumped up from his bed. "Are you sure? Come on; let's go to the bar for a drink, my friend."

Spire opened two bottles of *Kronenbourg* and handed one to Trimaud, then unfolded the piece of paper on the bar in front of them.

Trimaud stared at the paper for a while, analysing the words which Spire had formed *Liquid Carbon* from, before looking back up at Spire. "You mean *Oil?*"

Spire nodded. "Exactly, Francois."

"Good God, Robert, It certainly makes sense. I mean, if oil has been discovered, it would make someone very rich. I know that vast deposits probably exist under the Arctic, but I don't see how it correlates with the deaths of Jack and Dr. Stanton."

Spire shook his head. "Could there be oil around the Crozet Islands?"

Trimaud's eyes widened. "I've no idea, Robert. If there was, you'd have thought something would have shown up when searching the internet?"

"Unless, any discoveries made there have been kept secret."

They were interrupted by the gruff voice of Captain Deville over the P.A system, informing them that the necessary repair to the damaged engine had now been completed, enabling him to increase speed to twenty knots.

"Some good news at last," Trimaud said. "We should be at the seeding location early tomorrow afternoon. On the way back, if communications are still down, we can stop off in Canada or Greenland and call the UK to alert the police about the oil theory. What do you think?"

"I don't see we have a choice, Francois. If this whole thing is related to oil, then someone in the industry will surely know about it."

"It's all very puzzling, Robert. Listen, I'd better go and check on the container again, then go over my calculations in preparation for the seeding to take place. I'll see you at dinner later."

Spire finished his beer, wondering where Dr. McBride and Dr. Mathews were. He'd not seen either of them for some time. *Must be preparing for the experiment*, he thought. He checked his watch: it was coming up to four P.M. With another three hours until dinner, he decided to go and check the laboratories to see if anything was going on.

Both laboratories were empty, so he made his way back up to the lounge deck. As he passed the door to the port deck, he saw Dr. Sinclair, leaning over the railings with a pair of binoculars pushed to her face. He quickly returned to his cabin, grabbed his parka and gloves and made his way back to the port door. Dr. Sinclair was still there, looking out over the Davis Strait toward Baffin Island.

He walked out onto the deck and tapped her on the shoulder. She jumped, and turned toward him, almost dropping the binoculars. "Mr. Spire!" she said, taking a deep breath. "You shouldn't creep up on people like that; you never know what might happen."

"I didn't mean to scare you, Dr. Sinclair. Have you spotted anything interesting?"

Ksenyia looked back out to sea. "Not really. Baffin Island is about two hundred kilometres in that direction, but all I can see is ice. We should be heading into Baffin Bay soon, I imagine."

Spire looked out into the twilight. The light was beginning to fade, but it was about as dark as it would get for the time of year. The Strait looked grey and desolate. Every now and then a crack resonated up from the ship's hull as it smashed through a particularly resilient piece of floating ice.

"Do you really think global warming is melting all this?" she asked.

"Well, it's hard to believe looking out there, but that's what the science tells us. The Arctic has warmed by a massive five degrees Celsius, compared to the global average of zero point seven. Whilst it doesn't look like it now, this ice may not be here in twenty years time."

Ksenyia took a deep breath, exhaling a plume of mist as her warm breath condensed in the cold air.

The sky had turned a mottled dark grey in the short time Spire had been outside. A flash of light in the sky above suddenly distracted him. He looked up to see bands of green light twisting and turning in the darkened sky over in the north. "Look at that," Spire said, pointing up. "It's the Aurora Borealis - northern lights. Incredible, isn't it?"

"Do you know what causes the phenomena, Mr. Spire?"

"Something to do with particles of gas from the sun, I think."

"Not bad. The lights are actually caused by energised solar wind particles being funnelled down and accelerated along the Earth's magnetic field lines. They are beautiful," she replied, looking up at the green bands of light dancing in the twilight sky.

Spire smiled, impressed at her scientific knowledge. As he looked up, he realised that he hadn't spoken to her about the death of the scientists'. "I suppose you heard about the death of the American climatologist Dr. Jack Bannister a few months back? What's your take on it?" he asked.

Ksenyia turned to look at him, "I do recall hearing about that, yes. He died at a function in San Francisco, didn't he?"

"He was about to deliver a talk at a climate change conference, I believe - dropped dead before he had a chance," Spire said, studying Dr. Sinclair's reaction.

She turned her gaze toward the ocean, and the Aurora Borealis. A few moments passed. "Perhaps stress of the job, Mr. Spire?" she said, looking out over the grey ocean.

Spire followed her gaze. "You know, some people think there's oil down there. Imagine this beautiful wilderness, instead of ice, seeing the ocean covered with oil rigs. Kind of a shame, don't you think?"

Ksenyia turned to Spire, her green eyes sparkling under the shimmering northern lights, "I guess it would be...if you're right about the oil that is."

Spire looked into her eyes, feeling a lust he'd not felt in a long time. He felt frozen to the spot as Dr. Sinclair moved slowly toward him. Parting her lips, she kissed him passionately. Seconds felt like minutes, before he came to his senses. *What the hell am I doing?* He pulled away. "Listen Alice; I'm sorry, I can't do this, I'm married."

Ksenyia shrugged, then turned and opened the port-side door, just as a blast of icy cold air hit them both in the face. "It's getting cold out here, we should go in."

Spire held the door open and followed her in to the warmth of the ship's interior. "I'll see you at dinner," he said, as she walked off down the corridor.

Spire walked back to his cabin, an overwhelming sense of guilt welled up in his stomach as he thought about the beautiful doctor.

CHAPTER 56
London

INSPECTOR JOHNSON WAS seated at his desk staring at his computer screen. A desktop fan provided a welcome breeze to the recent increase in temperatures. The wet weather of April and May now seemed a distant memory, as June brought record temperatures to London, and other European cities. It was still only ten A.M, and was already approaching twenty degrees Celsius.

Johnson glanced at the BBC news website which was showing pictures of the ten warmest European cities sweltering under the hottest summer on record, comparing only with 2005. People were cooling their feet in the fountains of Trafalgar Square in London, with similar scenes in Berlin, Paris and Rome.

The ringing phone dragged him away from the computer screen. He closed the internet down and picked up the receiver; it was Professor Sammedi calling from the National Oceanography Centre. "Inspector, I just wanted to let you know that I spoke with Robert Spire and Professor Trimaud yesterday. They called from the *Mercure's* Inmarsat phone."

Johnson sat up. "Really; do they have any news? What's their location?"

Sammedi relayed the conversation he'd had with Trimaud about the seawater samples and about the brief discussion he'd managed to have with Spire before the line had gone dead.

"I've not heard anything since, I'm afraid. They haven't called back."

"What's your take on the low salinity levels, Professor?" Johnson asked.

"They are certainly odd readings. Well below the levels we'd expect for that part of the ocean."

"And that means?"

"It suggests a large influx of fresh water flowing into the ocean at the coordinates given. This is worrying as the only source of such a large amount of fresh water is Greenland. It indicates Greenland's glaciers are melting quicker than expected, Inspector Johnson."

"From global warming?"

"Global warming, climate change, call it what you will. The Arctic region is heating up faster than anywhere else on Earth. If the fresh-water influx continues, it could destabilise the Ocean Thermohaline Circulation, which would in turn affect Western Europe's climate in the long run. Ironically, it could become much colder."

Johnson sighed, as he reached over the desk for the copy of the *Oakdale Metro* given to him by Spire. "Very well, Professor. If you hear anything more from Spire, tell him I want to speak to him." Johnson placed the receiver back down and stared at the headline in the paper, which suggested that the Northwest Passage would be ice free in as little as twenty years. *Jesus, it looks like Spire might be right.*

The phone rang again. Johnson mopped his brow and answered the call. It was Marjorie on the front desk. "Inspector, there's a young lad just walked in; says he recognises the lady in the photo-fit picture. I think you'd better come and speak to him."

"Thanks, Marjorie, I'll be right out."

Johnson had only received about twenty calls since the

police artist's impression of the mystery woman had been released, but nobody had actually come into the station about it. He walked out of his office and down the corridor to reception. Through the glass double-doors, he noticed a teenage boy with curly brown hair sitting in the waiting room; a skateboard tucked under his left arm. Johnson walked through and introduced himself to the lad, who confirmed his name was Ben James, and that he was seventeen.

Johnson took him into one of the interview rooms off the main corridor where they both sat down. "So, Ben, do your parents know you have come down here?" he asked.

"Yes sir. I told them I'd pop in on the way back from the park."

"Very good. So, Marjorie tells me that you recognise the lady in the picture," Johnson said, handing Ben an A4 copy of the artist's sketch of the suspect. "Where do you think you might have seen this person?"

"Well, I'm sure she lives at the end of my street. I skateboard past nearly every day. She's kinda unforgettable. Looks like a FHM girl, you know…hot."

"I see, Ben. Can you give me a better description, and confirm where she lives?"

"Sure, she's tall; about your height, with shoulder length dark hair and green eyes. She looks like one of them super models. Lives in the flats at the end of Lords Lane, Mortimer Court, I think they're called."

"Ok Ben, if I give you a lift home, do you think you could show me the flats?"

"Yeah, I don't know the exact flat, but I can show you the building."

Johnson left Ben in the waiting room and went to see Superintendent Flint to brief him on the potential breakthrough, then returned to collect Ben.

Lords Lane was situated about four miles away from the station in a quiet part of St John's Wood. Johnson drove out of the car park, and turned left down Newcourt Street, eventually finding Lords Lane. Mortimer Court - a red brick 1960s apartment block - came into view on the corner. "Is this the block?" Johnson asked, driving slowly past.

"Yep," Ben said, pointing at the glass entrance door.

"Ok Ben, you've been most helpful. If I drop you here, can you get home alright? If this turns out to be anything, I'll be in touch to let you know if our inquiries got anywhere," Johnson said, as he pulled over and turned the engine off.

"No problem," Ben said, as he got out from the car and threw his skateboard on the floor. "Oh, sir, what did she do wrong?" he asked.

"Good question, Ben, maybe nothing, but we just need to check her out. I'll let you know."

Ben took off up the street; his skateboard rattling over the pavement cracks as he went.

Johnson walked the thirty metres or so back to the apartment building. The properties around the area were typically large, most of them detached. Mortimer Court appeared to be a well-kept block of twelve apartments, one of many similar blocks built in the area during the early sixties.

He walked up to the entrance. A stainless steel plaque with twelve buzzers, some with names, most without, was fixed to the side of the double-glass entrance doors. Victoria Boothroyd's name wasn't listed. He tried the door, it was locked. He pressed the buzzer for apartment one. There was no answer, the same for apartment two.

After a minute, an elderly-sounding gentleman answered from apartment three. Johnson explained who he was, and that he was there to investigate reports that drugs were being grown on the premises - not wanting to alert anyone of the true nature of his visit.

Leslie Palmer introduced himself, and buzzed him in.

Johnson walked into the spacious foyer and up to the well-dressed man and flashed his badge. "Sorry to disturb you, Mr. Palmer, but I just want to ask you a few quick questions if that's Ok?"

"Certainly, I'll do my best to answer them. You'll have to speak up though, I'm a bit deaf in my right ear," Palmer said, adjusting his tie.

"Ok, Mr. Palmer. Can you tell me who else lives in the block?"

"Well, let me see," he said, scratching his head. "There's Edith and Mrs. Banks who live on the ground floor here. They are both in their early eighties, like me. On the second floor you have one apartment empty I think, and a Mr. James lives in number five, works for Nat West, I believe. Top floor, well…let me think. Ah yes, Mr. Smith, he always seems to be away on holiday." Palmer scratched his head again. "Then you have Miss Boothroyd in flat eleven, very nice girl, not been here long, don't see too much of her."

"Could you describe Miss Boothroyd for me?"

"Certainly; tall, dark hair, very quiet, keeps herself to herself. I guess I'd say she was attractive, if I was forty years younger," Palmer said, his eyes sparkling.

"Thank you, Mr. Palmer, you've been most helpful," Johnson replied.

"Good day to you," Leslie Palmer said, lifting his hand to his head through habit to take a hat off which wasn't there. He smiled and shuffled back into his apartment.

Johnson walked up the stairs to the top floor. As he ascended, the heat inside the stairwell became unbearable, the air stale. He arrived in a spacious hall, and opened one of the double windows at the end of the corridor to let some fresh air in.

At the other end of the terrazzo-floored corridor was a collection of plants, all of which looked half-dead. Johnson found apartment eleven, walked up to the door and knocked.

There was no answer. He put his ear to the door and waited, but heard nothing. He knocked again, but Miss Boothroyd didn't appear to be home.

He headed back down the stairs and out through the entrance. He'd go back to the station to get a warrant sorted out as soon as possible, then come back and take a good look inside Miss Boothroyd's apartment.

CHAPTER 57

SUPERINTENDENT FLINT WASTED no time in applying, under The Terrorism Act, for a search warrant for eleven Mortimer Court, following Inspector Johnson's visit there. By four-thirty P.M, Justice Bridges had granted it without condition; on the basis that the occupier was wanted for questioning over the death of UK climatologist Dr. Dale Stanton.

Inspector Johnson and Sergeant Smith, together with three members of the Met's Armed Response Unit, arrived at Mortimer Court just before dawn the following morning. Leslie Palmer let them all in, and looked on perplexed, as Smith, together with a group of armed men, ascended the stairs to the third floor. Johnson, advising Palmer to return to his flat, then followed the armed unit upstairs.

Johnson followed the three armed officers as they crept stealthily up the hall stairs until they arrived at the third floor landing. One officer silently made his way to the end of the corridor and crouched down amongst the dying plants; the other two stood either side of the door to flat eleven, their guns drawn.

Johnson signalled to the armed unit, and then knocked on the door. He waited a few seconds - there was no response. "Miss Boothroyd, it's the Metropolitan Police, we need to ask you a few questions. Please open the door," he shouted into the keyhole. There was no answer.

Johnson nodded to Smith, and they both stood back, whilst

one of the armed response officers knocked the door in with a compact battering ram he was carrying. The door gave way easily, flying inward and hitting the rubber door-stop, which caused it to rebound, almost slamming shut again.

The officer with the battering ram moved back, allowing Armed Response Officer Sergeant Robertson to move into the apartment's dark corridor. He edged further in, keeping his back against the wall.

Inspector Johnson followed him in, felt for the light switch, and flicked it on.

Robertson called out, but there was silence. He came to an open door off the corridor, which Johnson could see was a bedroom, and went in. He quickly scanned the room, gun held out in front of him. The small bedroom was empty. "Clear!" he called out.

Johnson continued into the bathroom; it was also empty. "Clear here too," he shouted.

The second armed officer returned to the hall outside, the third tracked back to the entrance foyer, while Robertson, Johnson and Smith continued their search of the flat.

Johnson searched the bookshelves for any evidence of who might own the apartment, expecting to find a photo album or something, but there were just books; a mixture of novels and guide books on London, Paris and other European capitals.

Johnson and Smith entered the bedroom and continued their search. The wardrobe was filled with smart suits and tailored trousers. There was a box in the bottom of the wardrobe containing an old pair of ice skates and roller blades, but that was it. Smith started going through the top set of drawers opposite the bed. "I wish my wife wore this sort of stuff," he said, holding up an assortment of suspender belts and seamed stockings.

"You and me both," Johnson said, as he continued looking

under the bed.

A thorough search of the bedroom revealed nothing. "Whoever lives here is clean, or has done a good job of covering their tracks," Johnson said.

Smith moved into the kitchen and opened the fridge; it was empty apart from a six pack of eggs, jar of blueberry jam and a bottle of Stolichnaya vodka. He pulled it out. "Good taste in vodka," he said, noticing the label. He placed it back and checked the cupboards, finding nothing of interest.

Sergeant Robertson called out from the lounge. "Hey guys, take a look at this."

Johnson and Smith found him standing by the CD player studying a framed photograph. He showed the picture to Johnson. There was a little girl, standing next to a soldier and another very young girl. "See that uniform, I think it's Russian, probably Red Army."

Johnson studied the photograph of the man wearing full Russian Army uniform, flanked by two little girls. He held the framed photo closer, wondering if one of the small, pretty, innocent-looking girls could be the suspect they were looking for. "Here, take this," he said to Smith, who placed the picture into an evidence bag.

A further twenty minute search of the flat failed to find anything else. "Come on, let's get out of here," Johnson finally said. They all left the apartment, and Johnson taped a Metropolitan Police notice across the door, then called the station and requested a lock smith be sent over, as soon as possible, to repair the damage.

On the way out of the block, Johnson went to see Mr. Palmer, and asked him to call the police if he saw the girl come back. He told him to remain cautious and speak to no-one about the raid, until he heard further from the police.

As soon as they got back to the station, Inspector Johnson

and Sergeant Smith went directly to see Superintendent Flint to brief him on the search. They knocked and entered his room. Flint was sitting behind his desk, another man, six foot tall, dark hair and dressed in a dark suit was leaning against the back of a chair with his arms folded. He looked over at the detectives as they entered the room.

"Ah, here they are," Flint said, as they walked in. "Gentleman, this is Brad Mountjoy, he's with MI6 and will now be overseeing this investigation," Flint said, shrugging his shoulders, sounding tired.

"Take a seat please, gentlemen," Mountjoy said, as Johnson and Smith approached the desk.

They both pulled up a couple of chairs and sat down, awaiting an explanation. Johnson took out the evidence bag containing the framed picture, and placed it on the table.

Mountjoy waited until they were seated, before speaking. "In view of the direction that this investigation has taken, I've been asked to oversee things from now on. Your persistence in this investigation has proven invaluable, gentlemen, and I'd like to thank you both for that. We now believe that Dr. Dale Stanton was killed by the woman whose flat you searched this morning, and furthermore, that she might be a Russian agent, probably FSB." Mountjoy leaned over and picked up the framed photograph. "We've already analysed the pictures in this photograph from images sent back to us from the camera head-gear worn by the armed response team. The man in the photograph has been identified as Goran Petrovsky, an officer in the Russian Red Army, killed by a sniper's bullet whilst withdrawing out of eastern Afghanistan toward the end of the Russian-Afghan war. I'm afraid I can't say much more at the moment, gentleman, suffice to say, we believe the woman you have been looking for, might be his eldest daughter. The question remains however, why she would want to kill two climatologists, and whether she was working as a privately hired assassin, or more worryingly, the Russian government."

Johnson looked over at Flint, who shrugged his shoulders in response. "So, you're telling us that we are off the case?" he asked, looking at Mountjoy.

"Well, not off, exactly. You can still assist, but MI6 will be leading the investigation from now on. It's the same for your friend, Gus Mitchell, over in San Francisco. The CIA will be coordinating investigations over there, in view of the threat to national security that we now believe exists."

"I see," Johnson said, "so this whole thing is about global warming after all?"

Mountjoy glanced toward Flint, and then turned back to Johnson and Smith. "Let's just say gentlemen, we believe there is an imminent environmental threat to the UK and possibly the globe, and that the scientists' deaths are related to this. The quicker this woman is found, and detained, the better. That's what we need to work on now."

"Have you managed to make contact with Robert Spire yet? I assume you know of his involvement in all this?"

Mountjoy moved away from Flint's desk and walked over to a projector, which had been set up close to the wall at the end of the room. He turned it on and motioned for Flint to turn off the lights. The machine purred as it projected a satellite image of the Arctic region onto the back wall. Mountjoy stood at the edge of the image and, using a pointing stick, marked a spot somewhere in the Arctic Ocean. "We believe the US/French expedition is currently around here. We know from Canadian coastguards that the *Mercure Blanc* made contact with them at zero eight hundred hours on the fourth, that's three nights ago. There's been no contact since then. We assume she is somewhere around here," Mountjoy said, pointing at a location about a third of the way along the

Northwest Passage. "Our Canadian friends are in the process of sending a frigate to try and locate her. We believe she's just suffered a communications malfunction, but we aren't taking any chances. The area is also being monitored by the Canadians in view of increasing seismic activity, in and around the coast of Greenland, which is a concern." Mountjoy turned the projector off and walked back to the desk. "So, we are keeping a close eye on things, gentleman, but our priority right now is to find our Russian suspect, and bring her in for questioning, as soon as possible. All UK police forces are on alert, but links to the dead scientists' have been kept quiet for now. We don't want the press getting hold of the story; they'll have a field day." He paused. "Do either of you have any questions?"

"Just let us know what the next move will be," Johnson said, standing to walk out the door. "You know where to find us."

CHAPTER 58

Arctic Circle

THE MERCURE BLANC continued its journey, cruising at twenty-two knots through the Lancaster Sound, the eastern portion of the Northwest Passage, toward the seeding destination. The body of water off Resolute Bay had been chosen for the drop-zone, primarily because of its position almost halfway along the channel; and because the sea-ice at that location had - for the last few years - been melting quicker than anywhere else in the Arctic during the seasonal summer-melt. This, despite the location being one of the coldest inhabited places on Earth, with an average yearly temperature of minus sixteen degrees Celsius.

The mercury in the ship's external thermometer trickled to a relatively balmy ten degrees Celsius. The pack-ice, whilst still evident on the Baffin Island side, was virtually non-existent in the sea off Devon Island. Just the odd sheet of thin summer-ice remained on the surface, no threat to the *Mercure's* ice-strengthened hull.

Spire walked with Dr. Bonnet toward the bow of the ship and looked out over the clear, calm, azure blue water. The morning Arctic sun beat down overhead. "Sure is beautiful out here, Mari. Makes the journey all worthwhile," Spire said, looking out toward the pack-ice along the jagged coast of the approaching terminus of Baffin Island.

Dr. Bonnet pointed toward the island, handing Spire the binoculars she was holding. "Here, take a look, you should be able to see a magnificent glacial tongue coming down from the Barnes Ice cap in the centre of the Island."

Spire raised the binoculars, adjusted the magnification and focused on the sheer cliffs of the island. He moved slowly along the cliffs, and after a short while located a vast channel that appeared to have been cut out of the isle, no doubt by the retreating glacier within.

"The Barnes ice cap covers the central part of the island. It has been in retreat since the early nineteen-sixties," Dr. Bonnet said, as Spire scrutinised the awesome view.

"It looks absolutely fantastic," he said, handing the binoculars back. "No wonder you're so passionate about trying to preserve this wonderful wilderness."

"Let's just hope Francois' theory works, Robert," she said, looking out over the ocean.

Spire glanced at his watch; it was coming up to eight-thirty A.M. "Any idea how long until we get to Resolute Bay and the drop zone?"

"Well, it's around one hundred and fifty-five nautical miles from Baffin Island. So, another six hours at this speed and we should be there, hopefully by two-thirty."

"Now that *is* good news. I think I'll go and check if Captain Deville has managed to restore the communications system yet." Spire left Dr. Bonnet looking out over the channel at the bow of the ship and walked over to where Trimaud was inspecting the damaged side of the steel container. "Give me a shout if you need any help with preparations for the drop," he said.

"Will do, Robert. See you shortly."

Spire walked back along the deck toward the port-side door,

and entered the main cabin. He felt more alert and fresh than he had in a long time, despite only getting five hours sleep a night due to the increasingly light Arctic nights. He made his way to the science lab, to check if either Dr. McBride or Dr. Mathews were working down there. He opened the door, but the lab was empty, just a quiet whir from the computers and the centrifuge machine was just audible above the rumble of the ship's engines. He looked over at the table where the body of Luc Morel lay, covered in a white table-cloth, and felt a slight chill race up his spine. He closed the door and made his way up to the bridge to see Captain Deville.

Deville was staring through his binoculars, out across the channel of the Lancaster Sound, when Spire walked onto the bridge. He looked visibly tired.

"Ah, Robert, how are you holding up?" Deville asked, as he continued looking out to sea.

"Feeling pretty good, considering," Spire replied, straining his eyes as he tried to see what Deville was looking at.

"Good, I wish I felt the same. We're almost at the drop zone. Only one hundred-forty nautical miles to go," he said, lowering the binoculars. He screwed up his eyes, and rubbed them with the back of his hands. "It looks like we have company," he said, motioning out to sea with the binoculars. "There's another vessel in the middle of the channel, not far from Cornwallis Island."

Spire glanced out of the window, then back at Deville. "You look tired; perhaps you should take a rest?"

Deville sighed. "Boucher can take us back tomorrow morning. I can rest then."

"What's with the other ship, are we expecting company?"

"My guess is that it's a Canadian patrol boat monitoring the experiment."

"Do you mind if I take a look?" Spire asked, picking up the

binoculars.

"Be my guest, your eyes are probably better than mine."

Spire looked through the binoculars and adjusted the magnification. The channel remained ice free for the most part, but pack-ice was still evident close to the coast on the left hand side. He found the object visible on the horizon in the distance, and refocused. He could just about make out a grey-metallic ship in the middle of the channel, but couldn't see a flag or any other evidence of the vessel's identity. "Can't quite make it out," he said, returning the binoculars to the bulkhead. "It looks stationary. Like you said, probably just the Canadians in position to monitor the experiment."

"We'll find out soon enough," Deville said, pulling the microphone towards him. "Captain speaking; make initial preparations for drop-zone arrival in one hundred and forty nautical miles." He pushed the mike away and turned toward Spire.

"Stay vigilant, Robert. I have an uneasy feeling about this whole thing. This voyage hasn't gone quite how I planned, and it wouldn't surprise me if something else goes wrong before we get back to Marseilles."

Spire nodded. "I've got the same feeling. Have communications been restored yet?"

"Nope, the Inmarsat's fuse and main wiring is burnt through. I'm hoping to get replacement fuses on Cornwallis Island; there is a small weather station there."

"Good, I expect most of us need to use that thing. I'll see you in a few hours, Captain," Spire said, as he took one last look at the stationary vessel through the binoculars, before leaving the bridge.

The *Rezky* was anchored eighty nautical miles offshore from

Resolute Bay, waiting for the *Mercure* to arrive. Admiral Dashkov had received orders to pick up the Russian assassin from the ship, using one of the *Rezky's* Zodiac inflatables. The task of dropping the last OTM had been completed only hours before, and Dashkov had cruised through the night to reach their current location. At the bottom of the Northwest Passage, equidistant apart and stretching from Bylot Island to Banks Island, the OTMs lay ready to receive the incoming remote signal that would power up their internal nuclear thermal heaters.

Admiral Dashkov was now standing on the bridge, the binoculars held to his eyes; a Golden Fleece hung from his lips. He scrutinised the *Mercure Blanc,* closing in on their position at a confirmed radar speed of twenty-two knots. He inhaled on the cigarette then stubbed it out on the steel trim of the bulkhead. A pin-prick of light reflecting off something in the channel then caught his eye. He focused the binoculars, and saw a large, house-sized tabular iceberg drifting toward their position. He lowered the binoculars and turned to Tabanov, who was sitting at the chart table, shuffling a deck of cards. "Our friends should be here in a matter of hours, Captain. Have Charkov prepare the Zodiac; make sure the outboard motors are sufficiently fuelled for a twenty-kilometre round trip. I don't intend getting too close to the French ship."

"I'll see to it," Tabanov replied, throwing the cards down onto the table as he stood. He radioed down to Lieutenant Brilev in the communications room and asked him to keep a radar lock on the ice that appeared to be drifting toward their starboard side. "I'll go down now to help the men," he said, as he left the bridge.

CHAPTER 59

SUNLIGHT BLAZED THROUGH the glass roof into the landscaped gardens of *NewSaudOil Corp*, creating shafts of light that intersected the vast space at multiple angles. Below, Faric and his brother walked along the path in silence, savouring the serenity of the internal oasis. The only sound to be heard was the gentle hissing of the garden's water sprinklers, and the occasional squawk from a parrot as it flew across the large open space. Outside the compound, the sun baked the desert to an unbearable forty-five degrees Celsius.

Faric felt his Blackberry vibrate in his pocket, and pulled it out. It was an e-mail from Zoblozky, their Russian financier. "Excuse me, brother," he said, "I must go and attend to some business."

"So early in the morning, Faric? I think we can afford to relax a little now, everything is going to plan."

"Yes, brother, however there is something I must deal with."

"Very well. I'll meet you in the conference room in one hour. There will be a progress report on the drilling at eleven."

"I'll see you there, brother," Faric said, as he made his way to the hidden exit, in a shaded corner of the garden behind a large date palm. Back inside the building, he took the elevator to level three, where his office was located, sat down at his desk and powered up his lap top. He opened an e-mail, which confirmed that the *Rezky* was anchored off the drop-zone in the Lancaster Sound, midway along the Northwest Passage. All

OTMs were in position at their predetermined locations, and the *Mercure Blanc* was in view, some one hundred nautical miles behind their position. Further orders awaited, the message confirmed.

Faric responded; *Standby to pick up Russian agent. She will confirm when her mission has been completed. Do not activate OTMs untill I give the order.*

He sent the message, wiping away a bead of perspiration from his forehead, which had appeared, despite the cool air within the air conditioned office. He reminded himself that his brother would eventually thank him, should the OTMs need to be activated. He closed his laptop and made his way to the conference room on the second level, where the presentation was due to start in thirty minutes.

Dashkov walked over to the main windows and raised the binoculars to his face. The *Mercure Blanc* was moving at a fair pace, the spray from her bow shimmering under the Arctic sun. He replaced the binoculars into their slot on the bulkhead shelf and moved over to a steel cabinet against the wall behind the chart table. He took a key from a small metal tin in his jacket pocket, and inserted it into the cabinet lock. Inside, was the black book-sized control pad for the Ocean Thermal Modifiers.

He reached in and removed the device. A series of eight lights glowed green along the length of the unit, above them was the alpha numeric touch pad where the activation code needed to be entered. He kept the code, on a slip of paper, in the silver amulet around his neck. *The safest place,* he considered, as he fingered the pendant. He returned the control unit back into the cabinet and locked the door.

Tabanov appeared on the bridge. "The men are ready, Admiral. The Zodiac is fuelled and ready to launch on your order."

"Very well," Dashkov replied, offering Tabanov a Golden Fleece. Tabanov took one, lit it and inhaled deeply, letting the rich tobacco fill his lungs. "Have you met the Russian before, Admiral?" he asked, after a few moments.

"No, but I knew of her father. He was a Colonel in the Red Army, killed when his unit pulled out of Afghanistan in January nineteen-eighty-nine. I don't doubt that must have been a persuasive factor in our Russian friend joining the KGB."

Tabanov stared out along the Sound. "I look forward to meeting her," he said, exhaling the cigarette smoke through his nostrils.

Faric entered the conference room, his brother Fahim was already seated, along with Mousaf, the senior geologist and drilling operations manager, and Tarique and Moussad who had secured the mineral extraction rights licences, from the French and Cape Verde Governments respectively. A white pull down screen had been set up against the far wall, and a Samsung projector, connected to a lap top, projected a still image of *NewSaudOil Corp's* logo onto it. "Good afternoon, gentleman," *NewSaudOil Corp's* chief geologist said, as he stood up and walked over to the projector. "It is my honour today to brief you all on the status of the Crozet and Cape Verde sites, *NewSaudOil Corp's* historic discoveries," he said, a large grin forming across his bearded face.

Using the projector remote, he changed the slide on the screen - from an image of the company logo - to a photograph of the windswept Crozet Islands. "Our first discovery was, of course, made some eight months ago, following detailed seismic seabed sampling and geotechnical boring samples of the most promising leads, using the *Seahorse* submersible and *Plentiful* drill ship. Similar operations were being carried out over in the Atlantic Cape Verde site. Two vast oil bearing provinces were discovered, missed by BP, Chevron and Shell, with combined oil reserves of twice the size of our country's largest oil fields."

Fahim nodded at the men in the room, and smiled at his brother, as he leaned over the table to pour himself some coffee.

Mousaf continued his briefing. "Updated estimated reserves in the Crozet site amount to one-hundred-ninety billion barrels, gentlemen. The oil reservoir is contained within porous limestone rock. Over in the Atlantic site, sandstone rock provides the reservoir." He looked over to the two men sitting by him. "Praise to Tarique and Moussad, who persuaded the oil ministries in both nations to grant full exploration and extraction rights, the ministries oblivious of course to the extent of our discoveries," he chuckled, shrugging his shoulders smugly. "Well, they will regret that decision in due course."

An image of the drill ship *Plentiful* appeared on the screen, its drill-derrick fully raised in drilling position. "This was the *Plentiful* last Friday, gentlemen, drilling well number three on the Crozet site, which we have named *Macaroni*, after the indigenous penguin population that inhabit the islands. At least we can't be accused of ignoring the local wildlife."

Faric grinned at the comment. "Whose idea was that Mousaf?"

"Actually…it was mine, Abu Zamal," he replied nervously, bowing his head slightly toward Faric.

"I like it Mousaf, I like it a lot."

Mousaf smiled smugly before continuing. "Once all sites have been drilled and assessed, we will start the process of establishing fixed rigs at each well."

Fahim interrupted, "What news with the methane Dr. Bannister and his team discovered off the Crozet Island site?"

"Ah, yes, I was just about to mention that." Mousaf replied, switching the image on the screen to a satellite photograph of the coastline of Ile de l'Est. "As you know, large deposits of methane gas are believed to exist around this side of the Island. The gas is twenty times more powerful than carbon dioxide, and is of course highly inflammable. Our team has checked the geography of the deposits, and will continue to monitor them. The drilling is taking place at a sufficient distance from the islands, we believe, for it not to cause a problem." Mousaf smiled slightly and wiped away a bead of sweat that had appeared on his temple.

Fahim poured himself another cup of coffee. "At what time will the *Plentiful* being drilling the fourth well tomorrow?"

Mousaf picked up his papers from the table, a small tremor evident in his hand as he started flicking through them. "Ah, yes, here we are, the *Gentoo* well will spud at around three P.M local time."

"Very well," Fahim replied, sipping his coffee. "Keep me informed of any developments please. Thank you for the presentation, Mousaf, does anyone have any questions?"

The room fell silent, except for the whir of the air conditioning and the quiet hum of the projector. "Very well, gentlemen, we have reached the final phase of our operations. Well done, to all of you. We will announce to the King, and to the world, the extent of our discoveries once the fourth well at both sites has been drilled to target depth, and final reserve estimates at both locations have been calculated."

Fahim stood and left the room and Faric followed him out. Fahim turned to his brother, speaking in a low voice. "We should be hearing from our Russian friend any time now, following the completion of her assignment. When we do, I will let you know. Only then can we celebrate, brother."

Faric nodded in response. "Don't worry, Fahim; I'm sure she is on the verge of completing her task at this very moment."

"I hope so, Faric, I hope so," Fahim replied, as he turned and walked back down the corridor towards his office.

CHAPTER 60

Arctic Circle
June 9

ROBERT SPIRE SHIVERED as he zipped up his parka, a freezing gust of air gripping his torso. The sky above was a pale blue with not a cloud in sight. He checked the external thermometer, noticing the mercury had dipped slightly to just below six degrees Celsius.

He shielded his eyes, from the Arctic sun, as he looked out over the peaceful ice-free channel. Suddenly his thoughts were broken by a distant low rumble, coming from somewhere to the south of their position. *Was that thunder?* The cloudless blue sky suggested not. It was one of the calmest days they'd had. Again, a second rumble echoed along the Lancaster Sound, this time slightly louder, but still distant in origin. Spire didn't know why, but the ominous rumble made him feel uneasy. He turned and walked back toward the port-side door.

He found Captain Deville on the bridge, looking out over the ocean, a large mug of black coffee in his hand. He questioned him about the sound.

"I heard it, but the radar isn't showing any signs of adverse weather within two hundred nautical miles of here. There is a storm moving up from the Atlantic, but that won't be anywhere near us until late tomorrow, or even the day after. It's conceivable that we are hearing some distant thunder, but it's a little odd I must say."

Spire noted the time was just after midday. "What's our ETA?" he asked.

Deville squinted at the radar, appearing to carry out some mental calculations. "Just over one and a half hours to go," he said, handing the binoculars to Spire. "Here, take a look at the slab of pack-ice that has broken off the coastal ice-pack. It's drifting into the channel. Francois has suggested we pull up alongside it if we can. He wants to take some samples, measure its thickness, that sort of thing."

Spire stared through the binoculars at the shimmering sliver of ice now visible in the channel ahead. The ship behind was now also identifiable, her Maple Leaf flag flapping in the breeze off its stern section. "Looks like you were right about our Canadian friends," Spire said, handing back the binoculars.

"It looks like they are carrying out some observations, or perhaps taking supplies to the joint Canadian/US weather base on Resolute Bay," Deville replied.

"Good to see some signs of human life," Spire said, as he left the bridge to look for Trimaud and the rest of the group.

Ksenyia was in her cabin, preparing for her final assignment. She felt a renewed sense of confidence, after having seen the *Rezky* waiting for her in the channel up ahead. If she couldn't prevent the experiment from going ahead, she'd simply eliminate Trimaud, Deville and Spire the good old fashioned way – a bullet to each of their heads. No one else on board posed a threat to her. She'd signal the *Rezky* and wait for them to send a boat to collect her. She double checked the *Makarov* was loaded, and tucked it into the small of her back behind her belt.

She opened her wardrobe for the final time to check on Dr.

McBride. The light from the cabin illuminated the doctor's mascara-smudged face. Dr. McBride cowered further into the wardrobe as Ksenyia looked down at her. *McBride was proving to be no trouble at all.* She closed and secured the wardrobe again, blocking out the doctor's muffled groans which were barely audible over the ship's engines.

She checked her watch; sixty minutes to go.

Spire walked along the corridor and entered the bar. The French scientists' were all sitting and chatting together. "Ah, Robert, are you ready for the main event? Not too long to go now," Trimaud said, a look of excitement spreading across his face.

"I sure am. You couldn't ask for a better day for it. Looks like the Gods are smiling down on us after all."

"Well if they are, they clearly disapprove of something," Dr. Bonnet said, frowning.

"Oh, you mean the thunder earlier?"

"Thunder, you think it was thunder? On a clear day?" she said, shrugging her shoulders.

"Must be the storm moving in, I guess. Is there any word on Dr. McBride?" Spire asked, looking at all three of them.

"I checked on her thirty minutes ago. It looks like she's getting ready for the sampling experiment. Her cabin's empty," Girard said.

"I'll pop down and see if I can find her. See you all up on deck in thirty minutes. I want to see that stuff going into the water, after the effort I made to save it," Spire said, turning to walk out.

"Robert, I'll be giving a short briefing up here in twenty minutes, you might want to come and listen. And don't worry, my friend; you'll have the honour of pushing the button that releases the *Blankoplankton* into the ocean!" Trimaud shouted after him.

"I wouldn't miss it, Francois," Spire shouted back, as he left the bar and walked down the corridor toward the stairs. He found the stateroom corridor and made his way to Dr. McBride's cabin. Room number six was halfway along the short corridor. He knocked the door, there was no reply. He knocked again and put his ear to the door – silence. He tried the handle, and the door creaked open. He peered into the cabin, it was empty. Dr. McBride's bed was made, and her black case was resting on top of the small table by the porthole. He noticed Dr. McBride's parka jacket was still on the back of her chair, which suggested she was somewhere inside the ship.

He left the cabin, walked back down the corridor, and headed for the laboratory. Upon entering the lab, he saw Dr. Mathews hunched over one of the computers, checking out a series of graphs.

"Ah, Robert, it's you," Dr. Mathews said, turning around. "I was expecting Dr. McBride. You haven't seen her on your travels, have you?"

"Nope, I had assumed she'd be with you, she's not in her cabin."

"She must be around somewhere," he said, returning his gaze to the screen. "I was rather hoping she'd help me double check the plankton and salinity analysis software before we drop the sensors and Niskin bottles overboard," he said, shaking his head.

Dr. Mathews shut down the computer and turned to Spire. "Could you help me bring that steel container up on deck?"

"Sure," Spire said, grabbing one end. They both made their way to the starboard door carrying the heavy container down the deck to the stern, near to where Dr. McBride had carried out the earlier experiments.

Spire left Dr. Mathews unpacking the equipment and walked back along the deck, toward the bow of the ship, passing the large steel container as he did. The holding clamps looked tightly secured on each corner. The only evidence of the earlier disaster was a series of deep grooves cut into the steel deck, leading toward the buckled port-side railing.

Continuing toward the bow, he saw the large slab of ice come into view, floating in the ocean up ahead, looking oddly out of place in the otherwise ice-free channel. Looming up behind, some distance away was the stationary, gun-metal grey Canadian ship. He could just about make out gun turrets on the ship's bow and stern sections. The vessel's identity was also now just about visible: painted in faded black lettering on the bow was the name – *Rez*. He assumed the rest of the lettering was too faded to see. He stared at the floating section of ice, and the ship beyond for a few moments, both objects looking strangely out of place in the channel.

Shivering from the cold, he made his way quickly back along the deck, his thoughts pre-occupied by the experiment that would shortly be taking place.

CHAPTER 61

CAPTAIN DEVILLE HAD successfully brought them along the Northwest Passage to their current position, some twenty nautical miles off the coast of Resolute Bay. Officer Henri Boucher, who'd been resting for the previous twelve hours, was now on the bridge.

Spire could see the cliffs of Cornwallis Island, through the starboard porthole, as he sat down on a comfortable armchair in the lounge cabin. The rest of the science team was seated, waiting to listen to Professor Trimaud's briefing.

"Well, finally, we have arrived," Trimaud spoke, raising his arms jubilantly. "As Robert is here, I'll give the briefing in English. I'd like to congratulate everyone on their remarkable spirit of adventure for coming along in the first place. Without colleagues like you, this expedition, and my experiment, would never have been possible…"

Before Trimaud was able to get his next sentence out, another low rumble resonated along the channel, again from the southeast of their position. "Even the storm is trying to stop us," Trimaud said, making light of the ominous sound.

Deville shifted on his bar stool, scratched his beard and glanced out of the porthole at the blue sky beyond. As he turned back, Spire noticed the concerned look on his face.

Trimaud continued, explaining how the experiment would proceed and the stages involved. "Finally, I think it appropriate to dedicate this occasion to my good friend, Dr. Jack Bannister, and not forgetting Luc Morel, whose life was tragically shortened as a result of this voyage."

"Salute!" Deville said, sombrely.

"So, my friends and colleagues, without dwelling on the past, it's time to commence our long-awaited experiment. A little unexpected, but I thought the large tabular iceberg that has joined us in the channel would prove an ideal opportunity for us to get some additional data - ice core samples, measurements, that sort of thing. We will also take a small amount of the sulphate and see how it reacts when we add it to the ocean. Then, we will use the crane to manoeuvre the container over the side and release all ten tonnes of the modified iron sulphate into the ocean. Tomorrow morning, we will take some additional water samples, and hopefully see the first signs of the *Blankoplankton* forming. Transponders will then be dropped overboard, to mark the seeding location. After that's done, we will have to commence our long journey back to Marseilles. Are there any questions?"

"Isn't there a *Hilton,* on Cornwallis Island, we can spend the night in?"

"I'm sorry, Mari, but I promise to personally pay for you to stay in the Paris Hilton, when we all get back," Trimaud replied, chuckling.

Dr. Bonnet shrugged her shoulders. "That will do!" she said, smiling at the rest of the team.

"According to the ship's sonar, the iceberg is over two metres thick, but I'm not taking any chances. You get thirty minutes on the ice, that's it," Captain Deville said, a serious tone in his voice.

"No problem, Jacques, thirty minutes I promise, we'll be back on board. Are there any other questions?"

There was a few moments silence.

"Bon! Come on, let's get this job done safely and then we

can relax and celebrate tonight," Trimaud said, getting up.

Spire pulled on his parka and made his way along the corridor and out of the port-side door. He filled his lungs with fresh, cold air, as he walked along the deck to the bow. He checked the time; it was three-thirty P.M and the Arctic sun was low in the sky over in the northwest. He felt the deck beneath his feet suddenly vibrate as the *Mercure's* engines went into reverse, as they approached the metre high, flat slab of ice, drifting majestically a short distance ahead.

A flock of pure white Ivory Gulls flew from left to right, across the bow. Spire assumed they were on route to their cliff nests on Cornwallis Island, some twenty nautical miles to the east of their position. He directed his gaze back to the ice ahead. Small waves lapped the sides of the floating tabular iceberg, gently eroding its edges which had been slowly warmed by the Arctic summer sun. The Canadian ship was visible, some two nautical miles beyond the ice, its bow pointing toward them, sitting silently, as if abandoned in the channel.

The mercury on the ship's external thermometer had trickled down to four degrees centigrade, prompting Spire to zip up his jacket. The deck vibrated again, as the engines slowed the research vessel down to a crawl. The floating ice was now only ten metres or so ahead. Another rumble, this time from the *Mercure's* port-side bow thrusters turned the craft slowly toward starboard, Cornwallis Island could be seen directly ahead in the distance. An eerie silence descended as the large vessel drifted sideways toward the floating iceberg.

Trimaud and the others had now joined Spire out on the deck, their excitement clearly visible on their faces. Trimaud rubbed his hands together quickly, blowing into them in an attempt to warm them. "Coming onto the ice, Robert?"

"Francois, I'm not going to miss this for anything," Spire replied. "I don't think we have to worry about this thing not being safe, it's bloody massive!"

The *Mercure* gently thudded against the iceberg, followed by the sound of grating metal, as the vessel's anchor tumbled down into the cold waters of the Lancaster Sound below.

Captain Deville strode along the deck to the stern and unhooked the railed gangplank, before operating the hydraulic controls on the side of the hull, swinging the gangplank out from its housing and extending it ten metres down to the surface of the iceberg below.

On the bridge, Officer Boucher released the four large retaining clamps holding the steel container of iron sulphate in place. A succession of thuds resonated across the channel like gun blasts as the clamps released.

Spire watched the crane head slowly manoeuvre into position above the lifting eye situated in the center of the container.

Dr. Mathews and Dr. Girard had been busy bringing an assortment of instruments and containers out onto the stern deck. Spire spotted a pair of binoculars in one of the plastic containers and picked them up, hoping to locate the Ivory Gulls that had flown over earlier.

Amongst the excitement, no one had noticed that Dr. Ruth McBride still hadn't appeared.

Down in her cabin, Ksenyia checked her modified FSB tranquilizer dart gun, and quickly placed it into a green waterproof canvas bag. The gun was loaded with ten, self-degradable darts, which contained a powerful barbiturate - a non-lethal, but handy incapacitating weapon. She placed her laptop and other belongings into the bag, and slotted a throwing knife into a leather knife-pouch, which she'd tied around her right calf. She hid her empty case under the bed, placed the canvas bag over her shoulder and left her room, locking the door behind her.

On the deck, Roberto and Carlos, the ship's cooks, stubbed out their third cigarette and made their way back down to the galley. "Come on, we got lobster and pork cutlets to prepare for tonight's celebration dinner," Roberto said, as they descended the stairway.

They were startled by Ksenyia as she rounded the corner at the bottom of the stairwell. "Good luck with the experiment, Miss Sinclair," Roberto said, as she squeezed past them on her way to the main deck.

"You boys better get cooking," she replied, smiling.

"I certainly would," Carlos said, as he turned to look at Ksenyia's svelte figure, as she walked up the narrow stairway.

"You'd never get the chance," Roberto joked, as they both walked down the corridor, laughing together.

Ksenyia walked out onto the deck through the port-side door and spotted Spire handing something to Trimaud, who was standing at the top of the gangplank. Dr. Mathews was assembling some equipment on the stern deck.

It was finally time to end this experiment, she thought.

Returning through the port door, she crept up the steel steps to the bridge. As she reached the top she pulled the dart gun from the canvas bag and knocked on the door.

"Oui," Boucher shouted from inside.

Ksenyia released the safety catch on the dart gun, and walked in.

"Ah, Dr. Sinclair, aren't you going out on to the ice…"

Henri Boucher stopped speaking mid-sentence as he saw the gun pointing at him. The ballistic syringe was just a blur as it flew toward him, penetrating his jumper and embedding itself into his left pectoral muscle. He stared down at the biodegradable dart in disbelief, and then slumped to the floor as the barbiturates flooded into his bloodstream. Twenty seconds later, he was unconscious.

Ksenyia, stepping over Boucher's crumpled body, pulled the binoculars from their leather pouch on the bulkhead shelf. Glancing down, she saw Trimaud and Girard descending the gangplank onto the ice below. Captain Deville was looking on from the stern. She looked through the binoculars and focused on the *Rezky*. Taking a powerful compact spotlight from her bag, she pointed it toward the ship, sending three flashes, followed by five, then another three, the agreed pre-arranged signal.

She stared through the binoculars toward the waiting Russian ship. *What the hell are they doing?* She quickly glanced back down to the deck below. Focusing back to the *Rezky*, the return signal she'd been waiting for materialised. Five successive pinpricks of light flashed from the *Rezky's* bridge through the twilight.

She exhaled in relief; knowing her ride home was now on its way. She reloaded the dart gun and left the bridge, heading back down towards the deck.

CHAPTER 62

THREE FLASHES OF light caught Spire's eye as he looked through the binoculars toward Cornwallis Island. The gulls he'd been looking for were nowhere to be seen, but he was certain the flashes had come from the Canadian ship. He focused his gaze onto the vessel sitting silently in the channel, some two kilometres away. The vessel looked just as empty and unattended as it had earlier. *Just something shiny reflecting in the setting sun*, he thought.

Ksenyia exited onto the deck through the port-side door, focussed on the task in hand. She knew she needed to immobilise both Deville and Spire first, the two most troublesome targets. She proceeded along the deck to the stern, and saw Deville turn and walk toward the starboard door. She quickly slipped back in through the port door, and zigzagged down the corridors to intercept him on the other side of the ship. As she rounded the corridor, which took her to the starboard side, she heard Deville's footsteps approaching. Upon seeing his figure in the corridor, she fired the gun. The dart hit the mark, and her victim slumped to the floor, frantically grabbing for the syringe protruding from his left shoulder.

Ksenyia ran over to the body now slumped on the floor, and rolled him over. *It wasn't Deville!* Instead, somehow she'd hit Carlos; the cook who had walked past her earlier. "Let's see you try and fuck me now," she said, grabbing his ankles and dragging him off the main corridor into a small side-room used for storing life-jackets and netting.

Where the hell was Deville? She pulled back the reload slide on the dart gun and headed along the corridor to the starboard door. As soon as she walked onto the deck, she saw the captain, who was bending over an outside storage container searching for something.

He glanced up as he heard her walk onto the deck. "Ah, Dr. Sinclair, I think Dr. Mathews is looking for you," he said, pulling out a large red buoy from the container.

"Oh really?" Ksenyia said, firing the ballistic syringe into his left leg.

Deville stared down in bewilderment at the projectile protruding from his thigh. "What the hell?" he bawled, as he felt his legs weaken under him. He managed to pull the syringe half out, just before collapsing to the floor.

Ksenyia knelt down by his hulking body and pushed the projectile further into his leg, ensuring its contents would be fully absorbed into Deville's blood stream.

She then made her way along the starboard side to find Spire and the professor.

Intrigued by the flashes of light, Spire checked Trimaud and Girard were safely down on the iceberg and then shouted down to Dr. Bonnet - who was now also climbing down to the ice – to tell her that he was going to the bridge to check on something.

He knocked on the steel door at the top of the stairs, waiting for Officer Boucher to invite him in, but there was no response. Spire knocked again, still there was no reply. He tried the door, which opened with a load creak. He entered the empty bridge and walked over to the stern outward sloping windows, and looked down onto the vast iceberg, now extending out from the

Mercure's starboard side. He could see Professor Trimaud and the other two doctors setting up something on the ice, a short distance from the gangplank. Dr. Bonnet had just reached the iceberg. *Where was Dr. McBride?* Dr. Sinclair then came into view, walking along the deck toward the stern, carrying what looked like a duffel bag over her shoulder. He watched as she tucked something into the back of her jeans and stepped onto the gangplank.

Spire raised the binoculars and looked out toward the Canadian ship, but there were no lights, no sign of movement, nothing. As he panned the waters around the ship, he saw a small dark dot. *Could that be a whale or dolphin?* He magnified the view to get a better look at the object, which slowly crystalised before his eyes. Bouncing up and down on the surface of the water was a speedboat.

As he turned to leave the bridge, he noticed a pair of legs protruding from a pile of blankets over in the corner. *What the hell?* He ran over and pulled the blankets away and found Henri Boucher lying there, the remnants of an unusual looking dart sticking out of his chest. He felt for a pulse on Boucher's neck, and found one, very faint and slow, but definitely a pulse. He tried to pull the dart out, but it just disintegrated in his hands. He turned Boucher on his side and ran for the door, glancing out of the stern window as he did. His stomach turned over at the sight confronting him. Dr. Sinclair was on the iceberg, pointing something at Dr. Bonnet. A second later the scientist fell to the ice. Dr. Girard was also lying motionless a short distance away, and Professor Trimaud was slowly walking backwards, his hands raised in the air.

His head spinning with a myriad of questions, Spire rushed from the bridge and down the steel steps two-at-a-time. He reached the main corridor and ran out of the starboard side door, and turned to run toward the stern of the ship.

He didn't get very far. His feet were brought to a halt by what felt like a large sack. He tripped and flew onto the deck, landing on his chest. *"Shit!"* he shouted, as he hit the cold steel surface, spraining his left wrist in the process. He turned to see what he'd fallen over and saw the motionless body of Captain Deville sprawled on the deck.

He crawled over to him and found a similar dart sticking out of his thigh. He didn't bother trying to pull it out, assuming that it too would disintegrate if he tried. He checked for a pulse and found one. *Thank God, he's still alive.*

Spire jumped to his feet, and half crouching, inched his way toward the gangway at the stern of the ship, and peered over the edge. He could see that the three scientists had been shot and were lying on the ice, as good as dead. Dr. Sinclair had forced Professor Trimaud to the edge of the iceberg. Trimaud's hands were raised and he appeared to be trying to talk to her.

Spire now realised his instincts had been correct. *Dr. Alice Sinclair was clearly no marine biologist.*

He stood up and shouted over to them both. Startled, Dr. Sinclair spun around toward him, and then turned back toward Trimaud. She fired the gun, which let off a dull thud.

"No!" Spire shouted, as he descended the gangplank toward the ice. He reached the bottom and turned to see Dr. Sinclair crouched down by Trimaud's apparently lifeless body, pushing him toward the edge of the iceberg.

Spire half ran, half skidded, toward her, arriving just as she was about to push Trimaud's legs over the edge of the iceberg.

Ksenyia stood up and turned toward Spire, pointing the dart gun directly at his chest. "Well, well, if it's not Mr. Spire, the lawyer who thinks he's Superman. You always seem to be in the wrong place at the wrong time," she said, not attempting to conceal her now obvious Russian accent.

"I now see why you think the Arctic is a dangerous place,"

he said, glancing down at Trimaud who was lying perilously close to the edge of the melting iceberg, the freezing ocean lapping against it only a metre below.

Ksenyia moved toward him. "Quite. You don't appreciate the danger you have placed yourself in. Why did you ever get involved in Trimaud's desperate attempt to geoengineer the Arctic Ocean? His plan is destined to fail, and you and your clueless wife are lucky to be alive."

"Listen, Alice, whatever your name is, I don't know who you are, or why you're doing this, but please, just put the gun down and let's talk. There is no need for anyone else to die," Spire said, at a loss to know what do.

"Alice Sinclair, such a plain, boring name, don't you think?" Ksenyia said, smiling. "My real name is Ksenyia Petrovsky. I am a privately hired assassin, and you, Mr. Spire, are way out of your depth." She moved closer to Trimaud, and using her foot, started to shove him further over the edge of the iceberg, whilst keeping her gaze and the weapon fixed on Spire.

"Perhaps you can tell me why you are doing this?" Spire asked, desperately trying to buy more time. Glancing down, he noticed the small container of iron sulphate off to his right.

The sound of an outboard motor prompted Ksenyia to turn her head. About two-hundred metres or so away, the inflatable Spire had spotted from the bridge came into view.

At the same moment, Spire threw himself onto the ice, letting his body-weight carry him toward the plastic container full of sulphate.

Ksenyia turned, aimed the dart gun and fired, but failed to anticipate her target sliding so quickly. The syringe whizzed over Spire's left arm and embedded itself harmlessly into the ice. She cursed and quickly pulled back the reload slide, forcing another projectile into the gun's chamber - aimed and pulled the trigger again.

At that moment, Spire cupped a handfull of the whitened iron sulphate and threw the dense powdery substance into the Russian's face, temporarily blinding her. She fired the gun, but again the missile missed its mark, penetrating the surface of the iceberg instead, just millimetres away from his torso.

Spire watched as the Russian stumbled back, trying to rub the sulphate from her eyes, which were now clearly stinging with pain. He lunged toward her, forcing her to the ground, trying to pin her arms to the ice. As he tried to grip her wrists, he felt a sudden searing pain in the back of his left leg, and screamed in agony. *What the hell has she done?*

He moved his hand down to the area of pain and felt the cold steel handle of a knife protruding out, the blade fully embedded into his Gluteus Maximus muscle. Spire rolled off her, his left leg in agony and struggled to his feet, ready to try and bring Ksenyia to the ground again.

Out of the corner of his eye, Spire noticed the dark grey Zodiac a short distance away, pulling up to the side of the iceberg. *Whoever these guys were, they were coming to pick her up,* he realised.

A sudden cracking sound from the edge of the ice slab caused him to turn back to the Russian, who appeared to be smiling as she wiped her weeping eyes. Then; she suddenly disappeared from view, as if her legs below her knees had simply vanished. Spire then realised that the section of ice she was standing on had cracked off the main iceberg. The smaller block of ice started to topple and sink into the ocean. He looked on as Ksenyia Petrovsky was sucked into the freezing water.

He dragged himself to the edge of the iceberg and peered over. The Russian was in the water, gasping from the shock of the cold ocean. Irrespective of the havoc she had caused, he couldn't leave her there. He reached out to her. "Quick, take my hand, I'll pull you out."

Ksenyia looked up at him; the sound of the Zodiac's outboard motor seemed muffled and distant to her as she felt her limbs stiffen. She tried to lift her arm for Spire, but it felt weak and numb. "I…I just want to see my family again," she said, her voice weak and trembling. She tried to reach his hand but the metre-high stretch to the top of the iceberg was too great. She could barely feel her freezing arm, and knew she was losing all her strength. She tried again to reach out, but her arm muscles had frozen and she started to sink into the freezing depths. The reflex action caused by the freezing water triggered her diaphragm to contract, drawing air sharply into her lungs which now filled with icy water. As the darkness enveloped her, she thought of her mother, sister and father.

Spire watched as her head and shoulders slid silently beneath the freezing water. The canvas bag she'd been carrying slipped off her shoulder and started to sink. He just managed to hook the strap of the bag with the camera tripod that had been lying on the ice, before it went under. The chunk of ice Ksenyia had been standing on then bobbed back to the surface, and drifted back toward the main section.

Spire looked over to where Trimaud was still lying, and could see he was also about to slip off the iceberg into the water. He stood up; gritted his teeth from the electric shock he felt shooting up his nerves from the knife wound, shuffled over to Trimaud, and quickly dragged him away from the edge.

The men in the Zodiac looked on briefly, three metres or so from the ice plateau, before throttling the idling engine, turning, and speeding back toward the ship waiting silently in the channel.

CHAPTER 63

SPIRE DRAGGED TRIMAUD and the others, who were all still unconscious from the effects of the tranquiliser, over to the base of the steps. He looked down at his injured leg. The tourniquet he'd tied around the top of his thigh was stemming most of the blood, but the wound was now becoming agonising.

He slowly ascended the gangplank back onto the *Mercure* and lowered himself onto the deck. Looking out to sea, he could just about make out the Zodiac in the distance, moving toward the sinister ship, still stationary in the channel.

Dragging his injured leg, he shuffled to the starboard door. Captain Deville was still lying there, out cold. He stepped over him and headed down to the science lab. *Where the hell were the cooks, Dr. McBride and Marcus, the engineer?*

In the laboratory, Spire found the first aid kit and took out some gauze swabs, a paraffin dressing and a pair of scissors. He forced a rolled up bandage into his mouth, just in case he bit his tongue, and then reached down for the handle of the knife, and yanked it out. The pain was instant and sharp. He bit down on the bandage and pounded the workbench with his fist until the worst of the pain subsided. He placing the dressing over the five centimetre gash, and then wrapped the bandage tightly around the top of his leg, in order to prevent any further blood loss.

He hobbled out of the lab and carefully descended the steel

steps to the corridor that led to the ship's galley. As he neared the galley cabin, he heard whistling; a smell of freshly cooked tomato soup wafted into the corridor.

Spire entered the galley and saw Roberto the chef, chopping onions. "Thank God you're OK," he said.

Roberto stopped whistling and turned toward Spire, leaning against the galley door. "You look like you've done a round with *Mike Tyson!* What the hell happened to you, my friend?" he said, putting down the chopping knife.

"Haven't you heard anything down here? Dr. Sinclair, turned out to be a Russian assassin, decided to go crazy and shoot everyone with some kind of tranquilizer gun, before trying to kill the professor."

"*What?* You're kidding right?"

"Do I look like I'm joking," Spire said, pointing out his bandaged stab wound. "Dr Sinclair wasn't who she said she was. Appears she was attempting to prevent today's experiment from proceeding. Anyway, I need your help to get Professor Trimaud and the others off the ice. Captain Deville and Officer Boucher have also been hit, and are both out cold."

"*Oh, man!* What has happened to Dr...the Russian?"

"She's dead. Slipped off the ice and drowned. I tried to save her, but she couldn't reach my hand."

"You are not messing me around, Robert?" Roberto said, removing his chef's jacket and pulling on a jumper. "Here, drink some of this, it will help," he said, handing Spire a bottle of *Jack Daniel's*.

Spire took a long swig from the bottle; the whiskey slid down his throat, warming every inch of him as it went down. He took another gulp and handed the bottle back.

"You fit enough to show me what's been going on?" Roberto asked.

"I think so. Follow me," Spire said, hobbling back along the corridor.

Roberto followed Spire along the corridor and up one flight of stairs to the first deck, and out through the starboard door, where they found Captain Deville lying on the floor. Roberto rushed over to him and felt for a pulse. "Captain, are you alright?" he asked, lightly shaking him.

Deville opened his eyes and let out a deep groan, before closing them again.

Spire knelt down beside him. "Captain, you were shot with a tranquilizer dart by Dr. Sinclair. She's dead and you're in no imminent danger. I'll bring you some water shortly."

Deville groaned and nodded his head.

Spire and Roberto continued along the deck, to the stern of the ship. Roberto looked over the rail and down onto the iceberg. He could see the four scientists lying on the ice where Spire had said, but they had been joined by six gulls, which were pecking at their legs. "Get out of here!" he shouted as he descended the gangplank to the ice. He picked up Dr. Bonnet and lifted her back onto the deck, where Spire was waiting with warm blankets.

Forty minutes later, Roberto, who had been joined by Marcus Roux, the ship's engineer, had managed to get everyone off the ice and back onboard. Only a few items of scientific equipment remained on the tabular iceberg, artefacts left over from the unfinished experiment.

An hour after being rescued, the scientists and Captain Deville were slowly recovering in the warmth of the *Mercure's* bar, and being looked after by Roberto and Roux. A constant supply of warm coffee was being provided from the galley.

"Where the *hell* is Dr.McBride?" Trimaud finally asked, looking around.

"Bloody hell! We've forgotten all about her, she must still be onboard, hiding somewhere," Spire said, getting up. "Come on, we need to find her, she could be injured."

Roberto and Roux stood up. "We'll come with you," Roux said.

"Carlos is missing too," Roberto said.

"Very well, but you lot stay here, you need to rest for a bit," Spire said to the others, as Roberto and Roux followed him out of the cabin.

"I'll be along in a moment," Captain Deville boomed. "I just need another one of these first," he said, pouring himself a third whisky.

Spire left the bar and made his way down to the staterooms. Roberto and Roux walked in the opposite direction, heading down to the ship's laboratories.

Spire entered Dr. McBride's cabin and called out her name. He listened, but heard nothing. He checked under the bed and in the wardrobe. All her belongings were in the same position, as before. There was nowhere for her to hide, or be hidden. He left the cabin, headed for the Russian's room and opened the cabin door.

The room was empty. On the bed he spotted a large book on marine biology. He walked over, picked it up and flicked through it. Just as he was about to throw it back on the bed, a blue scrawl on one of the pages caught his attention;

-Operation Fonte d'Arctic-0600, 22 June-

He looked at the entry, written in felt-tipped pen. *What could it mean? 22 June was tomorrow!*

As he stood there he heard a very faint whimpering. "Dr. McBride!" he shouted her name again. This time the muffled sound was louder. *It was coming from the wardrobe.*

Spire then noticed the cord tying the door handles together. He tried to untie the knot but it was too tight. He felt his pocket for the lighter that Kim had given him; thankfully it was still there. He burnt through the tough cord in seconds and it fell to the floor in smouldering bits. He pulled both doors open and found Ruth McBride lying in the wardrobe in a crunched up foetal position, shaking. He pulled the gag away from her face. "It's ok, Ruth, you're safe now."

Back in the bar, Dr. McBride tearfully told everyone what had happened, and how she had feared for her life, when discovering the vial containing the clear liquid in Dr Sinclair's cabin. "I threw it at her," she said, sipping her coffee. "If there's any of it left in the vial, I can analyse it to see what it was."

"I have a hunch that you'll find nicotine," Spire said.

"Nicotine? Why do you say that?"

"Analyse it first, and then we'll explain," Trimaud interjected.

"Ok," Dr. McBride said, looking puzzled.

Captain Deville got up from the bar stool and walked over to the large porthole, on the starboard side of the cabin, and looked out. "So you think that Canadian ship out there has something to do with all this Robert?"

"Well, that's where the Zodiac came from. They were coming to pick up their Russian friend, I'm certain."

"The Maple Leaf has been hoisted only to deceive us," Deville replied, turning to everyone in the room.

"Well if that's the Russians out there, then we really are in the merde. We don't want this turning into World War Three now do we?" Dr. Bonnet said.

"I say we approach the ship, and find out what the hell is

going on," Spire said, shrugging.

"Come on, Robert, that is clearly dangerous," Trimaud replied.

"Listen, Francois, whoever she was, she clearly had orders to prevent your experiment from proceeding. She's surely involved in the deaths of your friend Jack, and Dr. Stanton. I say we dump your experimental sulphate overboard now, then go and investigate that vessel, and find out what the hell is going on."

There was silence in the room as everyone thought about Spire's comments. Finally, Deville took a deep breath. "I'm not going to endanger this ship or anyone on board, Robert. It seems a crazy idea. I don't mind continuing the experiment; we're here so we might as well get that done, but I say we get over to Cornwallis Island and radio for help."

Spire sat there for a moment. His instincts screaming that something was very wrong. He thought about the note in the marine biology book, *Fonte d'Arctic; what did it mean?*

"I found a note scrawled in the Russian's biology book. *Fonte d'Arctic*; what's the English translation? The note is dated the twenty-second of June."

"Well, the literal translation would be *Arctic melt!*" Dr. Bonnet said.

An icy chill shot up Spire's back. "I need to get aboard that ship, find out what the hell's going on," he said, looking around the cabin.

"I can't let you do that, Robert," Deville said, shaking his head.

"You're going to have to physically stop me," Spire replied. "Think about it, Professor," Spire continued, directing his gaze at Trimaud. "We have two dead climatologists, a Russian agent who almost succeeded in preventing your experiment from proceeding, and the business cards left on or near both murdered climatologists with the name *Arc Bin Quid Lo* embossed on them. First I thought these might be unrelated or just disinformation of some kind, but now I think the names are an anagram."

"An anagram? What for, Robert?" Dr. Bonnet asked.

"I think the letters spell LIQUID CARBON."

"Liquid carbon?" Everyone, but Trimaud, repeated in unison.

"Think about it - *Oil*. What if the Russians, or someone else, wants to melt the Arctic ice in order to search for, or recover oil? An environmental disaster, on a scale not previously seen, would occur."

"Robert, don't you think that's a bit farfetched?" Deville said.

"Well, it's not as farfetched as you might think, Jacques," Trimaud replied. "You see the Arctic's resources are well known. Trillions of dollars worth of natural gas and oil lie under the ocean here. It's quite possible that someone has made a discovery, and will go to any lengths to get it...even if it means killing for it. Clearly, whoever is involved has every interest in seeing my experiment fail."

The cabin fell silent.

Spire spoke again. "We don't have much time. It's already five P.M. I suggest the *Blankoplankton* experiment goes ahead without any further delay; then Captain, you can get me as close to that Canadian ship as possible on your way to Cornwallis Island. I'm going aboard to find out what's going on, whether you like it or not."

There was a few moments silence, and then Roberto spoke up. "I'll take you there myself in the inflatable. It's the least I can do...for Carlos, if nothing else."

"I don't know if you're brave or stupid, Spire, but you seem to have found support for your plan. I tell you what; I'll take you to within five hundred metres of the ship, and then proceed to the island to try and fix our communications. We'll return for you at eleven. That's my final decision. Accept it, or you're not getting off."

"You have a deal," Spire replied, nodding at Deville. "Come on, Roberto we don't have much time. Let's get some supplies and prepare the inflatable. I'll figure out what we are going to do on the way," Spire said, standing up.

"Take care both. We'll sweep the ship for Carlos one more time," Trimaud said, as they left the cabin.

Spire hobbled down the corridor to his cabin, an ominous feeling welling in the pit of his stomach.

CHAPTER 64

THE TWO RUSSIANS pulled the Zodiac onto the *Rezky's* rear hydraulic platform, and then elevated it to the docking area on the lower deck. Charkov unzipped his black waterproof jacket. "Useless bitch," he said to Donskoy, "I thought she was supposed to be good. What the hell was she doing standing so close to the edge of the iceberg?"

They both secured the inflatable, and turned to walk in through the stern door, when Captain Tabanov came striding toward them. "What the hell happened out there? Did my eyes deceive me, or did our contact fall off the ice?" he said, throwing the remnants of his cigarette over the side.

Charkov briefed Tabanov on what he'd seen. "There was a fair-haired man on the iceberg with her; it looked like he threw some substance into her eyes before she lost her footing, Captain."

"Very well, let's get inside. I need to report to Admiral Dashkov. Prepare the ship for departure, our work here is done," Tabanov said, as he turned and walked back along the deck. He climbed the rusting steel stairway to the bridge and walked in. Admiral Dashkov was seated at the chart table, manually plotting their return journey.

"You were right, Admiral; she slipped off the iceberg, overpowered by one of the ship's crew. Her journey has ended. She served mother Russia well."

"Very unfortunate, I must say," Dashkov replied, without looking up from the chart. "We depart in the morning at two, when the light is at its most dim. I have plotted the quickest route back. Please ask Lieutenant Brilev to keep me informed of any further seismic activity."

"Of course, Admiral," Tabanov said, as he scanned the horizon with the binoculars. After some seconds he spoke again. "Do we have orders to activate the thermal devices, Admiral?"

Dashkov looked up from the chart table. "I will find out soon enough. I am due to make contact at eighteen hundred hours. Do you have any doubts about the mission, Captain?"

"No, Admiral. I will be happy to enter the activation codes if need be," Tabanov replied, setting the binoculars back down on the bulkhead.

"Good. For now, see if the others require any help with preparing the ship for departure. I will go and make the call. I'll be in my cabin if you need me."

Captain Tabanov left the bridge and headed down to the *Rezky's* communications room to let the crew know the time of their departure.

Faric glanced at the clock on his marble mantelpiece and sipped his coffee, a knot formed in the pit of his stomach as the time ticked to eleven P.M. Rather than speak with his Russian contact; he thought it more suitable to speak directly with the admiral aboard the *Rezky*. He was expecting the call at any moment. Soon, I will be able to sleep soundly, he thought.

The house was in darkness, the only light coming from a small table lamp beside him. He was stretching his neck and looking up at the ceiling when the phone rang. He took a deep breath and picked up the receiver. It was the call he'd been waiting for, a personal call from Admiral Dashkov, a man he'd never met, but a man who impressed him by his flawless credentials. "Good evening, Admiral, I have been waiting for your call. I trust everything has gone to plan. Is our Russian friend enjoying your hospitality at last? I must say she deserves it."

There was a short silence. "Unfortunately, I am not able to bring you such news," Dashkov paused. "The Russian agent Petrovsky, it seems, was outwitted by one of the crew members on board the *Mercure*. She failed her mission at the last minute. Just as my men arrived, at a large iceberg the *Mercure* was anchored against, she lost her footing and fell into the ocean. A man on the ice tried to pull her back up, but was unable to do so. She wasn't able to last long in the freezing water. I am afraid she is dead."

Faric was silent as he digested the unpleasant news. He shifted on his chair, knocking the table next to him which sent his half-finished cup of coffee crashing to the floor. Shards of the bone china cup scattered across the marble slabs. "How could this have happened, Admiral?" Faric asked, his voice trembling with anger.

"Like I told you, my men were there, unfortunately, so was another man. A well-built man with fair hair, he threw something into Petrovsky's eyes. She lost her balance and slipped off the iceberg."

Faric cursed and mumbled in Arabic before answering. "Robert Spire; we should have eliminated him when we had the chance."

"Do you have any orders for me?" Admiral Dashkov asked, after a few seconds silence.

Faric sat there, nervously running his fingers along the raised scar on his face, a bead of sweat formed on his forehead. He remained silent for twenty seconds or so before speaking. "Activate the thermal devices, and then leave the area. The device control-pad has a signal radius of five-hundred nautical miles. As long as one device is activated, all others will automatically switch on."

"Very well, consider it done. When can we expect payment?"

"I will sanction it now with Zablozky. The money will be in your Swiss account by the morning."

"Good. Is there anything else?"

"I am sorry for the loss of the Russian agent," Faric said, through gritted teeth.

He slammed the receiver down.

Enraged, he stood up, and overturned the small table beside him, sending the lamp and phone crashing to the floor. He lifted the up-ended table by its legs and smashed it back down on the marble floor, sending splinters of wood in all directions. "Useless bitch," he shouted as he stomped out of the room.

Fahim will surely understand what I have done, he told himself.

CHAPTER 65

THE SLATE-GREY ship lay off their port side, now almost camouflaged against the darkening cloudy skies. Spire shivered as he checked his bag, into which he had packed a rope, flares, grappling hook and money. The cash was Trimaud's idea, in case he needed to bribe his way off the vessel.

Three hours earlier, just before they had left their make-shift iceberg dock, Spire had watched the joy on Trimaud's face as Captain Deville manoeuvred the container of sulphate over the side of the ship. The steel container had glinted in the low Arctic sun as it dangled from the crane's heavy steel chains. As promised, Trimaud had allowed him to activate the remote control hatch on the container's underside, releasing the white sulphate into the ocean below. The powdery substance had fallen into the freezing ocean, like billions of microscopic sugar crystals, where it immediately began to disperse on the surface.

The event had been over in less than twenty minutes. If it worked, this single action would lead to a larger seeding which could reverse the Arctic's declining ice pack, thus preserving the planet's most delicate ecosystem. Dr. Ruth McBride had completed the experiment by releasing her phytoplankton monitors into the drop zone, so that the rapidly forming *Blankoplankton* could be monitored.

Spire thought about the *Blankoplankton* as it went about its business of sucking up carbon dioxide, producing oxygen and reflecting light; before re-focusing on the dangerous task ahead.

Captain Deville brought the *Mercure* to a crawl, whilst Boucher lowered the Zodiac to the surface of the ocean. Spire and Roberto descended the rope ladder, to the tethered craft waiting for them below.

Dr. Bonnet shouted down from the deck above. "Please be careful, Robert, we'll see you in six hours."

"Don't worry about me, Mari, I'll be fine. You and Pierre take care of Francois, while I'm gone," Spire shouted back.

Roberto started up the Zodiac's Yamaha 350 engine and pointed the craft toward the Canadian flagged ship. The inflatable quickly picked up speed, and was soon skipping over the choppy grey waters of the Parry Channel toward the vessel.

Spire held onto the wooden seats to steady himself, whilst carrying out a final check on the contents of his draw-string canvas bag. Freezing ocean spray buffeted his face as the inflatable bounced across the waves.

The crossing took fifteen minutes, and as they closed in on the ship, Spire could see that the vessel's decals had weathered badly. The once jet-black lettering now revealed the ship's name clearly - *Rezky*. "That doesn't sound Canadian to me," Spire said, pointing up at the name on the bow, which rose menacingly out of the ocean above them.

"That's because it's Russian," Roberto replied, throttling back the Zodiac's engine to an idle as he steered them along the hull of the ominous vessel, hugging its port side. Continuing past the beam of the ship, they slowly made their way along to the stern, where they found what they'd been looking for. A series of small steel rungs set into the side of the hull ascended to the vessels deck above. "There's my way up," Spire said, pointing to the rusty steel ledges.

Roberto cut the engine, allowing Spire to reach out to the lowest rung, some two metres above the water line. Grabbing the Zodiac's lanyard, Roberto tethered them to the hull of the ship, pulling the inflatable tightly up against it.

"Ok, this is it," Spire said, pulling his gloves on and placing the canvas bag over his shoulder. He checked his watch; "I'll see you back at this precise point four hours from now."

"Be careful, I hope you make friends easily," Roberto said, untying the lanyard as Spire pulled himself up onto the first rung.

"Just make sure you're back here at eleven P.M," Spire replied, looking up at the vertical hull towering above him. He looked back at Roberto. "I'm very sorry about Carlos."

Roberto nodded and untied the Zodiac, as Spire slowly climbed up the side of the cold, steel stern section of the ship.

Inside the *Rezky's* communications room, Lieutenant Brilev had been monitoring the radar target moving toward them. He picked up the phone and called Admiral Dashkov. "The target is, no doubt, an inflatable - two occupants - which is now moving away from us again. It appears we have a visitor, Admiral."

"Thank you, Lieutenant," Dashkov replied.

Dashkov turned to Captain Tabanov. "Captain, have a welcome party greet our guest, but don't harm him. Keep a low profile initially; I want to observe our friend to see if we can determine his intentions."

"Very well, Admiral," Tabanov replied, checking that his *Stechkin* revolver was loaded.

Spire reached the final rung of the vessel's inset ladder and slowly pulled himself up using the ship's railings, where he rested on a small ledge to catch his breath, from the twenty-metre or so vertical climb. He looked down to the cold grey ocean; the waves were now larger, smashing into the hull below. A cold brisk wind was blowing down the strait, buffeting Spire as he held onto the flaking, rusty railing. He glanced down the deck toward the main superstructure; it was clear. He slowly lowered himself down onto the steel deck, remaining crouched whilst he orientated himself. He looked up and saw a pennant displaying the Russian flag, flapping violently in the wind. *What the hell were the Russian's doing here?*

To his right, on the stern deck, was a pair of old gunning turrets, which looked like they dated back to the 1950's. At least two of the guns were no longer operative; they had been filled in with concrete, or perhaps rubber. The rest of the deck was empty, apart from a couple of rusting steel crates stacked in one corner.

He estimated the distance to the superstructure to be about twenty metres or so. Half crouching, he moved across the deck to it, and then stood for a few minutes, his back pressed against the cold steel. The location afforded him some respite from the biting wind now howling east to west along the Northwest Passage. The Arctic sun hung low in the sky, but the storm clouds overhead made it one of the darkest evenings so far.

He edged along the back of the superstructure and peered around the corner, to look at the starboard side of the vessel. It was clear, so he continued slowly along the deck. He arrived at the first door, gripped the cold steel handle and tried it, but it was locked. Moving further along, he could see that the superstructure splayed out, and the angular edges of the bridge loomed above. The entire ship seemed strangely abandoned. He moved the canvas bag onto his left shoulder, and crept further along the deck, heading for another door in the superstructure. Reaching it, he yanked down the heavy steel handle; the latch made a loud clunk and the door swung open.

Spire stepped inside the dark corridor and closed the heavy door behind him, drowning out the sound of the howling wind. He checked the time; it was approaching eight P.M - almost half an hour had elapsed since he'd been dropped off, one hour since he'd left the *Mercure*. The stark corridor was lit with low wattage sodium lighting which hummed quietly above him. He headed left, down the shorter section of corridor toward the stern, and arrived at a right hand, ninety-degree bend. Peering around, he could see the corridor extended the width of the vessel, and it too was empty. He continued along and arrived at a metal door about halfway along. The corridor beyond appeared to bend around to the right again, presumably back along the length of the ship toward the bow.

Wiping perspiration away from his forehead, he opened the door. A steel stairway descended into the bowels of the ship, lit by the same dim sodium lighting. A faint drone emanated from somewhere deep within the vessel. *Probably a generator or engine*, he imagined, as he slowly crept down the steps. He arrived at the bottom of a large rectangular space, the floor of which was made from steel and painted in a deep red, possibly non-slip paint, now considerably faded. A stack of old crates were piled up in the right hand corner. Diagonally opposite, a large object was covered with a tarpaulin. Spire crept over to it and grabbed the dusty cover on the bottom corner, pulling it back. He was amazed to see an old car, which looked in almost pristine condition. He removed more of the cover to reveal a large six wheeled Land-Rover type vehicle. *How the hell did this get in here?*

He looked up to inspect the room, and noticed a crack running along the centre of the ceiling. He guessed he must be in some sort of hold, just below the main deck. Intrigued by the vehicle under the sheet, he grabbed the corner to pull the tarpaulin back. As he did so, a cold, blunt object was thrust against the back of his neck, causing him to freeze.

"Welcome aboard. I see you're admiring our ZIL-167 Mr…?"

Spire raised his arms and slowly turned around. The Russian voice belonged to a well-built man, with steel-blue eyes, who was now pointing an automatic pistol directly at his chest.

"Spire, Robert Spire. I was beginning to wonder where the welcome party was."

"This way, Mr. Spire, Admiral Dashkov would like to meet you," the man said, shoving him forward toward a door at the rear of the dark hold.

CHAPTER 66

A LIGHT MIST drifted down the sheer eastern cliff face of Cornwallis Island as the *Mercure Blanc* drifted towards the small stone quay, which extended out from the rocky cove to the east of Resolute Bay.

Captain Deville gave the screws one last nudge in reverse, slowing the ship, as her bow gently bumped into the rubber tyres that lined the stone wall of the makeshift quay.

Trimaud and Dr. Bonnet were out on the main deck, surveying the stark cliffs of the weather-beaten island. Herring Gulls and Ivory Gulls flew in and out of their clifftop nests, oblivious to the island's latest visitors.

"I do hope Robert is safe out there," Dr. Bonnet said, a look of concern evident upon her face.

"I'm sure he's fine. We did try and talk him out of it. Anyway, he can take care of himself. He is a lawyer after all. If anyone gives him trouble, he'll just threaten to bill them!" Trimaud said with a chuckle.

"That's hardly funny in the circumstances, Francois, but I hope you're right. I don't want to stay here any longer than neccessary," Dr. Bonnet replied, straining to see the stationary ship, still moored some ten nautical miles away in the Parry Channel.

With the *Mercure's* engines off, an eerie silence descended on the bleak cove. The only sound was the constant sloshing of waves hitting the quay, and the occasional cry from the gulls above. The mercury on the ship's external thermometer had moved down to minus one degree Celsius. Dr. Bonnet shivered and zipped her parka tightly up to her neck. "Come on, Francois, it's getting cold, I want to go back inside."

As they walked in, the ship's P.A system crackled to life. It was Captain Deville, asking everyone to assemble in the library for a quick briefing.

Trimaud and Dr. Bonnet made their way to the library, to meet up with the others. Just as they sat down, Deville entered with Roux, both of them dressed in Arctic weather gear.

"Ok everyone," Deville said, "listen carefully. Marcus and I are going ashore to the old weather base, located against the western cliff face. I have been there before and I'm hoping we'll find some fuses to repair the communications equipment. The main town of Resolute is about three kilometres away, but we're not going to have time to get there and be back to pick Robert up at eleven P.M. The weather station is much closer. Are there any questions?"

"How long will you be?" asked Dr. Bonnet.

"It's about sixty minutes, there and back. Officer Boucher is in charge during my absence."

The team watched from the top deck as the two men descended the gangplank to the stone quay below and made their way along the narrow manmade stone walkway carved from the cliff face, which ran along the eastern side of Cornwallis Island. Within five minutes, their silhouettes were barely visible through the grey mist cascading down from the cliffs above.

Deville and Roux slowly continued along the misty cliff path to the main walkway which traversed the small inlet to the western side, where the old Canadian weather station - built in the 1950's - was situated. Resolute Bay proper, and the town of

Resolute, consisting of a population of around two-hundred and fifty, was a ninety minute walk to the west.

Deville had stopped at the small weather station twice before, and the old outpost usually had a sufficient supply of electrical equipment and food for the two-man team based there.

Ascending a small ridge, they looked back toward the foggy cove and the *Mercure,* which was moored against the stone quay, now barely visible. The Parry Channel behind was shrouded in a light mist.

"Hopefully that fog doesn't extend too far out into the channel," Deville said, as they descended a set of stone steps cut into the rock face.

"Might take longer to find Robert, if it doesn't lift," Roux replied, eyeing the captain.

"Come on, it's only another twenty minutes from here," Deville replied.

They both continued along the damp, lichen covered path toward the weather station. As they walked on, the mist lifted, revealing the stone building about fifty metres ahead and nestled against the western cliff wall of the small bay. Three large antennas extended from the back of the stone building, behind an ancient satellite dish fixed to the corrugated roof - which pointed skyward. As they approached the stone hut, they could see light coming from a solitary window to the right of the main wooden entrance door.

"At least someone's home," Deville said, somewhat out of breath from the one kilometre trek along the cliff path.

"Thank God. I'd go stir crazy if I was based out here. Give me a twelve hour shift in the *Mercure's* engine room anytime," Roux replied, stopping to catch his breath.

After a brief rest, they continued down the steep path to the building. Deville slipped down the last metre of the path before steadying himself on an old weathered wooden post. They walked up to the salt-stained window and peered in. The light they'd seen was coming from a small lamp, which was on a desk at the back of the stone hut. The silhouette of a seated man could also just about be made out.

"There's someone in there," Deville said, breathing a sigh of relief. He thumped on the thick wooden door. "Bonsoir! Hello!" he shouted. There was no response. Deville tried the door, which opened with a loud *creak.*

They both walked in. "Hello, my friend - what's happened to the heating?" Deville asked, walking over to the man, who appeared to be engrossed in something at the desk.

Roux followed Deville over to the lit desk, at the back of the hut. A table against the side wall was laid out for two people. Arctic weather gear hung from hooks near to the door, together with ski poles and empty steel buckets. A damp, musty odour permeated through the small building.

Deville could see that the radio operator was wearing a set of headphones, which explained why he was ignoring them. Reaching the desk, he walked to the side so as not to startle the man. As he did, he could see that there was something very wrong. Deville saw it before Roux. The man's throat had been slit from ear to ear; congealed and frozen blood covered the desk and floor around him.

Roux turned away from the sickening sight and immediately saw the legs of another individual lying face down, half hidden in shadow, near to the cupboard at the back of the room. He felt his stomach churn. "Captain, there's someone else over here," he said, running over to the body. He turned the stiff, frozen corpse over. "Jesus, same thing's happened here," he said, looking down at the man's throat, which had been slit in the same fashion. "How long do you think they've been dead?" Roux asked, his heart now beating furiously.

"Difficult to tell, the cold will have preserved their corpses. I'll radio for help."

Deville rushed back to the desk and pulled the headphones from the dead man's head, and followed the headphone lead to the radio base unit. "Merde!" he shouted, as he pulled the lead from the smashed equipment. "Someone's destroyed the radio."

Deville quickly fumbled through the desk drawer in search of the fuses he needed for the *Mercure's* communications equipment, but found nothing. He walked to the back of the building where the storeroom was located and found two plastic containers on the shelves, labelled 'Fuses.' He pulled them out and emptied the contents onto the table. Four of the fuses he needed lay amongst the assortment of items. He grabbed them with shaking hands and shoved them into his pocket. "Allez – come on! Let's get the hell out of here. We can call for help when we get back to the ship."

"I'm with you there," Roux said, shivering as a column of ice rushed up his spine.

They left the weather station without looking back, scrambling back up the steep path, for the forty minute hike back to the quay.

CHAPTER 67

SPIRE WAS SHOVED through the doorway at the back of the cargo hold and down another set of steel steps to a lower deck.

"Take it easy, will you," he said, as his captor pushed the end of the gun deeper into his back.

"Take a left when you reach the bottom," the man sneered.

Spire wasn't about to try anything stupid and turned left as instructed, into another large space, which also looked like some kind of cargo hold. An overhead gantry was fixed to the ceiling, no doubt for the portable crane which he noticed at the far end of the room.

His captor moved alongside him. "Take a seat, Mr. Spire."

Spire was forced back into a chair, which he hadn't noticed when he first walked in. Another man appeared from a room off to the side, moved behind him and bound his wrists with a plastic tie. The two men then spoke to each other in Russian.

"No tea?" Spire asked, interrupting them.

The man holding the gun looked at Spire and smirked. The other man, who had tied him, up walked back into the side room. The brief silence was interrupted by the sound of clanking steel echoing in the large cargo hold, as someone walked down the steel stairway toward them.

Spire looked up to see a tall, formidably built man, wearing navy trousers, black boots and a thick grey trench coat step down into the room. The man walked over, placing a cigarette in his mouth, lit it and then pulled over a chair that was resting against the side wall. He turned it the wrong way around and sat down facing Spire, resting his arms on the chair's back support. "Welcome aboard the *Rezky* Mr. Spire. I am Admiral Dashkov," he said, drawing on his cigarette and exhaling a plume of smoke into Spire's face. "I am sure you didn't come all this way to drive off in my ZIL-167? So, may I ask, what are you doing aboard my ship?"

Spire's eyes watered from the cigarette-smoke facial he'd just received. He cleared his throat. "I was hoping you could tell me what the hell is going on around here?"

Dashkov took another drag on his cigarette, this time exhaling the smoke above Spire's head. "Did you kill Miss Petrovsky?" he asked, matter-of-factly.

"If you mean the crazy Russian who shot most of my colleagues, tried to drown my friend, kill me…then yes."

Dashkov smirked. "Then you're very lucky to be still alive, Mr. Spire. When Miss Petrovsky decided to kill someone, she rarely failed."

"Yeah, well, I can assure you that I'm not feeling particularly lucky right now," Spire replied, tugging on the ties binding his wrists together.

Dashkov took a last drag, and stubbed his cigarette out on the steel deck.

"So, are you going to tell me what's going on here?" Spire asked.

Dashkov narrowed his eyes, and scratched the greying stubble on his chin. "I'm afraid our business here is confidential, Mr. Spire."

"You realise my friends aboard the *Mercure Blanc*, together with the Canadian Navy, will be here any minute. I'm sure nobody wants an international incident out here, least of all the Russians."

Dashkov laughed. "I admire your tenacity, Mr. Spire, but I doubt very much whether your friends will be able to help you now."

"What the hell does that mean?" Spire asked.

Dashkov got up from his chair. "Mr. Spire, you will be wanted in Russia for the murder of Ksenyia Petrovsky. The Russian authorities do not take kindly to their citizens being killed by foreign nationals," he said, looking down at him.

He walked back into the dimly lit side room. Spire could hear him speak in Russian to the other crew member. Dashkov then re-appeared after a short while and went to ascend the stairway to the upper deck. "Goodbye, Mr. Spire, it was a pleasure meeting you."

Spire tried to remain calm, slowly inhaling the oil-contaminated air. He looked around the room. Steel racking lined the side walls and an overhead gantry ran along the centre of the room and out through a large opening at the end. Steel chains hanging from the ceiling at various points, swayed with the gentle rocking motion of the ship as it was buffeted by the waves outside. He could hear the faint sound of a radio coming from somewhere in the side room, but the language appeared to be Russian. He sat there, wondering how the hell he was going to get out.

Dashkov arrived on the bridge, took a Golden Fleece from the packet, and lit it. Captain Tabanov was sitting down at the chart table, the control pod for the OTMs on the wooden table in front of him. "How is our guest?" he asked, looking up at Dashkov.

"He's enjoying our Russian hospitality, Captain, tied to a chair in the weapons room. Charkov and Donskoy are watching over him for now."

Tobanov hesitated for a moment before asking, "What are we going to do with him?"

Dashkov looked at him. "We do nothing, until we leave Canadian waters. Our orders are to activate the OTMs and return to Severomorsk. We depart in ten minutes Captain, please alert the men," he said, his voice tense.

"Yes, Admiral, I will give the men the good news."

Tabanov addressed the crew over the *Rezky's* P.A system, telling them to prepare for immediate departure. He turned back to Admiral Dashkov, to see him enter the final digit of the activation code into the control-pad. A red light blinked on the pod, confirming that the OTMs had now been activated.

"It is done," Dashkov said, folding the paper containing the code and placing it back in the silver amulet hanging around his neck.

Down in the weapons room, Spire felt a powerful, low rumble as the *Rezky's* engines started up, causing the chains hanging from the gantry above to vibrate furiously.

He felt his heart pounding in his chest as he realised they were leaving. A renewed sense of dread washed over him as he tugged on his bound wrists.

CHAPTER 68

DEVILLE AND ROUX jogged the last few hundred feet along the cliff path, their movements made easier by the lifting mist. Arriving at the quay, Deville hurried up the gangplank and onto the deck of the *Mercure*. He got Boucher's attention up on the bridge and signalled for him to start the engines.

Roux undid the last rope on the quayside, and climbed on board, the deck vibrating as the ship's engines starting up.

Deville stormed onto the bridge, and updated Boucher about the grisly discoveries they made back at the weather station, yanking his Arctic weather gear off as he spoke.

Boucher listened in astonished silence, whilst raising the gangplank, and directing power to the bow thrusters. "But who could have done such a thing?"

"I don't know, I'm guessing it might have something to do with that ship out there."

"I've been watching her," Boucher said. "She's moved down the channel, perhaps five or six nautical miles."

"Merde! We need to get Spire off, as soon as posible. Find Marcus; make sure he stays down in the engine room. I'll need full power until further notice, and if you see Francois, tell him to get up here - now!"

Boucher handed the wheel to Deville and hurried off the bridge.

Deville manoeuvred the *Mercure* away from the quay and within minutes had turned her toward the open channel. White-crested waves were visible in the distance in the unprotected windswept part of the passage.

Five minutes later, the *Mercure* was cruising at twenty-two knots through the Parry Channel, toward the Lancaster Sound. The radar revealed that the *Rezky* was now some twenty nautical miles ahead of them, travelling at eighteen knots.

Deville activated the auto pilot, just as Trimaud entered the bridge. "Ah, Francois, you'd better take a seat to hear what I'm about to say."

Trimaud sank into one of the swivel chairs and listened as Deville told him about the gruesome discoveries at the weather station. He sat at the chart table, his head buried in his hands as he tried to process the terrible facts. "Merde! Merde! This is unbelievable. My best friend, Jack, murdered, and now this? And Robert is on that ship. If anything happens to him, I'll never forgive myself."

"Don't beat yourself up too much, Francois. It was his decision to come along, besides, he's a tough nut to crack, we'll get him back, don't worry."

Officer Boucher joined them. "I've briefed the rest of the crew and guests. They are aware we won't be stopping off at the seeding location in view of the circumstances."

"Very well, Henri, take over please, I need to try and repair the communication system, so I can get hold of the Canadians; we will need all the help we can get to intercept the ship in the channel."

Beneath the steel hulls of the two ships, in the depths of the Lancaster Sound, the freezing waters were slowly beginning to warm. A pod of beluga whales had started to gather around an alien object, its shiny black surface similar to one of their own young. The mammals had only ever experienced water this warm in their southern breeding grounds. The fish and other marine life migrating to the warming water provided excellent hunting grounds for the pod.

Unbeknown to the whales, the Ocean Thermal Modifier was slowly heating the waters of the Northwest Passage to a temperature it had not been for millions of years.

CHAPTER 69

FAHIM LOOKED UP at the sun's rays streaming through the semi-open glass roof, of *NewSaudOil Corp's* internal garden. He felt ecstatic. The news he'd been waiting for had come from Mustafa, forty-five minutes earlier. The first signs of oil were now flowing from the *Gentoo* Well on the Crozet site, following installation of the fixed rig two days ago.

Drilling on the third and final well had reached target depth at the Cape Verde site, adding ten billion barrels to the existing twenty billion already discovered. *The estimate, of probable reserves of thirty-five billion, had been accurate*, he realised.

He listened to the parrots squawking in the palm trees above, as he let the sun's rays warm his face. The only other sound in the tranquil gardens was the rhythmical *'cha' 'cha' 'cha'* from the water sprinklers, as they sprayed arcs of water onto the lush lawns.

Fahim had given his team, of thirty-five geologists and technical advisors, two days off upon hearing the news. Only a skeleton staff of maintenance engineers now occupied the desert complex. They deserved it. Two of the world's largest sub-sea oil provinces had been discovered, which were almost double that of the recent Tupi find - off the coast of Brazil.

As he sat alone, he considered the sacrifices that had been made; the lives of the three climatologists who had been killed. Whilst he was still waiting for confirmation on the death of the French climatologist, Trimaud, he was sure that their Russian friend had taken care of him by now. She was probably half way home, he thought.

The human sacrifice, when considering the amount of oil found, was miniscule. The greatest human achievements always involved sacrifice. *The human cost was acceptable.*

He wondered where his brother was, he should be here by now. A company of parrots flew over the lawn in front of him, distracting him from his thoughts.

Faric sat alone in the dark room of his apartment, his face expressionless, and his emotions numb. Upon hearing of the Russian assassin's death, he'd had no choice but to order Admiral Dashkov to activate the OTMs. He couldn't let the French climatologist's experiment jeopardise everything. If successful, the geoengineering plan could reverse the warming now occurring in the region. But now, the Northwest Passage would never freeze over again, not even during Arctic winter.

NewSaudOil Corp's oil would be transported quickly, and cheaply, between the Atlantic and Pacific Oceans'. A new and permanent route through the Arctic will have been created for the first time in modern human history. His brother would surely thank him for this intuitive plan.

Still, he knew he'd betrayed Fahim, which is why he felt tense and ashamed. He stared blankly at the fan on the ceiling, oblivious to the honking horn of the Mercedes outside. A dog barking, in the distance, brought him to his senses. He walked into the bathroom, splashed some cold water onto his face, wandered out into the heat of the afternoon sun, and over to Gomez, in the waiting car.

The Mercedes slid to a stop in front of *NewSaudOil Corp's* large glass entrance doors. Faric got out and walked through the automatic revolving door into the cool foyer of the complex. He passed through the security scanners and walked down the long corridor on the left hand side, which led directly to the internal garden. He passed through the air lock, into the temperature controlled oasis. A light twenty-four degree centigrade breeze brushed against his face as he strode along the shaded path toward the central garden, where he expected his brother to be. Emerging into the sun, he put his Ray-Ban's on, to shield his eyes. As expected, he saw Fahim sitting on his favourite bench, overlooking the large Koi pond.

"There you are, Faric! I have been waiting for you to join me. We should be celebrating the good news together," Fahim said, as he stood to hug his brother.

"Sorry, I am late. I have only just heard the good news about the wells. There was a few things I needed to do," he replied, his voice shaky.

"Is something wrong, brother? You don't appear to have received the news with as much joy as I?"

"Please, walk with me, Fahim. There is something I need to speak with you about."

Fahim stood, and removed his sunglasses, looking at his brother with trepidation as they walked slowly towards the central fountain. "As you can see, it is very quiet around here. I have given everyone a few days off, to thank them for their hard work," Fahim said, before hesitating. "So, tell me brother, what is troubling you?"

Faric felt his throat drying up as he started to reply. "Brother, I need your forgiveness for something I have done."

Fahim stopped walking and turned to his brother. "What is it, Faric?"

"The Russian assassin was killed yesterday. I received the news only one hour ago. Trimaud's experiment proceeded as planned, it seems."

Fahim stared at him blankly. "How could this be? How was she killed?"

"I believe at the hands of Spire, the meddling lawyer. She was forced off the ice into the freezing waters of the Lancaster Sound."

"How could you know this, Faric?"

Faric bowed his head, speaking hesitantly. "Brother, I have deceived you. I have engaged the services of our Russian investor...he has ex Russian Navy contacts, and they have helped us, brother. A back-up plan, in case of failure."

Fahim interrupted him. "What are you saying? What have you done?" he asked, the tone of his voice tightening.

Faric told his brother about the *Rezky*, the Ocean Temperature Modifiers, and the business cards he'd paid Ksenyia to leave at the scene of each killing. "Brother, now the Northwest Passage will remain open forever, allowing us to transport our oil cheaply and quickly through the permanently ice free route."

Fahim looked at him aghast. "Are you out of your crazy mind? How the hell do you expect to get away with that? You failed to prevent Trimaud's experiment, and you are a bigger fool than I ever thought. You have jeopardised the entire operation."

"Brother, I thought it was the right thing to do. I did it for *NewSaudOil Corp*...for us."

Fahim struck his brother across his face, sending his sunglasses flying to the grass.

"You did it for yourself. You lack the moral fibre that made our father great. You did all this without consulting me, your own brother, how could you?"

Faric walked over and picked his Ray-Ban's up from the manicured lawn, then walked back over to Fahim. "That was uncalled for; you will appreciate what I have done in time."

Fahim looked at him, eyes narrowing. "You have betrayed me, Faric. I sincerely hope that your stupidity has not affected our operation here. I need to know exactly what you have done, and I need to speak to whoever your contact is…now."

"Brother, it is Zablozky. He assumed that the operation had your blessing. He organised the Russian crew, they are his contacts."

"Zablozky!" Fahim shouted.

"Brother, he was happy to implement the plan, to protect his investment."

"The devices under the ocean; who developed them?"

"I believe they were built to order by a Russian engineering science team, again, Zablozky's contacts. They are experimental devices designed to thaw ice-blocked ports and inland waterways."

Fahim shook his head, a look of disbelief on his face. "And what about Spire? Where is he now?"

"I believe he is on board the *Rezky,* brother. The Russian's know what to do with him."

Fahim pointed a finger directly at his brother's forehead as he spoke. "I sincerely hope that for once, you are right, Faric. He must die for this."

Before he could respond, Fahim walked off, back toward the main complex entrance, leaving him standing in the garden. Faric closed his eyes, listening to the water jets in the fountain, the sun warming his face. *Oh yes, brother, you are right. Spire will certainly die.*

CHAPTER 70

THE *REZKY* CONTINUED along the Lancaster Sound, cutting through the two-metre high waves now traversing the channel. The sonic anemometer confirmed the wind outside was gusting to sixty miles per hour, almost eight on the Beaufort scale. The channel ahead was a mass of grey and white, the islands on either side, now obscured by low cloud and mist.

Dashkov picked up the radio and called down to Brilev in the communications room, "Give me thirty minute updates on the *Mercure's* position," he bawled.

"Very well, Admiral. Their current distance is twenty nautical miles, maintaining twenty-two knots," Brilev reported.

Tabanov hovered over the chart table, as he plotted their journey back along the shortest possible route. "Admiral, if current speed is maintained, the *Mercure* will catch up with us some twenty nautical miles north of Nuuk."

Dashkov turned to Tabanov. "They will be welcome aboard, but they won't find what they are looking for. Robert Spire will be somewhere at the bottom of the Davis Strait by then," he sneered.

Down in the weapons room, Spire continued to try and cut through the plastic ties binding his wrists. He was interrupted by the sound of footsteps, and looked up to see the man, he now knew as Charkov, emerge from the side room. Spire sat motionless, feigning defeat. The Russian looked at him for a few seconds, and then walked back into the room. Alone again, Spire resumed his frantic efforts to free himself, but the metal edge of the chair wasn't sharp enough. He sensed the friction from the rapid movement was however slowly starting to weaken the plastic ties.

Suddenly the ship lurched to port, sliding Spire, and the chair, into the metal racking that had housed the OTMs. After a few moments, the ship righted itself again, but Spire managed to hold onto the side of a vertical section of shelving, preventing himself from sliding back to his original position.

Charkov came out of the side room once again to check on him, before disappearing a few seconds later, leaving Spire sitting against the steel units.

Using the side of the steel racking, he started rubbing his wrists vigorously up and down. After a few minutes, he felt the weakened nylon tie snap, and fall to the floor. He listened for footsteps, but heard nothing. He reached down and picked up the nylon tie and created a new loop, this time large enough for both his hands to slip through easily. He placed the tie back over his wrists and put his arms back behind the chair.

On the *Mercure*, Captain Deville had replaced two of the missing fuses, but the Inmarsat system was still not functioning. He was now studying the *Mercure's* communications manual to check if there was a third fuse. *What could I have missed?* He wondered.

On the bridge, Officer Boucher was at the helm, maintaining twenty-two knots. Visibility ahead was down to one nautical mile. The ship's radar showed the channel ahead was virtually clear, the large tabular iceberg they'd anchored against earlier, was now ten nautical miles behind them. The harsh conditions left Boucher struggling to navigate, the horizontal sleet making visibility extremely poor. The foaming waters of the Lancaster Sound melted with the sky above in a mass of grey, the deep ocean swells buffeting the *Mercure's* bow every thirty seconds or so with a large wave, spraying white foaming water onto the deck.

Boucher glanced down at the sonar, and noticed an odd signal being picked up, which hadn't been present earlier. The sonar was identifying sound pulses, which appeared to be running down the channel from east to west towards their position, originating from somewhere in the Davis Strait. *What the hell now?* He picked up the radio, pushed the button for the P.A system, and called for Professor Trimaud or Dr. Mathews to come to the bridge immediately.

Trimaud and Mathews were talking together in the library when the message blasted out over the P.A system. They glanced at each other, before quickly making their way up to the bridge, two decks above. When they arrived, they could see Boucher was struggling with the ship's wheel, whilst also trying to flick various switches on the sonar control panel.

"Bonsoir Henri, what's the problem?" Trimaud asked, directing his attention to the sonar screen.

"These sonar readings, ever seen anything like them before? I can't work them out," he said, his voice laden with panic.

Trimaud and Dr. Mathews held on to the bulkhead to steady themselves as they studied the sonar screen, now displaying intermittent pulses, showing up as thickening green lines every forty seconds or so. "Surface waves or ambient background sound?" Dr. Mathews suggested, shrugging his shoulders.

"Non," Boucher said, flicking a switch on the console. "This turns off the sonar's ambient hydrophones, cancelling out any ambient background signal."

"Could the sonar be picking up pods of whales, or krill perhaps?" Trimaud asked.

"It's possible," Boucher replied, "but I've already considered that. The sonar is pre-programmed to recognise the broadband source levels from a number of targets, including beluga, sperm, blue, bowhead and humpback whales. Dolphin and shrimp too. The incoming signals don't match."

Trimaud scratched his head. "Can you set the sonar to the two hundred and sixty decibels range?"

"I believe so," Boucher replied, turning a dial on the console counter-clockwise a few notches. "That should be set now - two hundred-sixty DB only."

The images on the sonar screen remained the same, there was no change. "Merde," Trimaud cursed, his voice was tense. "I think the sound source is seismic. Can we determine the wave speed from this?"

"Oui," Boucher said, depressing two buttons.

Trimaud studied the digits on the screen, a look of panic spread across his face. "As I suspected, primary waves from seismic activity travel at around one thousand-fifty metres a second in water, confirmed by this readout. The wave pattern suggests an origin from the south-east, quite probably Greenland."

"This is bad news," Dr. Mathews said. "We've been picking up increasing levels of seismic activity from the continent for the last five years now. The entire continent appears to be rising as the weight of the ice covering it decreases, accompanied by a proportionate increase in seismic activity."

The *Mercure* suddenly descended into a deep trough, sending the three of them off balance. Trimaud and Mathews grabbed the bulkhead and managed to stop themselves from falling, but Officer Boucher lost his balance and fell to the deck. Water streamed down the windows from a large wave that hit the bow.

Just as Boucher got up from the floor, Deville burst through the door. "Getting rough out there," he shouted, seemingly unfazed by the worsening conditions. "I can't find that third blown fuse anywhere," he said, unlocking a cabinet under the bulkhead shelving. "Have you figured out what that sonar reading means yet Francois?" Deville asked, looking up.

"Oui Jacques, it's not good news. We could have a serious situation on our hands. The sonar is picking up increasing levels of seismic activity from Greenland. The rumbles we heard earlier, it wasn't thunder, but earthquakes. We need to find Robert as soon as possible and get out of the area."

"Pourquoi, what could happen?"

Trimaud looked at Deville. "Jacques, if there is a significant seismic event in Greenland, it could trigger a tsunami, and we will be directly in its path."

CHAPTER 71

THE *REZKY* CRUISED along the Davis Strait, having emerged from the Lancaster Sound some fifteen hours earlier. Greenland's capital Nuuk lay just fifteen nautical miles to the northwest of their position. Forty-eight hours had ticked by since Spire's capture.

An engine warning light suddenly blinked red on the panel, to the right of the wheel. Admiral Dashkov hit the panel with the palm of his hand, assuming a faulty connection, but the light remained on. He cursed, picked up the radio and called down to the engine room. "Is there a problem down there?" he asked Brilev. "I hav e an engine warning light just flashed red on the console up here."

"Hold on, Admiral," Brilev replied nervously.

There was silence for a few moments before Brilev returned to the radio, breathing heavily. "Admiral, there is smoke coming from the casing on the port-side engine. I'll need you to reduce power by seventy-five percent so I can examine it. Maybe just a coolant problem - the engines have been running at full power for thirty-six hours solid."

"Very well," Dashkov bawled. "See to it, but I need full power restored within fifteen minutes."

Captain Tabanov looked up from the chart table. "Is it anything serious, Admiral?"

"I hope not. Didn't we have the ship checked after the Morroco operation?"

"I believe so; it was only two months ago."

Dashkov reduced propulsion in both engines as requested, slowing the *Rezky* down to eight knots. He glanced at the radar; with each revolution, the sweeping line revealed the green smudge of the *Mercure* closing in on them.

"I think it's time to say goodbye to our English visitor, Captain. Make sure Charkov and Donskoy don't make a mess down there."

"Yes, Admiral," Tabanov replied, lighting a Golden Fleece cigarette as he left the bridge.

Spire heard the sound of heavy boots on the metal stairs, and the man who captured him -Tabanov - appeared, walked up to him and knelt down by his side. "Have they been treating you well down here, Mr. Spire?"

Spire raised his head, faking tiredness. "Please, I need some water."

"Don't worry; you'll be off the ship very soon. You're friends are coming for you," he said, grinning.

Spire nodded at Tabanov, certain he was lying.

Tabanov stood up, leaving behind an odour of stale cigarettes and alcohol.

"At least tell me what you're doing here," Spire demanded.

Tabanov hesitated for a few moments, and then turned back to Spire. "I guess there's no harm in telling you now. Our orders are to melt the ice in the Northwest Passage, to ensure it remains ice free…forever."

"How do you propose to do that?" Spire asked, perplexed.

"With Ocean Temperature Modifiers, basically nuclear heating devices to you and me. They are down there now, warming up the channel, as we speak." Tabanov laughed, and disappeared into the side room where the two Russians had been playing cards for most of the journey.

Spire tried to process what he'd just been told, he'd never heard of the existence of such equipment. He listened to the Russian's talking together. His heart rate accelerating, he sat there contemplating his next move.

Tabanov appeared again and went to ascend the stairs to the higher deck. He turned back toward him. "If I don't see you again, enjoy your trip home, Mr. Spire."

Spire felt ill, the fear of death growing inside him. He tried blocking the thought of never seeing Angela and his friends again from his mind.

Just as he was about to stand up and make a run for it, the two Russians came out of the side room laughing, one holding a gun, the other a half-empty bottle of *Jack Daniels*.

"Do not make a sound, Mr. Spire," the man holding the gun said, as the other picked up some heavy steel chains from the floor and wrapped them under and around his chair, pinning his legs in place.

"What the *hell* are you doing?" Spire demanded.

"Do you not understand English - I told you, shut up!" Donskoy shouted, placing the bottle of *Jack Daniels* on a small table next to the steel racking. He then helped Charkov wrap the steel chain around the chair. Spire heard a clunk, and looked up to see the overhead crane moving into place above him. Donskoy kept the pistol pointed at Spire, while Charkov gathered the chain, and placed it onto the large hook attached to the thick steel gantry cable. Spire heard another clunk, and was then lifted into the air as the cable retracted back into the overhead crane.

The two Russians laughed, sharing the bottle of whiskey as Charkov pressed a button on the hand-held control-pad. "It is time for you to disembark, Mr. Spire. You'll find this route very much quicker!" Donskoy laughed again, as the overhead gantry carried Spire down the centre of the weapons room and out into the corridor, where the overhead rail turned left towards the ship's hull.

Donskoy squeezed past him and walked ahead, Charkov followed behind, one hand on the control-pad, the other holding the bottle of *Jack Daniels*. He took a swig from the bottle. "Won't be long now," he said, gesturing toward the hull.

Spire heard a click, and then felt a blast of cold air hit him. He twisted in the chair to see a section of the hull slide open, leaving a car-sized opening in the side of the vessel. He calculated there was about five metres or so of rail left until the opening. "Listen, if you're going to throw me out, at least let me have a last cigarette," he said, stalling for time.

Charkov shouted to Donskoy in Russian. Donskoy laughed, walked over and pulled a cigarette out from a soft pack and placed it in Spire's mouth. "You have sixty seconds to enjoy it, Mr. Spire," he said, walking back to the opening in the hull.

Charkov stopped the crane, leaving Spire dangling in the chair, a metre or so above the floor. He pulled out a Zippo lighter, flicked it open, and leaned toward him to light the cigarette. As he did, Spire brought his untied arms around quickly and powerfully, smashing Charkov on the sides of his head, his cupped hands striking and rupturing his eardrums - a martial arts move designed to stun the victim.

The Russian staggered back in pain, dropping the control-pad, as he raised his hands to his injured ears.

Spire grabbed the cable above him, and using all his strength, lifted himself up, freeing the chain from the hook. He crashed to the deck, still in the chair. With the chains loose, he slipped one leg free, and then the other, just as Donskoy came charging towards him from the opening in the hull, gun held out in front of him.

A shot rang out, deafening Spire in the confined corridor.

The bullet whizzed over his head, ricocheting off the steel chair he was crouching behind. Spire reached for the bottle of *Jack Daniels,* lying broken on the floor, and threw its remaining contents into Donskoy's face. The liquor hit him in his eyes, temporarily blinding him. Spire then kicked the gun from his hand, sending it spinning down the corridor, and then followed up with a powerful kick to the Russian's solar plexus, sending him to the deck like a sack of flour.

Spire heard a grunt and quickly turned. Charkov, who appeared to have recovered from his ear punch, lunged at him, but the alcohol in his bloodstream slowed his reflexes, and Spire side-stepped out of the way, quickly kicking him in the stomach. Charkov flew backwards toward the opening in the hull; Spire followed.

As Charkov staggered to his feet, Spire punched him in the jaw, sending him further back toward the opening. Charkov then reached up, grabbed the overhead rail, and attempted to kick Spire, but Spire anticipated the move and got out of the way.

Spire leapt forward, jumped up and grabbed the rail. "This will sober you up," he shouted, lifting his knees and kicking Charkov in the chest with as much force as he could muster.

The Russian flew back through the opening, arms flailing as he tried to grab hold of something. His screams lasted the full seven metres, as he fell into the freezing waters of the Davis Strait below.

Spire spun around, just as Donskoy punched him on the jaw, temporarily stunning him. Spire felt his jaw bone - which didn't appear to be broken - then lunged at the Russian with his shoulder. They wrestled momentarily in the confined corridor, but were interrupted as Donskoy's radio - still strapped to his belt - crackled to life, and briefly distracted the Russian.

Spire seized the opportunity and landed a heavy punch on

the Russian's chin, knocking him out. Wasting no time, he then dragged Donskoy's limp body back along the corridor to the crane, hauled him up, and jammed the hook onto the loop of his belt. Spire pressed the button with an 'up'arrow on the control-pad, raising the cable, leaving the Russian suspended in the middle of the corridor, his legs just touching the floor. He depressed another button, and the crane sprang to life, moving the Russian along the gantry toward the opening in the hull. As the crane approached the opening, the rails automatically extended out, dragging Donskoy clear of the ship, suspending him helplessly above the ocean.

After a few moments Donskoy opened his eyes and quickly realised where he was. He screamed at Spire, a look of horror on his face.

"Sorry pal, I don't speak Russian," Spire yelled, pressing the buttons randomly on the control pad by the door, searching for the release switch. He hit the fourth button, and heard a loud click as the hook at the end of the cable hydraulically opened, releasing its grip around Donskoy's belt-loop.

Donskoy's eyes widened in terror as he realised what was happening, but his cries were drowned out by a large wave that smashed into the side of the ship, as he plunged to the icy waters below.

On the *Rezky's* bridge, Tabanov was still trying to get hold of Donskoy on the radio. "Has Spire been taken care of?" he shouted. There was garbled static on the other end. He asked again, but there was no reply. Tabanov threw the radio down onto the table and looked over at Admiral Dashkov. "I'll go down and finish the job myself."

CHAPTER 72

Greenland
June 13

THE VOLUME OF the Helhiem glacier had been decreasing steadily since 1990; the elevating Arctic temperatures melting it, at an unprecedented rate. As the weight of the central two kilometer thick slab of ice decreased, the continent of Greenland below had slowly been rising - a situation predicted by glaciologists for some time.

Three more large crevasses had opened up on the glacier, since the Danish team had placed seismic monitoring equipment there six days earlier. Moulin's on the surface of the five-hundred metre thick coastal glacier were letting torrents of melt-water flow down to the bedrock below, which in turn carved channels through the ice as it gushed towards the ocean beneath the ancient glacier.

The lubrication was now too much for the glacier to withstand. Suddenly, a tremor, caused by the rising continent was the last straw for the ice-mass. Its tipping point reached, a thunderous crack resonated up from the depths, as a five kilometre section split off from the main glacial tongue, sliding under its own weight slowly toward the coast.

Talirik and Uyarasuk were in their tent preparing for supper when they heard a loud, ominous crack roar down the valley.

"The children!" Uyarasuk shouted, "Where are they?"

Talirik jumped up and ran from the tent; other villagers had done the same. He shouted over to the children, who were playing on a grass mound, the snow having melted away a few weeks earlier. As they ran into the tent, another deafening crack from above, prompted Talirik to look up at the vertical cliff face. The last thing he saw was twenty thousand tonnes of ice and rock raining down on Samutaat.

With the settlement buried beneath it, the five kilometre section of ice continued to slide down the valley, over the cliff and into the coastal waters of the Labrador Sea. The massive displacement of water, caused by the mass of ice and rock, generated a forty-metre high tsunami, which fanned out in all directions as it travelled along the Davis Strait.

On the *Rezky*, fifty nautical miles from the ocean impact, Spire picked up the gun dropped by Donskoy and ran back to the weapons room. The sound of footsteps, echoing down the metal stairs, startled him, and he quickly ran into the side room and hid next to a large metal cabinet at one end of the room.

"Charkov! Donskoy!" He heard Tabanov shouting, as he ran into the room. Spire held his breath, as he hid in the shadows by the side of the cabinet. Tabanov peered into the bathroom, briefly looked around, and then walked back out into the main room. Spire listened to his footsteps fading as he heard him walk, through the weapons room, toward the corridor at the end.

Satisfied the route was clear, Spire ran from his hiding place and up the stairway to the deck above. As he reached the top he was deafened by the ship's alarm.

Lieutenant Brilev assumed the radar was malfunctioning when he first saw the fast moving mass of green on the screen in front of him. By the time he'd warned Admiral Dashkov, the image was only thirty-eight miles away, travelling at eight miles a minute.

"Admiral, I...I don't know what it is, but we have a target closing in on us at..." Brilev paused, "five-hundred miles an hour."

"It must be an error. What sort of target...range, size?" Dashkov shouted down the radio.

"Admiral, it's...the entire width of the Davis Strait! Range, thirty nautical miles, time to impact - three point-seven-five minutes."

Spire ran along the corridor, lit only by the *Rezky's* emergency lighting. Suddenly, a door opened in front of him, and a man, wearing an orange life vest and smelling strongly of oil emerged, a confused look on his face. Before the man could do anything, Spire pointed the gun at his head. "Bridge, where's the bridge?"

The man looked at him, blankly.

"Do you speak English?" Spire shouted, losing patience.

The man shook his head, "Russian...Ruskie!"

"Ok, give me that damn jacket," Spire said, ripping it off the man's body. "You go and get yourself another."

The Russian bolted off down the corridor.

Spire put the life vest on, secured it, and continued down the passage. He found a rusting stairwell leading up to a higher deck and ran up the metal steps, two at a time, before reaching a landing. Natural light poured in, through large panoramic windows. He glanced out, but the fog was limiting visibility to about a kilometre or so ahead. He moved along and found a carpeted stairwell leading up to the next level. *This must be the bridge,* he thought, as he quietly ascended the stairway.

He arrived at a steel door; a black notice in Russian was fixed to the front of it. He yanked the handle down, opened the door and crept onto the bridge, his gun raised.

CHAPTER 73

TABANOV MOVED TOWARD the opening in the hull, grabbed the safety handles on either side of the corridor and peered out, first looking toward the stern, then down at the ocean, which looked unusually calm and flat. He turned to look toward the bow; his first thought was that he was looking at very low cloud cover, but his confusion soon turned to terror as he saw a huge wall of water emerge from the fog bank ahead. He pushed frantically on the control-pad to close the hatch, but it was too late.

Spire edged onto the bridge to find Admiral Dashkov staring out of the port-side window at the fog bank. "Don't move," he shouted, thrusting his gun into Dashkov's spine.

Dashkov calmly raised his arms and turned toward Spire. "Ah, Mr. Spire, I see my men have failed me."

"Yep, I think they've all decided to go for a swim."

"Very amusing; no matter, I don't need them any more."

"Tell me where the control switch is for the temperature modifiers. Your crazy plan isn't going to succeed," Spire shouted.

"Oh, but Mr. Spire, it already has, you're too late. The OTMs have already been activated," Dashkov said, his cracked lips forming into a grin.

Spire glanced around the bridge, spotting the heavy steel cabinet. "Open that cabinet now!" he shouted, shoving the gun hard into Dashkov's rib-cage.

"I already told you, it's too late."

"Open it!"

Dashkov reached into his pocket for the key, unlocked the cabinet and pulled out the OTM control-pad, its eight lights glowing red, and handed it to Spire.

Spire shoved the rectangular box under his life vest. "Now, give me the code."

Dashkov laughed. "You're going to have to kill me for that, Spire."

Something out of the forward window caught Spire's attention. He turned to look, and as he did, Dashkov knocked his right arm up, jolting the gun from his hands. Dashkov then punched Spire in the jaw, sending him to the deck.

Spire reached up and grabbed the *Rezky's* wheel, yanking it down as he pulled himself to his feet. The ship reacted by turning towards port, but it was enough of a distraction to allow him to jump on Dashkov and wrestle him to the floor.

Facing the large forward windows they both paused as they tried to fathom what they were looking at. A wall of water, forty metres or so high and stretching the entire width of the channel, was racing towards them.

Dashkov broke free and went for the wheel in a desperate attempt to steer the *Rezky* into the wall of water in a futile attempt to prevent a broadside hit.

Spire lashed out at Dashkov; but instead his hand met the pendant hanging around his neck. He ripped it away, just as the huge wave struck, completely enveloping the ship. The windows on the bridge imploded in a cacophony of sound, throwing Spire backwards as foaming water gushed in from all directions. Spire braced and took a deep breath as the freezing water hit, just before being plunged into a broiling, swirling, black ocean.

On the bridge of the *Mercure*, Boucher had gone into a cold sweat, insisting Deville take control of the wheel. He picked up the radio to speak over the P.A. "God help us," he shouted. "We have an emergency situation. A wave...a very large tidal wave is heading down the Davis Strait towards us. Put your life vests on, get together at the stern of the ship and prepare for impact - ninety seconds."

Boucher was the first to see the wall of water emerge from the fog bank. Deville had reduced speed to ten knots, and had turned the *Mercure* directly toward the oncoming wave. He grabbed the radio from Boucher; "Fifteen seconds to impact...twelve...ten...eight..."

The massive wave hit, forcing the *Mercure* up through seventy degrees, her bow pointing skyward as she rode up the wall of water. Chunks of ice and debris crashed onto the deck and through the bridge windows, the ship groaning and creaking as it reached the peak of the tsunami. A split second later, the vessel teetered on the brink of the forty metre-high wave trough, before descending into the watery abyss.

CHAPTER 74

NEWS OF THE tsunami quickly spread to the media, and *Reuters* News Agency broke the story as it obtained data relayed to Denmark from their seismic transponders monitoring the glacier. Danish glaciologists' worst fears had been confirmed; the decreasing weight of the ancient Greenland ice sheet had allowed the continent below to rise; a process known as *glacial isostatic adjustment*. The earthquakes had simply been more than the glacier could take, and the tsunami was a natural consequence of the displacement, caused by the massive section of ice hitting the water.

Fahim stared at his monitors and the newsfeed in silence, his dreams dissolving. A faint sound, coming from somewhere within the internal garden, prompted him to turn around. Fanning out from one of the entrances, he could see a unit of the Royal Saudi Guard, moving into the garden, machine guns at the ready.

Faric was in his office when the call from Zablosky came through, telling him that the *Rezky* had been lost in the tsunami, and all attempts at contacting it had been met with silence. He thanked Zablosky, ended the call and quickly started scrawling a simple note to his brother; *Please forgive me, Fahim, I did it for us, for NewSaudOil Corp, for our beloved country.*

He left his office, taking the emergency exit up to the helipad on the roof of the complex. He staggered onto the roof, shielding his eyes from the bright desert sun as he ran over to the helicopter, jumped in and powered up the machine.

The rotors on the Robinson R22 began to whir and he yanked back the cyclic stick, just as two members of the Saudi Royal Guard burst through the steel door onto the roof, their Cal 50 machine guns aimed at the rising helicopter.

Faric ignored them and cleared the top of the building, banking hard left as he turned toward the desert.

Bullets sprayed out from the Royal Guard's machine guns, ripping into the fuselage and hitting the fuel lines. Faric grappled with the controls, but he knew it was useless. He was unable to control the helicopter, which was now burning and out of control. Seconds later, he was unable to prevent the aircraft plummeting through the glass roof of the internal garden below.

Fahim watched in horror as his brother's helicopter crashed onto the landscaped garden and erupted into a fireball, sending burning fuel and hot metal shards in all directions. Palm trees in every corner of the garden caught fire and burning wreckage laid scattered about the gardens.

Before he had time to think, three heavily armed members of the Saudi Guard burst into his room and forced him to the floor.

CHAPTER 75

CAPTAIN DEVILLE DRAGGED himself up off the floor of the bridge of the *Mercure Blanc* and looked through the smashed bridge window, cold air whistling in from outside. He brushed broken plexiglass off his shoulder and stood there, trying to comprehend what had just happened. The fog had now dispersed, pushed away by the force of the tsunami. The ocean was calm, as if nothing had happened. Broken ice and other flotsam lay scattered in the Davis Strait, as far as the eye could see, debris and pack-ice wrenched from the edge of the channel, smashed to smithereens by the powerful wave.

He heard a groan behind him, it was Boucher. "Are you alright, Henri?" he asked, helping him to his feet.

"Oui, a cracked head, but I'll survive," Boucher replied, wiping blood away from a cut above his eye.

"The *Mercure* survived, Henri, we survived. Please go and check on the others and report back to me."

"Oui, Captain," Boucher said, limping off the bridge.

Five minutes passed before Boucher reappeared, with Trimaud and Marcus Roux. Trimaud, clothes crumpled, his hair all over the place, said, "Well done, Jacques. I don't know of anyone else who could have got us through that. Thank you."

"We were lucky, Francois, very lucky. How are the rest of the passengers?" Deville asked, lighting up a cigar as he spoke.

"Everyone's fine, but scared. We also have some good

news. Carlos just turned up. He awoke in the small storeroom on the upper deck. The last thing he recalls is being shot with a dart, by Dr Sinclair. Roberto is with him now."

"I've told him before about sleeping on the job," Deville replied, with a slight grin.

The four of them hugged. Trimaud pulled back after a few seconds and looked at his friends. "We are safe, but we must search for Robert. He's still out there somewhere. Jacques, do we have power?"

Deville starting punching buttons on the panel in front of him, checking gauges and dials. "Give me a moment, Francois."

Roux grabbed the binoculars and started scanning the channel. "I don't see anything. No ship, nothing. How far ahead was the *Rezky?*"

"It should be visible," Boucher added.

"Power restored," Deville shouted. "Engine room is flooded, but the bilge pumps are working. Engines one and two will be back online shortly."

Trimaud checked the radar, its green arm sweeping the scope once again. He shook his head at what he saw. "Merde, there's nothing in the channel for fifty nautical miles in any direction. The *Rezky* couldn't have survived the wave."

Boucher and Roux looked at him, their expressions revealing their obvious fears.

"Engines are back online. Let's go and find Spire," Deville said, without taking his eyes off the ocean.

Trimaud, Girrard, Dr. Bonnet and Roux were lined up on the *Mercure's* upper deck as the ship powered through the debris field of ice that filled the channel, scanning the ocean in front of them.

As they approached the last known position of the *Rezky* - some eighteen nautical miles from where the wave struck them

- Deville slowed the *Mercure* down to five knots, and searched the ocean ahead for any signs of the vessel.

Roux was the first to spot what he thought was debris and other items from the missing ship. "I can see something," he shouted. "Oil drums, crates and other wreckage, eleven o'clock," he said, pointing to the flotsam a short distance ahead.

Trimaud focused his binoculars on the spot, scanning the ocean for any signs of life. He realised the chances of finding his friend alive were minimal, but the least he could do was recover Spire's body, if it could be found. He pushed the negative thoughts to the back of his mind as he focused on every piece of floating debris, every wave trough.

He saw a wooden pallet bob up and down on the light swell, and on top, an orange life preserver. He kept the binoculars trained on the spot, and then he saw it, a body in the life jacket - Spire's body, his mop of dirty blond hair just visible. "I see him!" he screamed, "I see Robert!"

Deville brought the *Mecrure* alongside the floating pallet. Spire was sprawled on top, as good as dead, drifting amongst a sea of debris and oil from the sunken mine ship.

Officer Boucher lowered the gangplank down toward the floating pallet, and Roux descended, wrapped a sling around Spire's apparent lifeless body, and with the help of the crane, winched him off the floating pallet and aboard the *Mercure*.

Dr Girrard was waiting with a stretcher and he and Roux rushed Spire down to one of the labs and quickly covered him with a thermal blanket. Dr Mathews had already set up a make-shift drip attached to a bag of saline solution. He inserted the drip into a vein on the back of Spire's left hand.

Sixty seconds passed. "I feel a pulse," Mathews said, looking at the rest of the group in relief, who had all now assembled around the stretcher in silence.

Dr Bonnet pointed to Spire's right hand. "Look, he's moving," she whispered.

They looked on as Spire's clenched fist opened slightly, just enough for a silver amulet and chain to fall out onto the floor of the lab, where it coiled up into a small pile.

CHAPTER 76

June 14

THE SOUND OF muffled voices materialised through the fog; dark turned to light, then darkness again. Images cascaded through his thoughts; first he was running, and then drowning. Spire gasped for air and opened his eyes in panic, the overhead fluorescent lighting blinding him. "Where am I?" he asked, shielding his eyes.

A familiar voice answered him. "Robert, you're safe. You're in the Queen Ingrid's Hospital in Nuuk."

Spire opened his eyes wider and saw Dr. Bonnet's soft brown eyes looking down at him. Trimaud was by her side. "Wh...what the hell happened?" he asked.

"Relax, Robert. The *Rezky* was hit by a massive tsunami, caused by the collapse of a tributary of the Helheim Glacier. We were further up the strait, and managed to survive the wave. We found you floating amongst the wreckage and fished you out; thank God you were wearing a life preserver. Looks like you were the only survivor, Robert, you were very lucky," Trimaud said.

"And don't worry about Angela," Dr. Bonnet added, "she knows you're safe. You will be flown back to the UK, in a few days' time."

"The bag, is the canvas bag safe?" Spire whispered.

"Yes, don't worry. We found the CD's containing Dr.

Stanton's and Jack's work. We also found the silver amulet with the OTM codes. You had it clenched in your fist."

"Thank God," Spire whispered.

Dr. Bonnet smiled. "Robert, please rest. You have a punctured right lung and a fractured left tibia, but you'll be fine."

Spire groaned. "I'm glad you think so, Mari."

He then closed his eyes and drifted off to sleep.

Spire limped into the hallway upon hearing the mail arrive. It had been a month since his flight back from Greenland, and he felt extremely glad to be home. A small pile of letters and *The Independent* newspaper lay on the hall mat. He picked up the post, hobbled back into the kitchen and placed the mail on the table. He put the kettle on, reached into the cupboard for a fresh pack of *Lavaza*, opened it, and inhaled the rich aroma of the Italian blended coffee.

It was Saturday morning, and Angela was working at the boutique. He glanced at the paper, not really taking much in, apart from the date - July 17. His thoughts wandered to the last few months, and all the injuries he'd sustained. His pneumothorax had healed, his lung expanded, and his leg was on the mend, but he'd spent two days in hospital in Nuuk, another ten in London, and he was now on his third week at home. He realised he was feeling much better though, as he glanced out the window at the parched lawn.

Whilst the first week of June had been very wet, the last six weeks had been scorching, and a hose pipe ban was now in place. Scientists were saying that the first six months of the year had been the hottest since records began.

Looks like global warming is here to stay, he thought, as he pushed the plunger down on the French press.

He took a gulp of hot coffee, the velvety taste immediately energising him. He opened the paper, but was interrupted by his mobile phone ringing. It was Kim.

"How's the patient coming along?" she asked.

"Kim, I've never looked forward to getting back into the office so much. I owe you a huge favour for everything you've done."

"Well, that will teach you for going off on a jolly to the Arctic, won't it! Anyway, I'm calling with some good news."

"That will make a change. What's up?"

"We've received an offer on the Taunton case - four hundred and eighty-five thousand."

Spire whistled. "Wow! Not bad. Have you spoken to the client?"

"Yep, he's very pleased and wants to accept. He sends you his best wishes."

"Fantastic news!" Spire said, eyeing the Cuban cigar lying by the wine rack. "Listen, I'm taking Angela out tomorrow night for dinner. We want you to come along too, a double celebration. How're you fixed?"

"Sounds great, Rob, count me in."

Spire ended the call, grinning broadly at the news of the Taunton settlement. "Well done Kim," he said, raising his coffee cup.

Moving the paper aside, he picked up an official looking letter, that had arrived with the morning post, and ripped it open. It was from the Arctic Marine Council;

Dear Robert Spire,

The Arctic Council would appreciate your attendance at our Paris headquarters on September 1st, to present you with a special award for retrieving the O.T.M codes and for your gallant

actions in the Arctic, which are truly immeasurable. R.S.V.P.
Yours Sincerely,
Claude Dupont- AMC secretary.
Francois Trimaud - counter-signatory.

Spire smiled. *At least, Angela might forgive me now.*

He opened the second letter, which was from MI6, also thanking him for his cooperation and assistance in bringing the eco-terrorists - in what was considered a grave threat to UK national security - to justice. The letter also contained an invite to MI6 headquarters at Vauxhall Cross, in London, for an 'informal chat.' Inspector Lance Johnson had been assigned as a first point of contact, and would be in touch.

Spire stared at the letter, shaking his head. *What next?*

He opened the last letter; it was from Doris Stanton, also thanking him for everything, and inviting him and Angela over for tea and scones, next time they were in Windsor. Smiling, he folded the letter and finished his coffee.

He picked up the cigar, removed it from its tube, cut the end off and walked into the lounge to check the news. He turned over to CNN. Aerial footage of what looked like Arctic landscape was being shown; a news anchor was reporting;

"The scene of utter devastation below is all that is left of the Inuit settlement of Samutaat following the collapse of the Helheim Glacier one month ago. It is believed that around two-hundred Inuit lost their lives here. The massive clean-up operation, following the havoc wreaked by the powerful tsunami, continues along the Davis Strait. Meanwhile speculation mounts as to what US warships and Canadian salvage vessels are doing positioned along the strait and Northwest Passage..."

As he listened, he heard a familiar rustling sound coming from outside the French windows. *Is that the fox?*

He placed the cigar down, slowly opened the French door and crept outside. The garden was quiet. The ice cream container he'd left out was still on the floor, a thin layer of dry, cracked milk covered the bottom. He heard the garden gate creak. *Odd*, he thought, there's no wind. He walked around the corner to close it.

The powerful blow came from nowhere and knocked him to the floor. It was followed by a painful kick to his side. *What the hell?* Completely stunned, he managed to shield his face and looked up. *Christ, no! He recognised the man stooped over him – the thug from the Louvre!*

Spire rolled out of the way and staggered to his feet, then quickly lashed out with a double punch, hitting Gomez on the nose and in the solar plexus. The stocky man stumbled back, clearly injured. Spire followed up with a thrust-kick to his stomach, sending him flying back into the shed by the side of the lawn. Gomez smashed through the wooden door, ripping it from its hinges. Spire hobbled over, his leg now in severe pain just as Gomez lunged at him, this time managing to wrap some cord around his throat.

Spire hit the floor, unable to breath. He struggled to pull the cord away, but couldn't get his fingers under it. He felt himself choking. Panicking, he reached behind into the garden shed for something, anything that might help. His hand landed on something soft, a plastic container of some kind.

Unable to breathe, he used his last bit of energy to bring his good leg up, kneeing Gomez in the forehead. It gave him enough time to roll away and pull the cord from his neck. With Gomez still stunned, Spire brought the container he was clenching into view. It was a two-litre bottle of car engine oil.

He quickly unscrewed the top and jammed the bottle into Gomez's mouth, pinning him down so he couldn't move.

Gomez struggled, but Spire had the full weight of his body on his chest. "Sorry, I'm all out of ice, you son-of-a-bitch!"

Gomez continued to struggle, his eyes bulging as the viscous oil ran down his throat, slowly choking him. Finally the big man stopped moving.

Exhausted, Spire made sure Gomez was dead, before rolling off his lifeless body onto the lawn. He stood up and staggered into the house to call the police.

Back in the lounge he slumped onto the sofa, reached over for the cigar he'd left on the side table and lit it. He sat there, enjoying the sweet, smooth, tobacco smoke as he waited for the police to arrive.

EPILOGUE

12 months later

THE SUPERTANKER *KHIONE* accompanied by two Canadian ice-breakers, slowly cruised along the Davis Strait to the seeding location, its adapted hull full of modified iron sulphate. The US/French mission to seed the Arctic followed on from the successful tests, carried out from the *Mercure Blanc,* the previous summer. Scientists, from the N.S.I.D.C, monitoring the Arctic sea ice confirmed that the previous summer's melt was the second largest on record, and forecast another record decline this year.

The *Khione's* mission: to seed the Arctic Ocean, creating the world's largest ever manmade phytoplankton bloom, using the newly developed *Blankoplankton* to absorb carbon dioxide and increase Arctic albedo levels. The aim: to slow global warming in the region, by restoring the Arctic's temperature to pre-industrial revolution levels.

In a small village, just outside the city of Novosibirsk in Siberia, an old lady, dressed head to toe in black and hunched over with scoliosis, walked along an overgrown path through the village cemetery. She passed a couple of ponies grazing on the long grass in the cemetery grounds and stopped to feed them some sliced carrots. She patted the ponies with her wizened hand whilst they grazed, before continuing along the grassy path. Passing numerous vine-entangled gravestones, she moved slowly along until arriving at a relatively new grave, situated next to three older, but well-kept headstones.

She carefully knelt down by the newest grave and pulled some freshly cut lilies from the bag she was carrying, and placed them on the grave of her granddaughter, lowering her head in prayer. *Rest in peace, my darling Ksenyia; you are back with your family now.*

The End – Continue below for links to your FREE e-book and Robert Spire thrillers two, three and four or check my website

–

www.sirosser-thriller-writer.com

Author Bio

Simon Rosser LIb, was born in Cardiff, South Wales, UK, in

1968. He is a personal injury lawyer and author of Action-Adventure-thriller novels with an Ecological/Apocalyptic theme.

If you enjoyed reading any of my books, and have the time, please stop by and leave an Amazon review. If you scroll to the last page on your Kindle now, you will be taken to a 'review' page, which you can also share with your friends on Twitter and Facebook if you wanted to – how cool is that? All reviews are much appreciated, thanks.

Author's Note…

Tipping Point was my first novel, and I hope you enjoyed the adventure. The book took me over 18 months to research and write, and I'd like to thank early reviewers for pointing out all the annoying typos and errors that were in the first edition – I have of course corrected them, and employed an editor; *Cheryl McLeod*, who managed to pick up the huge amount of typos I'd missed. I'm sure there are probably still a few errors hiding within the text, but I hope you, the reader enjoyed Robert Spire's first adventure. I would be eternally grateful once you have finished this book, if you would leave a review on Amazon, to let other potential readers know about my book. You can do this by clicking on the following link, or going to the final page of your Kindle, after the excerpt of IMPACT POINT –

Tipping Point Review (UK)
Tipping Point Review (USA)

Read an extract of IMPACT POINT below.

IMPACT POINT

Prologue

THE SMALL GATHERING of Evenki hunters finished erecting the last of their twelve birch-bark conical tents on a small hill close to the ancient Siberian boreal forest, before preparing to settle down for the night. The Podkamennaya Tunguska River flowed through the valley, some half a mile below. Aside from the faint gushing of the distant river, and the occasional hoot of a Siberian Owl, the night was calm and still.

Borya, one of the elder hunters, returned from the edge of the woods with a pile of branches, arranged them over a depression in the ground, and hastily lit the tinder underneath using a white phosphorus match. The sun had dipped below the horizon an hour earlier, and it was becoming desperately cold. Two huskies moved closer to the crackling fire to warm themselves, their ears twitching in response to the occasional sound emanating from the surrounding forest.

"Arkhip, please go and check on the reindeer, they appeared agitated earlier. There could be wolves around," Borya said.

Arkhip, a twenty-five year old member of the group, was warming himself by the fire. He nodded, stood up, and wandered down the hill to a flat grassy plain a short distance from the camp, where the twenty reindeer were tethered together. Most were lying down, but a few females close to the edge of the forest appeared restless; their heads bowed, and antlers scraping the ground in front of them. He checked the herd; apart from the two agitated animals, the rest appeared to be sleeping. Arkhip eyed the dark silent woodland beyond, but did not sense anything unusual. He sighed, and inhaled deeply. The smell of damp grass, mixed with smoke from the fire, filled the night air.

As he walked back up the hill toward the glowing fire, he looked up toward the night sky. The millions of pinpricks of light never failed to amaze him. Just like a plethora of animal eyes shining in the dark forest, Arkhip tried to imagine the countless number of stars up there; he wondered how far away they were, and where they hid during the daytime. Then, one object appearing much brighter than all the others caught his attention. As he gazed at it, he realised it was moving against the background of stationary stars. He ran the short distance back to Borya, who was still sitting by the fire.

"Borya, the star, it is very bright," he said, pointing in the direction of the glowing object. "Why is it moving when none of the others do?"

Borya stared at the object for a while before frowning. "It is too bright for a star. Perhaps it is the Moon spirit; a good shaman for tomorrow's hunting. Come on, let's get to bed, it is late. We rise at dawn to hunt in the forest."

Borya threw more branches onto the dying fire to keep it going for as long as possible. The two hunters then said goodnight to each other and went to bed.

A loud cry awoke Arkhip from his sleep. He looked over at his wife, who was still sleeping soundly under her reindeer pelt. *How long have I been sleeping?*

Again, a muted cry pierced the dawn. He crawled out from under the reindeer skin, taking care not to wake his still sleeping wife, and grabbed his wooden hunting pike, and left the tent.

The sun was rising in the east, its rays already fanning out across the valley below and touching the edge of the forest. He patted the tethered, restless huskies, now standing and growling in the direction of the woods, and walked to the brow of the grassy mound, when he heard the cry again.

He looked toward the herd of reindeer; all were now awake and agitated. As he ran down the gentle hill toward them, a grey streak flew out from the gorse lining the edge of the forest. A wolf from a hunting pack attacked, lunging at the neck of the female reindeer grazing along the margin of the grass plain.

"No!" he cried, as he tried in vain to prevent the attack. The large grey wolf ripped into the neck of the reindeer, whose attempts to gore it with her antlers proved futile, against the powerful, agile predator. The reindeer dropped to the ground, fresh blood oozing from her torn neck where she laid, her hind legs twitching.

Arkhip thrust the pike at the wolf, scaring it away, and then finished the reindeer off by driving the pike through her heart. The wolves would be back, he had no doubt, so he untied the other reindeers closest to the dead animal and moved them away from the kill.

An owl hooted, making its presence known from the depths of the forest. He hurried back up the mound to the camp, where the other hunters were now gathering, having also been woken by the reindeer cries. Arkhip went straight to his tent to check on his wife.

"What happened?" she asked. "Has there been another wolf attack?"

"Yes, by the edge of the forest. A wolf has killed one reindeer, but it could have been worse, we can carry the loss. The men are getting ready to leave, I must go. I'll be back before nightfall."

"Take care Arkhip," his wife said, kissing him gently on his forehead.

He grabbed his bloodied pike, left the tent, and walked over to join Borya and the others who were standing on the brow of the hill.

"Come, we are late, it must be close to seven o'clock," Borya said, looking toward the sun, rising in the east. Suddenly the reindeer on the grassy plain below became volatile, bucking and rearing, as if threatened by an invisible force. Half of the herd then broke free from their ties and bolted down the valley toward the river below, just as hundreds of birds flew out from the forest, their wings beating in a cacophony of sound.

The Evenki hunters looked on in astonishment as their reindeer stampeded.

Suddenly a column of bright, blue, light, streaking across the horizon, forced them all to look up. Then an enormous brilliant flash lit up the morning sky, more intense than the rising sun, followed by three successive deafening thunder claps. A massive shock-wave followed, throwing the hunters to the floor, whilst simultaneously blasting their tents from their securing poles, as if they were nothing more than paper bags.

Arkhip was thrown ten feet into the air, landing on his back in the soft grass. The ground rumbled underneath him. After a few moments he slowly opened his eyes, immediately covering them again as a strong hot wind raced out of the forest.

Shielding his face, he slowly got to his knees. All around, the forest was aglow, burning furiously like no fire he had ever seen before. He stood and looked down the valley, and was amazed to see the forest trees blown over by some incredible force, now lying like broken matchsticks, smouldering, and bathing in an eerie glow.

The time, and place, would be etched in Arkhip's mind forever – Tunguska, June 30th 1908.

Printed in Great Britain
by Amazon

72612306R00298